THE BARD

THE BARD

Dragonslayer
Book One

Jules Cory

Copyright © 2018 Jules Cory

The moral right of the author has been asserted.

Apart from any fair dealing for the purposes of research or private study, or criticism or review, as permitted under the Copyright, Designs and Patents Act 1988, this publication may only be reproduced, stored or transmitted, in any form or by any means, with the prior permission in writing of the publishers, or in the case of reprographic reproduction in accordance with the terms of licences issued by the Copyright Licensing Agency. Enquiries concerning reproduction outside those terms should be sent to the publishers.

Matador
9 Priory Business Park,
Wistow Road, Kibworth Beauchamp,
Leicestershire. LE8 0RX
Tel: 0116 279 2299
Email: books@troubador.co.uk
Web: www.troubador.co.uk/matador
Twitter: @matadorbooks

ISBN 9781 789014 310

British Library Cataloguing in Publication Data.
A catalogue record for this book is available from the British Library.

Printed and bound in the UK by 4edge Ltd.
Typeset in 11pt Minion Pro by Troubador Publishing Ltd, Leicester, UK

Matador is an imprint of Troubador Publishing Ltd

For those who believed

Chapter One

I have often wondered what they thought as they came out of the forest and saw the village for the first time. The vibrant greens of the oak and the sycamore highlighted by the bright yellow gorse; contrasted with the blackened, scorched ash left behind after the attack. Handfuls of ashes were blown like dirty snow in the light breeze. The acrid taste of burnt memories would have prickled the back of their throats, even though it had been over a day since the raiders had left.

There were twelve men riding under the banner that I recognised as the Faulknar marque; the white lion proudly standing on a scarlet banner above black and gold squares. Their soft chatter stopped abruptly as they left the forest and surveyed the scene of destruction. The charcoaled remains of twenty roundhouses dominated the meadow in front of them. Thatch had burnt away, crude stone walls were blackened, and basic wooden fencing had fallen over, allowing the livestock within to flee to the woods. More details were revealed as they rode closer. Within and between the houses were the charred remains of men, women and children, many cut down as they tried to run. There were no bodies of soldiers here. These were farmers. It had been a massacre.

Two men broke away from the group to approach the village first. The one on the left was built like a soldier – tall, muscular, with an air of contained power. Riding a large chestnut horse, he wore dark brown leather trousers and riding boots covered in a layer of dust from the journey. The summer afternoon was warm, and his worn leather gambeson was open to reveal a cream shirt stained with sweat and dirt. He carried a heavy sword sheathed at his side, paired with a hunting knife tucked in the waistband of his trousers. He sat comfortably in the saddle, moving fluidly as the chestnut shook to remove a fly from its mane. The soldier's blond hair was cut close to his head.

His companion was noticeably different. He rode a skewbald horse a handspan shorter than the chestnut, which fought the bit in its mouth, noisily chinking the metal against its teeth. The rider bounced in the saddle with each movement, a heartbeat behind the horse and lacking the effortless grace shown by the soldier. This rider carried no noticeable weapon and wore woollen trousers over leather boots, with a matching dull green tunic open at the neck. A pendant hung around his neck on a leather thong, knocking gently against his throat with each step the horse took. The base colour of his shoulder-length hair was brown, but age had sprinkled it with grey, particularly at the temples. His age was also shown in the wrinkles of his brown face, but his hazel eyes were clear and seemed to observe everything.

The riders came into the village. The blond soldier gave orders to take care of the dead and try to find evidence indicating who had attacked the settlement. The men complied with quiet respect.

'We're too late.'

The companion nodded. 'For many, yes. But perhaps not all.'

The first turned to his companion, who was squatting next to the entrance of a roundhouse a few steps away. The other man held a small knife with an elaborate hilt that caught the late-afternoon light as he raised it up.

'Laken, come look at this,' the smaller man said. 'Looks like the Lindvanes are active again.'

Laken took the offered knife and admired the workmanship evident in the decorated weapon. The blade was two handspans long, with sharpened edges of iron along both sides that had been nicked from frequent use. The blade was functional, but the hilt was a thing of beauty. The iron handle had been overlaid with bronze to enable the engravings of the boar that symbolised the Lindvane clan. They controlled the lands north-west of those held by the Faulknar clan, and often raided the villages on the border between the two kingdoms. It was unusual for them to raid this far into Faulknar territory, though. The centre of the knife's hilt was decorated with glass tiles of red and orange that represented the warrior God Camlun. A weapon that valuable would not have been left behind by accident.

Laken slid the knife beneath his belt. He watched his men go about their work efficiently, with a small smile of pride. But the smile faded quickly as he looked upon the numerous bodies that were scattered around – maimed, beheaded, burned.

'Why do you think they did this, Drey? Raiding for livestock is one thing, but this was…'

His companion shook his head. 'I don't know. To provoke a response from Kyllian, perhaps.'

'It would work. His Majesty is not going to let this go unavenged. There will be war over this.'

'You may be right. The Lindvanes have been spoiling for a fight for a while now. This could be the final push Kyllian needs to declare war on them.'

'May the Gods take pity on us.'

Drey gave his friend a gentle shove. 'You must be getting old. A captain fearing a battle?'

'Not for myself. Right now I would love to take a few Boar heads. But the cost of glory is often paid heavily by the women and children.'

Drey opened his mouth to reply, but closed it again quickly. He tilted his head to one side, listening, as a bird appears to listen for worms. A frown creased his forehead as he concentrated. 'Where are you?' he whispered to himself.

'What do you hear, Drey?'

The older man smiled. 'I think today is about to get a lot more interesting.'

'Why do I get the feeling I'm not going to like your "interesting"?'

Drey slapped him on the chest. 'Come on,' he said before marching off.

Drey led them to a small building at the eastern edge of the village, next to the manure heap and partially hidden from view by a mound of turf. The door had been torn off its hinges, but it looked otherwise intact. The inside of the hut was dim, with light from the doorway the only source of illumination. Pottery jars of different sizes lay scattered on the floor, smashed, and their contents spilled in piles of grain, dried herbs and seeds. Any liquids had seeped into the dirt floor, leaving darker patches around a few broken urns. First impressions suggested a seldom-used storage hut that had been quickly ignored by the raiders.

Drey closed his eyes as he stood in the middle of the building. He sniffed at the air; then sniffed again. He opened his eyes and looked at Laken, placing a finger on his lips to forestall any questions. He walked silently towards the wall furthest away from the door, which was hidden in darkness. Carefully he touched the wall and felt each stone in turn. His probing fingers found one, then another, then another of the loose stones.

'Go get a light,' he instructed, breathless with anticipation.

One by one he carefully removed the rocks and placed them on the floor beside him. By the time Laken returned with a branch holding a burning rag, there was a pile of stones next to Drey and a hole the size of a cartwheel in the wall, revealing the black cavity carved into the turf mound.

'Hello.'

I was momentarily blinded by the light and remained as still as I could – not even breathing – although it was obvious that he had seen me. I no longer felt the embossed dragon on the hilt of my father's sword digging into my palm as my mind circled round and round in panic. All three of us were motionless, frozen by the revelation of a seven-year-old girl hiding in a wall.

'You won't be needing that for us.' The man in front of me looked down at the weapon, as long as my arm, pointing at him. He spoke as if talking to a cornered fox cub.

I was ashamed to see my sword quivering in the torchlight, but did not lower the tip. The flames danced along the blade, making the engravings look like smoke over a midnight lake. My palms were sweaty and slippery, so I held tighter to the hilt, causing my fingers to turn cold as I compressed their blood supply. In contrast, my palm and wrist burned with the effort of holding the steel up.

'Now what are you doing in here?'

I looked into his hazel eyes and remembered to breathe. I was surprised by the detail I could see, even though the torch was behind him and shining into my face. He had long brown eyelashes that curved slightly away from his eyes. Laughter lines decorated the corners. The hazel of the irises dominated, with only a ring of white surrounding them. The background colour was accentuated by fine brushstrokes of darker brown, drawing my gaze towards the pupils. The black holes in the centre of his eyes seemed to expand as I looked at them, drawing me further into their velvety thickness, like dark molasses pouring over a waterfall...

'She told me to hide.'

I was surprised by the sound of my voice; the words falling out of my mouth before I realised I was speaking. I had not meant to tell him, or indeed anyone.

'And hide you did. The raiders never found you, did they?' He tilted his head to one side. 'Nobody found you until I did. Interesting.'

He suddenly stood up, making me jump and lift the sword in order to cover myself from any possible threat. The conversation, though, was over as he strode out of the hut, pausing only to clap Laken on the shoulder.

The taller man raised his eyebrows as Drey went past. 'What am I supposed to…?'

But Drey had gone.

Laken turned to face me. 'Well, what am I going to do with you?'

He walked slowly towards the hole and squatted down. Although he was taller and more muscular, he seemed less of a threat to me than the older man. His eyes were the colour of a faded summer sky and lacked the intensity of his friend's gaze. He had pale freckles scattered over his nose and cheeks. He was older than I had first assumed, aged by lines around his eyes and the corners of his mouth.

The sword was trembling now, and my arms were screaming from overuse. I lowered the point to the floor and relaxed my grip slightly, and I wasn't that reluctant to do so.

Laken smiled broadly. 'That's better.'

He waited, perhaps for me to speak, ask questions, but I had no intention of talking to him. He may have appeared less threatening, but I still didn't trust him. I didn't trust anyone. Everyone I trusted was lying outside. Dead. I bit my lower lip and refused to cry.

'I'll do you a deal,' he said. 'I know you're frightened of everyone, and that's all right. You've seen a dreadful thing and been very brave to hide in here. It's only natural you should be wary. But you can't do this alone. You have to trust someone at some point. Right?'

I waited a handful of heartbeats before nodding quickly.

'Well, let's agree that you stay on your guard and look out for yourself. You only have to come with me now. We'll get some food. See how you feel after that. You can leave if I do anything that makes you doubt me. What do you say?'

I closed my eyes and held my breath. I didn't want to trust him. That would mean admitting that I had no one else to trust. That my family was gone. That my friends and their families were gone. Everyone. And that I couldn't take care of myself. I squeezed my eyes against the tears that were threatening to spill and took a deep breath.

'All right.'

It was said so quietly I was surprised he had heard, but his smile widened. 'Fabulous! My name's Laken.'

'I know. I saw you coming. I heard you talking outside.'

The smile vanished and he grew serious. 'Did you now?'

He turned to look at my viewpoint from the hole in the wall. The forest from which they had arrived and first seen the village was clearly visible. He could see the soldiers gathering the bodies of the fallen for the funeral pyre that would be lit that night. Some were coming out of the forest carrying the wood that would be needed. He could hear the conversations of those nearest to us, even though they were speaking quietly.

'This is a very good place to hide. Did you find it yourself or did someone show you?'

I bit my lip again. I was not going to tell him. I had said too much already. He turned back to face me and tilted his head to one side, expecting my answer. He waited several heartbeats before giving a small smile.

'It's a secret, huh?' he whispered, accepting that I had said all that I was going to. 'Very well. Let's get you something to eat instead.'

My stomach growled at the thought of food, and he laughed his easy laugh.

Laken led me out of the hut. The men had been busy while we were talking. Without fuss they had separated into three groups: two, I had seen from the hut, caring for the dead and collecting pyre-wood. The third group had set up camp at the southern edge of the village, to the right of the woods where the soldiers had emerged. They had erected oil-treated wool sheets for shelter, but had placed them so that the huts were rectangular with pointed roofs, rather than the half-moon tunnels I had seen the Travellers use. There were six of these portable tents, five close together in a line, and one a few paces further away, facing the others. A midden trench had been dug to the west of the camp, partially hidden by bracken and ferns. The horses had been tethered at the other end of the camp, two hazel trees used to anchor the thick rope to which their headcollars had been attached. Several whickered as Laken and I walked past, some rolling their eyes to reveal large, cream sclera while others stamped their feet. We didn't have any horses in Methhold, but when the Travellers came with their horses to trade, I had seen the same reaction when I approached. For some reason horses didn't seem to like me, but then neither did the goats or the chickens we kept. I automatically moved to the other side of Laken, so that he was between me and the horses.

Between the row of five shelters and the solitary one facing them, a fire had been lit. A man of average height, but with a big round belly, was stirring a large iron pot suspended above the flames. On an already warm day the heat had turned his cheeks poppy red. His brown hair stood away from his temples in sweaty spikes. The breeze blew the scent of warm oats towards me and my stomach growled loudly as my mouth filled with saliva.

'Trail rations, I'm afraid,' said Laken as we approached. 'But Tad here is one of the best when it comes to cooking on the road.'

The cook looked up from his pot and smiled at the compliment, revealing a dark socket where his left eye should have been, and several gaps where teeth were missing. He reminded me of the ogres in the tales told by the fire on dark nights, and I shrank a little in fear, instinctively moving closer to the most familiar person I had – Laken.

He chuckled quietly. 'Don't worry about Tad. He may look like a daemon but he's a god when it comes to turning oats into a new creation every night.'

I was not convinced, but the porridge smelt good and I had not eaten for over a day. I was willing to take the risk, so placed my father's sword under one arm and accepted the bowl of steaming gruel from Tad. Maybe it was my hunger, or maybe Laken was right about Tad being a god, but the food was divine. The oats were soft and warming. They had been sweetened with honey and berries, and nuts added texture. My stomach growled once more, this time in appreciation of the offering, and the ever-present pain in my chest eased slightly. Although I was not cold, I could feel the warmth of the food oozing out of my stomach and into the tight muscles of my abdomen, arms and legs. The tension within them dissolved when touched by this heat, so that they became flaccid and heavy. I sat down heavily when my legs no longer supported my weight. The warm feeling was spreading through my veins to the tips of my fingers and toes, and I heard myself sigh as I watched the activity of the camp going on around me. Laken passed me a beaker of fresh, cold water that I knew to be from a spring a short walk into the forest. It sparked an icy chill in the core of me, halting the tendrils of warmth from the porridge. The effect was refreshing without removing the relaxed comfort now deep within my bones.

Soothed by the routine of people working around me, the blanket of warmth from the food within, and the sun on my face as it slowly fell towards the trees, it wasn't long before my eyelids grew heavy and my head began to nod. Aiming for comfort by supporting my head, I lay on the thick grass that released its fragrance as I crushed it. I curled around the sword, the dragon engraving providing reassurance as it pressed into my palm. My blinks become slower as my breathing settled into a deeper rhythm. I closed my eyes for a heartbeat…

I awoke with a start. Panic screamed incoherently in my head. My heart thudded painfully against my ribs, trying to escape the bony cage. My breathing was fast and shallow. Not enough oxygen was reaching my brain to process the images I was seeing. Blood pumped deafeningly in my ears. I could smell smoke. Burning. I tried to rise, but there was pressure against the centre of my chest. I could get no further than three or four handspans above the grass, even though I was using my forearms to gain leverage.

'Easy. It's all right.'

It took a while for my eyes to focus on Laken kneeling next to me. He had his hand placed on my chest to stop me from bolting. By force of will I slowed my breathing and willed my heart to calm. The pulsing in my ears gradually receded and I could pick out the sounds of the camp again. The sun had disappeared behind the forest and the muted colours of twilight enveloped the scene. The smell of smoke was not coming from the cooking fire. I looked at Laken for an explanation. His face was sad.

'It's time,' he said simply. I tilted my head to one side and frowned, not understanding what he was saying. 'It's time to say goodbye to your family.'

He removed his hand from my chest and helped me stand without the need to let go of the sword. We turned northwards and I could see, from across the village, that the funeral pyre was complete. My breath caught in my chest. My view of my home dived sharply as my stomach somersaulted and bile stung the back of my throat. I would have fallen without Laken's firm arm around my waist. I crushed the corner of my lower lip between my teeth. My eyes stung with tears trying to be shed.

The pyre stood one and a half times as tall as Laken, and twice that in length. Around the base, the kindling was burning. Young trees had been felled to provide the platform on which the fallen were laid. The bodies were placed head to toe across the mound, each covered by a thin sheet. They appeared to be arranged in size order, with the larger bodies on the left and the smaller ones on the right. The smaller ones must have been the children. My friends. My rivals. My sister.

Biting my lip could no longer stop the tears. The hot fluid burst the dam of my lower eyelids and cascaded down my cheeks. Tiny streams collected at the corners of my mouth, tasting salty, before dripping from my chin. Water leaked from my nose and over my upper lip, as if in sympathy with my eyes. I sniffed loudly.

Laken's firm arm gently pulled me around so I could look into his face. 'It's right that you should cry. You honour the dead with your tears.'

I collapsed into his chest as he hugged me tightly to him. My tears quickly soaked through his shirt. The coarseness of the material scratched against my face, dirt and tears mingling on my forehead, cheeks and chin. The fabric muffled the sobs that shuddered through my body, making it difficult to breathe as my diaphragm convulsed. The pain in my chest was unbearable, as if someone had pierced a red-hot boar spear through my heart. That pain alone should have killed me. But it didn't. And I cried, and sobbed, and wailed.

And none of it brought them back.

Eventually I ran out of tears. My breath hiccupped as I tried to control the overwhelming feeling of loss, replacing it with a seed of anger and hatred for those that had taken my family from me. Laken cupped my chin and raised my head, brushing the remaining tears from below my swollen eyes. He had not said a word, letting his solid presence provide all the support I needed. He gently turned me to face the fire and we walked slowly towards it. His arm wrapped around my shoulders, quietly guiding me.

The flames had passed the kindling and were sucking greedily at the wood of the platform on which the dead lay. As we reached the point where the heat from the fire prevented us going any further, the flames were licking around the top of the pyre. The sheets covering the bodies must have been soaked in oil, as the flames shot up into the sky as soon as they touched the material. Everyone gathered at the base of the pyre was forced to take a couple of steps backwards. Flakes of ash were caught by the wind and carried above the heads of the soldiers. Sparks danced through the air to land harmlessly in the grass.

This close to the fire, the bronze in the hilt of the sword in my hand warmed. It was my father's sword, and his father's before him. I changed the position of my grip, so the red stones in the dragon's eyes danced in recognition of the light. The flames called to the weapon, inviting it to join the dead; to journey to the halls of the Gods, reunited with its bearers, back to the time of its forging. I pulled away from Laken and drew back my arm to throw the sword onto the fire in tribute to my father and our ancestors.

A firm hand gripped my arm, preventing me from releasing the weapon. I turned to see Drey standing behind me. He had a powerful grip that was much greater than his size would suggest.

'No.' He softened his grip, but still held my wrist. 'I believe this sword is destined for other things.'

Giving a small nod in agreement, I lowered my arm and he released his hold. Taking a deep breath, I turned back to the fire. The bodies that I could see at the edge of the pyre were consumed by the sacrificial flames. The old religions believed that the smoke took the souls of the dead to the halls of the Gods. There they would meet their ancestors and loved ones and spend eternity in the company of lower deities, under the parental gaze of the Sun God and the Moon Goddess. Without the smoke, the souls would never find the way.

From behind, the haunting sounds of funeral keening began. This song of honour and respect should only be sung by the leaders of the old faiths, but the village Druid was among those needing to be guided to the afterlife. The small hairs at the nape of my neck and along my arms stood upright in response to the crystal-clear notes. The lilting melody weaved a magical spell as the words of the ancestors were made alive by the skill of one man's voice. Tears flowed from my eyes again as I watched the smoke rise and mix with the clouds, leading to the realm of the Gods. I said a silent prayer for those I had loved and lost, before turning to see who had taken on the duty of honouring the dead.

Drey stood with his eyes closed a few paces away from rest of the men. The purity of his voice pierced the core of everyone there. This man was a lot more than he seemed.

Chapter Two

I had never left Methhold, but as I looked around at the ruined settlement and the smouldering funeral pyre I realised there was nothing left there that I cared about. The morning had dawned, overcast and with an oppressive heat that suggested there would be a storm that day. The soldiers had started packing up the shelters, which were easily rolled and attached to their saddles. Each of the horses was groomed, tacked and ready to go by the time I had finished my breakfast of hard biscuit and fresh spring water. Some of the men were talking in a small group, frequently looking in my direction, and I guessed that they were discussing what was to be done with me. I was not interested in their opinions, so my eyes searched for Laken. I felt a bubbling panic when I couldn't see him.

That panic deepened, settling further into my abdomen, when I turned back to see one of the younger soldiers walking over to me. He was halfway between his friends and where I was sitting, and it was clear he was heading for me while the others looked on. I stood up when he was close enough that I could see the dark stubble on his chin, and the cold humour in his brown eyes that matched the smirk on his lips. I gripped the sword tightly, feeling the reassuring pressure of the embossed dragon on my palm. I bit the corner of my lip hard, to prevent my mind from convincing my body to run.

'Hey, little girl,' he said as he stopped a few paces in front of me. 'That's a really nice sword you've got there.'

I stayed as still as a deer that's heard a twig snap – expecting danger but not knowing from which direction it's coming. I, at least, knew my danger was right in front of me. The soldier was a handspan shorter than Laken, but lacked none of his power. The veins stood out from the muscles of his neck and upper arms. I concentrated hard on not being intimidated. I had met bullies before.

'Why don't you give it to me so I can have a good look?'

'It's not for you.'

He laughed. 'I just want a look. Isn't that right, boys?'

The group watching agreed enthusiastically.

'What are you going to do with a big, old sword anyway?'

He took a step towards me and I raised the blade. It was obviously too long for me, and trembled slightly in response to my rapidly beating heart. However, I had played with this sword for as long as I could remember. I knew her weight and balance well. And I knew I could use her to draw blood.

Everything went quiet and my attention was focused on the man in front of me. The smile had left his face and been replaced by a poorly suppressed expression of frustration. A muscle at the corner of his left eye twitched slightly. The rate of his breathing had increased, as had mine. He took a step towards me, reaching for the sword. I held my breath, preparing for what was about to happen.

At the same time, Laken's voice boomed across the clearing. 'Rolyan! What in the Seven Hells of Mobis are you doing?'

I breathed again as Rolyan stepped back and turned to face Laken, who was striding towards us. His face was stiffened by anger, and I thought of how it could change to so clearly reflect his emotions. It took no time at all before he reached us, standing protectively at my side.

'Well?'

Rolyan shrugged. 'I just wanted a look. What is a child supposed to do with a sword, anyway?'

'Anything she wants. It's her sword.'

'It's too good for her.' Resentment was causing his face to contort, and I moved a little closer to Laken.

Laken's voice was very low, and all the more deadly for it. 'It was her father's sword, and his father's before him. It belongs to her. You will not touch this sword. Do you understand?'

Rolyan hesitated, unwilling to be defeated in front of his friends. But he was not stupid, and when Laken repeated his question Rolyan nodded. 'Yes, Captain.'

'Have you and the others,' Laken acknowledged Rolyan's friends with a brief nod in their direction, 'got enough work to do, or shall I assign you new orders?'

The small group suddenly made much of checking the girth straps of the horses and ensuring their loads were securely attached. Rolyan mumbled incoherently before walking off. I suspected that I had made an enemy of that man.

'Making friends already, then?'

I turned to look up at Laken, wondering how he could have got it so wrong. But his expressive face had changed again, and he was grinning down at me. I smiled back, more at the release of tension than at any humour in his jest. Then I realised that this was the first time I had smiled since the raiders came. The smile evaporated.

'I have a present for you,' said Laken lightly, sensing my change in mood.

He held out his hand and I noticed for the first time that he was holding what looked like a leather belt. On closer inspection, I saw that it was a baldric with a round bronze buckle and a plain but functional scabbard. The leather was worn but had been well maintained, and was soft and supple when I touched it. Carefully, Laken placed the baldric over my head so it hung over my right shoulder, down to my left knee. It was too big for me, but he worked the buckle until it fit snugly between my shoulder blades, with the scabbard running along my spine.

'It will save you carrying it everywhere. You might need your hands free.' He hesitated. 'If you would ride with me to Liegeport?'

I had heard about Liegeport from the traders and Travellers that came to the village. The elders had travelled there once and had seemed to have been gone for a long time. Liegeport seemed a mythical place, a long way away. It was where the king lived. I nodded slowly, averting my gaze from the baldric around my neck to look for approval in Laken's eyes.

His big grin was back, and his eyes sparkled with joy. 'Oh, this is going to be so much fun.' The smile faded a little. 'But the gift comes with a condition. Do you accept?'

I thought about my life in Methhold, and my possible future in Liegeport. 'I accept.'

'The condition is that you tell me your name.'

My eyes widened. I hadn't expected this. Mamma had always taught me that names were special and those that knew your name had some power over you. Names were not to be given lightly, and only to those you trusted. It was an honour to be offered a name. But I had learned Laken's name through overhearing a private conversation. There was no honour in that. It wasn't fair that I knew his name, but he did not know mine.

'Tallen,' I said solemnly. 'Tallen nic Duane.'

The company of riders was soon heading out of the village and into the woods. I didn't know how to ride, and there were no spare horses, so I rode behind Laken. The chestnut was flightier with an extra passenger and I had to hold on tightly to Laken's waist. It wasn't long before my arms and upper back were aching from maintaining my grip, a fiery rod blazing between my shoulder blades. The pain had company as the width of the gelding tried to tear my hips from their sockets. This pain stabbed deep into the sockets with each step that the horse took. These two areas of torment were joined by a third as I was bounced heavily onto my seat bones. I never knew I had bones inside my bottom cheeks, but they were forcibly announcing their presence by sending flames of pain up my spine and down my legs. Moving to ease the pain there caused a cascade of fresh pain in my hips and shoulders, and a relay of torture circled around these three points, triggered by the slightest movement by myself or the horse. By the time the sun was a quarter of the way across the sky, sweat was dripping down my back as I laid my head against Laken's back and concentrated on keeping as still as possible.

The countryside around my home – what had been my home – was generally flat with only a few rolling hills to break the horizon. Although Methhold was surrounded by dense woodland, the Faulknar kingdom was mainly open heathlands and increasing areas of farmland. The woodlands provided a retreating industry of timber for building and plants for medicines. The new way was trade rather than self-sufficiency. The farmers grew abundant crops in the dark, rich soil that could then be bartered for other goods or traded for coins. The elders of Methhold had thought this dependency on others would be a short-lived idea, and held to the old ways of providing for the community. That way, when the floods came or snow isolated the village, we still had all that we needed. Riding through the countryside I could see that the views of the Methhold elders were not those of the majority. At any point in the journey I could see two or three farms, with their straight borders and linear planting forcing conformity onto the landscape.

The rain shower arrived during the middle of the afternoon. We had stopped briefly for a midday meal of biscuits, dried fruit and nuts. Most of the muscles in my legs and back were numb by then, and I had to be helped from the saddle. Drey prepared a tea for me from the store of dried herbs he carried, which tasted like the willow-bark tea that the village's healers had often used, but much stronger. It had a warming effect on my muscles and produced a light-headedness that was strange but pleasant, so that returning to the saddle was less painful than before the break. The rain, however, provided a new range of torments as the bruised skin of my inner thighs was softened by the moisture, and my leggings chafed it away to make multiple small sores. The afternoon dragged on miserably. The heavy grey clouds smothering the world reflected the depression settling into the very core of me. It was as if we were passing through sodden fleece, muffling sound and thickening the air that we breathed. My world shrank to the rhythm of the horse and the saturated back of Laken's gambeson.

Such was my state of mind that it was some time before I noticed we had stopped moving. Laken was giving instructions to get the horses stabled, groomed and fed. Someone was to stay with them to make sure none stiffened and became lame. All tack and weapons were to be cleaned and oiled before anyone was fed.

I carefully uncurled myself from the fixed position I had huddled into when trying unsuccessfully to prevent the rain soaking into my clothes. We had arrived at a long timber building roofed with thatch, like Methhold's meeting hall but with more than one level. There were stables to the side and a small enclosure containing a sow and her suckling piglets. As the first of the soldiers led their mounts into the barn, the sound of disturbed chickens could be heard as the roosting birds protested the intrusion. Tad entered the building carrying the perishable food, releasing the warm smell of roasting pork as he opened the door. My longing to get off the horse and out of the rain escaped me as a small whimper.

Laken turned and smiled at me from where he was scratching the chestnut's neck under the dripping mane. 'Journey's over for today.'

'Where are we?'

'This is Sharpie's Tavern. Sharpie's an old friend of mine. He and his missus will take care of us until the rain stops.'

He reached up to help me from the saddle. I had no strength left to help myself dismount, and my legs were as weak as a newborn goat kid's, so that I nearly collapsed when Laken placed me on the floor. Effortlessly, he scooped me up and carried me into the tavern. The warmth from the fire and the small number of people inside the tavern enveloped me like a comfortable blanket. I relaxed into Laken's strong hold and no longer cared that I was wet and aching.

'Oh my, Laken,' cried a woman's voice from behind me, to the right of Laken. 'What have you got there? Poor thing looks half drowned. Use the small room at the far end. I'll be right up with hot water and towels.'

'The towels will be good, but I think the bath may have to wait. She's just about asleep already.'

Laken's voice rumbled in his chest and tickled my ear. I tried to protest that I wasn't sleepy but couldn't summon the energy to form the words. My upper eyelids resisted all efforts to open them fully, slowly creeping towards their lower counterparts. I willed myself to take a deep breath and open my eyes as Laken walked up the stairs, his boots knocking hollowly on the wooden floor.

'I'm still awake.'

He gave me a squeeze. 'You're safe here. We'll be going nowhere until the morning. Enjoy the chance for some rest in a soft bed.'

I was carried into a room just large enough for a bed covered in soft blankets and a table with a washbowl, currently empty. The room smelt faintly of summer flowers, with more of the scent released when Laken placed me on the bed.

'Make sure you get out of these wet clothes before you fall asleep.'

'I'm not a child,' I mumbled, removing the baldric and my outer tunic with heavy hands. It took more effort than I had anticipated.

Laken chuckled as he left the room, and I was asleep before I had removed the next layer.

The room was dark when I woke, with the moonlight casting a silver sheen across the floorboards. I was naked under the soft blankets, but warm and dry. My muscles ached as I rolled out of the bed, and my bladder screamed to be emptied. My wet clothes had been replaced with clean leggings and tunic, folded neatly at the foot of the bed. They were a little big for me but fitted well enough with some rolling up of the legs and sleeves. I placed the baldric with my sword over my shoulder, unwilling to leave it behind even though someone had come in and undressed me without touching the sword that I had placed beside me on the bed. I left my damp boots on the floor and walked silently, barefooted, across the room. The hallway was deserted but voices were talking softly in the main room downstairs. The fire still gave off a warm glow, enough so I could confidently walk down the stairs. Laken, Drey and a man I hadn't seen before were sitting at the far end of the room. Laken had his back to me and the other two didn't see me as I stayed in the shadows and slipped quietly out of the door.

The night was still with only the rustling of the horses in the barn and the occasional soft hoot of a hunting owl. The rain had stopped and left the clear, fresh smell of wet earth. The mud squelched pleasantly between my toes as I walked towards the horses. The midden at Methhold had been behind the manure heap, which I could smell was behind the stables, so I headed in that direction. Fortunately, I found the midden easily and my bladder was finally silenced.

I was halfway along the barn wall, heading back to the tavern, when I saw Rolyan and a smaller, wiry soldier who had been in the group earlier that day. My heart rate increased rapidly, causing a sharp pain in my chest. I quickly searched for an escape route, but they were heading towards me. They would see me in a matter of heartbeats. I retraced my steps and entered the stables at the far end, hoping to pass Rolyan and his companion as they walked up the outside of the barn. But I had forgotten my effect on horses, and several of them whickered in alarm as I entered. In panic I ran towards the tavern end of the stables, and straight into the wiry soldier. I tried to squirm away from him, but he pinned my arms to my sides with an iron grip. He was smaller and leaner than most of the soldiers in Laken's company, but I was quickly and easily immobilised. My back was pressed against his chest and I could see Rolyan walking slowly towards me from the far end of the stables. He wore an arrogant smirk and, even in the low light of the barn, I could see a dangerous glint in his eyes.

'Well, what have we here? There appear to be little rats in this stable, Roaf.'

I struggled as hard as I could but Roaf did not show any signs of relaxing his hold. I tried kicking his shins, but my bare feet caused no harm. Rolyan stepped into a shaft of moonlight, so that I could see him clearly. He took his time, appreciating my helplessness.

'I think it's about time I had a look at that sword you so thoughtfully brought with you.'

Roaf spun me around so quickly my vision swam for a couple of heartbeats. Before I could mount any type of defence, Rolyan had removed the sword from the scabbard. The blade sighed as it was drawn out of the smooth, oiled leather. The engravings danced briefly, silver as the moonlight reflected in the polished iron. Rolyan smiled greedily as he admired the weapon, and his eyes lusted to possess it. He rolled his wrist, making the blade sing quietly as it cut the air, moonbeams dancing along its surface. He opened his mouth slightly in pleasure. His tongue wetted his lips. Having felt the weight of the sword, Rolyan next tested its balance. He tossed the weapon from hand to hand, gently holding it for a heartbeat before throwing it back to the other hand. The moonlight flicked over the red dragon eyes in the hilt, making them glint maliciously as the blade was thrown faster and faster.

He missed.

Rolyan's timing was out by a blink of an eye. The hilt twisted on the heel of his hand and rolled away from his grasping fingers. The deceptively sharp edge ran along his arm, leaving a crimson thread from wrist to elbow. Rolyan grabbed at the wound in an attempt to stop the blood, but it seeped through his fingers and dripped onto the blade now lying on the floor. The dragon eyes dimmed.

Roaf let go of me and went over to help Rolyan, who was now kneeling on the floor beside the sword. I seized my opportunity, dipped to collect the blade, then ran as fast as I could back to the tavern. I burst through the door, making it bang noisily against the wall. I had only been gone a few moments and Laken and Drey were still at the table, talking.

'Someone has been hurt in the stables,' I said as I ran up the stairs, not waiting to see if they heard or acted upon my words. I heard the scrape of chairs being dragged against the floor, and then I was in my small room at the far end of the hall. I jumped on the bed and pulled the covers over my head, desperately wishing that the last few moments had not happened. I curled myself protectively around the sword, and waited.

The pale grey of pre-dawn was starting to lighten the room when I heard the tavern door close and the sound of footsteps on the wooden floor. Drey was grumbling loudly as two pairs of feet climbed the stairs.

'I have better ways to spend my time than fixing fools that should stay out of affairs that don't involve them.'

The door to the room opposite slammed shut. I poked my head out from under the blankets to see Laken leaning against the doorway to my room, grinning.

He winked at me. 'He'll be back out again soon.'

At that moment, the door opposite banged again as Drey burst out. 'Soldiers these days don't know their place. They are to follow orders, not lark around doing what they feel.' He threw a small container at Laken before stomping down the stairs. 'It will be left to me to clear up the mess, as usual.'

Laken came into the room and closed the door. He laughed quietly as he sat on the bed. 'He may moan like a fishwife, but he likes to feel useful.' He handed me the container. 'Some ointment for your sores. We won't be riding for a couple of days and Drey says this cream will have them healed by then.'

'Why are we staying here?'

Laken hesitated. Looking deep into my eyes, he sighed. 'Rolyan has a nasty cut on his arm.'

I bit the corner of my lip.

'Will you tell me what happened?'

'I went to the midden.' I shrugged. 'I had to pass the stables.'

He waited, but I was unwilling to give more details.

'I specifically told him not to touch the sword. He disobeyed a direct order. You understand what that means?'

I nodded.

'But I can't have him flogged for disobedience on an assumption. Tallen, did he take the sword?'

I clamped my lip so tightly between my teeth that I tasted the metallic tang of blood. I did not want Rolyan touching my sword, but I didn't want him to be flogged either. I knew the rules of fighting men. I knew the need for discipline and unquestioning loyalty. But I didn't have to like them. A boy from my village had been flogged for killing a hunting hound in spite. I remembered the smell of blood, fear and pain. The swelling of the welts within moments of the lash-bite. The crack of the whip and the tearing of flesh. I swallowed against the bile that was rising in my throat at the memory. I had no wish to see that again. Not even for Rolyan.

Laken sighed and lowered his gaze. 'Very well.' He patted my knee through the blankets and left the room.

We spent the next two days at the tavern, and I did my best to avoid everyone. Laken was busy tending to the horses and men, organising work parties to keep them occupied. Drey spent most of his time away from the tavern, leaving early in the morning and returning late in the evening. By keeping quiet and out of the way, I was able to hear snatches of conversations and piece together the reason for the delay. A young woman had fallen ill on a small farm a little way further down the road, and Drey was offering his herbs and help to the family. He was well respected by the people working and drinking in the tavern for his skills with herbs and his knowledge of the old ways for using them. His opinion was sought on many topics, with his advice carrying the weight of a village elder's even though he looked to be no more than middle-aged. I found myself watching Drey whenever I could and studying how people acted around him. He was obviously important to them, although it was not clear why or how he had come to be that way.

Rolyan remained in the back room of the tavern with the other soldiers for the whole of the first day. His wiry companion avoided my gaze, quickly moving to avoid me when chance caused our paths to cross. I suspected Laken had increased the direct order to leave me alone as well as the sword.

I saw Rolyan the following morning as I went to the well to collect fresh water. He was sitting on a low wall, chewing a blade of grass. His left arm was bandaged from wrist to elbow and he held it protectively against his body. His face was very pale, with dark grey circles under eyes that shone a little too brightly. The kitchen boy had said that the wound may be infected, and that the healer was using magick to ensure it healed well. I didn't believe him, but Rolyan did look worse than a clean cut should have left him. He ignored me and I was happy to leave him alone.

By the third morning the clouds had changed from dull grey to fluffy white, promising an end to the intermittent showers and to be replaced with blue sky and warm sun. The efficiency at Methhold was demonstrated again, with the horses tacked and loaded soon after dawn. I was to ride behind Laken as before. My sores had healed as Drey had promised and my hips no longer ached. I was beginning to understand why he was so highly regarded. The man who had been talking to Laken and Drey on that first night was standing in the doorway to his tavern. Sharpie had spent several evenings talking in private to Laken, and with Drey if he was around. I had not been able to overhear their conversations, and no one at the tavern talked of their business either. The talks were always serious; Laken never showed his grin when in discussion with Sharpie late at night. Now Sharpie came over to clasp Laken at the wrist in the manner of warriors. The two men shared a long look, and I could see sadness in Sharpie's eyes as he held Laken's gaze. Then he nodded sharply, turned and disappeared into the tavern.

We travelled for three days through the countryside, sleeping in meadows sprinkled with buttercups while the weather remained warm and dry. Laken chatted easily, explaining points of interest as we passed them, and life as a captain in Kyllian's army. Most of the soldiers mainly ignored me, but were polite enough. Tad would often smile and give me an extra portion of berries or sweet cakes, and Gheth, a young soldier with a sun-browned face bordered by curly blond hair and highlighted by sparkling blue eyes, would help me when I tried to groom the horses. Drey did not spend time talking to me, but I often caught him looking at me with a frown on his face. It was as if I was a problem he had not yet solved. Laken would catch his eye, giving a slight shake of his head, and Drey would carry on with what he was doing. This happened more often than I was comfortable with, and I started to become nervous around Drey.

I fell easily into the routine of waking and breakfasting on biscuits before travelling late into the afternoon. A quick break, more to rest the horses than the men, provided the chance for a small meal of dried meat and savouries supplied by the cook at Sharpie's Tavern. We would then ride until dusk, finding a clearing to light a fire and tether the horses while Tad worked his magic on the ration oats and gathered roots, fruits and nuts. The conversation around the fire stayed merry as the men swapped stories of outrageous conquests – on the battlefield and in the bedchamber. I would fall asleep to the sound of male laughter.

The feeling during the days changed slowly as we got nearer to Liegeport. An air of expectation and anticipation developed as we approached the soldiers' home town. The countryside took on a more industrious look, with less woodland and meadow and increasing numbers of organised farmed fields. The individual plots of land were getting smaller as more people claimed territory. The road, which had been mainly worn grass around Methhold, became harder, the earth packed down by generations of travellers heading to the main trade port of Faulknar. The simple offerings to the Gods of food and water, commonly left by streams and hazel trees, were seen less often the closer we got to the port.

The final night before reaching Liegeport was spent in a small town containing many wooden houses built almost on top of each other. The neighbouring farms had supplied a surplus of food, so that the population had grown faster than the village. Two-storey buildings stood adjacent to each other on either side of the main road, with alleyways leading off in all directions between groups of residences. We had arrived at dusk and the dim lighting added to the feeling that the structures were about to fall over and crush me. There were more houses and people than I had ever seen before, and I didn't like the smell, noise and activity that went with a densely inhabited town. I shrunk a little smaller and squeezed Laken a little tighter, intimidated by the buildings and the people.

Laken led the company towards the main square where market stalls were jumbled together under a timber roof. The sellers were packing up their goods and I could see small, brightly coloured wooden toys, breads and pastries, caged chickens, leather goods, pottery, and ironware. There were more items available for sale than I had seen in the whole of Methhold. Men and women shouted to each other in obvious companionship, while children played around the stalls, screaming and generally getting in the way. Dogs ran between their legs, their barks and yips adding to the general chaos and noise.

To the left of the marketplace was an imposing building of large blocks of stone and flint. Heavy timber double doors, twice as tall as Laken, dominated the front wall, iron bars holding the wood to the hinges and attached to the wall. There was no carving on the doors and no ornamental brickwork, but either side of the doors, starting five handspans above head height and rising to as many handspans below the roof, were a pair of coloured-glass windows. The windows of the roundhouses in Methhold had been covered with sacking or timber shutters; only the meeting hall had had glass. These windows were at least four times the size of those, and bore vivid pictures displayed by the coloured staining. My mouth fell open as I gazed in astonishment at the beautiful images. Serene faces looked down on the people in the street. Impossibly fine wings spread behind their heads and down their backs to their outstretched arms. Birds with blue and green plumage soared above them, frozen in mid-dance.

'The Temple of the Holy Baila,' said Laken over his shoulder to me. 'If you think that's impressive, wait until you see the one in Liegeport.'

The old Gods were worshipped at natural wonders such as streams and hazel groves. It was considered an arrogance to build temples that could not possibly encompass the glory of the Gods. But the temple in front of me argued against that point of view. It was breathtaking in its size and beauty, and the amount of work that must have taken place in order to build such a place. The worshippers of Baila were a prosperous society, and they spent their riches in celebrating their God.

The tavern where we were to stay was down a side road to the right of the temple. The building and stables were squeezed in the middle of a row of houses that appeared to have developed as the need arose. The buildings along this road were a mixture of one- and two-storey houses, many leaning at an angle and propped against the neighbouring walls. Structures that had been well maintained sat between those with rotting timber and broken shutters. The tavern was small compared to Sharpie's, but the wood was well maintained and the main room was already full. The noise of companionable chatter spilled onto the street as the horses were stabled. There were no rooms available and we were to sleep in the hayloft above the stables. Two soldiers were left to look after the horses and guard our supplies while the rest of us ate in the tavern.

I sat close to Laken at the only available table in the far corner of the room. Drey sat opposite me, while Laken sat opposite his sergeant. Herron had the muscular build common to fighting men but seemed more agile than his size would suggest. His hair was cut close to his head so that the skin of his scalp showed through, but flecks of grey were still visible throughout his brown hair. He had an easy manner, but his eyes missed nothing and he had gained respect from the men by dispensing swift but fair discipline.

The men spoke quietly about military matters and I stopped listening almost as soon as they started talking. I was much more interested in watching the drinkers as I slowly ate the vegetable broth offered by the tavern's cook. There were men from a number of trades: slightly built men with calloused fingers from weaving or carpentry, larger labourers, and a bear of a man with spark-burnt tunic and leggings who must have been the town blacksmith. A group of young men at the bar were jeering at the pretty young woman behind the counter. She was one of three girls serving the drinks and food, and I could see no women customers.

I sensed more than heard the conversation between Drey, Laken and Herron stop. I turned to see Herron shifting uncomfortably while Drey and Laken stared at each other.

'We can't put it off any longer.' Drey leaned forward to emphasise his point. 'It's what we agreed.'

Laken looked at me. 'I know. It's just…'

'You're too soft. Always have been.' Drey placed a cloth of deep midnight blue, folded in half, on the table between himself and Laken. 'It attracts too much attention. It's a risk here and will be positively dangerous at Liegeport. We've already had one casualty.'

'I know.' Laken held up his hand in defeat. 'I know.'

Drey turned to me. 'I need the sword.'

My eyes widened. 'No.'

'Tallen—'

'No!'

Laken turned sideways on the bench so that he was facing me. 'Tallen. I know it belongs to your family, but you won't be able to keep it once we get into Liegeport.' His eyes pleaded with me. 'It would be better for Drey to keep it safe. It will be too much of a temptation in the armoury.'

It was my turn to show pleading eyes. 'No.'

Laken stayed silent. He had explained his case and waited patiently while I considered all the options and came to the only conclusion I could. I would not be able to hold on to the sword in a strange town, surrounded by strangers. I had no idea what my life was going to be like once we reached the port, but I suspected that it would not include the need for a sword that I could barely use. I looked at Drey, searching for the desire for the sword I had seen in Rolyan's eyes. But it wasn't there; just an undercurrent of concern. I was not sure if it was for me or the sword.

I unbuckled the baldric and laid it on the table between us, my fingers still touching the leather, unwilling to part with it. After more than a dozen heartbeats I pushed it towards Drey.

Drey nodded in acceptance and covered the blade and baldric with the blue cloth. The fabric flowed over the sword, suggesting a high quality of material. He quickly excused himself and took the weapon out of the room. Watching it go, I had a hollow feeling in the pit of my stomach but, strangely, did not feel sad at its loss. I knew I would see it again.

The tavern room was crowded and noisy, but my attention was caught again by the group of young men at the bar. There was palpable tension between this group and a group of Laken's men, including Gheth. Gheth was getting upset about how the boys were treating the barmaid, and was being gently restrained from attempting to teach them some manners. Insults were traded, progressing to shoves. Laken was talking to Herron and had not seen the situation developing.

'Silly old relic,' a youth with legs and arms that looked too big for him and a mop of unruly hair commented loudly as Drey left the tavern. 'When's he going to realise that he's part of history? His kind are a joke.'

The room exploded.

Gheth flew at the boy, hitting him in the chest and knocking him to the floor, then straddled him and started punching him in the face. Both groups took this as a cue to release the tensions that had built up during the evening. Men were knocked to the ground and fists connected with jaws, cheeks and eyes. The noise level rose as insults were shouted and howls of anger bounced off the timber beams. Another group of Laken's men were at the other end of the room, and attempted to go across and help their colleagues. Their way was blocked and another fight started.

Laken was now paying attention and vaulted over the table into the melee. He and Herron were pushing men out of the way, Laken moving towards Gheth's group while Herron headed towards the other. I saw Rolyan isolated in a corner but holding his ground, using a broken chair to protect his injured arm. Three men were closing in on him and I could see he would soon be overpowered. I moved towards him, collecting an iron fire-poker as I went. Being small I was able to move easily across the room, avoiding the groups of fighting men and flying furniture. I stood on Rolyan's injured left side and did what I could to even up the odds for him. He acknowledged me with a brief nod of the head before taking the legs out from under his remaining opponent with the chair.

There were three isolated groups – Rolyan and me in the far corner, Herron and two others to our right, and Laken, Gheth and the final three by the bar. The townspeople surrounded these groups, but Laken's men were holding their own. They moved instinctively to complement each other, containing their opponents but never overwhelming them. It was a while before I realised this was intentional. The fight was staged and controlled by the soldiers. The townsmen were bruised and battered, but no real harm was being inflicted on either side.

Laken caught my eye, smiling the biggest grin I had ever seen. His voice carried easily over the noise of the brawl.

'Told you this was going to be fun!'

Chapter Three

The next day was bright and cheery, which reflected the mood of the men as they prepared to leave before most of the townspeople awoke. There were cuts and bruises, split lips, scraped knuckles and black eyes, but spirits were buoyed by the expectation of being in Liegeport by sundown. The bruise on Laken's right cheek was mainly dark grey with purple touches at the edges, and he stiffly protected his left ribs where he had been hit with a chair. He was almost bouncing up and down as he merrily instructed the men, teasing them and laughing at their bad jests. The mood was contagious and although my arms and back ached from wielding the poker and I had a huge bruise on the top of my shoulder preventing me from raising my left arm, I couldn't help smiling at the men acting like little boys.

Drey seemed to be the only one who was immune to the mood of the soldiers. He was thoughtful and sombre as he loaded his gear onto his skewbald horse, its white patches blindingly reflecting the sunlight. I could see a corner of the midnight-blue cloth that covered my sword for a moment before Drey tugged at a fold of leather and hid it from sight. He turned and caught me watching him, and held my gaze for a handful of heartbeats before giving me a small nod. Then I felt Laken's warm hand on my right shoulder as Drey mounted his horse.

'Time to go,' he said as I turned from Drey and he carefully lifted me onto the front of the saddle. He winked. 'You'll see the sights better from here.'

We rode steadily all day, eating our midday meal on horseback. Although the landscape was still mainly flat, the horizon was obscured by the increasing number of farms, villages and small towns. The dwellings clustered around the main road to Liegeport, but spread further than I could see as the populations rose. Original mud-plastered roundhouses were surrounded by timber buildings, many with two storeys. In more than one small town I saw a stone building similar to the temple for Baila that I had seen the previous day. The people of the towns looked wealthier than those I had seen previously, their style of clothing more decorative and ornate than that worn by the farmers. Homespun and plainly weaved clothes were replaced by tight-fitting tunics and leggings, with the ladies wearing gowns of dyed felt or multicoloured woven material. As we got nearer the port, more than one man wore a rich doublet as if he was at the royal court.

The traffic on the road also changed during the day, with increasing numbers of horses as well as travellers on foot. Some men carried large sacks that bounced against their backs, hanging from a strap pressed against their foreheads. Others pushed rough wooden carts full of vegetables from the fields, or crates of chickens for sale in the markets. We once had to wait for an ox-drawn carriage that had blocked the road, with the ox refusing to move despite all the efforts of the driver and his stick.

By early evening, our pace had slowed to a crawl due to the volume of traffic heading towards Liegeport before the city gates closed at dusk. The late-evening sun was warm on our backs as we crested a small hill. The force of the wind had increased, and I tasted the sharp tang of salty air. Large white birds that I had never seen in Methhold cawed loudly, unafraid of people as they dove to the pathways to collect the scraps of food that had been dropped there.

From the foot of the hill I could see the top of a large stone building. The pale, sandy towers with a pointed centrepiece pierced the sky at the four corners of the building, each bordered by decorative stone crenulations atop a small wall. However, the scale of the building, and the coastal fortress that supported it, was not apparent until we reached the summit. The sandstone building with its pointed turrets dominated the scene, standing out against the grey-blue of the sea and the darker blue of the sky. The sun glinted on the windows that in places extended for two storeys, and a banner displaying the Faulknar colours flew proudly over a stone archway in its centre.

The rest of the building was hidden by the sprawling town that provided the workforce for the royal residence and the bustling port. A similar mix of the mud and timber houses that had been seen in the neighbouring towns was represented in Liegeport, although there were several large stone houses near the centre of the town. A network of pathways and alleys could be seen radiating in all directions. The main road was at least twice as large as the connecting roads and ran from the dominating stone building to the encircling flint walls. The city gates were double doors of heavy oak strapped with iron hinges. They stood open as late travellers made their way through into the protected streets.

To the right of the city was the port that provided trade for the Faulknar territories. Large-sailed ships could be seen within the natural harbour that served as a dock. The white birds were more numerous around the dockside as they circled the people working below. The noise of the men, unloading goods and transferring them onto waiting carts, could be heard as far away as we were on the hilltop. The sight of the ships, the intimidating number and grandeur of the buildings, and the bustle of all the people were overwhelming for me. I had seen so many sights in the few days since I left Methhold, each new encounter bigger and bolder than the previous one. I shrunk back into Laken, feeling the reassurance of his warm chest and scratchy shirt. He tightened his hold around my waist.

'Welcome to Liegeport.'

The sun had dropped behind the horizon and the light was starting to fade as we passed through the city gates. The soldiers were well known and passed through without challenge. Playful banter was exchanged between the men and the guards who were leaning, relaxed, against the wooden gates.

'Any later and we would have barred the gates on you, thinking you common outlaws.' The larger of the two guards grinned, stained teeth splitting his thick, black beard.

Laken laughed. 'I'm surprised the gates are still open, and you're not in the Blue Boar already.'

The smaller, younger guard nodded towards me. 'You picking up strays now, Laken?'

'My cousin's child. Half the village died of the wasting disease. She's got no one else.'

I stiffened. Laken had lied so easily. The guards accepted his story with a sympathetic nod. Without question. The soldiers paid no attention, although they had surely heard the lie. It reminded me that there was a lot I didn't know about this man that I had been so quick to trust.

We rode through the city, where buildings were used as businesses as well as homes. These houses had double wooden shutters covering most of the front of the building, with only a smaller door left on the first floor. Many had their shutters closed, having finished trading for the day, but a few were still pushed open to allow passers-by to view their goods. The shops seemed to specialise, so that I saw one containing pottery, another with candles, and another with shoes. The horses picked up their pace as I smelt the tang of metallic smoke and heard the ringing blow of the blacksmith. We turned off the main road and rode down a side street that opened up into a small courtyard. The forge was the first building we came to, but my attention was caught by the other two sides of the courtyard where large barns contained the heads of horses looking over the gates to each stall. There were examples of every colour and shade. There were fine-headed horses in one barn, while another housed ones that were much larger and had wider heads. A chorus of shrill whinnies greeted the returning horses, who responded with equal enthusiasm. I was bounced as Laken's chestnut shook in anticipation of clean straw to roll in.

We left the horses in the care of the grooms. Three young boys were supervised by an older lad, and they efficiently collected the horses. They led them to their stables before removing their tack and grooming away the sweat and dirt from the day's riding. The men disappeared through a stone archway between two barns, while Drey carried his belongings through a more ornate archway between the far stables and a plain building on the fourth side of the courtyard. Laken disappeared into this building briefly and returned without his saddlebags. He still carried his sword in the scabbard on his belt, although his men and the guards were the only ones I had seen carrying weapons.

He held out his hand. 'Come with me.'

I took it and held tightly as we quickly walked through the decorated archway, following Drey. The arch lasted fifteen paces. I was momentarily blinded by the darkness but welcomed the coolness that radiated from the stone. As my eyes adjusted, I saw carvings on the inside of the tunnel showing scenes of battle and of hunting large game. The images of the horses, boar and stag were so finely detailed that I wanted to reach out and touch the fur, imagining it to feel soft and warm.

Laken led me into another courtyard, this one almost twice the size of the stable courtyard. The three sides opposite us as we emerged from the tunnel presented beautiful two-storey houses with window glass and two colours of stonework. The main doors to the house on my left were guarded by two rearing sandstone horses. The house in front of me was guarded by two sandstone men, twice the size of Laken, brandishing spears. The one to the right was guarded by two giant sea serpents, mythical creatures said to protect sailors from the dangers of the deep ocean. Laken ignored these buildings and led me down a passageway between the house with the horses and the one with the men. High flint walls enclosed the backs of the houses so that I could not see behind them. However, the green tops of a few trees could be seen, and the smell of scented flowers suggested ornamental gardens.

The alley opened into a small rectangular courtyard, directly in front of the three-storey house I had seen from the hill. I felt as if I had shrunk to half my size as I looked at the scale of the building with my mouth hanging open. I could hear Laken chuckling beside me but could not take my eyes away from the largest building I had ever seen. There were at least ten windows along the front of the building on each floor. The central two windows on the second floor were taller and wider than those on either side of them. The third storey was only gained at the towers standing at the corners of the main building. In each of these towers glass windows reflected the torches starting to light the city, before the building was crowned with pointed spires and decorative borders. Different shades of stonework created patterns at the edges of the building and beneath the windows. The main feature, however, was the archway at the centre. The pale sandstone rose to the sill of the second-storey windows and was breathtakingly decorated with carvings of hare and hound. Some were captured mid-chase, as if time had suddenly stopped. I forgot to breathe for a couple of heartbeats as I was captivated by the spell. This stillness was broken by the flapping of the Faulknar banner, proudly displaying who owed this magnificent house. If further reminders were required, these were offered in the paired white-stone lions either side of the main doors. They were standing on their hind legs like kittens reaching for a thread to play with, the paw furthest away from the door on each lion extended as if to salute the Faulknar banner.

Laken gently guided me away from the majesty of the front of the house to a small wooden door along the left side. He had to stoop to go through it. We entered a corridor where men and women, boys and girls, all wearing matching pale yellow leggings and black tunics with the Faulknar crest on the left side of the chest, ran around looking very busy. Several greeted Laken with smiles and a pat on the back or arm as we passed. The heat from the cooking fires felt as if it was melting my face as we walked into the kitchen. This was a large room with two fires burning at the far wall. A deep pot was being stirred above one of these fires, while a pig was being roasted over the other. The smell of cooking meat made my stomach growl in anticipation. I could almost taste the juices contained in the succulent meat.

A high squeal on my right made me jump, and I had to move quickly out of the way to avoid being pushed over by a young woman running full speed at Laken. Her long blonde hair was tied back in a ponytail, exposing a pretty face with the blue eyes of a summer's day. From three paces away, she launched herself at Laken, forcing him to catch her by the waist as she curled her arms and legs around his body. They kissed fiercely. Urgently. Passionately.

'Oleana,' called a commanding female voice. 'Leave the poor boy alone. He's barely made it through the door.'

They broke the kiss and smiled sheepishly at each other. Laken moved Oleana to his right hip so he could see the lady who was so obviously in charge of the kitchen. A small, plump woman with light brown hair piled on top of her head and held there with broken wooden spoons, stood with her hands on her hips.

'Mistress Narran.' Laken smiled warmly. 'I hope you are well.'

'I was until ruffians came in and distracted my girls!'

Oleana whined in Laken's arms. 'Mistress, it's been two months. I've missed him.'

'Well, miss him somewhere else.'

Oleana squealed again. 'Really?'

'You're not much use to me sulking in a corner. Your miserable face would turn the sweetmeats sour.'

Laken mouthed a thank-you to Mistress Narran as Oleana leapt from his arms to smother the older lady in a warm embrace. She left a quick kiss on the cook's cheek before darting back to Laken. Mistress Narran flapped her hands at the pair, shooing them from her kitchen.

I had been completely forgotten.

I started to feel sick as a tight band constricted around my stomach. My heart hammered against my chest as it increased its rate. I swallowed, trying to slow my rapid breathing. Laken had gone. I had no idea how to get back to the stables or find the soldiers I had travelled with. I didn't know what to do. Was this it? Had Laken only planned on bringing me to Liegeport for me to take care of myself from then on? My stomach growled again, reminding me that I did not know where I could get food to eat. No one was eating in the kitchen despite the volume of food present.

'Don't just stand there, child.' Mistress Narran was looking at me. 'Come and help me with this.'

Relief flooded through me so that I was left feeling light-headed. The cook had offered me the opportunity to forget my problems and concentrate on the tasks she found for me. I quickly transferred the responsibility for my care from Laken to Mistress Narran, and focused on the now, rather than scaring myself with the thought of what could happen next. I readily walked over to the large wooden table to help mix the contents within a bowl.

I was achingly tired by the time Mistress Narran had run out of jobs for me. It was fully dark outside and the sounds beyond the kitchen had fallen quiet a while ago. I finished wiping down the tabletop while others returned pots and dishes to the shelves. A large pot of rabbit casserole was simmering over one fire, while the other burnt down to glowing embers.

'Here.' Mistress Narran passed me a bowl of casserole. 'Go sit by the fire. You've earned your supper.'

I smiled gratefully, still too intimidated by the woman to say my thank-you. I joined the small group of kitchen girls by the smouldering fire, sitting a little to the side. A young girl with fiery red hair and a face covered with freckles passed me a chunk of grainy bread. The smell of the stew made me feel sick with hunger, and I greedily shovelled the food into my mouth, then sighed deeply as the warmth radiated from my stomach and spread through my tired muscles. The gentle conversation of the kitchen girls and the cooks bubbled over my head as my limbs grew heavy and my blinks began to slow. My bowl had been wiped clean with the bread and I lay down next to it on the floor, watching the small flames flicker and dance in the embers.

I awoke to the smell of baking bread. It was still dark outside, but the people in the kitchen had changed. Mistress Narran was not in sight. Someone had placed a blanket over me during the night, but I was the only one lying on the floor. I watched the early-morning kitchen routine as bread was kneaded and placed on a shelf above the fire to rise. Smaller loaves that had been prepared earlier were already enclosed in copper pans and being heated over the flames. There were three young men taking care of the household's bread, while two boys washed the bowls and spoons used to make the dough. I quietly watched them go about their work, snuggled under my warm woollen blanket. The sky outside had turned the pale grey of dawn before more people came into the kitchen to prepare breakfast.

A young boy, about the same age as me, entered the kitchen, stole a small loaf and came to sit on a chair next to me. He had dark blond hair, long enough to tickle his ears, and sea-green eyes in a tanned face. He smiled a wide, open-mouthed grin, winking at me as he pulled the loaf apart and handed half to me. No one in the kitchen paid any attention to him or the fact that he had just helped himself to the freshly cooked food.

'Good morning.'

'Morning,' I mumbled around a mouthful of bread.

'I'm Tawpin,' he said cheerily. 'Drey sent me to find you. He figured that Laken may have been distracted by the charms of the beautiful Oleana.'

I nodded.

The grin returned. 'He wasn't at the Blue Boar last night so Oleana must have kept him *very* busy.'

I scowled, remembering how Laken had left with Oleana without thinking about me. Tawpin playful cuffed me on the arm.

'Cheer up. Drey sent me last night, so will have forgotten by now. I guess we've got until late afternoon until they come looking for me. And anyway, he never said to bring you *straight* to him.' He winked at me again. 'Which of Liegeport's many sights do you fancy seeing?'

I shrugged. 'I've seen the stables.'

'Pah! The stables are boring.' He frowned thoughtfully. 'I could take you to North End. That's where all the fun is, but it's probably not the best place for your first day. You being such a country girl.' He laughed as I scowled at the implied insult. 'The docks aren't particularly safe…'

I took the bait. 'I can take care of myself.'

The grin returned, wider than ever. 'Brilliant. The docks it is, then. The *Golden Lady* has just returned from Gallowgla. She'll be full of gold and treasures.'

He jumped up and pulled me to my feet. Keeping hold of my hand, he dragged me away from the dropped blanket before I could tidy it away. We ran out of a door to the rear of the kitchen, through a storeroom with stacked wooden barrels and jars of pickled fruit. My head banged against the hanging vegetables as Tawpin took me out of the side door and into the street. There were fewer people around than the previous evening, as it was still early morning, but already there were many men and women rushing towards the main house or opening the shutters of the business-houses. Tawpin didn't slow as he guided me between buildings and down side alleys, and I was soon breathing hard from the exertion of our flight through Liegeport, and also from the excitement of running through the streets with Tawpin. He had a contagious personality and I was soon grinning alongside him, even as my legs screamed with the effort of keeping up.

We raced through the rear city gates to the shouts of the guards, and continued up the sharp incline that led to the coastal road, before turning towards the docks. Timber platforms jutted a long way into the harbour to avoid the rocks littered around the coastline. Three of the five platforms contained a large ship, with canvas sails closely tied to the mast. Two of the vessels lay quietly at their moorings, while activity buzzed around the third like bees around a hive. This was obviously the *Golden Lady*, as there was a female statue carved at the front of the ship. She was covered in what looked like bright yellow paint that reflected the rising sun so it hurt to look directly at her. She was nearly twice as tall as the men working on the platform, with long hair carved to fall over her bare shoulders. Her arms stretched behind her, pressed against the side of the ship, while her bare feet peeked out from the hem of her gown to cross delicately above the waterline.

'That's gold,' said Tawpin, slowing to allow me to drink in the sights of the magnificent ship. 'The *Lady*'s carved from timber, then covered in a thin sheet of gold.' He pointed. 'You can just see the rivets used to hold the gold in place.'

I didn't know whether to believe him or not, but the figure was the most beautiful thing I had ever seen.

'The Gallowglass have more gold than they know what to do with.' He looked at me, raising his eyebrows. 'Fancy a closer look?'

Reluctantly I took my eyes away from the *Golden Lady* to look at him and smile. I nodded enthusiastically. 'Yes please.'

Tawpin laughed and we raced down the slope from the clifftop towards the wooden docks. Mules and small carts were being laden with chests of cargo taken from the ship. A small man with rusty brown hair inspected each container before it was loaded, making thin marks on a sheet of paper as each one was approved. The goods were then taken by a road, wider than the coastal path we had used, that ran directly to the city. Tawpin playfully pushed me into the path of a cart heading towards the ship, and I apologised to the carter before turning to glare at Tawpin and slap him on the arm. He offered up one of the two apples he had taken from the cart as an apology.

We watched the *Golden Lady* all morning. The sun rose over the sea, glinting gemstones of light on the ripples of the water and the gold of the *Lady*. The men sweated on the docks and most had removed their shirts by early morning. Those that remained fully dressed appeared to be in charge – the man inspecting the loads before they went to Liegeport, another checking the food provisions being loaded onto the ship, and another two organising the gangs of labourers. Tawpin chatted merrily about the town and docks, explaining the buildings I pointed to and the people working in them. We kept the conversation light, and did not ask questions about each other, Laken or Drey.

A box was dropped from the docking plank onto the dockside. The lid fell open and the contents spilled onto the walkway. My heart rate instantly gained pace as the sun reflected on the gold and gems fashioned into a variety of decorative items. My fingers flexed at the sight of the treasures being frantically picked up and replaced in the chest. Fine necklaces, thick torcs, arm bangles, rings, buckles, plates and goblets. The gold was highlighted by reds, blues, greens and ambers. The way they caught the morning light suggested these were precious stones, not coloured glass.

'Merciful Mother,' I breathed, biting the second knuckle of my first right finger.

'Sure is a pretty sight.'

The last of the treasures was carefully replaced and the lid strapped over the precious cargo before I began to breathe normally again. Tawpin laughed at me.

'I see you like the pretty things, Magpie. You are going to be so easy to corrupt.' He laughed again as I frowned at him. 'How about we go and find some real treasure? I'm starving. The Blue Boar will be serving lunch now.'

He led me back to the city along the wide road that was used to carry the cargo to the markets. We again passed through the rear city gates, which were much smaller than the front ones but made of equally stout oak panels. The guards playfully checked Tawpin to see if he had stolen anything from the dockside. It was clear that he had a reputation for taking things that did not belong to him, and the two occasions I had seen suggested a lot of practice. With loud protestations of his innocence, Tawpin was eventually allowed to follow me through the gates into the city.

He led me on a confusing route around the city, and within a few steps I was hopelessly lost. I knew if Tawpin left me I would not be able to find the city gates again, much less the stables or the kitchen. One street looked very much like another, with mud and timber houses clustered together against the pathway. These dwellings were not as well maintained as the ones I had seen on the main road, and their plain walls showed signs of neglect. Many of the shutters on the lower floors remained closed throughout the day. The atmosphere was more suffocating in these back alleys, although Tawpin continued on confidently. With the convoluted journey, I was starting to think that he had lost his way, but eventually we emerged into the bright midday sun. We left the dark lane and stepped onto a wider road with a variety of townspeople walking and talking companionably. Opposite to where we had come from was a small barn containing five or six horses, and next to this was a long, two-storey timber building. Cheerful banter and out-of-tune singing drifted out of the main door that stood open at the far end of the building. A wooden sign with a painted blue pig hung above the door and swung slightly in the gentle breeze.

'The Blue Boar. Home of all the lowlifes, ruffians and wastrels. The only place to be.'

Despite Tawpin's introduction, I found the atmosphere inside the Blue Boar friendly and welcoming. There were only a handful of men in the tavern, but they were making the noise of a whole company of soldiers. The banter between them and the serving girls was gentler and more jovial than I had seen in the tavern where the fight had happened, with the girls, on more than one occasion, getting the better of the men teasing them. Tawpin led me to a small table set into a curve in the wall, tucked behind the main door. It was easily overlooked by both the drinkers and those behind the bar, and no one bothered us as we watched. One man was singing and playing a stringed instrument lying across his lap. The notes appeared random, with those being sung not matching those played on the instrument. The song told of a young girl trying to get a husband, with increasingly more outrageous exploits in her attempts to snare a man.

'Here.' Tawpin passed a plate over the table towards me. It contained a thick slice of bread, cold meats, cheese and an apple. An identical plate sat in front of him.

'Where did you get these?'

He grinned. 'They were destined for the pair of wool dealers over there. Shanna got distracted.' He shrugged.

'How do you not get caught?'

He stuffed a chunk of bread into his mouth and grinned widely, showing soggy bread stuck between his teeth and lips. I giggled. He didn't tell me the secret of stealing food without being seen.

We spent the afternoon watching people come and go from the tavern. Some men left on their own; others were collected by their wives or sweethearts. More men always came to replace those leaving, so that the tavern was constantly busy with drinkers and diners. Tawpin identified the main players as they entered.

'The wool dealers in that corner are plotting against the tanners over there. They think the tanners pay less tax and can afford to sell their goods cheaper than the wool dealers can. They pay the same, but the tanners get cheap leather from the poachers. Many a fine lady in this city is wearing squirrel.'

He indicated a small group of men wearing sailors' loose trousers and tunics, standing by the bar. They were tanned, and I could see they were barefooted. 'Those are the sailors from the *Golden Lady*. My guess is that they will be causing trouble later tonight. The drink is already making them louder than anybody else. By nightfall they will be itching for a fight, or a girl.'

I looked at my new friend and wondered how he knew such things, but he had moved on to the next group. He nodded towards a couple of thickset men, one of whom had a scar running from his right ear, along his jawline, to the point of his chin. 'Those two are traders that carry the goods from the docks to the rest of the kingdom. They will be taking goods from the other ships. Those that trade goods from the *Lady* don't drink at the Blue Boar. It's been said that Abe got his scar from fighting off twenty bandits trying to steal his load.'

I couldn't count to twenty, but it sounded like a lot of men.

'Now, that's interesting. That skinny fellow in the black leggings and tunic.'

I looked towards where Tawpin was staring and saw a thin man with a slight stoop at the shoulders. He had a sharp, angular face exposed by a receding hairline so that his mousy brown hair formed a horseshoe around his head. I noticed he was wearing shiny leather shoes with silver buckles.

'That's the temple scribe. I wonder what he's doing here.'

We watched as the thin man slowly slid a small purse across the counter. Brethick, the tavern owner, dropped the cloth he was using to clean the tankards over the purse and continued talking to the scribe. A few moments later he left to serve a customer. He took the cloth with him, and the purse was gone.

'Very interesting.' Tawpin grinned at me, knowing I had seen the purse disappear as well.

The scribe casually left the bar, climbed the stairs at the far end and entered one of the rooms on the second floor. We continued watching and were rewarded shortly when one of the older serving girls followed him.

'Naughty scribe,' mocked Tawpin, before suddenly cursing. 'Horse dung!'

He was looking over my shoulder at a group of three men walking through the door. I took a breath to shout as I recognised Laken and Herron, although I did not know the third man. Tawpin reached over and gripped my arm, hard.

'Don't.'

'But Laken—'

'I know. But he's a busy man. He'd have sent for you if he could spare the time.'

I glared at Tawpin, feeling this wasn't the truth.

He shrugged with one shoulder. 'He'll kick us out of here if he finds us. Things are just starting to get interesting.'

I did not believe him, but I nodded in agreement. I was content to see Laken again. And he did look busy. The three men sat at a table far from the bar and ordered drinks but no food. Shanna brought the tankards over and spoke to Laken while draping herself over his shoulders. He mumbled something that made her laugh. But she removed her arm from his neck and patted him on the shoulder as she left.

'What?' laughed Laken as Herron rolled his eyes.

The men talked in quiet voices and I could not hear what they were saying. I watched as they sat comfortably in each other's company, although there was an intensity to what they were saying, and several times one of them leant forward to emphasise a point. Laken wore a similar serious expression to the one I had seen when he had talked to Sharpie late at night. Herron stayed quiet for most of the discussion, only occasionally contributing a point. Laken paid attention to these comments.

Tawpin sat quietly in front of me, and it was a while before I realised he had stopped talking. I turned away from Laken to see Tawpin watching the stairs. I twisted slightly so that I could see what he was looking at, but there was no one there. Tawpin caught me watching him and smiled.

'Fancy a little more adventure?'

I was reluctant to leave Laken, but Tawpin's smile as ever offered untold wonders. I grinned back at him and nodded.

We slipped out of the door without anyone noticing, and Tawpin led me to the stables. Seemingly without effort, we entered and climbed up into the hay store without being seen.

'Hey, Magpie, how are you with heights?'

I had climbed trees in the forest behind Methhold and knew I wasn't scared of heights like some of the other children. I had never climbed onto the roof of a two-storey building, however, and I hesitated before following Tawpin onto the tiled roof of the barn. The experience was different to that I remembered from climbing trees. The wind was stronger as there were no branches to provide shelter. There was nothing to hold on to, and my feet slipped on the smooth baked-mud tiles. I looked out across the city. It was much more beautiful up here. The people disappeared, and the rooftops flowed like waves on a lake. The large white birds perched on the chimneys, squawking at the smaller birds that may have wanted to join them.

Tawpin was leaning precariously over the side of the stable roof, kneeling on one leg while pushing away with the other. The only thing keeping him on the roof was a handhold on the corner of the tiling. I strained to see what he was looking at, but could only see the top of the tavern wall where it joined its own tiled roof.

'What are you looking at?'

'Shush!'

I sighed. This was not as exciting as I had thought. The view was good, but nothing was happening up here. I quickly grew bored of watching the birds squabble.

After a short while I heard a wooden shutter slam, and Tawpin quickly spun around to join me.

'Time to get you back to the kitchen, I think. And Drey will definitely be looking for us by now.'

We climbed off the roof and ran through the stables. Tawpin quickly returned me to the kitchen, which was again full of people, activity and noise. Mistress Narran scolded him as soon as we walked through the door.

'Where have you two been all day? Getting up to mischief if I know you, Master Tawpin.'

He dodged out of reach of her swatting arm and ran laughing out of the room, leaving me to feel awkward under Mistress Narran's gaze.

'Come on then, lass. There's plenty of work to be done.'

Chapter Four

As I had fallen into the rhythm of a company of soldiers on the road, I also quickly adopted the routine of life in the city. I would wake early so that Tawpin and I could explore the city and docks. We watched the cargo ships in the harbour and helped the fishermen unload their catch in the bay further up the coast. We spent time watching the people selling their goods in the marketplace, a gathering of stalls covered by brightly coloured wooden roofs to protect from the heat of the sun in summer or the rain and snow in winter. There was so much on display – food, clothes, weapons, gifts, household items. I watched Tawpin stealing food when we were hungry, and it wasn't long before I could take it as easily as he could.

We would run down the alleyways and call to the merchants selling from the open-fronted houses. We saw the rich people that gathered around the centre of town, near the royal house. And Tawpin showed me the poorer side of town – the North End. The houses in this part of the city were smaller and almost all had only one storey. The timber buildings were heaped into houses, looking more accidental than planned. They huddled together in the narrow streets, making the area darker and more claustrophobic. The air smelt damp and musty, and breathing seemed difficult. The bright, cheery colours of the market were replaced by browns, blacks and greys. The few people we saw, lurking in doorways or scuttling down side alleys, looked wary and suspicious, but Tawpin seemed as comfortable here as he was everywhere else.

By midday I would return to the kitchens and Tawpin would run off to perform his duties. He never told me what they were, but I was kept too busy by Mistress Narran to spend much time thinking about that. The kitchen tasks were never-ending, but boring. Due to my exploits with Tawpin in the city, I soon knew the layout and where all the household merchants were. I readily volunteered to run messages or collect items, happy to be running around outside rather than being in the hot, bustling kitchen. In a short space of time I was spending more of my day being a runner than I was being a kitchen hand.

Late evenings were spent in front of the fire, eating the leftovers from the royal family and their guests. The household staff would join us and tell stories of the family – Kyllian, the king and ruler of the Faulknar kingdom, and his two sons, Kerk, the eldest by four years and the king's heir, and Kade, who was the same age as me. I was told of how the queen had given birth to a daughter, but both had died soon after. It was said that Kyllian had been a jovial and carefree man before the tragedy.

Tawpin would often join us and would whisper in my ear the gossip surrounding the officials and dignitaries that visited Liegeport. Kyllian had firm control over his kingdom, but there were constant tensions between his dukes and retainers to gain favour. Land and influence were exchanged regularly, depending on the desires of the king at any particular time. Only blood kin were guaranteed their lands and place at court. Valour in battle, bravery in a crisis, successful merchants and personal friends were as likely to gain favours as ancestral pageantry. Tawpin had an amusing story for all of them. It was generally late before I retired to a small building to the side of the house, where I slept with three other kitchen girls.

I didn't see enough of Laken. He would send for me in the evenings, once or twice a week, and I would tell him all that I had done. He would seem interested in how I was getting on and if I'd made friends, but I could tell I was a distraction from his work with his company of soldiers. He bought me coloured ribbons, but I had to wrap them around my wrists as they would slip out of my short, straight hair. He bought me dresses that didn't fit and that I never wore. The evenings would often end awkwardly as we ran out of things to talk about.

The times I treasured were when Tawpin and I would sneak into the training grounds to watch Laken and the soldiers practise. Langdon, the Master of Arms and head instructor, would scowl at us and threaten to throw us in the city gaol. His brown eyes were overshadowed by his big, bushy eyebrows, making him look almost comical. However, his large arm muscles that were generally on display below a sleeveless gambeson, and the fact that he always carried at least two weapons, ensured that he was always taken seriously. Laken always convinced him to let us stay, and the soldiers would bicker over which one of us would be their lucky mascot for the day.

I watched the men practise with sword and spear, throwing knives and rapier, on horseback and on foot. I learnt about lunges, feints and counter-feints, forward thrusts and backhand follow-throughs. I could describe the techniques to disarm and to kill. The practice sessions were controlled and technical. The killing strokes were clothed in grace and beauty.

The uglier side of combat was shown to me when Tawpin would take me to the North End on fight night. Occasionally the soldiers would fight, but mainly it was the dockers and sailors who fought for extra coin. A circle would be roped off in the Mermaid tavern, and the men and women of North End would come to cheer the local who would take on the visiting sailor or trader. The fights were short and bloody. Bare knuckles connected with the flesh of cheeks, eyes, jaws, abdomens and lower backs. Bare feet kicked at shins, knees, thighs and ribs. It was primitive and brutal. It made me feel sick. But the power and the passion of the bouts kept me coming back for more.

It was an early winter's day, cold, windy and grey – reflecting my mood. My day off had coincided with Tawpin's and he had several plans for how to spend the day. He wanted to take the ponies to the forest south of Liegeport where goblins and trolls were meant to live, but I couldn't ride. He wanted to explore the caves hidden in the cliffs where stolen treasure was kept, but the tide was in and I didn't want to get wet. He suggested throwing mud at Crazy Vinik who was in the stocks for stealing a merchant's purse, but he scared me and I thought he could curse me just by looking.

Tawpin sat heavily next to me and sighed dramatically. 'Well, what do you want to do then?'

I shrugged. I wanted to see Laken. He hadn't sent for me in over a week and I was missing him. We had already been to the Blue Boar and the practice grounds, but he had not been there. I wanted to sulk and be miserable.

'Why are you so grumpy today?'

I shrugged, causing Tawpin to groan and roll his eyes.

'I miss Laken. He didn't send for me last night.'

'They've all been busy lately.'

'I know.'

'He probably just forgot.'

I huffed, drawing up my knees and wrapping my arms around them. We were sitting at the back of the market, letting the stalls divert the wind around us. The low clouds threatened rain, but the dry weather had held so far. People were hurrying to get their jobs done and did not pay us any attention.

Tawpin turned to look at me. 'Have you been in the royal house?'

I rolled my eyes. 'I work in the kitchen, stupid.'

'I didn't mean the servants' wing.'

It took a couple of heartbeats for me to understand what he was saying. 'You mean the main house? The royal rooms?'

Tawpin smiled. 'Yes.'

'But we're not allowed in there.'

'We're not allowed in the Blue Boar either.'

Despite my poor mood, I felt my heart increase its rhythm in anticipation of seeing where the king lived. The one place in the whole city I had not explored. I couldn't hide the excitement in my eyes. Tawpin laughed and hit me on the shoulder.

'Come on then!'

We ran back to the royal house, but then Tawpin led me down the far side, opposite the kitchen and staff accommodation. The house on this side was extended by a stone wall, and Tawpin took me through a wooden door into the private gardens of the royal family. The central lawn was cut short, and was crossed by narrow stone pathways to enable access to the numerous flower beds without stepping on the grass. Even this late in the year, there were several plants in bloom and the leaves of the bushes were various shades of green and yellow. We walked down the pathway closest to the wall and I was finding it hard to breathe amidst the fear that we would be discovered. I avoided making eye contact with anyone, but the few people that were working in the garden did not pay any attention to us. We ducked under a rosebush archway and crossed a small courtyard, before entering the house.

We entered at the far end of the servants' hallway, which ran along the back of the house and allowed the staff to move around without being on public display. Tawpin grinned at me, his eyes flashing with the excitement of entering forbidden areas. He confidently walked over to the wall in front of us, checking that no one was walking down the passageway. He pressed a wooden panel, four handspans in from the end and a third of the way up. A quiet click was heard deep within the wall. A panel the size of a small table, rising from the floor to the height of my waist, moved into the masonry by the width of my fingernail. Tawpin pushed against the right side of the panel and it swung smoothly inwards to reveal a passageway within the wall.

I turned to Tawpin, my eyes wide as I found it hard to believe what I was seeing. 'How do you know about this?' I whispered.

He held his finger to his lips before gesturing that I should go through. I had to bend almost in half but was able to stand straight again once I was through the panel work. He followed me and closed the panel so that I could no longer find the hidden door. As my eyes adjusted to the darkness, I could see spears of light coming from holes halfway up the far wall so that spots highlighted the passageway for several paces in front of me. I could feel Tawpin's hot breath in my ear as he leaned close to whisper.

'Sounds carry really well in here, so you have to be very quiet. But look through the eyehole.'

I leaned over to place my eye against the hole in the wall. I had to stretch slightly to be able to look through, but the holes were obviously made for children as they were too low for an adult to comfortably see through. I looked into a small room richly furnished with tapestries, rugs and soft chairs. Deep blues and reds predominated, but gold and green threads highlighted the details within the designs on the chairs and the hunting images in the tapestries. No one was in the room.

I grinned at Tawpin. I had never seen such a beautiful room. He took my hand and led me towards what would have been the outer wall. He placed my hand on a wooden ladder bolted to the wall, before climbing up out of view. I quickly followed him. My feet made no noise as I climbed into the darkness. Tawpin took my arm as I started to see another row of lights coming from the eyeholes and helped me off the ladder. I guessed we were on the second floor.

The secret passageway ran within the dividing wall between the main hall and the private rooms. I was surprised to find the doors into rooms were hollow to allow easy movement around the house. We had to turn sideways to squeeze through and push on false panels that made the door look solid when it was opened. Tawpin stopped after we had walked through the second door and indicated the eyehole. I looked through. My heart leapt, and I took an instinctive step back when I saw a well-dressed man sitting at a writing table, his back to me. I felt, rather than saw, Tawpin's grin get wider. The man could not see us. I looked through the hole again.

The room was again richly furnished like the one I had seen below. Rugs and tapestries stopped the cold creeping in from the stonework. The writing table was in front of the window and through the glass I could see the top of the neighbouring house. The man was average height but slight of build. His hair was neatly trimmed so that it just touched the collar of his felt jacket. The stitching detailing the panels in the back of the jacket spoke of the quality of the garment more than the fine material. To his right was a fireplace, with a small fire burning in the grate. A couple of thickly padded chairs were positioned either side of it. To the man's left was a large bed, covered in layers of blankets and three deep-filled pillows. A carved wooden clothes chest stood at the bottom of the bed. A thick woollen cloak had been carelessly thrown over it so that half of the cloak was on the floor.

Tawpin showed me three more rooms on the second floor. Each contained expensive furnishings but lacked any personal touches to indicate who lived in them. Then we climbed down a ladder on the opposite wall to the one we had climbed up, taking us back down to the ground floor.

We were heading back along the servants' corridor passageway to the panel where we had entered, when I heard a voice I recognised. I grabbed Tawpin's arm so he wouldn't leave me, as I stopped to peer through the nearest eyehole. My palms became clammy and my heart was hammering so loudly in my chest I was sure everyone in the room could hear it.

Laken was standing, facing me, holding a glass of wine. Herron and Langdon were seated in the chairs either side of him. Langdon was scowling. I could see the outstretched legs of another man sitting next to Herron, but not his face. I was not certain, but the voice of the man talking did not seem to come from him.

'We don't have the resources to…'

'You've said that already,' said Laken, shaking his head. 'But people are dying.'

'You know as well as I, if we send troops to the north it will leave the south dangerously exposed. We need more time to train the companies from the summer recruitment.'

'So we do nothing.'

Langdon raised his hand to placate Laken. 'Be easy. The new companies will be ready by the spring. We can cover the whole western border and Hayton will not be able to sneak in behind us.'

Laken sighed before draining his glass of wine. 'We lose territory while we wait. Hayton's taken most of the fenlands. Westford and Nenbarrow have gone. The people have deserted half the villages on the border. Yarebridge and Black Lodge have been attacked, well within Faulknar lands. Not to mention Methhold.'

'I hadn't forgotten Methhold, Laken.' A chair creaked and a man I had not seen before walked into view to refill Laken's glass. He was as tall as Laken, with close-cut grey-and-white hair. His back was towards me, but his voice was clear. It carried the authority of the man who had been talking to Laken from the start. 'And I know how much territory I've lost.' He gently shook Laken's shoulder before disappearing out of view again.

Laken smiled sheepishly. 'My apologies, Keenan. Patience has never been my greatest gift, and I never meant to imply...'

Lord Keenan was the king's brother and lord General-in-Chief of the army and cavalry. I was stunned that Laken was so familiar with such an important man. I had seen Laken's company call him by his name, and titles were only used during matters of discipline. Langdon was the Master of Arms and soldiers rarely called him by his appointed title. I had not realised the relaxation of formality would extend all the way to the top.

'So what is the plan, then?' Herron's quiet tones commanded more attention than their volume would merit. Extra emphasis was given due to the scarcity of his involvement in any discussion.

Another chair creaked as the legs I could see next to Herron were pulled out of view. 'A quiet one,' said the man who had remained silent until this point. I recognised the voice from the practice grounds but did not know who he was.

'I just need to do something.' Laken sat down on the vacant seat between Herron and Langdon.

The nameless man continued. 'The fenlands are providing a base for Lindvane to attack deep into Faulknar. We do not have the resources to protect the waterways. The horses are as good as useless there. We need to shake their confidence in holding those lands.'

Keenan continued. 'General Pirellin is controlling the fenlands. He is a key asset to Hayton and responsible for a number of important raids against our borders.' He paused. 'He needs to go.'

Laken leaned forward, resting his elbows on his knees. 'How?'

'Quietly.'

Laken smiled.

'He's camped just outside Marshland. Take a few men. See how closely he's guarded. With luck he'll feel well protected deep in the fens and you'll be able to get to him.'

'Just like that,' Laken mocked.

The owner of the voice leaned forward, and I could see the side of the man's head. He had short, dark hair and a long face with a prominent chin. 'It goes without saying that if you are seen, Hayton would love to have your head.'

'I'll make sure I'm not seen, then.'

'Don't take risks. This is a distraction strategy. It won't win the war.'

Laken nodded. 'When?'

'You leave tonight.'

I stopped listening. My heart was beating out of control. The temperature in the passageway had risen by several degrees and I had started sweating. I stepped backwards and pressed my back against the far wall. I was shaking so hard I thought I was going to fall down. Or be sick. I knew Laken was a soldier, but I had just realised what that meant. The thought of him amongst people who wanted to harm him made my head swim.

Tawpin grabbed my arm and dragged me through the passageway and out into the servants' corridor. The light stabbed my eyes after so long in the dim passageway. I was still thinking of the conversation I had overheard as he guided me out of the house and into the garden. We were outside the stone wall before he turned to talk to me.

'You can't mention this to anyone.'

I stared at him, not understanding what he was saying.

'I mean it. You can tell no one about what you heard in that room. We should not have been there. We *really* should not have been listening.' He gently shook me. 'Do you understand?'

I nodded, not trusting my voice to remain steady. My mind was conjuring up images of Laken bleeding. Broken. Dead. Tears started to sting my eyes and I bit the corner of my lip to stop them flooding over the dam of my eyelids.

'I have to go.' Tawpin hesitated. 'Will you be all right?'

I nodded again, and he squeezed my arm before running down the alley. I leaned against the wall, stabbing the jagged edges of the stone into my back to force my mind to concentrate on something else. I couldn't face the thought of losing Laken. I couldn't bear the thought of being in Liegeport on my own. I had started shaking again. I slid down the wall to sit on the floor, scraping my back and making it sting. I hugged my knees as close to my chest as I could manage. Nothing helped. The day had promised so much. A day free to do as I pleased. It was my birthday. I was eight years old.

I don't know how long I sat there. The pale sun had dropped below the rooftops and I was shivering. I was hungry, but not yet ready to return to the kitchens. I decided to walk through the market. Some stalls had already packed up, but many were still open. I took an apple from the first stall and slowly chewed on the sharp flesh as I walked between the clothes and the pots. I did not plan my journey and let my feet take me where they would. A handful of people were still browsing, but the market was mainly empty and I could have a good look at the items on display. No one paid any attention to me.

I stopped at a stall selling jewellery and decorative items. The coloured glass in the pendants, vases and clay bowls caught the last shards of evening light and flickered in the glow of the torches that were beginning to be lit in the darker corners. The light reflected in my eyes and my fingers stretched slightly with the need to touch the delicate items. I was mesmerised by the reds, greens, yellows, blues and oranges. The way the colours were placed together, complementing shades interlocking with contrasting colours. The shapes made by the patterns and designs. The tips of my fingers prickled as if stabbed by uncountable numbers of needles. I bit my lip, trying to decide the impossible. Which one was my favourite?

A pendant was sitting close to the edge of the table, about two paces away from me. The chain was fine silver; delicate links interwoven. Suspended from it was a teardrop of cut glass, the colour of juice from late summer blackberries. The depth of colour pulled me in, as if I could fall into the heart of the pendant and be enclosed in that bubble of coloured glass. The market seller was facing away from me, talking to another stallholder. I turned away, brushing the tabletop with my right hip. My right hand swept across the rough wood, ensnaring the pendant and hiding it in my pocket without slowing. My heart beat so hard that it hurt my chest. I concentrated on walking away slowly so I wouldn't draw attention to myself.

I was four stalls away and three stalls over before I dared to turn back. No one had noticed a thing. A grin exploded on my face as I stroked the pendant within my pocket.

It was fully dark by the time I returned to the kitchen. The last of the pans were being dried and returned to their places on the shelves above the sink. The kitchen girls had settled by the fire and had started eating the evening meal of the remains of roasted pig and coarse bread. I sat in my usual place to the side of the group. I thought about the pendant as I chewed the food, barely tasting it, and had almost finished when Mistress Narran came in.

'Where have you been?'

Everyone turned round to see who she was talking to. My hand went reflexively to my pocket when I realised she was looking at me.

'It's my day off,' I stammered.

'I know that, child.' She took a rag from her belt and cleaned a surface that already looked spotless to me. 'Laken was here earlier, looking for you.'

I jumped up, suddenly remembering the conversation Tawpin and I had overheard. I threw the last remnants of my meal into the fire, to the protestations of Mistress Narran regarding wasted food. I ran out of the room, pumping my legs as fast as I could, and through the corridor, bouncing off the stable runner-boy as I turned the corner. I reached the stable yard in my fastest time and raced into the administration building opposite.

'Where's Laken?'

The clerk looked up from his ledger. 'Not here.'

I darted out of the building, across the courtyard and through the archway to the barracks. Several soldiers were lazing on their bunks, some cleaning boots, others polishing belt knives. I searched for Gheth and saw him at the far end of the room.

'Where's Laken?'

Gheth looked at me, apologising with his eyes. 'He's not here.'

'Where is he? I need to see him. He was looking for me.'

Gheth looked past me, to see who was listening. 'I'm sorry.' He lowered his voice. 'I shouldn't be telling you, but…' He checked again to see if anyone was listening. 'He's left Liegeport. He could be gone for a while.'

The kitchen was buzzing with the activity of organising the food and drink for the midwinter festival. There was to be a parade along the main road, with market stalls offering free food and trinkets to the inhabitants of the city. The gamekeepers had filled the stores with fowl, rabbit, boar and stag in preparation for the feast to be held in the big house. The bakers had been busy from the early hours. Loaves of every size and shape had been stored at the cooler end of the kitchen, to be joined by cakes, pastries and sweetmeats. Root vegetables from the surrounding farms had been cleaned and sliced, stored in large bowls of water. Mistress Narran worked her magic producing sauces, pastes and dressings from herbs in the kitchen gardens and expensive oils from the far south. There was not a surface that was not used for preparing or storing delicious food for the royal family and their guests.

I had been running all morning, fetching ingredients that had run out or been overlooked. Extra plates, bowls and pots were constantly needed, and I was sent for more deliveries. The streets were crowded with people. The Blue Boar and other taverns had already donated barrels of watered-down ale, which were being readily shared. Children were running everywhere, and I joined their crowds as I darted through the alleys to the business-houses. Guards from the city watch were wandering around, quietly keeping order and ensuring the main road stayed clear. Everybody was happy and relaxed, enjoying the chance for a free party.

I returned to the kitchen and stopped dead.

Laken had returned.

Oleana had buried her head in his shoulder while Laken slowly stroked her back. He smiled sadly at Mistress Narran as she pounded grains in a shallow bowl. When Oleana moved her head to look into his eyes, I could see hers were red and puffy. She had been crying. She had missed Laken too.

'Hey, Tal.' Laken continued stroking Oleana's back, seeing me in the doorway.

He had a stubble of beard covering his lower cheeks, upper lip and chin. There were dark circles under his red-rimmed eyes, making him look tired. He had lost weight and the bones were starting to stick out on his cheeks and hands. His clothes were covered with stains and the dirt from the road. His right arm was bandaged. But it was the angry scar above his left eye that made my stomach lurch. I couldn't stop staring at it and was only vaguely aware of Mistress Narran calling Oleana back to work. Laken gently removed Oleana's arms from his waist. They kissed, slowly and tenderly.

Laken came over to me and knelt so that we were eye-to-eye. The bustle of the kitchen disappeared as his wound became my only focus. I tentatively reached out and touched the raw edges with my fingers. He closed his eyes and I could feel him shudder. I quickly withdrew my hand.

He took both my hands in his. 'It could have been worse,' he said quietly. 'Marron and Jacen won't be coming back.'

I threw my arms around his neck and held him tightly as he trembled. I knew I should feel sad about Marron and Jacen, but I was so glad to have Laken home. He sighed deeply, before gently kissing my forehead and removing my arms from his neck.

'How do you fancy watching the parade with me?'

A smile exploded on my face. I couldn't think of anything better. I nodded enthusiastically.

He smiled back at me. 'Do everything Mistress Narran says, and I'll come for you at midday.'

He winked at Mistress Narran as he left the kitchen, and I was quickly given a list of tasks that had to be completed.

I had no time to anticipate the festivities of the afternoon and it seemed like moments before Laken was back. He had bathed, shaved and dressed in clean leggings and tunic. His wound was less inflamed and glistened slightly. I suspected that one of Drey's salves had been applied. I was almost bouncing up and down with frustration by the time Mistress Narran allowed me to go.

People had lined the main street, standing four paces deep. The city watch were standing between them and the main street, but there was evident respect and the people did not push the limits. Coloured banners hung from the houses and children waved bright ribbons as they ran up and down the streets. Laken guided me to a spot a third of the way down the main road, where we would have a good view of the procession moving up towards the main house. I pushed through to the front and was protected from the crowd by Laken's comforting bulk. I found it hard not to continually press against him, reassuring myself that he was still there.

The noise of the crowd rang in my ears as the horses approached the top of the main street. The household guard came first. All rode black horses, their coats shining like puddles at midnight. The bronze on their uniforms reflected the pale winter sun, little points of fire dancing in time with the horses' movements. Each rider looked straight ahead, not acknowledging anyone in the crowd despite the cheers and whistles.

The next group were the foot soldiers, led by Lord Keenan. The Lord General-in-Chief walked alone, his ceremonial sword banging gently against his leg as he strode proudly forward. The men followed behind, synchronised in every step. The sight of so many men marching in perfect time was breathtaking, and I felt the hair at the nape of my neck rising. Halfway down the street, Lord Keenan drew his sword. The crowd gasped with a collective intake of breath in appreciation of the salute. The gold on the hilt competed with the precious stones as they flashed at the sudden movement. The iron of the blade reflected the colours from the hanging banners, swirls of colour slipping over its surface.

The third group was the royal party. Laken pointed out the important people as they came into view, and I felt my jaw dropping at the beauty and elegance of the spectacle. The king came first. Kyllian was riding a striking stallion, black with a white star half hidden by his flowing forelock. The long hair at the horse's fetlocks accentuated his every footfall. Kyllian was wearing a black military uniform, with the purple sash of royalty running from right shoulder to left hip. The Faulknar crest was clearly visible on the sash over his chest. A black coat with gold lining hung from his shoulders and over the rump of the stallion. His features were similar to Lord Keenan's, and the family resemblance was clear. His grey-white hair was longer than Keenan's and his eyes were brown rather than blue, but the intensity of the stare was the same. As his brother had, Kyllian looked ahead but saluted the crowd as he passed by. The cheers were louder than they had been for Keenan.

Behind Kyllian were the royal brothers. Kerk was nearest to me, astride a chestnut mare. As the heir he wore the colours of Faulknar, with black leather leggings, a richly embroidered golden tunic and a red sash with the family lion embroidered in white. His back was rigid, his knuckles white as he gripped the reins, and his jaw was clenched as he concentrated on his father's back. In contrast, Kade grinned at the crowd. His relaxed posture flowed with the movements of his horse, whose russet rump had areas groomed counter to the flow of hair so that striped patterns were visible on both sides. Kade's hair was a much darker brown than his brother's and worn much longer. His eyes were the colour of roasted chestnuts. They sparkled with mischief as he acknowledged the crowd with a slight nod of his head. I couldn't help but smile back as he revelled in the attention.

Between the young brothers but riding a horse-length behind was a beautiful girl. She looked to be older than Kade, possibly the same age as Kerk. Her blonde hair bounced at each step of her horse, rippling halfway down her back. The pale colour was complemented by the dark blue cloak hanging from her shoulders. The violet lining matched her eyes to stunning effect.

'That's Lady Breya of Greenwood,' Laken said in my ear in order to be heard over the crowd. 'She's the king's ward, sent to Kyllian to seal a treaty with her father and secure lands for him. She has been betrothed to Kerk since she was a year old.'

I was only half listening as my attention had been caught by two boys who were riding behind Breya, one behind Kerk and one behind Kade. I stared at the one behind Kade.

Laken chuckled beside me as he saw who I was looking at. 'Oh yes. That's your fellow street rat, Master Tawpin, Earl of Kingsport. Page to His Grace Kade Faulknar.'

I couldn't believe it. Tawpin was dressed in fine leggings and tunic. He sat on his pony well and matched its pace to Kade's. He looked straight ahead, seemingly unaffected by the poisonous glare I was giving him.

Two men walked behind the pages. Drey was closest to me. He wore a full-length white cloak, with white robes showing at his feet as he walked. The image of the sun and its rays, embroidered in gold thread, covered almost the entire back of the cloak. His head stayed facing forward but I could see his eyes taking in the crowd. The man next to Drey was taller. His dark blond hair brushed the collar of his plain grey cloak. He had a long, narrow face with a prominent nose that was slightly hooked at the end. His eyes were the colour of slate, and just as hard. He also surveyed the crowd, and my blood turned to ice as his gaze found me. I couldn't break the stare as my heart lurched painfully in my chest. I only realised I had held my breath when his attention moved on to the next person.

'That's Villermir.' There was a stony undercurrent to Laken's voice that I had not heard before. 'He is the high priest of Baila for Liegeport. He advises the king on matters of the soul.'

I turned to look at Laken. He was scowling at Villermir.

'Best to avoid him. He has considerable influence over the king.'

My attention returned quickly to the parade as the cavalry brought up the rear. Chestnut and bay horses trotted alongside grey and coloured ones. The riders looked splendid in their dress uniforms; coloured sashes denoting rank, brass buttons glinting and the golden stripes on their leggings running perfectly straight. The horses tossed their heads at the colours, movement and noise of the crowd, but maintained their lines and pace.

The procession disappeared along the far side of the main house and the street lost some of its colour as they moved from view. People started moving away from the main road and towards the food stalls set up in all the side streets. Laken took me to a nearby stall for bread and roasted fowl, and I was allowed some watered-down ale to honour the celebration.

Chapter Five

The war on the border grumbled on for two years. The new recruits promised by Langdon arrived and troops were placed along almost the entire length of the border between Faulknar and Lindvane. The Lindvanes, however, added soldiers of their own and a stalemate resulted. There were skirmishes into Faulknar, followed by revenge attacks into Lindvane. But neither side obtained a clear advantage. Laken would leave the city for weeks at a time, returning with new scars and a more pronounced limp.

I saw less of Tawpin as the months passed. His duties as Kade's page increased as the prince grew older. The times we had to run the streets were treasured and I missed his company. I distracted myself by stealing everything that I desired. Initially I tested myself by taking items from market stalls – pendants, bracelets, jewelled belt knives, brushes containing coloured glass, bronze buckles and gold buttons. Taking items from distracted stallholders became less of a challenge, and I increased the excitement by stealing items while being watched. It was a natural progression to move on to stealing from the business-houses.

I stored my treasures in a hole in the wall behind my sleeping area. I had removed the wooden plank and carefully took out the stones in the wall. During my time off when no one else was around, I chipped away until there was a large cavity, taking care to replace the outer stones and wooden plank when I left. The false wall was barely visible, even to me. Such was my desire to obtain pretty things, I was continually removing more stones to store my secret treasure.

I eventually tired of the items readily available for purchase. The merchants commonly kept the best stock for themselves, so I developed new skills to exploit this new market. I would creep out of the sleeping area while the other girls slept. I had memorised each of the creaking floorboards and avoided those on my way out. The streets were quiet at night, but often those that were about were as unwilling to be seen as I was. We all stayed in the shadows, dodging each other while avoiding the city watch. The business-house merchants lived above their shops, making it easy to identify which premises would provide the best haul. I avoided the clothes shops and those selling household wares. More often than not I would head for those that stocked decorative items.

One merchant was renowned for collecting small statutes of the lesser deities. The Sun God and Moon Goddess were rarely cast into decorative items. Their touch was present in everything, and therefore negated the need to produce specific idols. The lesser Gods were produced in a variety of different forms, however, from simple clay images to ornately decorated statues. The inhabitants of Methhold had kept a number of the Gods to encourage fertility, successful hunting or good health. I had seen a few on the journey into Liegeport, although there was a scarcity within the clan capital. The religion of Baila was gaining dominion in the larger towns and cities, and dictated that it was sacrilege to create images of their master. Renis kept the statues as decorative items rather than as religious objects.

The shutters at the front of the shop were well bolted and did not offer a way into the building. Fortunately, many buildings had easy access at the rear of the properties that were not on public display. I could safely climb into the back courtyard of Renis' house, gently shake the bolt behind the shutters of the ground-floor window and slip into the house. The room was dark, but my eyes quickly adjusted to the dim conditions and I easily avoided the furniture in the reception room. The stairs were located to the left. I carefully tested each step before putting my full weight on it to avoid any creaking that might alert the shop owners to my presence. The house remained quiet as I crept along the hallway at the top of the stairs. I could hear soft snoring through the door into the first room. I moved on. Moonlight poured through the window at the far end. I kept to the shadows.

I listened at the door of the next room I came to. All was quiet, so I carefully lifted the latch and slipped through. No moonlight came in through this window and I could only make out basic shapes. The square of a chair. The length of a table. I moved to the fireplace where the dying embers gave out the smallest amber glow. I gently felt along the shelf above, exploring with my fingers, searching for the smooth, silky surface of silver; the cold corners of coloured glass; the contours of pitted bronze. I removed a couple of small items to allow a closer look in the dull glow of the dying fire. One was a statue the size of my hand. The figure was of a woman with the head of a hawk: Arduinna, the Goddess of hunting. The bronze rippled in the ember light. The stones in the bird's eyes sparkled. My heart beat a little faster as I placed it in my pocket. The other piece was a circular disc of bronze, polished so it gleamed like water. Silver strands were braided around the outside, intricate woven patterns. I placed it in another pocket to avoid the two rubbing against each other.

I turned to leave with my treasures, but had yet to find the truly fine piece that I had expected from Renis. The best items would be the most guarded. He would keep them in his bedchamber at night. I needed to look there. I crept back along the hallway and listened again at the first door. The soft snoring was steady and rhythmic. My heart started hammering in my chest as I slowly lifted the latch. I pushed the door and listened. The snoring remained uninterrupted. I squeezed through the tiny gap I'd made and waited until my eyes adjusted. As with the previous room, there was no moonlight and the only illumination came from the fireplace. The fire was larger in this room and I could see the outline of a statue on the small table beside the bed. My breath caught in my throat. The embers made the twisted serpents writhe as I moved around the figure. Their warm glow identified them as gold. The numerous snakes intertwined and reared up to support a round disc, slightly larger than the palm of my hand. This disc shimmered with pearlescent hints of rose and peach. The reflection of the Moon Goddess.

My fingers itched and I knew I had to take this. I walked round the bed, keeping to the thick rug that covered the sounds of my footsteps. Two small mound shapes were covered by the blankets, and I nervously watched their breathing. The blankets rose and fell, rose and fell, the shape nearest to me rasping with each intake of breath. I eventually stood beside the table and reached out to grasp the statue.

The snoring stopped.

I froze and stopped breathing.

Renis mumbled incoherently before turning over to face his sleeping wife. It was several heartbeats before I silently let out my breath. My vision blurred and my head started to swim. Waiting several heartbeats more, I advanced my hand and took hold of the item. It was heavy. It was beautiful. I smiled in the darkness.

I quickly retraced my steps and silently closed the door behind me. I had to concentrate on not running down the stairs, but again tested the wooden boards to ensure I made no sound. I left the window open as I slipped out of the house, then ran as fast as I could to my hole in the wall. The two items taken from the living room made me smile as the moonlight highlighted the detailing. They were safely stored with my other treasures. I hesitated over the Goddess statue. The serpents seemed to sing to me, their lithe bodies reaching towards the moon disc. I lovingly stroked the gold, my sensitive fingertips caressing each bump and indentation. It was quite a while before I could place it in the cavity and cover it with the stone and planking.

As well as spending my nights stealing, I also developed my skills by sneaking into forbidden places and hiding. When Laken was home I would pass the evenings in the Blue Boar. I learnt to be invisible in crowded places. Avoiding eye contact, staying in secluded corners, moving around the tavern so I was never in one place too long. I would watch Laken laughing and relaxed with his men. They teased the serving girls. They heckled the minstrels. They brawled with other drinkers. But I could see a constant hint of sadness in his eyes. He seemed to be ageing quicker than the years should have made him.

Laken would not talk to me about the war that was being fought on the border. He never mentioned his role in the skirmishes. I learnt everything from using the secret passages that Tawpin had shown me and sneaking into the administration building opposite the stables. Eavesdropping gave me warning when Laken was about to leave and it kept me informed when he was away. I learnt of the raids on villages just like Methhold: the men slaughtered, the women taken as hostages, the children seized to trade as slaves in the far south. I learnt of the casualties for Faulknar: those that had lost arms or legs, the head wounds that got infected, the gut wounds that took weeks to kill a man, the heads taken as trophies from the dead, used to demoralise the men. I understood the sadness in Laken's eyes. I found it hard to sleep most nights. I had night terrors whenever Laken went away.

Midsummer was a chance to forget the traumas of the war and celebrate with friends and family. The townspeople held small festivities for neighbours and kin. The royal family held a ball for the kingdom's landowners, who would renew their fealty to Kyllian before feasting and dancing. Bards would sing tales of ancient heroes and the jealousies of the Gods. Minstrels would entertain with rowdy ballads and crowd-pleasing songs. Finally, the finest musicians would play while those of high status danced well into the night. The military officers were invited and Laken was to go. He took Oleana.

I was kept busy during the day, running for supplies and passing on messages. By early evening the kitchen tasks had been completed and the staff were able to return to their families. Having no family to spend midsummer with, I decided to sneak into the ball and watch the evening's entertainments. I had not planned on the increased presence of the city watch, specifically instructed to let no one except the recognised guests enter the royal house. The staff corridors were too busy to gain access to the secret passageways and even if I could have sneaked in, the view would have been too limited. I could think of only one way of seeing the jesters, jugglers and dancers in the main hall. I would have to climb onto the roof.

I had never been on the roof before and was not sure how I was to gain access. It turned out to be easier than I expected. A barrel had been left near a corner of the house, where the rear wall joined the main building. After spending a few moments ensuring no one was looking my way, I jumped up on the barrel and pulled myself onto the wall. The stonework provided the smallest of hand- and footholds and I had to concentrate in order to clamber up to a ledge between the two storeys. Fortunately, everybody was busy with the festivities and no one looked up. I could straighten up on this ledge, but still had to stand on the tips of my toes and reach as far as I could to hook the roof with my fingertips. For a handful of heartbeats I thought I would not have the strength to drag myself up, but I scrabbled around with my toes and eventually found a foothold to lever myself onto the roof. I lay on my back and breathed heavily, relief flooding through me. It took a while for my legs to stop shaking.

The view from the top of the building was beautiful. The more mundane and grimmer details of city life were diluted by distance and the graceful lines of the rooftops predominated. Looking east I could see, far out over the ocean, the seabirds wheeling and diving for their final meal before roosting. Looking south I could see the top of Cloud Mountain poking through the trees, so called because an optical illusion made it look like a cloud resting on the horizon. To the west, the flat lands of Faulknar stretched as far as I could see. The farms were deserted, the forests darkening as the sun dropped low in the sky.

I moved to the centre of the roof where the large glass windows allowed the evening light to illuminate the main hall. I lay on my stomach, peering over the edge of the glass. The spacious room was decorated with banners that were the bright colours of summer – buttercup yellow, poppy red, cornflower blue and lush grass green. Bouquets of flowers decorated pedestals, bringing a little of the countryside into the royal home. Wooden benches were arranged along the outer walls so that the area in the middle could be seen by all guests. Jesters tumbled and entertained as the guests ate.

The main table was opposite the large windows that could be seen from the main street. Kyllian sat in the middle, his jewelled crown flashing in the light with each movement of his head. He wore a deep red doublet over an embroidered white shirt, the ties tipped with silver. Breya sat to his right. She radiated in the glow of the candles. Her long-sleeved cream gown was flecked with stones, giving a hint of lilac each time she moved the fabric. She wore a silver chain with a small locket that hung between her breasts, but was otherwise without jewellery. Sitting next to her was Kerk, dressed in a golden doublet with cream material showing through slits in the sleeves. His royal signet ring flashed as he stabbed items on his plate and raised them to his mouth. I jumped when I saw Villermir sitting next to Kerk. His plain grey robes stood out amongst the finery of the other guests. His hawk's eyes were surveying the crowd suspiciously, and he occasionally leaned towards Kerk in private conversation.

On the other side of Kyllian sat Kade. His carefree nature was evident as he laughed freely at the jesters. He wore a dark blue doublet with pale blue material showing through the numerous small slits on the front of the garment. His plain white shirt was open at the neck, revealing a triangle of tanned skin. He playfully cuffed the shoulder of Drey, sitting on his left, as the jesters imitated members of the court. Drey wore a smart white tunic with a high collar. He beamed back at Kade, sharing jokes with the king's younger son. The jesters started juggling and Kade leapt over the table to join them, expertly joining in with the complex manoeuvres. Kyllian glowered at him and barked a command. Kade reluctantly returned to his chair. Drey grinned at him, making him smile again.

I quickly scanned the rest of the room, not interested in the nobility that had joined the royal party. I found Laken halfway down the far side of the benches, with Oleana sitting next to him. Despite my resentment that he had taken Oleana and not me, I had to admit they made a handsome couple.

Oleana's blonde hair shone like faded gold, lightly curling against the collar of her pale yellow gown. There were numerous shiny buttons down the front of the gown. Laken was wearing a matching yellow doublet. It was good to see him relaxed and smiling at the entertainers.

My attention returned to Kade. He was tapping the table in time with the dancing jesters, although his eyes were scanning the guests. Despite his relaxed posture I got the feeling he was searching for something, or someone. Beside him, Drey had his head tilted slightly to the right, as if listening. He closed his eyes and sat stone-still for a moment before lifting his head and snapping open his eyes. And looking directly at me.

My heart leapt in my chest and I rolled over to hide myself from view. How could he have possibly known I was watching him? I convinced myself that he was just looking at the sky in my general direction, that was all. Controlling my breathing, my heart rate slowed again. I rolled back to look through the window once more. Drey's attention had returned to the entertainment. The jesters had been replaced by acrobats, twisting themselves in positions I had not thought physically possible. I was fascinated by their ability, and it was some time before I realised that Kade was no longer sitting next to Drey. I searched the hall but could not see him anywhere. I was a little saddened by his absence but was soon distracted by the acrobats again.

'How did you get up here?'

I rolled away from the window and jumped up in the same movement. I crouched slightly, preparing for any threat. My mind raced at the thought of what those threats might be.

Kade leaned against the base of one of the towers, where a door I hadn't seen before stood open. 'You have a good view, but I'm not sure my father invited you.'

I had lost the ability to speak. My mind was still racing with the possible consequences of being discovered on the roof of the royal house, while also trying to plan escape routes.

Kade smiled. 'It's all right. I won't tell him.' He walked towards me. 'What's your name?'

I stopped thinking about dangers and noticed how soft his voice was. 'Tallen,' I said, the word out of my mouth before I realised I was speaking.

'Good evening, Tallen.' He bowed to me. 'May I welcome you to the Faulknar Midsummer Ball?'

He stopped a couple of paces away, and I could see the small, intricate detailing on his doublet and the quality of the shiny material poking through the slits. He had a thin sprinkling of freckles over his nose and cheeks, and long, dark eyelashes. His smile revealed small white teeth.

'Shall we watch the entertainment?' He lay down where I had been earlier. 'Earl Reed should be well into his drink by now. He'll probably start dancing on the tables soon.'

I hesitated, not quite believing that the prince was on the rooftop with me. I stared at his back. I didn't know what to do. I had always been forbidden to enter the main house and had therefore never been taught the appropriate way of behaving around the royal family. I didn't know whether to take him at his word and join him, or if I should leave while I still had the chance. Kade's quiet giggling decided it for me. My curiosity got the better of me, and I lay next to him to see a portly man with a long beard hopping from leg to leg on a bench. Food and plates were flying everywhere, but he had a firm hand on his tankard. I couldn't help giggling either as Kyllian's face coloured from pink, to red, to purple.

The festivities ran late into the night. Kade talked about the important people there, many of whom were getting very drunk. I watched Laken dance with Oleana, feeling strangely happy and sad at the same time. Villermir left early in the evening, but Drey enjoyed the good company until well after dark. Kade and I laughed a lot, sharing stories of our lives and the people around us. I was sad when the night ended and he escorted me through the house to my sleeping quarters. He hesitated a while, before quickly kissing me on the cheek. I was so shocked that he was long gone before I thought of a suitably cutting reply involving many of the words I had learnt in North End.

The stalemate lasted until the following spring. Lindvane gained an alliance with Gallowgla, who then attacked our south-eastern shores. Lord Keenan was forced to split his troops between the western front against Lindvane and the southern ports against Gallowgla. It left the defences perilously thin and the attacks within the heart of Faulknar increased. The atmosphere within the city grew tense as the merchant ships from Gallowgla stopped arriving at the port, reducing the availability of work for the dockers. This tension boiled over in the Mermaid, where tempers were easily provoked. The fights became more violent, both in and out of the roped-off area. Men started to carry weapons, and this was only partially discouraged by the city watch, particularly in North End. Women and children spend less time on the streets and were always home before dark.

The talk in the meeting rooms of the administration building was sombre. I overheard reports of the heavy losses in both the cavalry and the foot soldiers. The troops were being pushed back from the western border, losing ground to the greater number of Lindvanes. The south-eastern coast was repeatedly hit by skirmishes from the sea. The Gallowglass chose a different village each time, so the cavalry was never sure of where they would strike and consequently would always arrive too late. The morale of the people was being attacked as well as their families.

Laken was in discussion with Herron, Langdon and Keenan. It was late, and the dim room added to the weight of their conversation. Laken and Herron had just returned and looked like they hadn't slept for days. Herron kept rubbing his shoulder as if it pained him. Keenan's face was becoming more lined.

'We lost another two lads,' said Herron. 'I swear they knew we were coming.'

'We have spies in their court, they will have spies here.' Langdon rubbed his eyes. 'We have to be even more vigilant, it seems. No more gossiping at the Blue Boar.'

Herron smiled politely at the familiar jibe, but no one was in the mood for teasing. The room was silent as they became lost in their own thoughts. The muscles in Laken's jaw tensed repeatedly as he unconsciously ground his teeth.

Keenan looked up at Laken. 'We need to repeat the success of the Pirellin attack a couple of years ago. Cut out the heart of the Lindvanes.'

'And how do we do that?' asked Herron. Laken stayed silent.

'Handera is planning a morale-boosting visit to the front line. He left court two weeks ago, so should be almost at the border by now.'

'King Hayton's brother? Are you mad?' Herron shook his head to emphasise his words. 'It can't be done.'

Keenan continued to look at Laken. 'We have to try.'

The two men exchanged a long look, before Laken gave the smallest of nods. A block of ice lodged in my stomach. I felt sick. Tears burnt hot tracks over my cheeks. I had a really bad feeling about Laken going after this man.

'I'll go alone.'

'Oh no!' Herron stood up and started pacing the room. 'Going is a suicide mission. Going on your own is... is...' He blustered, trying to find the right words.

There weren't any.

I was waiting for Laken when he returned to his rooms. I sat on the floor with my back to the door. I didn't think it would be appropriate to enter his rooms, although I knew he never locked the door. I sat in the dark and waited. Laken almost tripped over me before he realised I was there.

'Tal, what are you doing?' He stopped, a frown forming on his face. 'How did you get in?'

I avoided looking at his eyes – and answering the question.

'I shouldn't be surprised, I suppose. You spend enough time with Tawpin. I swear that boy could get into the Seven Hells and back without Mobis knowing.'

He opened the door and we walked into the reception area of his apartment. He was allocated three rooms within the main barracks, upstairs from his men. They were functionally decorated, with four leather chairs and a table in the reception room. The floor was wooden boards, but a thick rug bearing the Faulknar crest covered a third of it. It had been a present from Oleana.

Laken lit a couple of candles as I slumped in the nearest chair. He came over to kneel before me.

'So what's all this about?'

I shrugged. 'Haven't seen you since you got back.'

'It was late, Tal. I'm surprised you knew I was back at all.'

'I saw your horse.'

Laken smiled. 'Clever girl.'

I fell silent, not sure of what I wanted to say, let alone how to say it. Laken's smile faded.

'Are you in trouble?'

I shook my head. 'No.'

'So, what is it that couldn't wait until the morning?'

I hesitated, then took a deep breath. 'I've brought you something.'

I reached into the inside pocket of my jacket and removed the silver warrior's arm-ring that I had taken from my treasure store. It was not elaborated decorated, but the quality was good. I rubbed the smooth surface with my thumb, unable to feel the tiny lion engravings. Even though it was for Laken, I still had trouble parting with it. I eventually passed it to him.

'Thank you,' he said, taking the gift. 'Where did you get this?'

I looked at the floor, scraping some dirt from under my thumbnail.

'Thank you.'

He took me into a tight embrace and I could not stop the tears from flowing. I held him as tight as I could. I felt him tremble beneath my grip. He gently stroked my back and murmured in my ear, as if quieting a spooked horse.

It was the first day of summer when the news came. Handera was dead. Stabbed in the heart in his own bed. The streets were full of gossip and the gory details; details the people had no way of knowing. I was glad Handera was dead, but I still had a sick feeling about Laken. Distracted, I completed my errands and returned to the kitchen for something to eat that might settle my stomach.

I froze as I entered. The kitchen was quiet, which in itself was suspicious. Herron was standing by the big table that was covered with half-peeled vegetables. The hair on the left side of his head was matted with a dark substance. His face was pale, contrasting with his swollen, red-rimmed eyes. He distractedly weaving his fingers in and out of each other.

Oleana was slumped against Mistress Narran. Her back was to me and her head buried in the older lady's embrace. Her body shook with tremors. She was sobbing without any energy to make a noise. Mistress Narran looked towards me with puffy eyes and tear tracks smearing her face.

'I tried...' began Herron. 'He knocked me out... Why would he do that? I could have...'

He appeared to be talking to himself, but the words echoed around my head. My vision blurred and I fell backwards, resting my back against the door frame to stop myself falling over. My head was frantically telling me that my heart could not be correct. That there was some mistake. That this wasn't happening.

Herron looked at me with the saddest eyes I had ever seen.

'I'm so sorry.'

I ran out of the kitchen. And kept running.

Chapter Six

I spent two seasons lost in North End. It was a good place to hide. No one looked too closely. No one was interested in other people's business. No one cared about a girl who had lost everything. I walked the streets until I got tired, then crouched in doorways until I was moved on. The dark alleys hid other homeless – men, women, children – curled against walls, hidden behind street rubbish, huddled under torn sheets. I anonymously joined their company. The hunger in my belly became a welcome distraction from other pains.

I wallowed in my misery for a long time before accepting this was my future and I had to learn to survive in it. I thought of my skills that I could trade for food and shelter. It was a neighbourhood of thieves, so possessions were well protected. The only other experience I had was in the kitchens of the royal house. I thought of the times I had spent with Tawpin in the Mermaid. The dull ache of the loss of a friend was buried in the deep place with all the other pain. The Mermaid was the most likely place I knew in North End that would hire staff. They would probably need someone to wash dishes and tankards.

The tavern looked unfamiliar without its rowdy customers. The dirty windows let in little light and the main room smelt of spilt ale that didn't quite cover the smell of stale human odour. I tried not to wrinkle my nose as I searched in the gloom for the tavern owner.

'Get out.'

I turned to see a young woman behind the bar. Her curly brown hair was piled on the top of her head, a few unruly strands curling around her face. She had brown eyes that contained a hint of hardness. Her full lips complemented her long, narrow face. But her beauty was marred by an old scar on her right cheek that twisted the corner of her mouth.

'You're too young to drink in here.' She looked me up and down and was not impressed by what she saw. 'Even if you had any money.'

'I need food.'

'We ain't a charity.'

'I thought you might need someone to wash… clean?'

'Then you thought wrong.'

Dag, the tavern owner, came out of the back room at the sound of voices. He was a solidly built man, with a shaved head and a mean face. I instinctively took a step back.

'Kia? What's this stray doing in my tavern?'

'She wants a job.' She wrinkled her face as if she'd eaten something rotten.

'Does she now?'

'I told her we ain't no charity.'

'Mmm…'

Dag looked at me with his head tilted slightly. I felt like a horse being assessed by a trader. I half expected him to ask to see my teeth. Eventually he gave a lopsided sneer. A tremor rippled down my back.

'Now, Kia. Let's not be hasty. We can always use more hands to wash and clean.'

'Really?' Kia put her hands on her hips.

Dag turned to her and winked. 'Think of it as a long-term investment.'

Kia turned back to look at me. The hardness in her eyes was replaced fleetingly by a sadness, a sorrow. She brushed past Dag on her way out.

He smiled a more genuine smile at me. 'When can you start? Now?'

I washed dishes, cleaned tables, tidied the upstairs rooms. I kept quiet, avoided looking anyone in the eye, and ate my meals alone. The other girls ignored me. That suited me fine. I survived. That was all I was planning on doing.

It didn't last long.

The tavern had closed for the night, but Dag was drinking with a small party of customers that had stayed after locking up. I quietly cleared the tables, wiping their surfaces free of dropped food and spilt ale. Dag and the other men were laughing loudly as they finished their drinks. I looked desperately for tasks so I could avoid going to their benches. But Hama would be angry if I neglected tables, and would tell her husband I was lazy, and I would be out on the streets again.

I could avoid it no longer. I silently approached the table and started collecting the empty plates and tankards.

'Gentlemen, have you met my new girl?'

The man on Dag's right was a small man with dark stubble over his chin. His eyes had the glassy look of the drunk and he had difficulty focusing on me. 'Dag, you dirty old man. She's a child.'

Dag snickered. 'But what a child. Look at her.'

The man tried but was too drunk to understand what Dag was looking at. Dag sighed dramatically. He cuffed the man on his left before grabbing my arm as I tried to move away.

'Imagine – longer hair, pretty dress…'

The other man looked me up and down slowly, examining every part of me. I felt unclean under his gaze. 'Those eyes.'

'Aren't they something?'

'They look into my soul. They burn my heart.'

Dag giggled. 'I know. Picture her in a few years.'

A slow smile drifted over the stranger's face as he considered Dag's image. 'Playing the long game, then?'

Dag leaned in conspiratorially. 'How much would you pay for the first taste of her fruit?'

I dropped the crockery and cutlery.

I couldn't believe what I was hearing. Tawpin had told me tales, but I never thought such things happened. And why would anyone… with me… my eyes… It was too disgusting to comprehend. I tried to remove my arm from Dag's grip, but he held it firmly. A predatory smile revealed his stained teeth as he increased the pressure of his hold, making my skin burn and my bones ache.

'Quite a prize,' agreed the man opposite. His tongue darted out to lick his lips.

'And with years of anticipation boosting the price.'

Ice water was poured down my spine. This was no drunken bragging. Dag was deadly serious, and the men were dangerously interested in his proposal. I started to panic. I was all alone. There were four of them. I doubted the girls in the kitchen would come to my aid. I increased my struggles against Dag's grip, but he laughed at my pathetic attempts. My heart was beating out of control, my breathing so fast that my vision blurred. My mind was racing with all the horrible connotations of what was being discussed. I thought of Laken's disappointment in me.

Time slowed.

The pain of Laken's loss turned the ice water to steam. My mind cleared of the possibilities and looked for ways of freeing myself from Dag's hold. I stared at him with all the hatred I felt for those that had killed my only protector. Dag stopped laughing. His face paled as I felt his hand grow cold on my arm. He did not slacken his grip, though. It seemed I had all the time in the world as I held his gaze. My free hand reached for the belt knife he had been using to eat his food. I was surprisingly calm as I stabbed the knife into his arm.

His howl of pain broke the spell, and time rushed up on me again. All four men jumped up, knocking over chairs in their haste. Having broken free of Dag's hold, I darted for the door, expecting to be grabbed at any moment. The men's curses were loud and explicit, but nobody followed me. I slammed the door behind me and ran into the dark streets. I didn't stop until I was deep within the maze of the North End alleys.

After the events at the Mermaid I was reluctant to work anywhere else in North End. With my first option closed to me, I resorted to stealing what I needed. It suited me better. I needed no one; I just needed to improve my skills. Everyone in North End was suspicious, and consequently watched. Especially strangers. Many times I was chased away as I moved in to take bread or meat. Many times I went hungry. I was not the only one. The alleys were littered with children, running the streets during the day, running scared at night. The dirt didn't quite cover their bruises; the darkness couldn't quite cover the hollowness in their eyes.

The market in North End was enclosed in a large building, containing only one room filled with small stalls. Entrance was through wooden double doors that could be closed and barred at night and guarded by two large men during the day. Anyone caught stealing would not leave the building. These guards also meant I could not visit the market too often. I took only small items, never from the same stall. I would often huddle in corners as if sheltering from the weather, to reduce the suspicions of the traders.

When the market was not an option for me, I looked for resources elsewhere. As with the main city, North End had a rigid structure of prosperity. The street people, with whom I shared doorways and hidden corners, had nothing. The next social tier involved lean-to shelters with cloth hanging over the doorway to provide a little privacy. The traders and labourers lived in the ramshackle houses forced into every available space within the neighbourhood. These provided a new source of revenue for me, and I would sneak in to take some of their meagre provisions. Some were protected by dogs, and in those cases I would have to avoid the whole alley to prevent them reacting to my presence. But these homes provided enough to supplement my gains from the market and stop me from starving.

But this was North End. The dogs were not the only hazard.

On more than one occasion I was caught by the homeowner. The city watch rarely ventured into the area and the residents dispensed their own justice. The first time I encountered this justice I vowed never to steal again. But hunger drove me back, time and again.

I had selected a house deep in the heart of North End. The owner visited the Mermaid most nights and would drink late into the night. His wife would be home but was such a timid thing that she would not investigate if I made a sound. I waited a long time after the man had left before creeping towards the house. I silently lifted the latch and slipped into the dark front room. The layout of these houses was very simple – a front room that served as a kitchen and living area, and one or two rooms at the back for sleeping. I moved quickly to the larder where the meat, cheese and bread would be kept. I had taken chunks of bread and cheese and placed them in a small sack I carried, and was about to take some dried meat too when I heard the door open.

I froze.

I heard a deep cough and heavy footsteps as someone shuffled around the room lighting candles. My blood turned ice-cold. The houseowner had returned early and was going to find me. There was nowhere to hide. The candle in the kitchen was lit and highlighted me against the far wall. My heart thundering in my chest, I darted for the door while his back was still turned.

He turned faster than I could blink. His large left hand whipped out and grabbed my arm as I tried to get past him. His grip crushed as he turned me to face him. A vicious grin revealed broken teeth.

'I got kicked out of the Mermaid,' he growled. 'Seems Dag did me a favour.'

He brought up his right fist and smashed it into my jaw. Pain I had never experienced before exploded across my face, causing my eyes to water. I was sent across the room by the power of the blow, slamming against the wall. The breath was forced out of my lungs by the impact. The crushing agony in my head and shoulders where I had hit the wall competed with the stabbing in my jaw, split lip and lungs. I was just recovering my breath when he kicked me in the stomach as I lay crumpled on the floor. The remaining air in my lungs was expelled as a grunt. My vision dimmed as my brain was starved of oxygen. The cacophony of sensations being screamed by my body weaved into one large fireball of pain.

The man stood over me as I lay panting on the floor. Very slowly, he removed the wide leather belt from his waist. He wrapped the buckle end around his fist and looked at me dispassionately.

'Justice for taking a man's food.'

He whipped the belt down across my back. My skin flashed in response as I cried out. Two tracks were made in my flesh by the stiffened leather at the edges of the belt, as if a dog had scratched its claws across my shoulder blades. My eyes burned and tears flowed readily down my cheeks as I lay helpless on the floor, whimpering as the belt came down again and again.

Eventually it stopped. I was tensed into a ball, my head protected by my arms, my eyes shut tight. I panted to restrict the movement of my aching ribs, lungs and back. It was several heartbeats before I realised the beating had finished.

'Get out of my house.'

My muscles had cramped and each tiny movement sent a lightning storm of pain rippling across my back. The first explosion caused the neighbouring muscles to spasm, repeating in all directions. The man grabbed the neck of my tunic, constricting my throat as he lifted me up and dragged me across the floor. I was thrown onto the street outside, awakening new elements of pain. I lay curled where I fell, trying not to move my body by crying, but failing.

It was past dawn before I could crawl to a more secluded place.

The chronic aches of hunger and old beatings were nothing compared to the torments I subjected myself to. The fear and the loneliness produced a hard scar deep in my chest that constricted each beat of my heart and caused a catch in my breath when inhaling. I felt the emptiness that I saw in the others. I knew my eyes looked as flat. I didn't care. Happiness seemed a faraway world, lost in the mists as I fought to survive. My life shrank to the moment. I gave no thought to the next day; never considered the future.

I slept little. The fear of attack and the crushing hunger kept sleep at bay. When exhaustion would not be refused, my rest was interrupted by nightmares. The dreams that had haunted me since I learnt the horrors of war took on a new twist. They became more personal.

The background would vary – sometimes a forest, a battlefield, a crowded marketplace. Otherwise the dream was always the same. More often than not, it would start with me at the foot of a mountain that towered over everything. The view showed the sea glistening all around the island either side of the rock I was to climb. The breeze whipped the wave crests into white foam as the seabirds floated on the wind. The sun was hot, and I felt sweat on my upper lip and between my shoulder blades. My legs were trembling from the effort of climbing up the steep path that circled the mountain.

In the way of dreams, I was instantly standing on a ledge halfway up the mountain. I faced a half-moon-shaped entrance into a cave. The roof was several handspans taller than me and I could stand upright to the back of the cave. I had no torch to light the way. As I stepped into the darkness, my eyes adjusted to reveal various shades of dark grey; enough to prevent me from bumping into the boulders and overhangs that were scattered around. I walked to the back of the cave where there was a tunnel leading deep into the mountain. The darkness smothered me like a blanket as I entered. I stretched out my hands to touch the walls either side of me, guiding myself forward. My ears strained to hear any noise beyond my breath and the gravel beneath my feet as I walked. In the absence of anything else, the repeated placing of my feet became hypnotic.

The path led round and round, down and down. I lost all sense of direction. My breathing became more erratic as I increasingly felt like I was being crushed by the weight of the mountain.

Then I heard it.

The soft sound of someone crying. The rocks caused the sound to echo around the narrow chamber and I was unable to determine where it was coming from. The only option was to walk forward, but within a handful of steps there was a dividing of the path. I took the left track, seemingly heading toward the voice. I was encouraged by the sound growing a fraction louder as I walked down this new avenue. My pace increased, but within another handful of steps I was faced with another splitting of the path. The choice was less clear than at the previous junction. I hesitated before choosing the left path again. The crying grew fainter and I was about to turn back when I faced another division. I took the right path, hoping to correct my earlier mistake, and was reassured by the voice gaining volume again, but this was short-lived as I banged against a stone wall. The path was a dead end.

I retraced my steps, taking the left turn to correct my initial mistake. But this led to a dead end as well. My way back to the cave was blocked. I was forced to take the left path, away from the crying. The tunnel looped round and down. Sometimes the sound grew louder, sometimes quieter. It seemed independent of the path I was travelling. I was beginning to panic. I was totally lost. I could not get closer to the crying. I could not get back to the surface. Each time I turned around I would be faced with a blocked path.

Slowly the voice grew louder, identifying itself as male. His crying carried a deep resonance that reminded me of a man I knew but could not quite place. I was carried further into the heart of the mountain. The sobs were interspersed with cries for help. The voice sounded frustratingly familiar but was still too distant for me to place. I quickened my pace as my feeling of unease grew. A person I knew was in trouble and I couldn't get to him. Round and round I was led. Down and down I went.

'Tal, help me.'

The knife of pain was twisted a little further into my chest. I shivered as my blood ran cold.

It was Laken.

I started running, calling out to him that I was coming. I grew more frustrated with each junction, each turn that took me away from his voice. I called out reassurance but could not keep the hint of desperation from my voice. My breath became ragged and my legs burned with cramp as I ran further and further into the mountain. Each junction took me left. Solid barriers and rockfalls blocked every right turn. Tears of frustration left warm streaks on my cheeks, my sobs mixing with Laken's.

I stumbled into a cavern, larger than I could imagine, lost in the darkness. Laken's cries echoed around the rocky void. All sense of which direction they were coming from was lost. I collapsed to my knees, gasping for breath, my mind racing with impossible options to get to him. I banged my fists against my head in frustration, screaming just to release the pressure.

My scream was answered by one from Laken. That scream told of indescribable agonies. The coherent cries for help transformed into mindless babbling. My heart ripped apart, my scream of agony joining Laken's. I forced myself erect and ran down the nearest left-hand path. The darkness blurred before me as tears ran unchecked from my eyes.

I ran and ran and ran, never getting closer to the screams, but I couldn't stop running.

I would wake screaming and struggling for breath. My knuckles would be scraped raw from where I had been fighting against the walls that sheltered me. An unbearable feeling of loss lodged in my chest, making the scar there that little bit harder.

My face became known as that of a thief, making it harder to find food within North End. The guardians of the indoor market refused to allow me entrance and I tried to restrict taking from homes because of the beatings. I fought with the other street kids for scraps of food dropped by traders or rotten food thrown out by homeowners. I grew a little more feral every day.

I was forced into the main city to look for other opportunities to find food. Taking items had been so easy when I worked in the kitchen of the main house. It was much more difficult to hide in the crowds with dirty clothes, cuts and bruises. I was readily identified as coming from the North End and was consequently watched with suspicion. If I did manage to steal the food, I was often spotted and chased. I darted down alleyways and side streets before disappearing into the darkness of North End. I would often use up more energy than I could recoup from the small items I had taken.

The city watch increased their presence on the streets between the main city and those of North End. There would be at least two guards patrolling the area, with more on the days after I had been spotted taking food. Several other guards wandered the markets, so that I had to dodge them as well as the stallholders. Many times I left with nothing. I grew increasingly desperate, darting up to stalls even though I knew I would be seen. I trusted my knowledge of the backstreets of Liegeport to provide a means of escape. My luck was always going to run out at some point.

Winter was beginning to show, with shorter days and the nights getting colder. I was not eating enough to keep warm. I had lost so much weight that a piece of string was needed to hold my trousers up. The scraps of cloth

I used to cover myself at night were too thin and let the cold air through no matter how I huddled underneath them.

I had smelt the food before I left North End and was salivating heavily by the time I saw the market stall. It was early morning and the stall was selling hot meat pies. There were a few stallholders setting up. A couple of guards walked casually around the stalls, talking to the owners. The odds were more favourable than usual. I took the chance. I darted from my hiding place and ran towards the hot food. I had reached out my hand to take a pie when the shout went up. Two more guards appeared from a side street, joining the two I had seen earlier. All four were running towards me.

I left the pie and ran down the nearest alley. I darted left and right, hoping to lose anyone that was following me. Winding a convoluted path back to North End, I skidded to a halt as I saw more guards at the end of the alley. I backtracked, hoping to use another entrance, but that avenue was guarded as well. I cursed in frustration, and looked for another way in. Twice more I was blocked by the city watch. I was forced to retrace my steps again, but the sentries had been closing the net. A soldier was standing at the far end of the alley in which I was hiding. Realising that I could not go forward nor retreat, I cursed again. Quickly looking around the alley for an escape route, I saw an opportunity. Keeping to the shadows, I climbed onto a barrel that had been left next to the second house along. The extra height allowed me to reach for the second-floor window, and from there heave myself onto the roof. I closed my eyes for a heartbeat, allowing the cool breeze blowing over the rooftops to calm me. Then I carefully crept over the gable to peer down into the alley and check for guards. I could not see any, so rolled over the side of the house onto the second-storey windowsill, then onto the first-storey ledge before dropping to the ground. I crouched for a handful of heartbeats, listening for sounds of approaching watchmen. I heard none.

I slipped along the alleyway, looking for another way into North End. As before, the way was blocked by guards. There was no way I was getting into North End any time soon. I turned and walked away from the neighbourhood, looking for a place to hide until the watch grew bored and left. I had made it over halfway along the passage when a soldier appeared at the far end. He shouted to his colleagues and ran towards me. I panicked and ran back towards the men guarding North End. Half them came at me to block off my exit, while the remaining men prevented any attempt to gain access to North End. I ran parallel to the approaching guards, hoping to find an alleyway that would offer a chance to disappear. There were so many men. Too many men. It was not long before I was surrounded and all escape routes were blocked.

I circled, desperately looking for a way out. The guards stopped a few paces away, encircling me. They hesitated, confident I was trapped. One stepped forward, grinning. I recognised the angry scar on his left forearm.

'Rolyan? What are you doing here?'

'Hello, street rat.'

He came towards me, sure that I would come quietly. He had not taken account of the time I had spent in North End. My feral side took over as soon as he made a grab for me. I punched. I kicked. I bit. I scratched. I fought like a cornered cat, using all that I had learnt in order to survive. Rolyan was losing his grip. Two of the city watch saw what was happening and came to his aid. Against three I was easy overpowered. Rolyan pinned me to the floor with a knee in my back, while one of the others bound my hands behind my back with his belt. I still bit and kicked when Rolyan turned me over, but the battle was lost. He threw me over his shoulder, laughing at my ineffectual kicks to his chest and my bites into his leather gambeson. I didn't stop, though. I was determined to make this journey as difficult for him as it was uncomfortable for me.

I was quickly carried to the city gaol. Rolyan dumped me on the floor hard enough to make my teeth crack together. I glared at him but could do nothing else. I had lost all feeling in my fingers. He laughed at me as he turned to leave.

'All yours, Sergeant. Be warned, she fights like a vixen.'

The sergeant looked at me over the worn wooden table. He rested his elbows on the tabletop as he leaned towards me. His disinterested grey eyes inspected me from top to bottom. He didn't seem impressed by what he saw.

'So, Tallen. You decided to grace the *good* people of Liegeport with your presence once more.'

I stayed silent, glaring at him. It was all I could do not to hiss at him.

'A lot of people are very interested in you. Seems you've been a very naughty girl. If it was up to me I'd have you thrown in the deepest dungeon until you're old and grey.' He sniffed. 'But it's not up to me, so I have to put up with you in the meantime.'

He stood up suddenly, making the chair scrape across the stone floor. He was an intimidating man. Very tall. Reflexively, I scuttled backwards until my back pressed against the wall. As if I hadn't moved, he walked slowly and purposefully around the table and over to me. He grabbed the shoulder of my tunic, effortlessly lifting me off my feet. I had to stand on the tips of my toes to get any purchase on the floor as he strode across the room to a door in the far wall, dragging me with him. He unlocked the door, walked through, and then locked it behind us. Torches provided light as there were no windows in the corridor. The air smelt stale, of damp straw. Stone steps led down, and a right turn opened into a corridor with a row of stout wooden doors, each with thick iron hinges and a grille at eye level. At the sound of our footsteps, those inside the cells started shouting and cursing. The sergeant ignored them.

We stopped at the farthest door. Still holding me almost off the ground with one hand, he unlocked the door and pushed me through. The cell was long and narrow, empty apart from a pile of old straw and a bucket. He untied the belt from around my wrists, then locked the door behind me. Little light came through the grille and I was left standing in almost complete darkness. I slowly brought my arms in front of me, the stretched muscles of my shoulders screaming in protest. I rubbed my wrists where the leather had chafed against the skin, leaving it warm and puffy.

I started to shake uncontrollably.

It was a long time before I stopped shaking and sat on the straw. I could hear the occasional moans of the other people in the cells, but nothing of the city above. The rats scratched in the straw out in the corridor, but they avoided my cell. I was grateful. I curled into a small ball, covering myself with the straw, trying to keep warm. I lost all sense of time. Nothing changed.

It seemed as if days had passed before I heard footsteps on the stone stairs leading to the cells. I huddled further into the straw, certain that no one would come for me. After so long in the dark, I had to close my eyes against the burning brightness of the torch as it was held to the barred window of my cell. I heard a familiar grunt, and sighed as the torch was lowered and I could see Drey's face through the bars.

'A lot of people are very angry with you,' he began. 'We found your little store of treasures. Well, not-so-little store of treasures. I see why Tawpin calls you Magpie now. The city watch had a jolly time trying to return it all to its rightful owners. You have been very busy.'

I stayed silent. Although I should not have been surprised that my hoard had been found, I was still sad to think that I would not see the trinkets again. Especially the Moon Goddess statue. I would have to steal that back.

Drey had continued talking. '…what to do with you. There were some colourful suggestions, but you needn't know about those. I finally got them to agree to one night. I'll send someone for you tomorrow morning.'

He turned to leave, then turned back again. 'Oh, almost forgot these.'

He bundled a small sack through the bars of the grille. It fell to the floor with a soft thud. Drey left and the cell returned to darkness. I crawled on my hands and knees to the sack. It contained a small loaf of bread, some meat and cheese, and an apple. My stomach growled in anticipation, as my salivary glands filled my mouth with fluid so quickly it made them hurt. I gobbled the food as quickly as I could get it in my mouth. I regretted eating so fast almost immediately, as my stomach started to hurt and I felt sick. It was not a large amount of food, but I had been deprived of a significant meal for so long.

I returned to the straw and snuggled underneath. I was warm, full and safe. Inevitably I started to drowse. I didn't want to fall asleep. The darkness reminded me too much of the cave under the mountain in my dream. But it had been so long since I had felt this warm and safe.

Sleep came quickly, and the dreams came as expected.

Chapter Seven

True to his word, Drey sent someone to collect me in the morning. Tawpin stood outside the cell as the door was opened by a guard. He turned pale when he looked at me, avoiding my eyes. I waited until he spoke before moving.

'Drey says you are to come with me.' He stepped back to allow me to pass through.

He must have been very disappointed in me. There was no sign of his usual jovial self. I could feel his eyes boring into my back as we climbed the stone stairs. It hurt that I had lost the approval of my friend, but I knew I had brought it on myself. I ignored the sergeant as I walked through the office, squinting as I walked into the light. Within a few steps Tawpin was walking next to me.

'You look like horse dung.'

I turned to see the corner of his mouth twitch in a ghost of a smile.

'Thanks very much.'

He hesitated before adding, 'You smell like horse dung too.'

He could contain the grin no longer. I smiled back, relaxing as it became clear I had not lost my friend after all. I shoved him playfully. He shoved me back.

We continued shoving each other until we arrived at the main house. Tawpin led me through the side entrance that we had used when investigating the secret passages, before using the servants' access up to the second floor. We crossed behind the main hall to a flight of stairs leading up to the far tower. The tapestries along the walls of this staircase had less detail and looked older than those surrounding the main hall. At the top was a functional wooden door.

Tawpin knocked. We waited. Tawpin knocked again, rolling his eyes at me.

The sound of shuffling and muffled cursing was heard through the wood, but it was still some time before Drey called for us to come in. Tawpin opened the door and motioned for me to go through. I turned as I heard the door close behind me. He had not followed me in.

'Ah, there you are,' Drey began as he placed a small leather pouch in a drawer. 'Come in, come in. Come on through to the back room on the right. Don't touch anything.'

I followed him through the main room, which was plain and functional, but spotlessly clean. Nothing was out of place – not a chair, a book or a shoe. It did not look as though anyone spent a lot of time there, although there were numerous small items that looked to have personal meaning and the furniture was comfortable and well used. There were two rooms leading off the main chamber. The one on the left was hidden by a closed door. The other doorway led into a small room, again sparsely decorated and surprisingly tidy. A simple bed was against the wall, under the window that looked out over the roof of the main house to the opposite tower. A plain chest rested against the foot of the bed, with a table and matching chair standing next to it facing the far wall. The remaining wall included the fireplace that backed onto the other room. There was a reasonable fire burning in the grate, reflected on the iron bathtub that stood in the middle of the room. Steam curled gently above the rim from the hot, soapy water within it.

The outer door banged open and a woman's voice called out. 'Those stairs will be the death of me,' she puffed.

Drey turned to meet the new arrival. 'Ah, Tarra. Perfect timing as usual. Tallen is ready for her bath now.'

Tarra walked into the room carrying a bundle of towels. She was a small woman with flushed cheeks, and she brought the faint scent of lavender with her. She wore a long, faded grey dress that was gathered at her ample waist by a chain of brass rings. Her long brown hair was tied into a neat plait with a yellow ribbon.

'Oh my,' she gasped as she looked at me, making me feel very self-conscious. 'I think a bath is long overdue.'

She bustled into the room as Drey left, closing the door behind her. Tarra laid the towels on the bed and came over to stand in front of me. She placed her hands on her hips as she looked me up and down, and shook her head slightly as she clicked her tongue against her teeth.

'My, my, this will never do.'

She moved towards me and I instinctively moved back, away from her reaching hands. She looked at me with such surprise I nearly laughed.

'Come on now.' She reached towards me again. 'No need to be shy. I've been bathing children for more years than I care to remember. I had only just finished bathing Mistress Breya when I got the message from Master Drey to come and assist you.'

She lunged for the hem of my tunic before I could move away again and lifted it efficiently over my head. I had not been naked in front of anyone since I was a small child. I felt my cheeks burning. Tarra appeared not to notice. She stood still, holding my stained tunic, looking at my bruises with an expression that was a mix of horror, shock, sorrow and anger. My bones stood out at my wrists and were easily visible along the length of my arms. I could see my ribs poking through my skin.

'Oh, my poor child.'

I was embarrassed by the bruises and healing wounds as well as Tarra's reaction to them. I crossed my arms over my chest to try to hide some of them.

'I can bathe myself,' I grumped.

She recovered her mild expression and folded my tunic on the floor. 'I'm sure you can. But I think it may take two of us to get rid of all that grime.'

She reached for my trousers, but I stepped back again and removed them myself. I quickly slipped into the water while she was busy with my clothes. The heat of the water made me sigh deeply. Tarra chuckled. She picked up a small towel from the bed, dipped it in the water and began scrubbing me like a dirty pan. I wanted to protest, but found I was enjoying being cleaned. I lay back and savoured the sensations of the dirt being scoured from my body. Tarra gave a sharp intake of breath as she moved to my back and saw the welts and scabs from the beatings I had taken. Her hands didn't falter though as she gently smoothed the ridges with the towel.

I ducked under the water so she could no longer see my skin. I held my breath for as long as I could before surfacing. Wise to my attempts at distraction, Tarra poured scented liquids on my head and began to scrub firmly at my scalp. She scooped the bathwater over my head, causing it to run down my face. My eyes stung and the back of my nose and throat burned as I inhaled some of the fluid. I screwed my face up, causing Tarra to laugh.

'Don't be such a baby,' she scolded mildly.

Every part of me was scrubbed and pink before Tarra was happy that I was clean enough. I had to admit it felt good to have the soft towel wrapped around me as I stood dripping from the tub. She rubbed my body dry before taking the final towel and drying my hair. I finger-brushed it into less of a haystack, tucking wet strands behind my ears and brushing the overgrown fringe out of my eyes. Tarra removed a clean set of clothes from the chest and placed them on the bed.

'Would you like me to dress you?' She laughed at my scowl. 'I thought not. I'll collect the bath towel later.'

She picked up my stinking clothes from the floor, and the other two towels, before leaving the room. It seemed empty and sad without the small woman's bustling presence. I dressed quickly, and the clothes were only a little too big for me. I sighed again from the warmth that went deep into my bones; the first time I had been truly warm in long time. I was tempted to lie on the bed but knew I would fall asleep if I did. I folded the towel and placed it on the chair in front of the table. My bare feet made no noise as I crossed the room and quietly opened the door.

I could see Drey at a table. His back was to me and I watched him for a number of heartbeats as he studied a book that was lying open. He was soon aware of my presence. He closed the book and turned towards me.

'Tallen, I...' he began, before stopping and closing his mouth. He looked at me with sad eyes for a moment, as if about to speak. But then he rejected that train of thought. He indicated the stuffed chair in front of him. 'Please, sit down.'

The chair was so comfortable it felt like I was sinking into it rather than sitting on it. I sat cross-legged, tucking my feet under my legs as they were getting chilly. Drey looked at me for a long time without speaking. His hazel eyes gazed deep into mine. I felt the same falling feeling that I had felt the first time I saw him; his dark pupils seeming to expand to fill my whole vision. I gripped the arms of the chair to stop myself from toppling forward into those dark lakes.

'Humph.' Drey's voice broke the hold of his eyes. 'Seems you've been having lots of adventures.'

I took a sharp intake of breath, blinking rapidly and swallowing to shake the feeling of nausea. I made a mental note to avoid direct eye contact with him in the future.

'It also seems you have developed quite a skill for taking things that are not yours.'

I stiffened, expecting the anger I knew had to follow the discovery of the stolen items hidden in the wall. I braced myself for the punishment that had to be dispensed. I silently prayed to the Goddess that it would not involve flogging. My heart raced at the thought of opening up the wounds on my back.

Drey watched me intently. 'Fortunately for you, I think I have a need for those talents.'

It took a while for me to realise what he was saying. I broke my vow not to look him in the eye. 'You want me to steal for you?' I asked cautiously, thinking that it might be a trap.

'More… special services to the crown.' He arched his fingers, tapping the two first fingers together. 'There are occasions when our liege may need to acquire certain… items. It would be helpful to be able to call on someone with your… speciality. It would mean you staying here, and you would have to study with the others. Can you read?'

I shook my head.

'Humph, some catching up to do then. Can you ride?'

I shook my head again.

'Oh dear. A lot of catching up, it would seem. Never mind. I'm sure you'll do fine.'

My head was spinning. It appeared that not only was I *not* going to be punished, but I was going to be taught to read and ride. I suspected that there would be a payback at some point, but for the moment I was happy to go along with whatever Drey wanted. I was free of North End for the time being. I was willing to see where this road would take me.

Drey noted my acceptance and nodded once. 'Good. Let's get some food.'

Drey took me to the main dining hall to the right of the royal house. The room was large, twice as long as it was wide. Wooden tables were arranged lengthways so that four long tables were available for people to come and get their meals. The hall contained a variety of diners – soldiers, clerks, ladies' maids – all mixing with each other without any regard for rank or profession. The food was presented on large silver platters at the far end of the room, with everyone helping themselves to whatever they required. There seemed more than anyone could possibly eat.

After we had cleared our plates, I was sent to find Langdon at the training grounds. I had not been to the arena since Laken had left, so I was a little apprehensive as I walked through the stone archway. I was beginning to wish I hadn't eaten so much. The food was churning in my stomach. I could hear the sound of iron ringing against iron long before I could see the practice arena. It was a clear, crisp winter afternoon and the sun shone brightly, pinpoints of light reflecting in the swords as they clashed together. I had to climb the wooden steps to the viewing platform before I could see who the combatants were, and was surprised to see the two princes fighting with real swords; lethally sharp edges flashing close to royal skin. Kerk had an expression of focused determination, while Kade was characteristically more flamboyant. Kerk was taller and, consequently, had a longer reach. Kade was light and agile on his feet. Their skills were evenly matched. I was enthralled by the intimacy of the contest, each one reading his opponent and devising new strategies to disarm him. The shifting of weight onto the balls of the feet. The dipping of a shoulder before a lunge. The focus on the face rather than the weapon. A deadly dance requiring the full attention of each participant.

Kade saw me watching from the platform and his attention was removed from Kerk for a second. Kerk saw the opportunity and lunged for his brother's head, the blade whistling as it sliced the air. Without taking his eyes off me, Kade bowed extravagantly so his head almost touched his knees as his arms swept out to the sides. Kerk's blade sliced through the space that Kade's head had occupied a moment earlier.

'One of these days I'll get you,' snapped Kerk. 'I did not hold my swing.'

Kade grinned at him. 'I know.'

The princes sheathed their swords and walked over to the side of the arena where a few benches had been placed. Tawpin was sitting on the nearest bench. He handed a water skin to Kade before waving at me to come and join him. I had seen the young man who sat next to Tawpin walking behind Kerk in the midsummer parades, so I assumed he was Kerk's page. He also offered a water skin but Kerk refused, taking the one from his brother instead. I went to sit next to Tawpin, nodding to the other page as I joined the group.

Tawpin leaned towards me and started sniffing at me as if he was a dog. 'Much better. No hint of horse.'

I tried to look disapprovingly at him and failed. I resorted to punching him on the arm instead.

'So, just waiting for Lady Breya. Again.'

Langdon's voice boomed across the grounds as he emerged from the hidden entrance under the viewing platform. The tunnel connected the arena to an outside practice area, running under the platforms and big enough to allow horses to enter by this route. It gave the illusion that Langdon had appeared from nowhere, and this added to the spectacle when tournaments were held there. He strode across the sand towards us, his arms bare despite the chill in the air. He wore his knife and sword sheathed at his belt, but also carried a number of swords. He placed these on the bench on the far side of Kerk's page.

'I'm here. On time. Precisely.'

Breya flounced into the arena using the same route that I had. Her blonde hair was held in a ponytail by a lilac ribbon that matched her gambeson. Her leggings were cream, to match the shirt that ruffled at her neck and ballooned at the sleeves. She wore soft leather boots that extended to above her calf muscles, accentuating her small feet. The leggings fitted closely over her hips as she swayed across the arena. The jewelled hilt of a rapier sat atop an elaborately crafted scabbard, which bounced gently against her leg. The gambeson emphasised her tiny waist and fully developed breasts. She looked stunning.

'My Lady Breya,' Langdon began with a heavy note of sarcasm. 'So nice of you to join us.'

She glared at him, then pointedly turned her back on him to stand with the princes. Langdon picked up two swords from the pile on the bench and handed them to the two pages. He looked at me for a few heartbeats, his head slightly on one side, then rummaged through the pile until he selected the sword he wanted. Balancing it in his hand for a moment, he then passed it to me. I took it hesitantly, not quite believing that he wanted me to use a weapon so close to important people. It was heavier than the ones I had played with as a child, but it was well made and had a good balance. It felt very strange to hold a blade again.

'Right.' Langdon moved a few paces away so he had room to swing his sword, but also to make sure we could all see him. 'We will work on backhand lunges today. I want to see smooth lines. No jabbing or shortening of the swing. Kerk and Kade, you take the far corner. Tawpin and Jeck, you two over there. Breya and Tallen can practise here.'

'I'm not practising with her,' snapped Breya, looking at me as if I was something unpleasant. 'She's hardly going to test *my* skills.'

'Well, I'm not practising with you,' replied Tawpin. 'I'd hate to damage that fine tunic.'

'You couldn't get near me, runt.'

'True. You'd be too busy running away.' Tawpin ran in a small circle, exaggeratedly lifting his legs high and squealing. 'Oh, my pretty buttons. Don't mess up my lovely ruffles.'

'You little…' Breya went to move towards Tawpin but found Langdon in the way.

'Holy Mother's tears. Give me a company of new recruits and save me from the young!' Langdon glared at Tawpin, so did not see Breya stick her tongue out. 'Breya can practise with Kerk. I take it that won't offend your sense of fair play?'

'Not at all.' Breya walked over to stand next to Kerk as if she was marching in a state parade. Her head was held high and she gave an imperious look at me as she went past.

Tawpin skipped over to me. 'I'll fight with Magpie.'

'Magpie?' Kade went to stand by Jeck.

Tawpin grinned. 'Magpie likes to take pretty things.'

Kade grinned back. 'Oh yeah. I heard about that.'

'Can we *please* focus on the practice session?' boomed Langdon. 'Breya and Kerk can demonstrate what I'm looking for. Breya can show off some of those skills she's so proud of.'

Breya beamed at the compliment as she and Kerk moved to a clear space. Langdon stood at the far side of the pair while Tawpin, Kade, Jeck and I formed the other two points of the triangle, with Breya and Kerk in the middle. Langdon instructed Kerk to make a backwards sweep, downwards as if to slice Breya from her right shoulder to her left hip. Breya had drawn her rapier and it looked pitifully small compared to Kerk's broad blade. I was impressed by the way she used the momentum of the swing to slide the sword down her blade, removing its power before twisting her wrist to force the sword away from her. She expertly deflected the force of the lunge by using her opponent's strength against him, compensating for her and her blade's weaknesses.

'Go practise those moves.' Langdon gestured for us to split into our pairs and repeat the exercises that had just been demonstrated. He stayed with Breya and Kerk to provide small corrections in posture and grip.

Tawpin gave me a gentle shove. 'You be Kerk and I'll be Breya.'

He was grinning as if his face was about to burst. I was instantly suspicious but assumed the position I had seen Kerk take. I raised my sword, adjusting my grip to account for the unfamiliar balance. Tawpin stood in front of me, holding his sword in a relaxed grip, the point resting on the floor.

'Ready?'

Tawpin nodded. I brought the sword down, letting the weight of the blade carry the momentum towards his shoulder. The weapon had moved less than a finger's breadth when Tawpin dropped his sword, threw his hands in the air and started running around screaming. I burst out laughing at the ridiculous spectacle, then laughed again as I caught Breya's furious face. Langdon sighed, shaking his head slightly as he walked over to us. I saw Kerk lean in to speak to Breya, preventing her coming over and skewering Tawpin with her rapier.

'You would be wise not to make an enemy of her,' Langdon said quietly to Tawpin.

'I know,' said Tawpin, only partially apologetically. 'But she's such an easy target.'

I was tired deep in the core of my bones when Langdon was finally happy with our efforts. My arms felt as if they weighed five times more than usual. My back and thigh muscles throbbed with each heartbeat, and my fingers tingled from the repeated concussion of my blade against Tawpin's. But it was an exhaustion that felt good. Productive. I was pleased with how much I had remembered from my play fights with the children of Methhold and my father.

I returned my sword to the pile on the bench and turned to follow Breya, Kerk and Jeck. Tawpin was returning his own sword and grabbed my arm.

'Wait a moment.' He nodded towards Kade, who was still talking to Langdon. 'We'll have to carry the blades back, but it will be worth it.'

I was a little confused as I followed Tawpin to the nearby bench and sat next to him. It was not long before I found out what he was talking about. Kade and Langdon moved to face each other, and both adopted a relaxed stance with their swords hanging low. Each focused on the other's eyes, waiting for the telltale indicators of a forthcoming lunge.

It was several heartbeats before Langdon made the first move. He moved to the left, bringing his sword down behind him towards Kade's head. The blade was moving with some speed and had no respect for royal lineage.

Kade parried, turning a half-circle to deflect the blow so that he finished standing where Langdon had been. Wasting no time, Kade sliced against Langdon's blade, forcing him to turn around and face the prince. Following through, Kade slashed the blade towards Langdon's head, causing the older man to step back.

The hairs at the base of my neck rose with the intensity of the fighting. The blades screamed as they dragged against each other. Spears of light flashed as the swords changed direction faster than I could blink.

Regaining his balance, Langdon lunged towards Kade, holding his sword with both hands. He chopped at Kade's abdomen, swinging the blade back and forth. Kade was forced to take several steps backwards, turning in a small circle so that he ended up behind Langdon. He also changed his grip to a two-handed hold as he smashed the sword across Langdon's back.

Langdon was made to turn and drop to one knee to contain the force of the blow on his blade. My ears hurt with the howl of protest from the iron as the two swords stilled for a heartbeat. Quick as mouse, Langdon turned the blades and harmlessly released the hold. He sprang back up onto his feet. The two combatants faced each other as at the start, taking the opportunity to catch their breath.

It was the first time all afternoon that I had seen Kade truly focus on his fighting. More telling was that Langdon was also forced to concentrate. Kade was demonstrating the skills of a man many years his senior and was providing a fair test for the Master of Arms. I was held spellbound by the grace and beauty of the exchange.

Langdon broke first again. He brought his sword across to decapitate the prince. I gasped, convinced he was going to make contact. Kade waited until the last moment before taking a half-step backwards to avoid the swing. He aimed for Langdon's exposed right side. Langdon twisted away, circling a finger's breadth in front of the blade so that his weapon sliced towards Kade's exposed neck. Kade was still carried by the momentum of his swing and was unable to change direction fast enough.

I held my breath, horrified by what I was certain was about to happen.

Langdon twisted the blade so the flat surface smacked the back of Kade's head, sending him sprawling across the floor. I breathed again. Kade was laughing as he turned to sit on the sandy ground. He rubbed the back of his head.

'Your confidence will be the death of you,' the Master of Arms warned.

Kade would not be chastised and continued to grin. 'Made you work for it though, didn't I?'

Langdon smiled affectionately. 'Yes, you did.'

I was still finding it hard to breathe, my heart pounding with the excitement of the fight. Langdon rolled his shoulders to stretch out the muscles before leaving the arena. Kade came over to sit between Tawpin and me.

'That was really good,' I said hesitantly.

Kade shrugged. 'Yeah, I know.'

Tawpin groaned and dramatically held his head. 'Don't tell him that. He's unbearable as it is.'

Kade shoved him in response. 'And you show no respect, Master Tawpin.'

Tawpin jumped up and performed an elaborate bow in front of the prince. 'My apologies, Your Grace. Let me make amends by buying you a tankard at the Blue Boar.'

'A fabulous idea.' Kade jumped up and slapped Tawpin on the shoulder. Tawpin gathered up the blades left by Langdon, leaving nothing for me to do. I remained sitting on the bench as the boys walked across the arena, not yet wanting to return to Drey.

Halfway across, Kade turned back to call to me. 'You coming, Magpie?'

I was too surprised that he had asked me to go with them to be annoyed that he had used Tawpin's name for me. I quickly caught up with them, knowing I was grinning ridiculously but not caring.

The Blue Boar was busy when we arrived, although I knew it would get busier still later in the evening. The heat in the room caused my cheeks to burn and my nose to drip after the chill of the air outside. I automatically went to the hidden table that Tawpin and I would use when sneaking in. Tawpin took my arm.

'We get to sit at the good tables tonight.' He grinned.

We followed Kade to a table in the heart of the inn. It was far enough away from the fire not to be uncomfortably hot, and had a good view of the cleared area at the far end of the tavern where a young minstrel was tuning his stringed instrument. Shanna came over with three tankards of ale before we had even sat down. Kade slipped his arms around her waist while her hands were full with the tankards and could not dislodge him. He squeezed until she squealed.

Tawpin sat to one side of me while Kade sat on the other. The ale tasted very good, the cold liquid flowing down my dry throat. It had been a long time since I had drunk any alcohol. My head felt warm almost immediately, my muscles relaxing after the afternoon's exertion. I only half listened as Kade and Tawpin chatted animatedly. I felt comfortable in their company.

The food arrived and was as good as I expected to feed the prince. The minstrel had finished tuning and started playing an upbeat melody that had the early drinkers tapping their feet. The mood in the tavern was light, although there was a subtle undercurrent of sadness as most of the customers were soldiers that had been fighting on the borders recently. The minstrel kept to jolly, crowd-pleasing songs throughout the evening as the tavern filled up. Soon it was standing room only and the noise level rose with the increased numbers. The minstrel struggled to be heard at times, and his voice was starting to suffer from the strain. At my side, Kade was growing increasingly agitated.

Eventually he could resist no longer. He jumped up and quickly crossed to the minstrel, patting him on the shoulder as he joined him. Kade effortlessly harmonised with the singer, adding depth to the song and cutting through the chatter. Tawpin smiled, a strange mixture of pride and affection I had not expected from him.

'He just can't help himself.' He turned to me. 'Now you're in for a treat.'

Kade's voice was rich, with a soft, gravelly quality. His harmonies raised the hair on my arms as I was captivated by his performance. The merchants and soldiers lowered their voices, maybe out of respect for the prince but I suspected it was due more to his singing. He was very good; better than he had been with the sword earlier that day. But his expression now was very different. When fighting Langdon he had looked focused, determined, professional. When singing, he seemed to grow in height and presence. His eyes sparkled, as those of a person suffering from a fever might. He responded to subtle changes in the audience, acknowledged those that cheered him, and directed playful gestures at those not listening, to the amusement of those that were. The minstrel was reduced to a supporting act within moments.

'He does it every time.' Tawpin had to shout in my ear as the songs got rowdier and the crowd cheered enthusiastically. Almost everyone in the tavern was now paying attention to Kade. The serving girls were running around trying to keep everyone supplied with drinks, while Brethick smiled broadly at the increased custom. A pretty young serving girl took drinks to the singers, smiling coyly at Kade as she passed him a tankard. She blushed cherry red as he winked at her.

Tawpin said something but I could not hear over the noise. I turned and leaned towards him to hear him better.

'What?'

He hesitated. 'It was good to hear you laughing today.'

I frowned in confusion. 'I always laugh.'

He looked deep into my eyes, uncharacteristically serious. 'No. No you don't.'

I dismissed his concerns and turned back to Kade, who was demonstrating a particular position being sung about. But Tawpin had not finished.

'Tallen…' he began before pausing again. 'Since Laken—'

'Don't.' I held up my hand to emphasise the point.

'But I—'

'Not now, Tawpin. Not today.' I was having too good a time to be brought back to reality by Tawpin's overprotective concerns. What difference did it make if I laughed or not? Didn't he realise there was not much to laugh about, with the war…?

I stopped that train of thought and concentrated on Kade.

'I'm sorry.'

I pretended not to hear him. Kade was in total control now, and the minstrel was barely keeping up with him.

It was getting late and the minstrel had almost lost his voice by the time Brethick called for the tavern to close. The customers complained loudly, until Kade agreed to sing one last song. He leaned down to the minstrel and whispered in his ear. The singer turned quickly to look at Kade, questioning his request. They looked at each other for a handful of heartbeats, before the minstrel nodded in agreement. He took a deep breath before starting to play.

The strings vibrated gently, releasing soft tones that brought a revering hush the room. Kade added his voice, made huskier by the night's singing. The effect raised the hair on my arms again and I shuddered at the chill that raced down my spine. The melody was slow and haunting, the strings interplaying in complex harmonies. Kade's voice weaved through the notes, telling of battlefields and battles, families left behind, loss and heartache. The room was transfixed by the images sung with passion and pain; the crescendo of power released by his voice during the climax of the song, followed by the softest whisper that broke everyone's hearts at the conclusion.

The tavern was frozen for several heartbeats, each person lost in memories of their own pain and loss. Quietly, they started leaving.

Kade slumped back in the seat next to me, draining his tankard. Brethick placed a pouch of coins at the minstrel's feet before continuing to our table.

'I feel I should pay you after your performance tonight.' He nodded slowly. 'Very special, Your Grace.'

Kade dismissed the suggestion with a wave of his hand.

'But I pay enough money to your father in taxes.' Brethick clasped the prince's shoulder, then walked away.

Kade chuckled quietly, then turned to Tawpin and me. 'Time to go home, I think.'

I blinked. I did not want to presume that I was staying with Drey. It had been implied but not explicitly stated. I turned to Tawpin with my eyes wide. He laughed as he understood.

'Drey forgets to tell us mortals the little things. Forgets we can't all read minds.' I was pleased to hear his words slur slightly. 'You get to stay with him.'

'Fabulous.' Kade stood up and banged on the table. 'I'll walk you two drunkards home.'

'I'm not drunk,' I protested, but swayed slightly as I stood up.

Kade chuckled again, looping his arm through mine. He raised an eyebrow at Tawpin, who then stood to take my other arm. Enclosed by the two of them, we made our way back to the royal house. Tawpin took his leave as we approached the main doors. I moved to go around to the servants' entrance, but Kade had a firm hold on my arm.

'May I escort you to your door?'

He smiled at me and my face that clearly displayed my surprise. I nodded, not trusting my voice not to squeak. He gently led me up the steps to the doors, through the entrance hall and up the main staircase. I nervously waited for someone to tell me off for being in the main house when I should be in the servants' quarters. But I was with Kade. No one challenged me. They only acknowledged him with a deferential dip of the head. It felt very strange.

Kade stopped outside Drey's door and finally let go of my arm.

'It is here I must bid you goodnight.'

He bowed elaborately before me, and caught my hand in his as he rose, bringing my fingers up to his lips. His warm lips pressed against my knuckles, his breath tickling the sensitive skin.

Then he was gone.

I stood frozen for several heartbeats, trying to make sense of the exchange. I gave up and leaned against the door. It was not latched and opened easily. I fell in through the door as it banged against the wall, and cursed quietly. Closing the door silently, I crept across the room to the far corner. A small fire was burning in the grate of the room I had bathed in so many hours before. It gave off a soft glow, enough to be able to see clearly. I walked over to the window, not ready to sleep. The night was clear and the breeze cool. It cleared my head and I felt refreshed as I leaned out of the window.

The railing around the base of the spire was just visible above my head. I grabbed a blanket and climbed onto the stone windowsill, reaching for the rail. My foot slipped, causing me to push against the bed. It scraped on the floor, making a loud rasping sound in the quiet of the night. I winced and tried again. My fingers clasped the railing tightly, allowing me to pull myself up onto the roof below the spike. I walked round to the front of the tower, so I could see over the black sea and forget the town behind me. I curled up under the blanket.

It had been a tidal wave of a day, starting in a city gaol cell and finishing with me being walked to my door by Faulknar's youngest son. I hadn't had time to think about what Drey was offering me or expecting me to give him in return. I smiled as I remembered Kade fighting Langdon and singing in the Blue Boar, but it faded when I thought of Tawpin's words. Maybe he was right. It had been a long time since I had laughed. It seemed a lifetime away when we ran the streets together, helping the fishermen and stealing apples. That was before. Before I knew about the war. Before Laken went away. Before Laken never came back.

Chapter Eight

If the previous day was a tidal wave, the one after was the storm-wrecked beach. The day started badly and got progressively worse. I awoke, chilled and stiff, on the roof of the royal house. I could hear Drey banging around in the rooms below. The noise echoed round my head. I groaned.

I climbed back in through the window as quietly as I could. I hoped to sneak out without Drey noticing, but there was a small chance of that. He turned on me as soon as I entered the main room.

'There are rules,' he growled. 'This house is not to be treated like some barracks that you can fall back to at any hour of the night.'

I started to apologise, but Drey continued, reeling off a long list of dos and don'ts. Mainly don'ts.

'If you are to continue to stay here you need to treat this place with a bit of respect. There will be no crashing about when you get in. Don't touch anything. There are valuable and delicate items here that I don't want damaged. You are not to enter my private room unless accompanied by me, and then you will not touch anything. There are things here that you couldn't possibly understand. I don't like a mess, so don't leave things lying around. If you must come in late, be quiet. I often work late into the night and cannot be disturbed. Did I mention not to touch anything?'

'Once or twice.'

He stared at me for a heartbeat, before blinking. 'Oh… yes… well. I'm not used to company. I like it quiet.'

'I'm sorry.' I finally got to apologise. 'I didn't mean to disturb you. It's just Tawpin and Kade took me to the Blue Boar, and Kade started singing. He's really good.'

The distraction worked and Drey smiled. 'Yes, he is, isn't he? That boy should be a bard, not a prince.' He sighed. 'But we can't change what we are.'

I hesitated before asking, 'Drey, why am I here? I disturb your work and you don't need the company. Why do you care what happens to me?'

I was scared to hear the answer but had to know why he had taken me from the cells. Surely there were others who could have provided for his needs. North End was full of thieves. Why was I so special? Why go to all this trouble?

Drey waited a long time before answering. He looked at me with eyes that probed the soul. His head was tilted slightly to the side, and his forehead was crinkled by a frown. It was as if he was considering telling me an important secret. But then he rejected the idea. The frown disappeared and the eyes lost their intensity.

'Laken was a good friend. He cared for you deeply.'

I knew that was not the full answer. But I also knew it was the only answer I was going to get. I changed the subject. 'So, what do you do here?'

He smiled at me and I knew he was not going to answer that question either. 'This morning you have reading lessons with Villermir.'

He laughed at the face I must have pulled. Villermir scared me. I got the distinct impression that he didn't like me, although we had never met.

'Oh, he's not that bad.' Drey's tone did nothing to convince me. 'Anyway, it will only be for a while. Just until you get the hang of it.'

'Do I have to? Couldn't you teach me?'

He smiled gently. 'You'll be fine. Villermir is very good at teaching. You'll be reading in no time.'

I doubted that. Very few people in my village could read. It was not a skill required for hunting or raising goats, so was not encouraged. The Druids kept the oral traditions, and that was all we needed. Since arriving at Liegeport it seemed there was a hierarchy, even within the servant ranks, regarding skills such as reading. Reading was not needed to clean dishes or chop vegetables, but many household staff could read and write. I hadn't cared for the skills until it was pointed out that I didn't have them. Now, I worried that it was too late and I would never learn, particularly under the tutelage of Villermir. He did not seem tolerant of other people's failings.

'Go get some food and meet Villermir in the library.' Drey looked at me in a way that made me suspicious. 'Do you know where that is?'

I had the feeling it was some kind of test, but I was unclear of the correct answer. I went for the truth. 'Yes.'

He nodded, seemingly satisfied with that answer. 'Good. Now get out of my chambers so I can do some work.'

He turned back to his desk, but I could tell he was smiling.

I was not very hungry, so I avoided the main dining hall with all the people and noise and went instead to the kitchen to get a drink and a light snack. The usual bustle of activity was familiar and welcoming. The feeling did not last long. The atmosphere became colder as I entered, with conversations stopping in mid-sentence. Many turned to stare at me. The looks were mainly suspicious, but some were almost hostile.

'Can I get you anything, miss?' I turned to see Mistress Narran looking at me, flour all over her hands.

'I wanted a drink,' I replied, confused at her change of attitude towards me.

'There's fresh water and watered wine in the main hall, miss.'

Her tone and formality made it very clear I was not welcome in the kitchen any more. I turned to leave, wondering what I had done to warrant such a response. Was it my time in North End? Was it because I was living in the main house now?

'Just make sure you leave the silver behind.'

I didn't recognise the voice behind my back, but it didn't matter. No one volunteered to correct him. I was just a thief to them. The time I had worked alongside them meant nothing. I had hidden my stolen gains in their sleeping quarters. I had betrayed their trust, and they would never trust me again. Another small sorrow to add to those already lodged in my chest.

The library was to the right of the main entrance hall. The room was large but appeared smaller due to the bookcases that lined every wall. There was a large, dark wood table in the middle of the room with chairs along both sides. Plain parchment, inkpots and quills were arranged along the centre of the table. There were four reading lecterns, one in each corner of the room, in the same wood as the table and chairs. In the centre panel of the long walls, there were slots for rolled parchment, all full of scrolls. I inhaled the musty smell of the books, enjoying the tingle it caused in my nose. I gently rubbed my fingers along the leather spines of the books, feeling the ridges of the embossed lettering.

'Don't touch what doesn't belong to you!'

I jumped at the sound of the deep, nasal voice that came from behind me. I had not heard anyone come in, and the fears of North End came stampeding to the surface of my mind, causing my heart to beat painfully. I turned slowly, half expecting a blow across the face. Villermir was standing very close to me, a full head and shoulders taller. Although his posture was intimidating, his hands remained at his sides. I relaxed a little, although not before I saw a glint of triumph in his eyes at my reaction to his presence.

'Sit down.'

He gestured to the nearest chair and I sat obediently. From behind me, he dropped two large books on the table, making a loud bang as the leather hit the wood. I jumped, and again saw the flash of triumph in his eyes. My body tensed reflexively. This was a game to him. He enjoyed causing fear in others. I felt my back arch slightly, like a cat that is being threatened.

He opened the top book and indicated the top of the page. 'Read this aloud.'

My cheeks grow hot as my heartbeat increased its rate again. My hands started to shake as embarrassment mixed with anger. He must have known, but would make me say it. 'I can't read.'

'What?'

I took a deep breath and looked him in the eyes. 'I can't read.'

He hit me on the back of the head with enough force to send me face first onto the table. The blow stung my scalp, but I was more outraged that he had struck me. I could not understand why he had.

'Show respect,' he barked. 'Do not look at me as if I was a common servant. I am the high priest of Baila. You will keep your eyes averted when I am in your presence.'

I clenched my fists in frustration, but kept my eyes lowered.

'It seems we will have to start at the beginning,' he continued as if nothing had happened. 'Copy out those letters. Let's see if you can do that.'

I took a piece of parchment and dipped a quill into the inkpot. I looked at the letters on the first line of the page indicated. Initially the individual characters stood out clearly, but as I continued to look they seemed to vibrate. The vibration increased until the letters were jumping around the page, mixing up the order.

I was hit on the back of my head again. 'Have you lost your wits? Start copying the letters.'

My hands shaking with anger, I concentrated again on the letters. Focusing on one letter only, I was able to copy the shape onto the parchment. It took a long time to complete the line. Pressure was building up behind my eyes, giving me a headache as I strained to keep the letter still long enough for me to copy. As I grew tired, the letters shimmered until they changed completely. The text looked more like lines or scratches on the parchment than the characters I had drawn. Triangles, squares and five-pointed stars replaced the curling script I had copied.

I paused to rub my eyes and relieve some of the pain that was growing there. I had thought Villermir was standing on the far side of the room, but he managed to strike the back of my head again. Black spots danced in the centre of my vision for several heartbeats. I was shaking with rage, but still lacked the courage to do anything about it. I returned to the book and tried to copy the next row of letters. Just as I was about to place the quill on the parchment, Villermir snatched the sheet away and tore it up.

'Enough of that. Your lettering is worse than an infant's. Practise in your own time, do not waste any more of mine.'

I had a flash of hope that the lesson was over, but my heart dropped several finger-lengths into my stomach when he placed the second book in front of me. He opened the first page and read the first line. He waited for me to repeat the words, indicating each word as I spoke it. He then read the next line. I was memorising his words rather than understanding the patterns in the book that were still jumping around and turning into boxes and stars. But Villermir seemed content with my efforts and did not hit me any more.

Eventually, the lesson was over. He closed the book with a slap, the puff of air making me blink. He instructed me to practise my reading and writing, and stated that I was to demonstrate improved skill when we met again in two days' time. He then left the room, closing the door quietly behind him. I closed my eyes and rested my head on my folded arms on the table. The pressure behind my eyes was subsiding, but the back of my head was still sore. I was dreading returning in a couple of days and was feeling more inadequate than ever. I groaned. It was better than being in North End, so I had better get on with it.

The afternoon brought new torment in the form of horse-riding lessons. The group lesson consisted of the six of us who had had weapon practice the day before. Kade, Kerk and Breya rode their own horses, while Tawpin,

Jeck and I had ones loaned from the stables. Tawpin had picked a flighty chestnut mare who danced around at the slightest pressure from his legs. I was given Legend – the only one that would tolerate my close presence. He was a retired battle mount, large and steady. My hips felt as if they were being pulled apart with each step, but the grey obediently followed the others and I had to do little work.

We gathered in a large sandy arena behind the cavalry stables. Baden was the Master of Cavalry and stood in the middle of the arena. He was a lean man with dark hair and piercing blue eyes in a tanned face. He had the longest legs I had ever seen on a man, which he used to great effect when riding. We circled him, guiding our horses into a trot. I bounced a heartbeat behind Legend, uncomfortably jostled. I tried to keep my arms down and my legs extended, as Baden instructed. But my legs continuously rose up the sides of the horse as I tried to grip, pushing me further out of the saddle. My hips and thighs started to ache almost as soon as the lesson began.

After warming the horses up by walking and trotting in a variety of patterns, including walking over poles to help improve the placing of their feet, we were arranged along one side of the arena for individual work. I watched while Kerk and Kade collected rings from a pole whilst galloping at full speed. The horses seemed an extension of their bodies; a drop of the shoulder to shift weight in the saddle and the horse turned obediently. Breya got her horse to dance. Gentle play on the reins combined with instructions from her legs had the mare turning in tight circles and high-stepping with her feet. The pair performed graceful manoeuvres demonstrating a great deal of skill from Breya. Tawpin and Jeck raced each other around barrels, jumping on and off their mounts at blindingly quick speeds. Jeck was a conscentious rider, and his calm manner and quiet instructions easily gained the trust of his horse. The gelding was steady and attentive. In contrast, Tawpin was as erratic a rider as he was in everything else. His commands were exuberant and the mare responded dramatically, spinning and rearing. But she was fast, and Tawpin won many of the races despite her antics.

I just walked and trotted around the arena as before, although Baden did not make an issue of this. He offered advice in the same manner as he did everyone else. I was very grateful, especially after the morning's session with Villermir.

We then repeated the exercises with Baden correcting mistakes and improving posture, hand position, extending the horses' paces, and so on.

Tawpin leaned back on his chestnut to talk to me. 'What exciting things did you get up to this morning?'

'What, after the lecture I got from Drey because I was home so late?'

Tawpin grinned. 'Oops.'

'I then had the joyful company of Villermir.'

He winced. 'Ouch. What did you do to deserve that? Surely it wasn't punishment for coming home late?'

'He's teaching me how to read.'

Breya laughed. 'What kind of country simpleton are you?'

I felt the poorly suppressed anger from the morning rise within me again. 'We don't all need books to tell us how to do things,' I snapped back.

'No, I suppose chasing a few goats around is easily mastered.'

'Whereas you need a team of people to be able to coordinate your riding gloves with your outfit.'

Tawpin snorted as he tried to stifle a laugh. Breya's face glowed red, clashing with the matching shades of blue in her gloves and tunic. I saw a dangerous spark in her glare but chose to ignore it.

'When did you learn to read, anyway?' I asked, innocently enough.

With more than a hint of pride, she replied, 'I could read the teachings of Baila by the time I was five.'

'So even if it takes me four years to learn, I'll still be beating you.'

Tawpin snorted again, almost doubling over in the effort not to laugh out loud. It was obvious that Breya did not have to defend herself often, and she was lost for words for several heartbeats.

'You will never understand the complexity of the text of Baila,' she spat. 'You will still be on recipe pamphlets when I'm in my grave.'

'Oh, I'm sorry, Breya. I didn't realise you were planning on dying so soon.'

Her horse shuffled underneath her as she became more agitated. Legend was ignoring everything, his bottom lip drooping contentedly. It was Breya's turn to demonstrate her moves again, but this time her commands were short and sharp. The horse responded accordingly, and the movements were far less graceful than before. Baden quietly corrected Breya's grip and posture so that horse and rider were working in harmony once more by the time she had finished. She was more relaxed when she rejoined the group, watching Jeck and Tawpin control their mounts.

She moved closer to me so she could speak to me without the princes hearing. 'You play a dangerous game, street rat.'

'And what game is that?'

She smiled sweetly, causing the hairs at the base of my neck to stand up. My heart rate increased in anticipation of what she was about to do, only I had no idea what that was.

Jeck was about to jump over a low pole, with Tawpin following him. I watched Jeck fly confidently over the jump with room to spare while Tawpin readied his mare to follow. He was two paces away from the jump when movement flickered in the corner of my eye. I turned towards Breya as she pulled backwards on the reins and kicked with her heels. With nowhere to go, her sandy mare reared up, kicking out with her front feet at Legend. Legend moved calmly to the side, purely due to his battle training as I was unable to do anything to help him.

Tawpin's mare, however, was young and inexperienced. At the commotion caused by Breya's horse, she spooked midway through her jump and twisted sideways, unseating Tawpin as she kicked out her hind feet. Tawpin had turned as he flew over the jump without his horse so he fell awkwardly, his left arm tucked under his body. There was a loud crack as he landed – the sound of a tree branch breaking.

I was frozen for several heartbeats, not believing what had happened. I looked at Breya, who sat calmly.

'You stupid…'

Breya shrugged but looked me straight in the eye. 'It was an accident.'

I jumped off Legend and ran over to Tawpin. Baden and Jeck were already kneeling beside him, as Kade, Kerk and Breya dismounted. Tawpin's face was grey and his eyes looked like they were seeing something far away. He cried out as Baden gently turned him over. It was clear that his arm was broken. Jeck's face paled and I saw him swallow several times.

I clenched my jaw so hard my teeth hurt. I was so angry that Breya had hurt my friend to get at me. She could have killed him. My muscles tensed, shaking under the strain. My anger exploded and I lunged for Breya. I wanted to break her nose so that she could have a share in Tawpin's pain. I wanted to rip her hair from her scalp. I wanted to gouge her eyes out.

Breya remained unconcerned as my charge was halted by strong arms around my waist. Kade had crossed both arms across my middle and had to turn sideways to stop me from dragging him towards Breya. He was not much taller than me, but his grip was as if iron bands had fixed around my body. I could not break his hold no matter how much I struggled and pushed and cursed. The energy I had gathered to confront Breya was being used harmlessly trying to break free of Kade. Defeated, I stopped fighting.

The corners of Breya's mouth twitched in a small smile of triumph. The rage ignited once more. Again, I struggled against Kade's immovable hold. Frustrated, I twisted this way and that in order to break his grip. Breya's triumphant smile flashed again. She could control me so easily.

'Tallen,' barked Baden. 'That's not helping Tawpin. Kade, get her out of here.'

I was still cursing at Breya as Kade dragged me out of the arena and threw me towards the wall of the stable block.

'What under the Heavens do you think you are doing?' he demanded.

As soon as he released his hold I pushed against the wall to dive past him, with the intention of getting back to Breya. He saw the move coming and easily blocked it.

'Are you insane? She could have your head if she wanted.'

'She did it on purpose,' I spluttered. Tears of frustration were very close to escaping but I would not give Breya the satisfaction of knowing she had made me cry. 'She tried to get Legend to buck me off but got Tawpin instead. The stupid sow could have killed him.'

'And how are you going to prove that?' He was staying irritatingly calm. 'You will never win against her, Tallen. Never. Stop trying.'

'So, she just gets away with it?'

Kade looked deep into my eyes. I saw a hint of sorrow in his, along with a lot of resignation. 'We are who we are.'

'How can you say that?!'

I was not so ready to give up on making Breya pay for what she had done. But I was beginning see that I could not go head-to-head with her. I was going to have to be more subtle. Her time would come. I'd see to that.

Kade noticed the relaxation of my posture that indicated I was ready to listen to reason. 'Go and get Drey. They will have taken Tawpin to the infirmary. He will be needed there.'

I sighed. 'All right. But this isn't the end of it. She will pay for this.'

Kade slowly shook his head. 'Why doesn't that surprise me? Now go!'

I ran to the tower, using my simmering anger to pump my legs. I burst through the front doors to the main house, getting some satisfaction from the shouts of the doorkeepers. I crashed through the door into Drey's chambers, slamming the door behind me.

'Breya has broken Tawpin's arm and you're needed in the infirmary.'

I spoke on the move, not waiting for Drey to turn from the desk where he was working.

'Did I mention not slamming doors this morning?'

'No!'

I slammed the door behind me again as I entered my room. I threw myself onto the bed, breathing heavily. My fists clenched, and I banged them against the blankets. Getting no relief, I banged them down again. And again. I growled in my frustration. How could it be so unfair? How could she get away with that, just because she was the king's ward? Tawpin was an earl; did that count for nothing?

For lack of anything better to do, I climbed onto the roof and plotted ways of getting even with Breya.

I was cold and hungry by the time I finally came down from the roof. The night air had cleared my head and I felt much calmer. Even though I had not thought of a practical way of dealing with Breya, I had thought of several things I would like to do to her if I ever got the chance.

Drey was sitting in a comfortable chair by the fire when I walked into the main room.

'You've been up there a long time. You must be frozen.' He knew I had been on the roof.

He indicated a bowl of soup that was keeping warm next to the fire. My stomach growled loudly in appreciation.

'I had some thinking to do.' I sat on the floor to eat the soup.

'Come to any conclusions?'

I stared at the soup. 'No.'

He nodded. 'Probably for the best.'

He waited for me to say it. 'How is he? How's Tawpin's arm?'

'Clean break. It will mend.' He paused, studying me as I ate slowly. 'He insists it was an accident.'

I kept my eyes on the soup.

'That's not what you said. What happened?'

I tried to separate fact from the emotion of the incident. And failed. 'It was all her fault. She was angry at me, so made Tawpin's horse spook. Legend was too well trained, but she wanted me on the floor. Tawpin had done nothing. She was just being spiteful. She could have killed him.'

I stopped myself, knowing I was ranting. Drey stayed quiet for several heartbeats, waiting for me to accept the childishness in my accusations. All I saw was Breya's triumphant smile. I glared at the fire.

'It's a dangerous game to tweak that particular tail.'

'So everyone keeps telling me.'

'And yet you still persist.'

I turned to him, my eyes pleading for him to understand. 'It's not fair. I can't just let it go.'

He shook his head sadly. 'No. I don't suppose you can.'

My dream that night took on a new, painful aspect. It started the same, with the summer sun producing an oppressive heat. The mountain stood like a giant, hunched troll in front of me. I could feel the jagged stones scratching the palms of my hands and scraping my fingers before I had even started climbing. The scrubby grass poking out of the cracks made the rock face look unkempt. I hesitated before entering the gloom of the cave, my heart constricting inside my chest, making it difficult to breathe. I knew what was to come.

As so many times before, I followed the left path, travelling deeper and deeper into the mountain. My fingers stroked the moist rock walls, guiding my journey. The only sounds were the rasp of my breath; the hitch as I inhaled. I chewed the corner of my lower lip, drawn endlessly forward.

Knowing it would happen, I still went ice-cold at the sound of Laken's voice. The pleading was unbearable. It felt as if a pair of large hands had dug deep into my body, ripping the two halves apart. Tears streamed down my cheeks, dripping off my chin. But I continued to walk, unconsciously increasing my pace.

My route led me to a different part of the mountain. The cavern I had expected, where Laken's screams always started, did not arrive. Laken continued to plead with me, begging me to help him, his voice cracking with despair. The path curled round and down in an ever-descending spiral, making me feel nauseous and dizzy.

I was physically and emotionally exhausted by the time the tunnel flattened out into a small, enclosed cave. The rocks glowed with a green phosphorescence, giving the cavern an otherworldly feel. I could see no other entrance than the one I had walked through, but there were several dark alcoves that could contain hidden tunnels. I paused, unsure of what to do next. Laken had fallen silent and there was no obvious left turn.

A flicker to the right of my vision caused my head to turn. A tall figure walked out of the gloom. The person wore black robes that brushed the floor, and the hood was pulled down to cover the face. The slight curve at the waist and the delicate hands folded in front were unmistakably female. I took a step towards the woman, but she took a corresponding step backwards, back into the dark. I returned to my original position, and she stepped forward again. I frowned in confusion.

Before I could consider who this person was, my attention was drawn by a movement to my left. Laken stepped out of the shadows.

My breath caught in my throat.

His leggings were stained with the dark brown of old blood. His shirt was dirty and ripped, revealing a bleeding wound slashed across his chest. His hands hung limp by his sides, the knuckles scraped and swollen. His face was bruised, with a split lip and a crooked nose, blood caked at the nostrils. His left cheek bore a puckered scar. The right side of his head was ripped open and bleeding, a flap of skin folded down.

I vomited. My throat burned with the acidic fluid brought up from my stomach. Sweat oozing from my temples mixed with my tears. My cries strangled into hiccupping sobs. I closed my eyes tightly, not wanting to see his damaged face.

'Tallen, look at me.'

His voice was hoarse and raspy. Glacial water trailed down my spine as I heard the disappointment in his voice.

'Look at me!'

I forced my eyes open and slowly turned back to face him. My heart was shredded by the look in his eyes. Sadness. Loneliness. But also anger.

'How could you?' he demanded.

My forehead wrinkled in confusion. 'What?'

'You let me down, Tallen. You let everyone down.'

'I don't understand,' I pleaded.

'I took you in. I took care of you. And you did nothing!'

The tears flooded down my face. 'I—'

He held his hand up to stop me. 'I don't want to hear it. Always with the excuses. You're lazy. You care for no one but yourself.'

I felt physically crushed. The core of me had been ripped out and ground into the floor. I walked backwards to escape Laken's disapproval but found a solid wall at my back. The entrance that I had come through was now part of the mountain. There was no escape. I had to listen to him.

'You're so stupid. I had thought better of you, but you let me down.' His face contorted into an ugly mask of rage. 'You always let everyone down. You can't be trusted. You take advantage of everyone.'

My knees collapsed and I slid down the wall onto the floor. I curled up on my side under the onslaught of abuse Laken was aiming at me. I tried to block out his voice by covering my ears, but it did not help. I couldn't bear the hurt I had caused him.

'You're useless. Rubbish. No wonder the raiders left you behind. Seems they were smarter than me.'

'No, Laken,' I whispered. 'Please.'

But he continued, over and over, reason after reason for my failures and disappointments. I was broken again and again by his words. The laziness, the let-downs, the selfishness, the disapproval, the worthlessness.

I wanted my heart to stop beating. Wanted the pain to go away.

I woke up, curled under the blankets in the room at the back of Drey's chambers, the pillow soaked with my tears. My knees were pulled painfully close to my chest, my arms covering my head protectively. My breath catching in my throat, forcing me to pant for small volumes of air. My heart still shattered into an uncountable number of pieces.

Chapter Nine

The months passed, the seasons changed. Tawpin's arm healed but he would still rub at it distractedly at times, as if it still caused him pain. I would also catch him staring at me when he thought I wasn't looking. Another layer of guilt to wrap around my soul.

The lessons continued. I was never going to be a good reader, but Villermir seemed content with my progress and stopped hitting me so much. As well as reading and writing, I learnt to always defer to his opinion and never question his ideas. He taught me to act submissive and obedient when I felt defiant and confrontational. He taught me about the religion of Baila – the one and only God. The priests acted as the mouthpiece for the Truth. Their word could not be disputed. They had a direct connection to the deity and spoke His words. I found it a very masculine religion, with male priests and a domineering hierarchy. This contrasted sharply with the teachings of the Druids I had heard as a child. The old religions involved a balance: up and down, right and left, male and female. The Sun God cared for the day, guiding all of creation in the daily struggle for survival. The Moon Goddess cared for the night, offering protection and shelter. Lord Sun of the Hunt, Lady Moon of the Home.

As I spent less time with Villermir, I spent more time with Drey. I copied his scribbled notes into bound ledgers, learning the value of herbs for healing and of those that could cause illness. I could identify the most commonly used plants for wounds, stomach upsets, headaches and eye infections. I learnt the advantages of drying and powdering, when to use a plant as a tea and what to use as a poultice. Once satisfied with my basic knowledge, Drey allowed me to enter his private room to help crush the dried flowers, stems, leaves and roots, storing them individually or as mixtures.

Drey's room was immaculately tidy, as I had come to expect. The bed was pushed against the wall that separated his room from mine. The corners of the blankets were neatly tucked under the feather mattress and the pillows were fluffed so that they were the same size and shape. It looked as if he never slept in the bed. The remainder of the room was full of tables and shelves. Dried plants covered the long table under the window that overlooked the coastline. A smaller table next to it held empty jars and bottles, all standing in a line ready for use. Fresh herbs hung to dry from hooks on a shelf above the fire. A small table stood next to the grate, covered with pruning knives, laid out neatly; string, tightly coiled; and a pestle and mortar, spotlessly clean. Shelves lined every available space, holding glass bottles and clay jars. These were arranged in size order and clearly labelled. A plain wooden door led from Drey's to another room further up the tower. I was repeatedly told never to go up there.

I became a competent, if not a confident, rider. The horses remained suspicious of me despite extended periods of time spent grooming and feeding them. I envied the easy trust Jeck had with the horses. No matter how hard I tried, the animals were still prone to shy, kick or bite if I moved too quickly. Weapons training went a lot better and I demonstrated some skill with the sword and throwing knives. I was quick and agile in unarmed contests, allowing speed to make up for what I lost in power. I liked Langdon's quiet humour and always looked forward to my sessions with him.

Many nights were spent in the Blue Boar. Kade would always sing. Tawpin and I would shout insults, trying to put him off. It never worked. He never faltered. He read the audience perfectly every time, matching their moods to upbeat, rowdy sea shanties or heartbreaking ballads of love and loss. Time and again the hairs on my arms and at the base of my neck would stand up, giving me pimpleflesh. His voice became deeper and richer as he grew older, with the power to melt my heart with a simple phrase or a single note. Occasionally Kerk and Jeck would join us, and those evenings were generally very noisy. It was nice to see the two young men, usually so serious, enjoying themselves without the pressures of state. The Blue Boar became a safe haven for the princes, allowing them to be young and reckless for a short time.

Rarely, Breya would come as well. She would sing with Kade, her clear soprano complementing his deeper tones; another perfect gift she had that I hated her for. Stunning looks, effortless horsemanship and the privileges of rank were not enough; she also had to be able to blend her voice with Kade's at the time he was happiest. I was almost able to accept that the failing was my jealousy, but after a few tankards of ale I was happy to convince myself it was all her fault.

My relationship with Drey changed over the next couple of years. We would often spend time powdering dried herbs, comfortable in each other's company. But the day finally arrived when I was required to earn my privileges within the royal house. The deal was that I would obtain items for Kyllian when required. I was a little over thirteen years old when Drey asked me to steal again. I was fit and lean from riding and weapons practice, and my agility had been maintained by my desire to climb – trees, walls, houses, everything. I easily fell back into the habit of creeping around the city at night, avoiding the city watch. To begin with, Drey asked me to take small decorative items. I suspected it was a test of both my skills and my ability to give up the treasures once I had taken them. As I grew older, I was asked to obtain more politically useful items from merchants and traders.

The city was getting ready for the midwinter festivities and parade. Food was going to be scarce as more land had been lost to the Lindvanes or destroyed by the Gallowglass raids. But the parade gave an opportunity for the royal family to acknowledge the citizens of the kingdom and the continued sacrifice of the soldiers. Kyllian was determined to boost morale after another year of hard losses. The occasion was also to include the official announcement of the betrothal of Kerk and Breya. All the influential families had been invited for the festival period. Tawpin was unbearably excited at the thought of being able to spend time with his family. He had not seen them for several years.

It was a couple of days before the parade and I was daydreaming in front of the fire in the main room of Drey's chambers. I had curled up in the comfortable chair, letting my mind drift as the dancing flames glowed white, yellow, orange and red as they lapped against the firewood. The flicker of the flames, the swirl of the lazy smoke, the shifting shadows all became hypnotic as my mind conjured images of burnt villages, scorched pastures and blackened forests. High above the ground, I glided, swooping and soaring, over the destruction.

'Tallen!'

I blinked and the images vanished. Drey had walked into the room, closed the door behind him and sat in the chair opposite me. I had not noticed his arrival. From the expression on his face, I guessed he had been speaking to me for some time before he caught my attention.

'Have you been listening?'

'Sorry, Drey. I didn't even know you were back.' I rubbed my sleepy eyes and sat straighter in the chair. 'How'd the meeting go?'

'Lots of boring detail about who is going to sit next to whom, and what savouries the meal should start with. I have no idea why I had to be there.'

I smiled, imagining Drey nodding in agreement with the small matters of hosting a feast, while not listening to a word of the discussion.

'But back to what I was talking about.' He took the opportunity to give me another chastising glare to make sure I was paying attention. 'Kyllian has a job for you.'

The last of the blanketing fug of sleep left my brain. My full attention was on Drey as my heart rate increased in anticipation of another theft.

'This is not like your previous jobs, Tal. The game has become serious. You are about to enter a dangerous world. Do you understand?'

'Not really. What do you want me to steal?'

Drey hesitated, considering his next words. He rubbed his first finger backwards and forwards over his bottom lip, then took a deep breath.

'There are a number of important people due to attend the betrothal feast of Kerk and Breya. We suspect one of them may be planning on disrupting the ceremony. We need you to search Lord Bridgeford's rooms for poison.'

I blinked in shock. 'Why would anyone want to do that? I know Breya's poisonous, but really?'

'Since Laken… since Handera was killed there have been several attempts to assassinate Kyllian. Hayton was not happy to have lost his brother and has sent many renegades to kill our king as a result. Those were handled by the royal bodyguards. Bridgeford needs a little more… diplomacy.'

I grinned. 'So you thought of me and my famous diplomatic skills?'

He raised his eyebrows at me. 'Hardly. But this does have to be handled quietly.'

I lost the grin to reassure him I was taking this seriously. 'What am I looking for?'

'You know that the seeds of the foxglove can be used to treat heart irregularities?'

I nodded.

'Too many and the heart will stop completely. I suspect that will be the method of choice. Although I do not suppose he will be so obliging as to leave labelled seeds lying around. You will need to use your knowledge of herbs to identify anything suspicious.'

I nodded distractedly, already thinking of ways of concealing adequate quantities of seeds. Drey remained quiet while I explored different options in my mind.

'When?' I asked eventually.

'Mid-morning tomorrow. Bridgeford will be in a Council of War. You will have a couple of hours to look around. Please leave the place as you found it.'

I grinned again. 'Are you trying to say I'm messy?'

He rolled his eyes, shaking his head slightly. I grew anxious with the sustained look he gave me.

'You know Kyllian cannot be associated with this, whether you find something or not. Bridgeford is a duke. If you get caught, you're on your own.'

And there it was. The payment required for my past mistakes and the reason for the second chance I had been given. I already had a reputation for being a thief; for having spent time in North End. It would be easy to disown my future actions. Drey was just trying to help the kin-child of a good friend. How was he to know she was continuing her criminal activities? There would be no comeback for him; no suspicion of Kyllian. Neat and tidy. I would hang and Drey would do nothing to help.

The game had become deadly serious.

I readily embraced the risks.

The next morning, I awoke early and went down to the main dining hall. The room was busy with the usual Liegeport staff as well as the important families that had come for the feast and betrothal. It was some time before I saw Tawpin waving to me. I went over to where he was sitting, and he introduced me to his parents. His father was so similar to Tawpin that the family connection was obvious. He had an easy smile and pale blue eyes that had a mischievous glint. His dark blond hair matched Tawpin's, down to the curl at the forehead that refused to conform. He had a soft, round belly that caused his embroidered tunic to bulge, complementing his jolly appearance and making me want to hug him. His wife was also small and round. She had Tawpin's sea-green eyes in a moon-shaped face, bordered by loose pale blonde curls. She smiled warmly at me, gesturing for me to sit next to her. I liked her instantly.

'So, you are the one constantly getting my boy into trouble?'

Her smile made it clear she was teasing as I replied.

'Sorry.'

'Tawpin is more than capable of getting himself into trouble, Elissie.'

Tawpin and his father were busy making disgusting noises like little children, causing both of them to giggle helplessly.

Elissie rolled her eyes at me, disowning the pair of them. 'Taw's told me all about the adventures you two have been up to.'

Horrified, I looked towards Tawpin, who shook his head. He hadn't told his mother *all* that we got up to.

'Tawpin is a good friend,' I conceded, leaning in conspiratorially. 'But don't tell him that.'

Elissie chuckled and proceeded to tell me all about Tawpin as a very young child and how much trouble he got into. Tawpin squirmed with embarrassment as his father teased him mercilessly. She told me how his father, Luart, had been so proud when Tawpin went to become Kade's page. Tawpin immediately pounced on the opportunity to tease his father.

I spent a long time enjoying the warmth of the family. Elissie told me about their home at Kingsport, on the border of the fenlands. She told me about her elderly mother who suffered from joint aches, and I suggested some of the potions Drey used for such ailments. She told me about Tawpin's younger sister who had been unable to travel to the feast because of the contagious child's disease, red-spot. Apparently, the temper tantrums were something to be seen. I was quite sad when Luart got up to leave for the War Council, and I made my excuses as well. Elissie insisted that we meet up the following day, and I was happy to agree.

Bridgeford's rooms were easily found. The guests had all been accommodated along the east and west wings of the second floor. Drey had given me instructions as to which room it was – the fourth door in the west wing. The lords were all convening in the lower meeting room. The ladies had arranged a tour of the gardens. The second floor was empty as I made my way to Bridgeford's rooms. I listened at the door for any noise that may suggest servants were still preparing the chambers. After one final check down the hallway to make sure I had not been seen, I slipped into the room.

The main room contained a table and chair for writing correspondence, four comfortable chairs in a half-moon formation around the fireplace, and a chest to hold personal belongings. The rugs on the floor and the tapestries on the walls were richly woven, thick wool producing the images and patterns. A decanter of wine and two clean glasses were on the writing table. I checked the chest, not expecting to find anything so easily. Anyone clever enough to poison the king during a festival would be too smart to hide the poison just inside the door of their quarters. As expected, the chest held spare cloaks and riding attire. Nothing suspicious was hiding there.

I moved into the back room that served as a sleeping area. A large bed dominated the room, covered in thick blankets over a deep feather mattress. Another chest, similar to that in the main room, stood at the base of the bed. There were also two smaller ones under the window. I looked in the one near the bed first. Spare blankets were neatly folded and stored. I had removed the top two before I found something. Covered by a plain sheet of cloth was a small dagger. The hilt was engraved with curling patterns and designs but had no clan identification. The blade was thin and sharp, with a burnished edge that contrasted with the silver iron of the shaft. Being careful not to touch the edge, I picked up the blade and sniffed the point. It had a musty, woody smell unlike the metallic tang associated with weaponry. I wrapped it in the cloth again before placing it in the top of my boot. I then rummaged further into the chest, feeling all the way to the bottom past cushion covers and towels. Tucked in the far corner was a glass vial with a sealed lid. The light from the window reflected in the container as I removed it from the chest, making the liquid in the vial shine the same colour as the edge of the dagger. I tucked that in a pocket inside my tunic, then moved on to the smaller chests. Both held only clothes and small personal items. I stopped to think where else Bridgeford may have hidden his poison.

Then I heard the door to the main chamber open. My heart pounding in my chest and the pulse in my ears drowning out all other noise, I scanned the room for a place to hide. There were no other exits and the tapestries did not extend to the floor. I dived under the bed just as the inner door was opening. Holding my breath, I heard soft footsteps approach the chest by the bed. Praying to The Lady of The Moon that the person would not look under the bed, I strained to hear what they were doing. The chest lid bumped against the bed and I heard the whisper of cloth being smoothed. The lid was replaced and the footsteps left as quietly as they had arrived.

I breathed out slowly. It would seem that a housemaid had brought fresh sheets. I waited several heartbeats without hearing a sound before scuttling out from under the bed. I was almost out when I saw a darker shape against the wooden slats of the bed frame. I reached out to investigate and felt a package wedged in between two slats. Carefully wrapped in a cloth was a packet of seeds. There was a surprising amount of them, weighing as much in my hand as a horse's bit; far more than could possibly be needed for medicinal purposes. I placed the packet alongside the vial in my pocket.

I quickly searched the rest of the room but found nothing else that could cause harm to Kyllian. Checking that I had not disturbed anything, I slipped out of the room and headed towards the servants' corridor. It had been a long time since I had sneaked around the royal house and I could not resist the temptation to visit the secret passageways. The upper rooms were deserted and did not hold my interest, so I climbed the ladder down to the ground floor. The main meeting room was the second room along, and the voices of those in the Council of War were easily heard. I placed my eye to the hole in the wall and watched the important men discuss the future of Faulknar.

I could see Kyllian sitting in a high-backed chair, woven with the colours of his clan. Kerk was sitting on his right side. Baden and Langdon were also there. Tawpin's father was at the limit of my vision to the left. He was arguing with the man opposite.

'The lands around Bridgeford have not been raided as much as those on the coast.' Luart was waving his hands around in frustration. 'We need more troops to cover the northern towns. The fens are almost totally controlled by Lindvane. It makes it too easy for Hayton to move into the heart of Faulknar.'

The man opposite, who would appear to be Bridgeford, glared at Luart with dark eyes that were difficult to read. 'Meaning, we should sacrifice the rest of the kingdom to protect your town.'

'Meaning, if we lose Kingsport we will have no access to the Northlands. Liegeport's trade has virtually dried up since Gallowgla joined forces with Lindvane. We cannot produce enough grain to survive without outside sources.'

Bridgeford sat back and folded his arms, as if he had scored a point. 'Our soldiers are stretched to breaking point and you're worried about your profit margins and trade with the Northlands.'

Luart banged his fist on the table. 'That's a cheap shot, Bridgeford, even for you. Perhaps we should be looking at why your lands have been spared when others have fallen.'

Bridgeford's face contorted into a murderous look of rage. His voice was pitched dangerously low. 'And what exactly are you saying, Kingsport?'

Luart refused to be intimidated, leaning forward over the table. 'Maybe you could share your secret, so the rest of us could be protected from Hayton's raids.'

The duke shot up and seemed about to leap over the table to throttle Luart. Kyllian held his hand up and Bridgeford stopped, glaring at his rival.

'Gentlemen,' Kyllian began in a mild tone that nevertheless carried to all in the room. His authority was clearly evident. 'This is not helping. We are all frustrated at the lack of progress. That is, after all, why we are here.'

It was a mild reprimand but Luart had the grace to lower his eyes and nod in acknowledgement. Bridgeford continued to glare at him for a handful of heartbeats. His fists were clenched on the table. A muscle twitched in his jaw.

'I want a retraction,' he growled.

'You haven't been accused of anything. Sit down.'

Bridgeford remained where he was.

Kyllian's tone lowered, becoming more menacing. 'Sit down or leave.'

Again, Bridgeford stood as still as a statue for a number of heartbeats. It became clear that he was not going to get an apology from Luart, and that he was alone in feeling wronged. He turned his back and stormed out of the room, the door slamming against the wall as he yanked it open.

I did not wait to listen to the rest of the meeting. I suspected that Bridgeford would return to his chambers and find his dagger and seeds missing. I wanted to be safe in Drey's quarters before he raised the alarm. Or came looking for the thief.

Drey was not in the main room when I returned to his chambers. I walked into his bedchamber, but he was not there either. Accepting that he would return soon, I decided to examine the seeds to determine whether they were foxglove as Drey had suspected. I opened one of the ledgers I had written in and scanned through the pages until I found the entry on foxglove. Tracing my finger down the page, I found a description of the seeds.

I looked up as Drey entered the room through the door leading to the higher tower. He was followed by Kade.

'How come he gets to go up there?'

Kade grinned at me, delighted by my indignant reaction. 'Because I'm Faulknar's son.'

'Oh yeah, then why are you not at the War Council?'

The grin turned into a grimace. 'Because I'm only the second son.'

'So not as important as you think you are, then?'

'I still get to go up the tower and you don't.'

Drey threw up his hands in exasperation. 'When you two have finished...' He looked at each of us in turn to make sure we were paying attention. 'How did your morning's work go, Tallen?'

I looked at Drey, then at Kade before returning my gaze to Drey. 'Fine.'

Drey waved his hand in dismissal as he looked at the ledger I had been reading. 'You can speak openly in front of Kade. I have nothing to hide from him.' He tapped the page as Kade stuck his tongue out at me. 'You found the seeds, then?'

I removed the packet of seeds from my tunic pocket and placed them on the table next to the ledger. 'I don't know if they are foxglove, but there's an awful lot of them.'

'Indeed there are.' Drey picked up the packet and poured some seeds into his palm. He closed his eyes as he curled his fingers over the seeds, gently moving them around his hand. 'They are foxglove.'

Kade winked at me. 'Magick,' he whispered.

'So Bridgeford was going to poison the king?'

Drey nodded. 'With this amount of seeds, he could poison the whole festival.'

I looked at Kade who was, for once, serious, thinking of the implications of the most important families in Faulknar being incapacitated. Even if the poison only produced cramps and vomiting, the kingdom would be defenceless against an attack from the Lindvanes. They could march right up to the front door. If the poison killed...

'That's not all I found.'

Both men looked at me with their full attention.

'Really?' asked Drey. 'What else?'

I removed the dagger from the top of my boot, unwrapped it and placed it on the table next to the seeds.

'All weapons should have been left at the gatehouse.' Kade went to pick up the blade, but Drey knocked his hand away before he could touch it.

'That's what I thought. Why would he want to keep a dagger hidden in his clothes chest?'

Drey smiled. 'You always were a clever one.'

'And this was with it.' I passed the vial of brown liquid to Drey. 'I think it has been smeared on the edges, where they are a different colour.'

Drey removed the seal and smelt the contents. His mouth set in a hard line. 'Monkshood. If the poison didn't work, one nick from the blade would paralyse.' He looked at Kade. 'This was a serious attempt.'

Kade returned his gaze. 'So what do we do now? We can't accuse Bridgeford without condemning Magpie.'

Even now he couldn't resist mocking me.

'I need to speak to your father. We may not be able to accuse Bridgeford, but we can watch him closely. He will not have planned this alone. Perhaps we can use him to lead us to the centre of this spider's web.'

Bridgeford left Liegeport later that day. Rumour said that Luart of Kingsport had offended the duke and Bridgeford had left in a rage. No one was particularly upset to see him go. The rest of the festival ran smoothly, and nothing was mentioned regarding the seeds or the dagger. Life carried on as before, with the troops preparing for the summer campaign against Lindvane.

The first attack from the Lindvanes came before the snows had fully melted from the farmlands. Word travelled quickly of the destruction of a town; the burning of all buildings so that nothing was left to salvage; the slaughter of men, women and children. No one had been spared. It was common opinion that the town had been made an example of what would happen to those that stood against the Lindvane advance. It was said that it was a revenge attack.

The town was Kingsport.

'It's all my fault.'

I had run to Drey as soon as I heard the news. I felt sure that Bridgeford had blamed Tawpin's family for the theft of his poison and blade. The theft that I had done.

'It's not your fault, Tallen.'

'But I took the poison. I messed up his plans. It had nothing to do with Kingsport.'

Drey gently took my shoulders and sat me in one of the upholstered chairs. I was shaking and very close to tears, both at my guilt and because of my anger at Bridgeford. I took a deep breath.

'Bridgeford made his choices knowing the consequences of his actions. He is to blame for this. Not you.' Drey sat opposite me. 'Kingsport was too strategic as a port; vital for resources we can barely supply for ourselves. Lindvane had taken the fens. It was logical to go after Kingsport next.'

'But did they have to kill everyone?'

Drey seemed to age in front of my eyes. The lines on his face deepened as the muscles of his face drooped. He slumped a little more in his seat. His eyes betrayed a deep sorrow. I understood that there was guilt there too. He had sent me to retrieve the seeds.

'Luart was never going to surrender his town or his people.'

I avoided Tawpin for several days. I did not know what I was going to say to him. He did not know of Bridgeford's poison and dagger, or of my part in it all. But I did. I couldn't bear to look at him; to see the hurt I had caused.

My dreams took on another element to ensure I took responsibility for my actions. As well as Laken reminding me of how useless I was, Luart and Elissie stood before me battered and bruised. They accused me of having the blood of their family on my hands; the blood of the people they were responsible for. As they uttered the words, my hands were indeed covered in blood, dripping onto the floor. I was to blame for so many deaths. Each morning I would scrub my hands until they were raw, but I could not remove the sticky feeling left on them by the congealing blood.

I eventually ran out of excuses to avoid Tawpin. My dreams had woken me early and I had gone down to the stables to attempt a truce with my horse before that morning's riding lesson. I was forced to stay calm and patient as I groomed and tacked the little grey who I had been riding for the last few months. She was a quick, responsive horse but was still suspicious of me, especially when I was on the ground. Once she had accepted I was on top of her, she would settle, and I enjoyed riding her.

I led her out of her stable and into the yard. I saw Breya walking towards me as I lengthened the stirrups prior to mounting. Rolyan was following a few paces behind her. He had been promoted to her royal bodyguard after the official betrothal and took pleasure in the tension between Breya and myself. My back stiffened in anticipation of trouble.

'I'm riding her today,' commanded Breya as she reached me. She held her hand out for the reins.

'Baden said for me to ride Nalya. She's just settled.'

'That may be so,' Breya said with no hint of regret. 'Shuree is lame. I'll be riding Nalya today.'

I was just tired enough to pick a fight. I had just drawn breath for a stinging comeback when Rolyan casually walked in front of me. He folded his arms, flexing his biceps. I released the breath. I would not give him an excuse to bully me. Reluctantly, I handed over the reins.

Breya leaned in to me, speaking quietly so Rolyan would not hear. 'You forget. There is nothing you have that I cannot take.'

The calm and patience I had nurtured whilst caring for Nalya withered. My shoulders ached with tension as I watched Breya ride out of the yard and through the archway. I went to find Legend. The old horse was rarely ridden any more, and my skills had progressed so that I no longer needed his steady presence. But the way this day was going, I was going to need all the help I could get.

The lesson had started by the time I arrived with Legend. Baden instructed me to ride without stirrups for the remainder of the session as punishment. I sent silent thanks to The Lady that I had chosen Legend and not one of the younger horses. Tawpin sat quietly on his chestnut mare. He was pale and his posture was more slumped than normal. The sight of him did not improve my mood. Neither did the fact that Baden placed us in pairs to complete a series of exercises. Tawpin and I snapped at each other, bickering over whose fault it was that the baton got dropped, who was slower and consequently caused us to come last, who was not staying in time with the other. We even argued over who was to blame for the punishments Baden handed us for bickering.

Soon neither of us was listening to the other's jibes. We knew each other well enough to find all the hidden soft spots, and strike for those. Each of us was too numb from their own pain to consider what they were inflicting on the other.

'It's hardly surprising your horse spooked,' I threw at him. 'One look at your miserable face and I'd try to buck you off as well.'

'At least I don't need the stuffed horse to carry me around. Legend is the only horse that won't throw you.'

'Breya took Nalya. Legend was the only one left.'

'I'm sure Nalya is much happier for that. She finally gets someone who can actually ride on her back.'

'I wouldn't call your pathetic attempts at rounding the barrel riding. More clinging on as if your life depended on it.'

'Better than going so slowly that it seems as if time has stopped.'

'What a thought.' I held my head dramatically. 'Time stopping with your face forever set in that self-pitying expression. May the Gods spare us that fate.'

Tawpin's eyes took on a dangerous quality as his voice dropped, but I was too angry to notice. 'Excuse me for having just lost my family.'

'Oh yeah,' I carried on obliviously. 'I forgot privileged families are not supposed to be attacked. Nobody cares when it's the tiny villages that get destroyed, but Gods forbid that those in their big, safe houses find out they're not so safe after all.'

'My mother, my sister...'

'Anyone would think you were the only one to have lost someone. What makes you so special?'

'I bet your family were so glad to be rid of you.'

Faster than he could blink, I reached over, grabbed his tunic and pulled him to the floor. Using his weight to pull me from Legend, I fell on top of him and punched as hard as I could. The shooting pain as my knuckles connected with his face extinguished the burning pain in my chest. I punched again before Tawpin rolled me over. Sitting astride me, it was his turn to throw the punches. My lip split and I tasted iron.

We fought dirty. Punches were aimed under the diaphragm. Kicks connected with knees. Hair was pulled. Insults traded. We were both bruised and bloody by the time Kade and Baden pulled us apart. The blood was pumping so loudly in my ears that I could not hear what Baden was saying until Kade shook me, breaking my glare at Tawpin.

'Tallen!' Baden was red in the face, more with anger than with the effort of restraining a struggling Tawpin. 'Get out of my sight.'

Kade turned and shoved me towards the archway leading into the arena. I collected Legend and left. The pain in my chest had come back stronger than ever, so that I could feel it at the back of my throat. My steps matched the throbbing of my cut lip, swollen eyebrow and smashed knuckles. I failed to see how the day could get any worse.

I retreated to the roof of the tower. I wanted to jump off the edge, catching the wind and soaring out over the dark sea. I wanted to fly so very far away. Away from the memories. Away from the pain I was causing my friends. Away from the disappointment of those I cared about. Away from caring about people and what they thought.

But I had nowhere to go. Although years had passed and I was a different person now, I was still unwilling to repeat the mistakes of North End. I was scared. Scared to be on my own. Scared to be without the protection of Drey. Scared of what might be waiting out there for me.

The sky had darkened so that it looked like crumpled velvet; pale grey layered with dark grey clouds. My muscles ached from maintaining the same position for so long. I was beginning to get hungry.

I turned at the sound of a soft thud as someone jumped over the railings onto the roof. Tawpin stood uncomfortably, waiting for me to accept his presence. I patted the roof beside me, encouraging him to come and sit next to me. He held out an apple.

I smiled. 'It's been a long time since you've given me an apple.'

'Peace offering.'

I took the apple. 'Accepted. But it's not you who should be making peace.'

Tawpin shook his head. 'I'm sorry, Tal…'

'You have nothing to be sorry about. I'd been pushing for a fight all morning. I really shouldn't have said those things about your family. I liked your parents. And your sister sounded really nice.'

He nodded, looking out over the sea.

'The things they are saying about your father. They're not true. It wasn't his fault.'

Tawpin turned to look at me. 'What do you mean?'

I hesitated, wondering how much to tell him of what I had seen and done that day. 'Luart argued with Bridgeford before he left. But I don't think that was why Bridgeford left.'

He tilted his head, listening closely but with a frown of confusion.

'Tawpin, it was my fault.'

'What are you talking about? How could it be your fault?'

I took a breath, changing direction. I wanted confirmation of a theory before revealing the theft. 'How did you find out about the secret passageways? How did you know they were there?'

His frown deepened. It was his turn to hesitate. 'Drey told me about them.'

I nodded. 'Drey asked me to look around Bridgeford's rooms while everyone was in the meeting.'

A small, sad smile flashed across Tawpin's mouth. 'Drey has you doing his dirty work as well, does he? Should've known. Drey is many things to many people, but mainly he gathers knowledge. I've been using the passages to listen in on meetings for as long as I have been in Liegeport. Being Kade's page allows me access to a lot of places, and people forget I'm there. What does he get you to do?'

'What I'm best at. I… confiscate things.'

'And what did you *confiscate* from Bridgeford?'

'Drey thought he might want to harm Kyllian at the feast. I was sent to see if there was anything that would reveal what he was up to. I found a lot of poison and a poisoned dagger. Tawpin, I think Bridgeford thought your father had taken them, and that was why he attacked Kingsport. I never thought…'

The sky had grown darker and Tawpin's eyes had become black holes in the darkness. I forced myself to watch his face as it developed new shades of sorrow. As he considered this new information.

Eventually he shook his head. 'You weren't to know what would happen. It was only a matter of time before Kingsport was attacked. The blame lies with the traitor and with Hayton.'

I was surprised by the harshness of his tone. The carefree Tawpin I had grown up with had become something sharper; more dangerous.

'I'm really sorry. For everything.' I gently touched his bruised cheek. 'You bruise like ripe fruit.'

I could hear the catch as he took a deep breath. 'Well, you don't look much better.' He grinned briefly before the sadness returned. 'Tal, the reason I came up here was to apologise to you.'

'For what?' I tried to dismiss the concern, but he would not be turned this time.

'For things I should have said a long time ago.' It was my turn to frown in confusion.

'When Drey sent me to get you from the cells… after Laken… you looked so wild. So damaged.'

'That was long ago.'

'Let me finish. Please. I thought you would always be broken. I'm sorry I took you to the North End.'

'What?' I didn't understand. 'How are they connected?'

'If I hadn't taken you there, you would never have run away. You would have stayed here and we could have looked after you. You wouldn't have…'

'I made my choices, Tawpin. It had nothing to do with you.'

'But I took you there. You never would have seen—'

'I would never have survived.' I couldn't believe he was taking the blame for my stupid mistakes.

We both looked out over the water, lost in our own worlds of guilt and shame; the tangled responsibilities in our bond of friendship. The sky had darkened so much that the crumpled velvet had reversed – the sky was almost black and the clouds had become the lighter grey in contrast. The first stars could be seen sprinkled between them.

'I don't know how you can stand it up here,' he said quietly. 'I keep thinking about what would happen if I fell off.'

I grinned. 'Don't fall off, then.'

He smiled back. 'I'll see you later. On the ground.'

He squeezed my shoulder as he left. I was not sure what had been accomplished. I still felt guilty about the attack on Kingsport, and I now felt guilty that Tawpin blamed himself for my stay in North End too. But I also felt like something had been achieved; that the thread of tension that had been present in my friendship with Tawpin for some time had dissolved.

I was not alone long. Tawpin had been gone for less than a handful of heartbeats when Kade joined me. The features of his face were shrouded by the darkness, but the flash of white teeth let me know he was incredibly pleased with himself.

'You two made up, then?'

'You told him I was up here?'

'Of course.'

'And how long have you known I come up here when I want to be *alone*?'

'Years. Your room is opposite mine, so I can see when you climb out of the window.'

'Great. It seems I am to have no privacy.'

'Not from me.' The teeth flashed again. 'Oh, come on. I had to make sure you were all right.'

'Really?' I was trying to make my voice sound annoyed but failing. 'And you appointed yourself the person to make sure I'm all right?'

'Yes. I hate it when you two fight. I'm never sure which side to support.'

'Thanks very much.'

'You're welcome.' He was irritatingly cheerful. 'Why were you in such a bad mood this morning?'

'Have you come here to see if I'm all right, or to annoy me some more?'

He hesitated too long over the answer to my question. I hurried him up by punching him lightly on the arm. The tight muscles of his bicep felt solid under my knuckles.

He laughed. 'I can see you are fine. So, time to annoy. Why were you being so miserable?'

I considered what to say. I wasn't prepared to tell him about my guilt over Kingsport. But I had told no one about my dreams. He waited patiently, his dark eyes exploring my face, the sea breeze lifting his hair slightly, his hands lying relaxed in his lap.

'I was tired. I don't sleep very well.'

He waited, the silence encouraging me to continue.

'I have dreams. Not nice ones.'

Kade reached up and touched my face. A reflex made me jump, but his warm touch remained against my cheek. The contours of his fingertips and their calluses from handling swords burned into my skin. I leaned, ever so slightly, into the palm of his hand. Slowly, he stroked with the touch of a spider's silk. I could feel my breath quicken as his deepened.

The moment lasted a lifetime before he cupped my chin and drew my face towards his. I could smell the gentle fragrance of berries over a richer, masculine scent. Our noses rubbed briefly before our lips bumped together; his pressed against mine with urgency and I instinctively responded. My lips tingled with the sensation. His adolescent stubble scratched my upper lip pleasantly. My closed eyes pictured his soft brown ones, before my mind was lost with the brush of his tongue parting my lips. He tasted sweet, warm, and vaguely of ale as his tongue explored mine.

He broke the kiss. Murmuring huskily, he said, 'Let's see if we can get you to dream about something else tonight.'

He gave me a last tease of a kiss and then left.

Chapter Ten

Lightning ripped a jagged tear across the dark, brooding sky, followed almost instantly by a crashing boom of thunder that caused the windows to rattle.

It was early morning in midsummer. The night had been hot and oppressive, making sleep difficult despite the sea breeze coming through the open windows. I was curled up on the ledge beneath the window in the main room, hugging my knees to my chest, watching the dark clouds roll over the sea as they were blown by the wind. The rain painted fine lines across the glass connecting the clouds to the sea, both the colour of muddy bathwater. I breathed in the scent of fresh, damp earth, feeling revitalised by the energy of the storm.

Drey burst through the door, letting it bang against the wall as he stomped over to table. 'Irritating, interfering, meddling… man!'

I smiled at his blustering. 'Good morning.'

He looked up at me, surprised I was there. 'Well, that's about to change.'

'Who's rattled you this morning?'

'Villermir.'

'That will do it. Villermir before breakfast is never a good omen.'

'Humph. That man could curdle the porridge.'

I laughed at the image of Villermir glowering at the simmering porridge, causing it to congeal and solidify. Drey noisily searched through the drawers of the table, moving aside papers and quills, removing crystals and silver bowls. Eventually he found what he was looking for and placed the red velvet pouch on the table. He stroked the material reverently, a look of sadness and loss on his face. He took a deep breath before looking up at me.

'Villermir wants you to take this to the temple.'

'Oh, Drey. That place hates me. Does it have to be me?'

'How can a place hate you?' he snapped, harsher than I had expected. Then continued in a softer tone. 'And yes, it has to be you. Villermir was quite insistent.'

The skin on my back prickled with suspicion. My stomach tensed in anticipation of what Villermir was planning. I looked at the red pouch.

'What is it?'

Drey looked at me for a long time. 'You're going to look anyway, aren't you?'

I smiled apologetically. 'You did teach me to be inquisitive.'

'I did, didn't I?'

He held out the pouch and I stood up to take it. It fitted comfortably into the palm of my hand and was heavier than I expected for an object that size. I pulled the material against the cord drawstring to allow access to the item within, tipping it into the palm of my other hand. It was a circular box of gold, with a hinged lid that bore the design of an oval eye. The white sclera contrasted with the black pupil and green iris. I stroked the smooth surface of the eye, unable to feel the joins between the different colours. My fingertips tingled as if stabbed by numerous tiny needles whenever they touched the box.

'The Box of Binhos,' murmured Drey. 'It is said that the eye can see into the future. You fill the box with spring water, close the lid, and when opened it reveals images of things yet to come.'

I opened the container, half expecting to see mysterious images held within. Drey chuckled.

'It's not been used for some time.'

'Why does Villermir want it?'

'He thinks it represents dark magick; an offence to the One Truth. He wants to cleanse it of evil.' He raised his eyebrows. 'He wants to see if it works.'

'Will it?'

Drey just smiled in reply. 'Go. Villermir is waiting for you.'

I replaced the box in the pouch and headed towards the door.

'Tallen, don't touch anything while you're there.'

I turned back and rolled my eyes as I slumped my shoulders. 'Drey…'

'I mean it, Tallen. This is important. Don't touch anything.'

'Fine.'

It was still raining heavily so I tucked the pouch inside my tunic to keep it dry. The lightning flashed less and the thunder had moved further away, but the sky was still menacing and the morning was dark. I hurried along the alleys to the Temple of Baila to the west of the city. The top of the temple could be seen above the rooftops, gleaming with coloured tiles that coated the spire roof. The vibrant reds, golds and blues testified to the wealth and power held by the priests of Baila. Devotees were obliged to donate a portion of their earnings to glorify the presence of their God on earth. It screamed pretentiousness to me, but then I never expected to be invited to spend eternity with that God.

As I got closer to the temple, more elaborate decorations were revealed. Statues of perfect men and women, wings spread majestically from their shoulders, guarded the corners of the building. Carved patterns of interlocking chains and circular mazes ran the length of the border between the roof and the walls. The large windows were almost as tall as the building itself, reflecting what little light was available that morning so that the coloured-glass faces within them shone with heavenly grace. It was a very impressive structure, both in grandeur and craftsmanship. The feeling of anxious anticipation increased to a physical sensation as I approached the large oak double doors. The hairs on my arms raised and it felt as if ants crawled over my skin. My stomach tensed and clenched as nausea swept up my throat. I had to fight the desire to walk away as I pushed against the brass handles and opened the doors.

Once inside the sensations vanished, leaving me thinking I had imagined them. The inside of the temple was as impressive as the outside. The entrance area extended to the spire, standing impossibly high above me. The hushed silence bore down on me, making me lower my stance without realising it. The temperature had dropped and the oppressive stormy weather outside seemed leagues away. Soft light came through the coloured-glass windows to diffuse throughout the temple in shades of gold and crimson, adding to the sense of splendour. Stone statues were set into recesses along the walls, each life-size and detailed enough to include fingernails and eyelashes. Dark wood benches were positioned in rows either side of a aisle leading to the main altar. I walked towards this long table, which was covered in a white cloth topped with golden bowls and goblets. Two candles burned in golden holders. The ants had returned to crawl over my skin as I approached the altar and I felt my hair lift slightly away from my head.

My attention focused on the centrepiece. It was an oval object, about the size of both my hands laid fingers to palm. The inner oval looked like polished silver, but it appeared to move and flow like water as I changed my position in front of it. The border was made of pearl, the hints of rose shimmering in the candlelight. My fingertips prickled with the need to touch it.

I placed the velvet pouch Drey had given me on the altar, reaching for the oval. My fingertips were almost touching it, closer than the length of my thumbnail, when a bolt of lightning sparked from the disc to my fingers. I yelped as I pulled them back, inspecting them for burns. There were no marks and the sting of the attack had disappeared. Placing my head on one side as I concentrated, I let my vision blur in an attempt to see hidden tripwires or poisoned powder. I could see nothing around the object. Slowing my breath, I reached forward again. I emptied my mind of all distractions, focusing on touching the oval. Picturing my fingers stretching away from my hand and extending towards the prize, I imagined a tiny, fluid barrier around my hand to repel any attack. It appeared to conceal my approach as no lightning struck this time. Tentatively, I brushed the surface of the silver. It felt wet. Small waves rippled out from where I touched.

'I believe you have something for me.'

Guiltily, I jumped and retracted my hand. I turned to see Villermir walking towards me. My body hid the oval from his sight and I was sure he had not seen me touch it, or the ripples my touch had caused. I picked up the pouch and walked to meet him away from the altar, trying to deflect his attention from my intrusion. I held out the pouch as I passed him, but his hand covered mine, securely grasping it as well as the pouch. The box pressed uncomfortably into my palm.

His eyes flashed with something indefinable. A chill raced down my spine as a small smile flickered at the corners of his mouth. A triumphant expression.

'Thank you, Tallen.'

His voice was soft, making me more suspicious of his intentions. I forcibly removed my hand from his and rushed out of the temple.

'Don't make me go back there again,' I demanded of Drey as I stormed into the room. 'The temple makes me feel uncomfortable. Villermir makes my skin crawl. Especially when he's being nice.' I shuddered at the thought.

Drey looked up from the desk where he was sitting. He looked at me for a long time, apparently searching for something in the way I was standing or how I held my hands.

'What?'

'Did you touch anything?'

'Oh, Mobis' torments. I didn't take anything. If you don't trust me, why did you send me?'

'I didn't ask if you took anything, I asked if you *touched* anything.'

I stayed silent. I had forgotten his instructions before I left. His *specific* instructions. I bit the corner of my lip, which was as good as a confession. He sighed.

'Oh, Tallen.' He sounded more disappointed than angry. 'You have no idea what you have done.'

'No, I don't,' I snapped back. 'You are so secretive, plotting away. If you don't tell me what you are getting me into, how am I supposed to know?'

He walked over to me and took my hands to inspect my fingers. 'I told you not to touch anything. I expected you to listen.'

'I thought you meant not to steal anything. I thought you'd be pleased that I didn't steal it. What harm can come of touching it?'

'More than you can ever know. The Ki Oval holds more power than you can comprehend.'

I threw my hands up in frustration, snatching them from Drey's grip. 'Don't you dare use me, train me to spy and steal on your command, then blame me for doing exactly what you would normally expect, when it doesn't suit you! I'm not a mind reader!'

I left the room, letting the door slam behind me.

Kade found me by the dockside, dangling my feet over the sea wall high above the water. He sat sideways on to me so that he could slip his arms around my waist and rest his chin on my shoulder. Since the kiss on the rooftop, he had been more demonstrative with his affections, often draping an arm across my shoulders and hugging me in public. He delighted in the disapproving looks when people witnessed these displays. But then the looks were not directed at him.

'It took me ages to find you.'

'And yet find me you did.'

'I looked on the roof where you normally go to be alone.'

'It was getting crowded up there. I needed to find a new place to be *alone*.'

He chuckled, his breath tickling my neck. He had spent a lot of time with me on the roof. He would name the different groups of stars, telling me the myths and legends associated with each. The comforting presence of his chest pressing against my back as he wrapped his arms around me would relax me like nothing else could. I had come to depend on his presence to make me feel safe from imagined terrors.

'I argued with Drey and stormed out. Thought it would seem stupid if I stormed back in to get to the roof.'

I felt him smile. I continued to look out over the sea, unwilling to lose myself in his melting brown eyes and the kiss that would inevitably follow.

'Did you come here for a reason?'

He sighed dramatically. 'Always straight to business with you.'

I smiled, still refusing to look at him.

'Ride with me tomorrow.'

That made me look at him. 'What? Where? How can you get away from your duties?'

His eyes sparkled with poorly contained mischief, while his suntanned face wrinkled with a smile that revealed his small, perfect teeth. 'Villermir would be pleased with your grasp of language.'

I punched his thigh playfully. 'Tell me.'

'I unexpectedly have a free day. Baden has agreed to let you have Nalya. Tarra will pack some food. Thought we'd go for a ride in the country. Just you and me.'

'Really? Just you and me?' I could not believe the Gods would favour me so much.

The inevitable kiss was as delicious as I was expecting.

We left early the next day while the town was still quiet. It took most of the morning before we emerged from the forests to the south of Liegeport. Kade was in a good mood and chatted easily about the plants and animals we encountered in the forest. I was happy to let him carry the conversation, enjoying the sound of his rich voice; the freedom of being out of the city. The day was warm and the sun cast rippling shadows onto the trail through the leaves of the canopy. I had a ridiculously large smile covering my face.

The forest gave way to a small clearing leading to a lake. Cloud Mountain stood proudly on the far shore. The sun reflected on the craggy ridges, making it shine like polished silver. It contrasted perfectly with the cloudless deep blue sky. The lake was the shape of an hourglass, with fir and beech trees encroaching into the waist. Diamonds studded the water where the sun's rays caught the small ripples on the surface. Lush green grass grew to the rocky shoreline. There was one small path to the lake from the trail we were riding. The rest of the shoreline was unbroken without so much as a deer trail.

I stood by the lake, soaking up the tranquillity of the scene. Kade tethered the horses to a nearby tree before joining me by the water's edge. He slipped his arms around my waist and rested his chin on my shoulder. The breeze lifted strands of his hair so they tickled my face.

'It's wonderful here, isn't it?'

I squeezed his arms. 'It's perfect.'

'Knew you'd like it.' His kissed the base of my neck where it sloped into my shoulder. 'The old name for Cloud Mountain is Arach Beinn. Legend has it that the Ancients buried a dragon under a pile of rocks, building it so high that it left a mountain in the flatlands of Faulknar. People have searched the tunnels under the mountain for generations.' He lowered his voice. 'Some never returned.'

He laughed quietly as I shuddered, not realising the parallels to the dreams that had tormented me for years. It was hard to reconcile the darkness of my nights with the splendour of the view before me. It was easy to ignore what might lie beneath the mountain and enjoy the beauty of the silver summit shining in the late-morning sun.

I turned within his embrace so that I was facing him. 'Thank you for bringing me here.'

'You are very welcome.'

This time I made the first move, reaching up slightly to press my lips against his. I closed my eyes to savour the taste of his lips, slightly salty from the sweat on his top lip. His breath tickled my skin as his tongue teased open my lips. Warmth radiated from him as I felt myself falling into his firm embrace. Strong hands roamed down my back from my shoulders, stopping briefly in the curve of my lower back before resting on my bottom. He pulled me gently to him as I weaved my fingers in his hair, massaging the base of his skull. He pressed my hips against his for a heartbeat before pulling away and breaking the kiss.

I groaned. 'You are such a tease.'

'I know,' he whispered. He took a deep breath and stepped back a short distance from me. 'Come on. I've got something else to show you.' He smiled at me suggestively. 'Before we both get distracted.'

We remounted and rode back into the forest, following a small dirt trail eastwards. The horses picked up on our mood and jogged along, challenging our control and each other. The trail led to a small stream with clear, bubbling water, passing alongside it to a clearing further into the forest. A timber cottage nestled at the far side of the clearing. A well-tended path led from the trail to the front door, with stacks of wood piled to the left of the building. There was only one door visible, with a single window next to it behind wooden shutters. The walls and thatch around the chimney were well maintained.

Kade tethered the horses to a rail on the right wall of the cottage as I walked through the door into the single room inside. The fireplace was at the far end, with a bed pushed against the wall to my right. A second window was set in the left wall, casting sunlight onto a wooden table and the two chairs in front of it. Kade had opened the shutters. Below the window at the front of the house stood a large wooden chest that could be used to store bed linen and clothes. Kade joined me, carrying the saddlebags containing the packed food Tarra had provided. He laid them on the table and looked inside.

'Oh. Blessings upon Tarra.' He rummaged through the bags, admiring the contents within. 'Cold meats, fresh bread, cheese, fruit, pastries. I think she thought we were staying for a week.'

I joined him at the table, placing the food on the wooden surface. 'So much food.'

He smiled at me. 'Hungry?'

I bit my lip, nervous about what I was going to say. Wanting it so badly, but unsure of how it would be received. 'Not for the food.'

Kade's grin stretched so far across his face I thought his skin would tear. The sunlight reflected in his eyes, making them sparkle. He reached out and held my chin tenderly before leaning in and kissing my lips. He took a step towards me so our bodies were touching, as he caught my bottom lip between his teeth. He squeezed gently, as his hands stroked down my back so slowly. The soft tickle of the touch made me arch my back as he brushed the spot just above the curve of my lower back. I pressed harder against him, my lips playing greedily with his, forcing my tongue into his mouth to run along the insides of his smooth teeth. His tongue met mine and we chased each other around his mouth.

I broke the kiss in order to breathe. I sighed happily as I leant back to see his face better. I used the tips of my fingers to explore the curve of his jaw, the crease that ran from his nose and around his mouth, the curl of his ears, the firm ridge of his brow. He captured my fingers in his warm hands, taking them to his mouth and kissing them. Releasing my hands, he let his fall to the front of my shirt, undoing the ties. I smiled back at him as I reached down to follow his lead and undo the ties of his shirt. He was much more skilled than I was, and had my shirt undone before I was halfway down his. He slipped the material over my shoulders, and burst out laughing.

'What?'

'I could ask the same,' he choked. 'What in the name of The Father of The Sun is *that*?'

He pointed to the strips of cloth strapping my breasts down. Adolescence had brought with it the practical problems of a girl growing up with a surrogate father.

'What else was I supposed to do with the damned things?' I pouted childishly. 'They were getting in the way.'

He laughed again. 'Oh, Magpie. You are brilliant.'

I scowled at him, making him chuckle. He quickly kissed me, dissolving the scowl and pout. He kept my mind focused on the kiss while his hands removed the bindings. With increased urgency, I removed the ties on his shirt, and then the shirt itself. We stumbled towards the bed, struggling to remove each other's leggings without falling over. He lifted me up to his waist with ease, my bare legs wrapping around him. Warmth spread from the very core of me, radiating out to the tips of my fingers and toes. The nerve endings in my skin screamed with every sensation, every touch causing explosions of pleasure. The urgency and passion increased until everything was forgotten except the taste of his skin. The tickle of his tongue. The burn of his lips.

Much later we lay wrapped in each other's arms. He tenderly stroked the raised scars on my back, as I played with the short, curly hair sprinkled over his chest. My fingers absently traced the damp hair across the top of one nipple, down the dip between the halves of his ribcage, and over the top of the second nipple. I retraced the movement in reverse to take my fingertips back to the starting point. My head rose and fell in time with his deep, rhythmic breath as I rested against his chest, inhaling the many layers of his scent; warm and fuzzy, with a hint of something sweet. My leg was draped over his, resting between his muscular thighs, our hip bones fitting together comfortably.

He sighed deeply. 'Oh, Magpie. What am I going to do with you?'

I smiled and tilted my head to look at him. 'Anything you like.' I let the smile slip. 'Why do you call me Magpie? Tawpin called me that to tease me.'

'I know, but it suits you. Your black hair and white skin.' He stroked my pale arm that contrasted with his tanned chest. 'And your obvious liking for shiny things.'

'Yeah. But I keep thinking of that rhyme. *One for sorrow...*'

He sighed again, shifting so he could see my face better. 'That fits too. You bring such a sweet sorrow with you. We both know that we shouldn't be here, that there will be no happy ending for us. Yet, here we are.'

We were silent for several heartbeats, each thinking about the consequences of the day's events. Kade broke the mood.

'Your eyes aren't like a magpie's. They are something completely different.'

'Oh, what is so special about my eyes? Everyone is always on about my eyes.'

'Do you *have* a mirror?'

'Do I *look* like Breya? Always preening and fussing about whether my hair is just right; whether my dress matches my sallow complexion?'

He laughed, bouncing my head against his chest. 'She's not that bad.' He paused. 'Actually, yes she is. But back to your eyes. Tallen, you have the most amazing eyes.'

'So everyone keeps telling me.'

'Tal. Your eyes are orange.'

'Don't play with me,' I snapped, slapping him lightly on the chest. 'No one has eyes that colour.'

'Exactly.' He gazed into my eyes, stroking the soft skin below my lower lid. 'They are the colour of amber warmed almost to the point of melting. Black bubbles rising to the surface around the unknowable depths of your pupils.' He took a shaky breath.

I didn't know what to say. What could I say to that? Kade leaned forward to kiss my eyelids. All thoughts of the colour of my eyes were banished as I lost myself in the sensations arising from the connection of our bodies.

Our lovemaking was as intense and passionate as the first time. The urgency had gone, however, and we spent time exploring each other's sensitive areas that would cause lightning storms deep inside. Time lost all meaning. The only thing that mattered was what was happening in the small woodcutter's cottage in the forest.

Chapter Eleven

I was awoken early the next morning by the door to the main room in Drey's chambers banging against the wall. Kade and I had returned to Liegeport late the previous evening and I had been careful not to disturb Drey. I cringed under the blankets at the thought of the lecture that would surely result from the 'blatant disrespect for his property'. My sleep-fogged brain did not realise that if it was not me banging the door, then it must be Drey. I was surprised, therefore, when Tarra bustled into my room carrying a small bundle of clothing.

'Tarra!' I burrowed further under the blankets. 'What are you doing?'

'What am I doing?' she chirped back at me. 'What are you still doing in bed? The day has been awake for ages and you should be up enjoying the lovely weather.'

She dumped the clothes at the end of the bed and opened the indoor shutters to allow the morning sunlight to flood the room. I groaned as tiny daggers stabbed my sleepy eyes, poking their sharp points into my brain. Tarra was oblivious to my suffering and continued to chatter to unseen people in the main room.

'No, don't leave it there.' She flapped her arms, ushering them into my room. 'Bring it in here. Be careful. Mind the door frame.'

I groaned again as one of the male servants who maintained the royal house walked backwards into my room. He was carrying a large mirror set within a beautifully carved, dark wooden frame. It was almost as big as he was. Another man was carrying the other end, both shuffling under its weight.

'That's right. Put it over here.' Tarra directed them to the corner of the room, by the table. She adjusted the position three times before she was finally happy. 'Thank you, Seton, Dech.'

She ushered them out of the room and closed the door behind them. She sat on the edge of the bed and looked at me for a long while before speaking. Her expression was a mixture of concern and sadness, with more emphasis on the sadness.

'A present from Kade,' she said eventually.

'I'll be sure to thank him.'

Tarra was still staring at me, appraising me for some quality I wasn't sure I possessed.

'Was there something else?'

She opened her mouth and took a breath as if to speak, then changed her mind with a small shake of her head. 'Maybe it's not my place to say.'

She turned to pick up one of the items of clothing she had placed on the bed. As she held it up, I could see it was underclothing by the delicate ribbons and lace bordering. My eyes grew wide as I realised what it was for. I felt my skin burn as the blood rushed to my cheeks and neck in my embarrassment. I was going to have to kill him.

'These were also suggested by Kade. Although how he knew you need them I will not begin to imagine.'

I wanted to die. I wanted the Gods to strike me down with a bolt of lightning.

'I'm disappointed in Drey for not sorting these things out for you. But then, how was he to know about such things? No, the fault is with me. I can't believe I didn't realise. But then, it only seems like yesterday when you came to join us—'

'Tarra,' I interrupted as the conversation was getting too uncomfortable. 'Thank you. But I think I should get dressed now.'

'Oh yes, yes. Would you like me to show you how—?'

'No! Thank you. I'm sure I'll manage.'

She smiled, patted my knee and then left. I pulled the blankets over my head and debated whether I could stay there forever. The inevitable conclusion was that I was going to have to get out of bed at some point. And now was as good a time as any. I threw back the covers and walked over to the mirror.

I was dressed in one of Drey's old shirts that fitted well enough, but only came to the middle of my thighs. My skinny, white legs and knobbly knees stuck out from under the hem. I lifted my gaze to look at my face. The skin was pinker than normal due to the ride in the sun the previous day. I knew it would soon turn white again. My arms never tanned despite being regularly burnt by the sun. My black hair framed my face, sticking out from my head like a small hawthorn bush. I brushed it into a more acceptable style with my fingers, tucking the longer ends behind my ears. It was cut so that it was all one length but fell no further than the base of my skull. I liked my hair. It was easy to take care of. The oils Tarra gave me to wash it in made it squeak when wet, and smell of flowers.

I wasn't so impressed with my face. It was a little too long and pointed. My mouth was too small. My nose was all right. And then there were my eyes. Kade was right – my eyes were a little unsettling. They were the colour of amber, complete with black bubbles within the orange irises. I had never seen eyes that colour. It felt as if they didn't really belong to me. I sighed, accepting that I couldn't change anything.

I turned to pick up one of the corsets from the bed. The material was a soft, white cloth with a lace border at the bottom and around the top, including two half-moon shapes at the front. Cream ribbons were woven into the lace where it joined the cloth, matching those that laced the front of the garment. Removing my nightshirt, I slipped a thin chemise over my head and let it fall to my thighs. I loosened the ribbons of the corset so I could lower it over my head and pass my arms through. Smoothing the material flat, I tightened the ribbons. The garment lifted and defined my breasts, while the ties accentuated my small waist and the curve of my hips. The corners of my mouth lifted in a small smile as I understood why Kade had suggested the items of clothing for me.

I quickly got dressed, throwing on woollen trousers and an oversized shirt. I still managed to sway more than normal when I walked, just with the knowledge that I wore the corset underneath, and the tickle of the lace against my skin.

I was surprised to find that it was almost lunchtime, and that I had slept much later than I had intended. It was the first time in as long as I could remember that I had slept soundly, without waking due to dreams. I hurried to the main dining hall, hoping there would still be food left from breakfast, and that I would not have to wait until the midday meal. I was so busy yawning that I almost ran into Tawpin.

'Hey, careful!'

I rubbed my still-sleepy eyes. 'Sorry, Tawpin. Late night.'

'So I hear.' He grinned. 'Come get some ginger tea and tell me all about it.'

I let him guide me to a nearby bench and he fetched me some tea. He thoughtfully brought me some fruit and nuts as well, and I chewed slowly on these as he bounced impatiently in his seat.

'Tell me.'

'Tell you what?'

'Tell me where you and Kade went yesterday.'

'We went for a ride.'

'A ride that kept you out most of the night?'

'Were you worried about us?' I teased. 'And anyway, we were back before dark.'

'Where did you go?' he persisted, bouncing in his chair like an angry bee.

'We went to the lake, in the forest to the south.'

'And...?'

'And we enjoyed the view.'

'Tallen, I'm dying here. Tell me what happened.'

'We went to a woodcutter's cottage. Ate the food Tarra had given us. Talked. Then came back.'

'Really?'

I took a sip of my tea, then smiled at him over the rim of the cup. He slumped in his seat.

'That's what Kade said. I'm sure there's more to it.'

'Poor Tawpin. And there was you thinking you knew *everything*.'

'Humph.' He suddenly sat upright. 'One thing I do know is that you should have been in a meeting this morning.'

I blinked at him. 'What?'

His mouth turned down apologetically. 'I forgot. I was supposed to find you and tell you to go to the king's meeting room.'

'Taw!'

'I know, I'm sorry.'

I gave him a glare as I took a final gulp of my tea. Grabbing a handful of nuts to eat on the way, I ran out of the dining hall and headed straight for the meeting room on the second floor of Kyllian's tower.

Kyllian's two bodyguards were standing guard outside the room as I skidded to a halt in front of the heavy oak door. The bronze buttons on their uniforms flickered softly as they breathed. Swords that I knew had seen action hung at their sides. Their still faces were not impressed as I caught my breath.

'You're late,' said Altes, his deep voice reverberating around his chest.

'I know,' I snapped back impatiently.

Altes nodded to his smaller colleague, who opened the door for me. The conversation within the room stopped as I entered, increasing my anxiety and self-consciousness. I nervously pulled at the hem of my shirt to remove any creases. I took three steps into the room, keeping my head down and my eyes lowered. The door was closed behind me with an ominous thud. My heart rate increased along with my breathing, and I trembled as I studied the rich woollen rug that covered the floor. The weaving was skilfully done, and apart from the change of colours it was hard to see where the different wools had been joined.

Kyllian cleared his throat after an unbearable length of time. 'You're late.'

Keeping my eyes lowered as protocol demanded, I replied. 'Yes, sire. I apologise for keeping you waiting, but I have only just received your summons.'

He waited again, purposefully increasing my discomfort. 'Sit down next to Drey.'

I was finally permitted to lift my gaze and note who else was in the room. Nearest to me was Drey, with an empty chair that was obviously meant for me. He gave me a look laced with disapproval, and I mouthed a quick *Sorry* as I sat down. The high-backed chairs were arranged in a square, with the side nearest the door remaining empty. Drey and I sat to the right of the room facing into the centre, while Kade and Villermir sat opposite. Kyllian and Kerk occupied the two chairs that faced the door. The window was behind them, causing them to be surrounded by a faint light. It added to the sense of splendour associated with the king and his heir. I did not think it a coincidence. Kyllian was dressed in formal clothes but there was no state finery about them. The circlet of engraved silver around his head was all that was needed to identify this as a meeting of importance. Kerk looked sombre beside his father, with his hands clasped in his lap appearing almost relaxed, in contrast to Kyllian's, which grasped the arms of his chair.

Villermir sat to the right of the king. His long-sleeved, austere grey robes covered most of his body, with only dark woollen leggings showing at the ankle. His grey eyes drilled into me as I glanced at him, piercing the core of me and causing an instinctual tensing of every muscle. The hardness of the stare remained as he slowly lifted the corners of his mouth. The small smile filled me with more apprehension than the stare did. With a small nod of acknowledgement, I turned to Kade. All thoughts of Villermir were erased by the look of anger on his face. I had never seen him wear such an expression. His normal relaxed features were well buried under a granite mask. The muscles around his eyes were so tight that their shape was distorted. The muscles of his jaw peaked and dipped like the ripples of ocean waves as he ground his teeth in frustration. The tendons in his neck stood out like the rope rigging on the ships moored in the dockyard. Kade's and my chairs were the only ones without arm supports, leaving him to cross his arms against his chest. The fine material of his dark green doublet was crushed as he folded his hands into fists. I could see he was trembling with rage.

Despite my purposeful staring at him that he must have been aware of, he avoided looking at me, instead glaring at a point in the middle of the floor.

'Villermir,' began the king. 'If you would be so kind as to repeat your recent understandings for the benefit of Tallen.'

I gave a polite nod of acknowledgement to Kyllian, despite the obvious chastisement. Villermir's responding nod to his king was much more elaborate.

'Thank you, sire. As I was saying, a junior priest has just returned from the Hilman kingdom, north of Lindvane. As I am sure you are aware, the holy priesthood of Baila has no political ties to any specific kingdom, and a number of priests are based in Hilman, as well as Lindvane.'

I felt Drey stiffen slightly beside me.

'This priest brought news of a recently discovered cavern deep in the mountains of Hilman. One of their mines was extended and revealed this underground cavern and the curiosities within it. Despite there being no obvious tunnels into the cave, the miners found a small hoard of precious gems, crystals and suchlike. Most of these stones are small and do not have much value. But there is tell of one stone, larger than the others, that may be worthy of note.'

Tired of Villermir's ramblings, Drey interrupted. 'The Hilman believe they have found the Empathy Crystal.' Seeing my confused expression, he continued. 'The Empathy Crystal is said to have been formed during the last firestorm age, when mountains were melted under rivers of infernal fire. The Ancients found this perfect quartz, the colour of the sun, and infused it with the power to control the ground of which it was made. Depending on the desire of the person bound to the crystal, it could produce earthquakes, floods, rockfalls—'

Villermir waved his hand dismissively. 'All stories to entertain children on a dark night. But the important point is the political power of this crystal. What if it did work? You really wouldn't want your enemies to use it against you. We could finish this war without the need for fighting. We could subdue the Lindvanes just with the fear of the possibility.'

The room was quiet while I considered the implications of this crystal. The potential.

'If this crystal is so important,' I questioned, 'valuable if nothing else, the Hilman are not just going to hand it over to us.'

Kyllian held my gaze, his face impassive while I calculated possibilities. My heart lurched and my eyes widened as I came to the solution. I glanced at Drey for confirmation. He nodded slightly.

'You want me to steal it?'

I looked at Villermir, unsure of whether he knew of the times I had stolen for Drey. His calm expression told me he was very aware of my activities.

'I'm sure your transgressions could be forgiven if they were to save the lives and suffering of many,' he conceded.

I turned to Kade. His face had turned pale, except for two blotches of red on his cheeks. So this was what he was so angry about.

Kyllian's voice was quiet as he confirmed my orders. 'This must be done with the utmost secrecy. It is not to be discussed outside of this room.'

He gave me his full attention, waiting for my acceptance of the task and my understanding of the consequences should anything go wrong. I had had this conversation with Drey a long time ago. There would be no support from Kyllian if anything went wrong. But this went further than taking a few documents and deeds. I thought about Tawpin's parents. It was not just my safety I was gambling with. Succeed or fail, the retaliation would be severe.

I looked up to find everyone watching me. Kyllian patient. Kerk uncomfortable. Villermir challenging. Drey apologetic. Kade pleading. I couldn't look at him. I had no choice.

'When do I leave?'

Kade exploded out of his chair. He had taken three steps before Kyllian spoke.

'You have not been given permission to leave.'

This was the command of a king. There was no paternal warmth detectable in his tone. Kade stopped but did not turn around. His back was held so tense I thought it would crumble from the strain. His fists were clenched so tightly I could see the skin of his knuckles turning as white as the underlying bone. My stomach spasmed in sympathy, and I felt like I was going to vomit on the expensive rug.

With a visible effort of will, Kade took a deep breath and slowly turned towards his father. He bowed deeply, acknowledging the break in protocol. 'My liege.'

Kyllian made him maintain that position for several heartbeats.

'This will be the end of it, Kade,' he said at last. 'You may leave.'

Kade again showed incredible will by resisting the urge to slam the door as he left. The conversation moved on to the time the journey could be expected to take, and whether the mild weather would hold. I stopped listening. I stared mournfully at the door. I didn't care about the details; I would deal with them at the time. I just wanted to follow Kade. To apologise to him. To promise I would stay safe. To stop his hurt. To erase the memory of his look of betrayal.

I turned to see Kyllian watching me, understanding my distraction. Maybe sending me after the crystal was less about my skills, and more about keeping me away from his son.

The discussion continued late into the afternoon. I grew impatient with the numerous tiny details that were debated; everything ranging from the route that the journey should take to the trail rations that would be needed. I concentrated very hard on not showing my frustration, but judging from the glares that Drey kept directing at me I must have failed miserably. I admired the way Kerk maintained his dignified expression throughout the afternoon, deciding I would have to ask him later how he managed this feat. By the time Kyllian allowed me to leave I had started to fidget due to an aching back and bottom from sitting too long, and my stomach was growling noisily. He declared that the others had business to discuss that did not require my presence and granted my excusal. I left with a little more speed than was appropriate.

I knew where to find Kade. While I longed for space and loneliness when I needed to think, Kade preferred to be among people. He gained energy from those around him. I went to the Blue Boar.

There were a handful of people in the tavern. A couple of men stood at the bar talking to Brethick, their clothing identifying them as merchants. Four cavalry soldiers were seated at a table drinking away their off-duty. Another small group of soldiers were at the far end of the tavern, playing a noisy game of dice involving too many players. Heated debates were had about the results of each round. I noticed Herron in the middle of the group and waved in recognition. He lifted his tankard in salute.

Kade was sitting at his usual table near the fireplace. There was no fire burning, but the grate had been stacked with logs to make it look more attractive. A plate of untouched bread and cheese was on the table in front of him. He sat slouched, staring into the tankard of ale that he was holding with both hands. His face was an image of unguarded misery.

'Hey,' I said quietly as I approached.

He jumped as if suddenly scalded with hot water. 'Hey.'

'Mind if I join you?'

His face relaxed and a small smile crept across his lips. He gestured to the empty bench next to him. 'Of course not.'

'Do you want that?' I nodded towards the food. 'I haven't eaten all day. I'm starving.'

He pushed the plate towards me and returned to his drink. I watched him while I chewed a mouthful of bread. The sadness had returned to his face. His eyes were distant, and a little too bright. I suspected he had been drinking steadily since he had left the meeting.

'It's not that bad, you know. Should be a straightforward steal.' My words were muffled by the bread.

He turned slowly to face me. 'You have no idea what they are getting you into.'

'No change there, then.'

Kade caught the eye of one of the serving girls and requested two tankards of ale. He sighed. 'Seriously, Tal. This is doomed to failure.'

'Thanks for your faith in my abilities.'

'You have to cross Lindvane. If you survive that, you need to find the crystal, deal with the professional soldiers that will be guarding it, come back through Lindvane with the armies of Hilman and Lindvane after you, and bring them flying into Faulknar! This is the stupidest plan I have ever heard. What in the Seven Hells of Mobis are they thinking?' He slammed his empty tankard onto the table to emphasise his point.

I sat very still. 'I think Villermir just wants to be rid of me. And I think your father wants me away from you.'

'What?' Shades of the anger that had transformed his face earlier returned in the tightening of his eyes and the fixed set of his mouth. 'Oh, that's just brilliant. He's going to bring untold destruction to his kingdom and people because he doesn't want me sleeping with a commoner!'

His volume had risen steadily as his anger grew. The last comment was heard throughout the tavern. Conversations stopped abruptly as everyone's attention focused on us for a handful of heartbeats. My cheeks flushed with embarrassment for the second time that day.

'Well, that's one way of telling the world.'

'What?' He had not noticed the effects of his words until I had pointed them out to him. He cringed in apology, taking my hand. 'I'm sorry.'

I smiled, dismissing the concern. 'At least you're not embarrassed by me.'

'Never.' He leaned forward to kiss me. The alcohol had affected his aim and he bumped against my mouth, squeezing my lips against my teeth.

'Your father's right in one way. He can't send an army after this. One person can sneak in where a full company can't.' I shrugged. 'I'm good at being invisible. No one is going to notice me.'

'I should go with you.'

'Now that *is* a stupid plan.'

His anger was easily provoked. 'Oh right, so sending you to your death is fine but I'd just get in the way?'

'That's not what I'm saying, Kade. I don't want to go any more than you want me to. But I can't tell the king that I've changed my mind. "I won't help you stop the slaughter of innocent people. I'd rather stay and sleep with your son instead, if that's all right?"'

'I can't just let you go. If anything…'

'Nothing is going to go wrong. Drey is going to come with me. Two unimportant people. Who is going to worry about a girl and an old man? We'll be back before you know it.' I reached for his chin, forcing him to look at me. 'I'll be careful.' I kissed him gently. 'And we have no choice.'

'Just because we have no choice doesn't mean I have to like it.'

I smiled as his body relaxed, accepting defeat. 'Nobody likes it, Kade. That's why we have ale.'

He smiled back, putting an arm around my shoulders and pulling me into his chest. He kissed the top of my head. 'You'd better be careful.'

I was still resting against his chest, playing with his fingers as they hung from my shoulder, when Kerk, Tawpin and Jeck arrived. Tawpin's grin grew wider as he saw Kade's arm around me.

'I really need a drink,' complained Kerk as he sat down heavily on the bench opposite. 'What a tedious day. The only interesting bit was when you stormed out, Kade.'

Kade nodded in gratitude at the comment. 'Glad to be of service.'

More drinks were requested while Tawpin and Jeck bickered about which one of them had had the most tedious day. Kade and Kerk were blamed for many of their problems. Kade remained quiet and seemed reluctant to let go of me, but he relaxed in the familiar companionship of his brother and the two pages. The tension left his face and his smile became less forced as the good ale and the bad jests flowed freely. The tavern steadily filled during the evening as people finished their daily chores and relaxed in the good company of their neighbours. Tawpin, Jeck and Kerk started a game of cards that led to a whole new level of bickering.

Breya arrived halfway through the evening, with Tarra acting as her chaperone. As usual Breya had selected a gown that highlighted the curves of her figure well. With her violet eyes and her cascade of blonde hair, almost every man turned to watch her as she walked across the room to join us. The glass beads on her bodice sparkled like stars in the flickering candlelight. I saw the desire plainly displayed on the men's faces, despite her being betrothed to the royal heir. Kerk was one of the few that did not watch her closely, continuing with his game of cards.

Breya's eyes narrowed as she saw me next to Kade. 'Comfortable?'

I smiled sweetly. 'Yes, thank you.'

'I assume the serving girls are too busy to attend to your needs tonight, Kade.' She sat next to Jeck, glancing at me with obvious disdain. 'One must take comfort where one can find it, I suppose.'

I felt Kade tense. 'Tread carefully tonight, Breya. I'm not in the mood for your games.'

'You prefer something simpler, I see.'

I noticed Brethick looking at Kade repeatedly, and guessed what he wanted. Hoping to prevent an argument before it started, I gently squeezed Kade's leg.

'Why don't you sing a few songs for the people? Bet it makes you feel better.'

He started to protest, but quickly realised that it would make him feel better. And it would get him away from Breya. He collected the lute that was kept behind the bar, receiving enthusiastic thanks from Brethick. He took his familiar position in the clear area reserved for minstrels, and I watched the rigidity in his shoulders dissolve as he tuned the strings. His face softened as he forgot the people around him and lost himself in the music produced by his fingers. A small crease formed between his eyebrows as he concentrated on the complex chords required for his chosen opening tune. His voice was not required, as the instrument sang under his expert handling, the notes producing a heartbreaking melody that captured the attention of everyone in the room. Conversations halted as people were carried away by the achingly beautiful music.

The room remained silent for several heartbeats after the lute fell silent, before breaking into appreciative applause. Kade chose to continue with the mournful tone for his next song, this time adding his voice to sing lyrics about the relentless inevitability of fate. I smiled, appreciating his choice of song and the parallels with our current situation, then looked up to see Tarra and Breya scowling at me.

'What?'

Breya rolled her eyes, giving a small shake of her head. She punched Kerk on the arm. 'Get me a drink.'

Kerk threw his cards onto the table and glared at her, before obediently complying with her command. He soon returned with a goblet of wine each for Breya and Tarra, smiling at Breya's scowl as he handed Tarra her drink. Kerk returned to his card game as Kade started another song, this time concerning the loss of a sweetheart to the depths of the sea. Breya had drunk half her wine before commenting on the evening's entertainment.

'Merciful Mother, what is wrong with him tonight? I'm sure Brethick is happy for his customers to drown their sorrows in his ale, but I require something a bit livelier.'

She went to join Kade, placing her hand on his shoulder as he finished the latest sad tune. For the benefit of the audience watching the exchange, she pleaded his indulgence in allowing her to sing the merry tale of the butcher's dog that ran away with the meat. Kerk winked at me, knowing that Kade had no choice in the matter, and that Breya was now in charge of the music. Kade conceded with good grace, and genuinely seemed happy to accompany Breya as she lightened the mood. She sang of how the butcher had to devise increasingly desperate schemes to stop the dog stealing his wares, and the drinkers were soon joining in with the rowdy chorus of the butcher chasing the clever dog, having been outsmarted yet again. They kept the rhythm by banging their tankards on the tables.

Tarra moved to sit next to me, so that she could talk without having to shout above the noise. 'You and Kade seem to be getting close.'

I turned to face her, suspicious of what she was trying to say. Tarra was a mild-mannered person who did not have a bad word to say about anyone. She seemed an unlikely person to criticise my relationship with Kade.

'Yeah, we are,' I answered cautiously.

She hesitated, her face clearly revealing her inner dilemma of whether or not to say what she was thinking.

'Tarra, just say it.'

She placed her hand on my arm. 'Kade is the king's son.'

'Are you saying I'm not good enough for him?'

'No,' she said hurriedly. 'No. That's not what I'm saying. It's just… It's not about what I think, or what you think, or even what Kade thinks. It's about what Kyllian thinks. Kade has responsibilities and will have to do as his father bids.'

I sighed, appreciating her concern but not wanting to acknowledge it. 'I know, Tarra.'

'He'll break your heart.'

I shrugged. 'Maybe I'll break his.'

She squeezed my arm. 'Be careful, Tallen. People like us are dispensable.'

I frowned in confusion and was about to ask what she meant, but she had turned away from me, making it clear that the conversation was over. She merrily clapped along to Breya's singing as if we had not spoken. The sudden change unsettled me, giving more salience to what she had said. I felt my mood darken, and it stayed that way despite Breya's cheerful, crowd-pleasing songs.

Chapter Twelve

Drey and I left a couple of days later. Drey took his familiar skewbald Mupp, while I was to ride Nalya. The horses were laden with sleeping mats and blankets, personal items and enough trail rations to last us for a week. Although our journey was expected to last weeks rather than days, the week's supply of food was to support the rumours that had been spread. Drey was said to be visiting an aged aunt who had fallen seriously ill. As his apprentice it was natural that I would accompany him. To any watching eyes, we easily assumed the roles appointed to us.

The charade, however, was only superficial. The day was hot and sunny, with most people wearing short-sleeved tunics and shirts. Both Drey and I were wearing light cloaks that covered us from shoulder to ankle. Beneath these cloaks was an assortment of weapons not required for visiting ailing relatives. Drey carried a sword and a dagger, while Langdon had given me a sword and three throwing knives as well as my dagger. Within their saddlebags the horses carried potions that could harm as well as those that could heal.

We left while the sun was still low in the sky. The horses' hooves clattered on the stones in the road as we rode through the main gates to the south of the city. Drey waved merrily to the merchants as we passed by, accepting their blessings for his aunt. The guards had already opened the gates and we passed through with a brief nod. Once outside, the full glory of the day became apparent. The puffs of white cloud moved lazily across the perfect blue sky. The small birds danced and dived after insects while butterflies searched for nectar. Flies buzzed around the horses' faces, making them shake their heads and swish their tails. The noise of their hooves was muffled by the dry dirt of the road, and grasshoppers could be heard in the tall grasses. The roadside was a tapestry of coloured flowers, with white daisies, purple lavender, pink foxgloves, red poppies and yellow clover. The sweet scents floated towards us on the slight breeze. The hedgerows were already preparing for autumn with rosehips and early blackberries. The Lady had nurtured her nature into a spectacular display of vibrancy.

Yet none of it lifted my mood. I hated leaving Kade. I had spent most of the previous two days arguing with him over irrelevancies, while carefully avoiding the real issues. We both knew there was a real possibility that I would not return, but we also knew there was no alternative. Perhaps this was how soldiers felt as they left their families, knowing the job had to be done but hating having to be the ones to do it; wishing someone else could go instead but knowing there was no one else. The soldiers were doing their bit on the border. Now it was my turn. Kade could not deal with having to be left behind. His part did not involve placing himself in danger. He had a responsibility to maintain the royal bloodline, to avoid becoming a target and placing others in danger as they protected him. The inability to act scorched the very core of him, smouldering within so that sparks could be seen in the depths of his eyes. I had fear, but could focus on the task ahead. He had fear, but with a frustration allowing no release. I considered him to have been given the worse fate.

'Tal.'

The word was said very quietly, but something in the tone cut through my thoughts and made me turn my full attention to Drey. He had moved Mupp closer to Nalya and was removing his cloak to allow easy access to his sword. His rose quartz crystal pendant bounced against his neck, reflecting shards of light now that it had been exposed to the bright morning sun. His face wore the faraway look he adopted when concentrating on something that was beyond my five senses to detect. I remained quiet, waiting for him to explain his sudden wariness. I folded back my own cloak and continued to ride with one hand on the reins while the other rested on the hilt of my sword.

'We're being followed.'

I unconsciously tensed the muscles of my back and thighs, causing Nalya to shy sideways. I consciously calmed myself, encouraging her to move forward again.

'Already?'

'I believe so.' Drey frowned slightly. 'I can't be certain. It's not clear. But I think there is only one.'

I rechecked the smooth running of my sword within the scabbard, desperately trying to remember everything Langdon had taught me, imagining different-sized assailants and which techniques would be most effective against them.

'How far away? How long have we got?' I asked.

'Not long. There's a clearing further up the trail. We can hide there and perhaps he will ride straight past.'

He didn't sound hopeful, but it was a plan and I accepted it readily. We pushed the horses into a brisk trot, their long-legged stride covering the ground quickly. We soon passed a tight bend in the trail where Drey brought his horse to a halt. With a little encouragement, Mupp pushed through the brambles and disappeared from my sight. Nalya was much more reluctant to enter the prickly bushes and needed the encouragement of Drey as well as myself to get her through. The bushes were deceptively small, and only a couple separated the trail from the clearing. The heath was bordered by trees and small patches of scrub on all sides, effectively concealing its presence from those on the road. Drey instructed me to tie the horses to a slender tree at the far end of the clearing, while he burrowed back into the brambles to observe the trail. I hurried to join to him, lying on my stomach and worming under the prickles until I could see the road. He had picked a good position, with a clear view of the road in both directions as well as the rider when he would have to slow for the bend.

We waited.

I slowed my breathing, straining to hear hoof-beats on the track. The air was still and the grasshoppers continued to chirp. I closed my eyes, concentrating on all the sounds I could detect, separating them and searching for any that should not be there. I had almost convinced myself that I could hear the soft thud of a horse's hooves.

'Oh, for the love of Mobis,' Drey snapped, reversing out of the bush.

I blinked in surprise at his sudden change of mood, torn between watching the road and following him back into the clearing. A horse nickered from back along the trail, immediately answered by an enthusiastic whinny from Nalya. It wasn't long before a muscular bay came into view. I frowned as it trotted closer, revealing a familiar white blaze. The rider was halfway between the limit of my view and the bend in the road when I finally realised who had been following us. I added a curse of my own, stronger than the one Drey had used earlier.

Kade slowed to a walk, and then stopped at the curve of the road. He had positioned Mael so that the gelding was facing the bushes in which I was hiding. I was certain that he knew of the clearing. Kade held his head at a slight angle, listening or trying to remember something. Drey was still mumbling as he brought the horses across the clearing, and Kade smiled as he heard this. I scuttled backwards to help Drey with the horses. His face was set in a mask of calmness that told of a seething anger under the surface. Quietly, I took Nalya and followed him through the bushes. He started berating Kade before he was fully through.

'What do you think you are doing? Have you lost all ability to think logically? You will be missed. Search parties will be sent. You will go straight back to Liegeport.'

Kade's smile melted from his face. His pleasure at finding us was quickly extinguished by the tirade of words aimed at him.

'I'm the *second* son of Faulknar. No one cares what I do, and for that I am immeasurably grateful.' He added quietly, 'I won't go back.'

'You stupid, idiotic boy. Think beyond your adolescent hormones and remember your station. You are second in line to the throne of Faulknar. You can't go gallivanting around the countryside on a whim. We are at war, boy!'

'I won't go back,' Kade repeated, just as quietly as before. 'Don't make me pull rank, Drey.'

For several heartbeats, Drey was actually speechless. He stared at Kade, who held his gaze calmly. I could easily imagine them puffing themselves up like two tomcats claiming territory.

Drey turned away. 'You increase the danger for her,' he said as he mounted Mupp and trotted along the road.

I quickly followed and Kade moved to ride beside me. We said nothing to each other as Drey continued to grumble ahead of us. I kept my attention focused on his back but could feel Kade watching me, waiting for my chastisement to add to Drey's.

'Do you have nothing to say to me?' he asked eventually.

I continued to look ahead. 'I think Drey has said it clearly enough.' I glanced sideways to make sure he was listening carefully. 'You know, I think this is the stupidest thing you have ever done.'

I could sense him shrinking a little in the saddle. His hands tightened on the reins and, from the corner of my eye, I watched the muscles of his jaw tense. I waited several heartbeats to ensure he had considered his actions fully, then turned my head towards him slightly, so I could see his reaction clearly.

'But it is good to see you.'

His smile exploded across his face like the sun coming out from behind a cloud on a rainy day. I could not help but respond, and we grinned ridiculously at each other. Drey's complaining grew louder to ensure we heard his thoughts on the lunacy of youth.

We travelled a good distance that day, partly due to the exuberant mood of Kade and myself being passed to the horses as they skipped and skittered along the road. Mainly it was due to Drey's anger with us and his reluctance to stop for a break. I'm sure he would have continued all day even if we had pleaded with him for a rest. The sun was starting to touch the horizon on our right when Drey finally suggested we set up camp by the river we had been following for some time. We travelled a short distance away from the trail, but as we were still well within Faulknar territory Drey was not concerned with hiding our presence. The evening was warm and still, so I left the oilcloth sheets that would provide our shelter with the saddles and placed only the bed-mats and blankets on the ground around the firewood that Kade had collected. Drey prepared a simple meal over a small fire while the sun melted into the distant fields.

I lay on my back, relaxing the tired muscles around my lower spine and watching the tiny flickering of the stars, so very far away. All three of us were quiet, lost in our own thoughts. I was thinking of the times when Kade had named the stars for me. I rolled onto my side, propping my head up on a bent elbow. He was staring into the fire's embers, the warm glow chasing shadows over his face.

'You need to know a few things before we reach Hilman.'

I turned my head so my gaze moved from Kade to Drey, who was watching me.

'We may as well start tonight.'

I lazily stretched my back muscles before pushing myself up to sit crosslegged. I had a feeling this was going to take a while, and I was already close to falling asleep.

'What do I need to know?'

Drey hesitated, trying to find the right words. 'There will be things that you will encounter on this journey that you will not understand.'

'More lessons, then.'

He sighed. 'No. That's not what I'm trying to say.' He started again. 'What do you remember of what was said about the Empathy Crystal?'

I shrugged. 'That it is politically important. Kingdoms will be fearful of the potential destruction that could be caused by the crystal. It's said to have the power to destroy mountains and open up the earth.'

'That's my point. The crystal *can* destroy mountains and open up the earth.'

A small laugh burst out of my mouth. 'What?'

I looked towards Kade, expecting him to be grinning at Drey's jest, but he continued to stare deep into the fire. I turned back to Drey, who showed no sign that he was teasing me.

'The old religions talk about the power of the Gods and their ability to control the weather, cure disease, predict the future. These powers did not belong solely to the Gods but were common among the Ancients. Our distant ancestors had a greater understanding of how the tapestry of existence weaves through everything and how it can be manipulated. There are still some that can practise these skills.'

My brain raced in every direction, searching for evidence that this could be true. I thought of the comments Tawpin and Kade had made about Drey. I thought of the depths of his hazel eyes, and how easy it was to fall into his dark, liquid pupils. I felt my own eyes widen as it suddenly became clear.

'You can read minds!'

A thin smile danced over his lips. 'Sometimes.'

'Fearsome Father.' I held my head in my hands as if that could protect my thoughts. 'You know everything.'

I heard Kade chuckling and turned to glare at him. 'You knew?'

He shrugged but continued to look into the fire. 'I have known Drey all my life. I knew his value to my father.'

I returned to Drey. 'Do you know everything I'm thinking? All the time?'

He shook his head. 'It doesn't work like that. Not for me anyway. I need permission to enter your thoughts. With practice, some can grant permission easily.'

'Helps relieve the boredom in really tedious meetings,' commented Kade.

I looked back and forward between the two of them. 'Can you talk to Kade as well as hear his thoughts?'

A flicker of pride infused Drey's smile. 'We're working on that. He needs more focus. But yes, on occasion we can hear each other.'

'And if someone doesn't grant permission, can you still hear them?'

'The mind has instinctive barriers, protective wards that prevent access if the person does not permit it. I can't get inside your head without disabling these barriers.'

'But I'm not aware of any barriers. How can I disable them if I don't know they are there?'

'*You* don't. You just need to stop blocking any attempts and allow me to remove the barriers. They are there to protect against threats. If the person does not perceive my access as a threat I can enter their thoughts. If the person resents my presence, the barriers will hold.'

I was quiet for several heartbeats, considering his words. 'You've been inside my head.'

'Yes.'

I hesitated again. 'You did something to me, to get information.'

Kade was very still as Drey shifted position slightly, uncomfortable with my accusation but accepting the need for honesty.

'You have an interesting mind, Tallen nic Duane. Your barriers repelled my every approach, no matter how subtle. I was required to actively lower your defences by placing you in a hypnotic trance. Even then, my access was restricted. That's unusual. There were areas, memories that were heavily defended. Even from you, I feel.'

'You can enter someone's mind, even if they do not want you in there.'

'Yes.'

The two men remained quiet and still, watching me while I explored all the implications of Drey's words. I eventually looked up to meet his gaze.

'Many of us believe it is a great gift to be able to see into the thoughts of others. One that comes with a respect for the individual. I fear, on this journey, we will meet those that hold no such concerns. There are those that believe every opportunity should be exploited to gain more money, influence, control. The privacy of the individual is brushed aside in the pursuit of the end goal.'

'How can you tell who these people are?'

'You can't. They could be anyone.' He shrugged. 'But often the knowledge of everyone's petty thoughts eats away at a person, leaving them suspicious or condescending.'

'Villermir.'

Drey released a bitter laugh. 'Perhaps. Despite his dismissive nature in front of the king, he is well aware of the capabilities of the Empathy Crystal and practises many forms of magick. I believe that is why the temple make you feel uncomforatble. There is dark energy in that building. Villermir has powerful wards protecting his secrets. Such as the Ki Oval.'

He watched me while I considered this new information. 'But I touched the Ki Oval.'

'Yes, you did.' He paused to ensure he had my full attention. 'And confirmed to Villermir that you have magick inside of you. Although I suspect he understands what you are capable of even less than I do. Nevertheless, he sees you as a threat. In being able to touch that oval, you have gained yourself a powerful enemy.'

I could feel Kade stiffen and hear a slight catch in his breath when he breathed in. 'You set her up for this.' His tone was soft but held an undertone of anger.

'I did not,' Drey snapped back. 'I was aware Villermir had his suspicions. I did not know she would be able to touch the Ki Oval. No one has been able to do that for over two generations.'

'You used her as a pawn in order to get the Empathy Crystal. Villermir is not the only one playing power games.'

'I got her away from Villermir! While she's useful to him, she's safe.'

I blinked, not believing what I was hearing. Why would anyone play power games over me? How could I have achieved something that no one else had done for more than two generations? Could I really have magick inside me?

The men had fallen silent, refusing to look at each other. I moved my sleeping mat over to Kade's, requiring the solidity of his presence in a world suddenly thrown off balance. He hugged me eagerly as I sat in front of him so that my back rested against his chest. His body trembled as if cold, although the night was pleasantly warm. We both stared at the small flames, hanging on to each other as if we would disappear if we let go.

Drey mumbled something about checking the horses and left. Kade kissed the slope of my neck. I felt the tickle of his long eyelashes as he rested his forehead on my shoulder. I reached up to stroke his hair.

'This just gets getting better.'

I smiled. 'Life is all about fun with me.'

'I just want to keep you safe, and Drey keeps putting you in danger.'

I squeezed his arms a little tighter. 'You don't have to keep me safe. You just have to be there to collect up the pieces.'

He groaned against my skin. 'Oh, Magpie. I'm so out of my depth.'

'*You're* out of your depth? The only reason I'm not babbling nonsense while rocking gently is because I have no idea what in the Seven Hells of Mobis is going on.'

He chuckled, which was what I was hoping for. He sighed deeply as I turned around to wrap my legs around him. He slipped his hands under my shirt, smoothing the skin of my abdomen with his thumbs. The kiss was deep and tender; urgent but allowing the time to explore all the sensations. His scent invaded my nostrils, smothering all thought of anything other than him. My skin crackled with energy wherever he touched, sending tendrils of pleasure throughout my body. Kade made love with a desperation I didn't fully understand, but my body responded, exulting in the intimacy; finding comfort in the familiar in denial of the uncertainty to come.

It didn't stop the dreams coming. The setting was a battlefield. Mist rose across the hilly ground, the view muted in shades of grey. Bodies lay mutilated on the ground, male and female soldiers wandering directionless around them. I was searching desperately for Laken, grabbing anyone within reach, turning them round to allow identification. Some were strangers. Some were known to me: Gheth, Herron, Langdon, others from the barracks. Their injuries ranged from bleeding wounds, to broken bones, to torn guts. I checked those that had fallen. Some of their faces were so disfigured they were unrecognisable. Others were friends: Jeck, Kerk, Tawpin. I ran faster and faster, this way and that. My brain screamed all the time – *It's too late, you're too late.*

Then I saw him.

He was on his knees, his arms dropped limply at his sides. There were no obvious wounds, but his face was so pale it looked grey. He was starting to sway as the life drained from his body. Sweat stuck his brown hair to his face. His chestnut eyes were losing their focus. I ran as fast as I could.

Kade died before I got to him.

I skidded to a halt and fell to my knees, grabbing his body and holding it to me as tight as I could. As if I could squeeze hard enough to make his unseeing eyes see, make his empty chest fill with air. A piercing scream echoed around the hills.

I became aware of his smell before the dream fully lost its hold on my senses. Clutching his warm, breathing body ripped my chest into shreds of raw tissue. Tears flowed uncontrollably into his already sodden shirt, his firm embrace keeping the fractured pieces of my soul together. I clenched his shirt within my fists, digging my knuckles into his back. It must have hurt and I knew I would leave bruises, but I wanted him to feel; to be alive and feel. He kissed the top of my head tenderly, again and again, as I trembled against him. I hiccupped to snatch air that my constricted chest needed but did not want.

The sky was lightening with the beginnings of dawn before my breathing calmed. I could have stayed wrapped in his arms forever. The warmth of his body and the rich musk of his scent enveloped me in a protective bubble I was loath to burst. Unfortunately, the more I snuggled against him, the more Kade squirmed away.

'Tal, I have to get up.'

I moaned, burying my head in his chest. 'Just a little longer.'

He gently removed my arms from his waist. 'I would stay here all day, but my bladder is being very insistent.'

I could not argue with that and let him go. I rolled over to see Drey already up. His sleeping mat was rolled and he was heating water over the fire. I watched him making tea with powdered herbs, and it was reminiscent of the times we had spent working in his chambers. His hands moved smoothly and confidently as he removed the hot kettle from the fire and poured water into a clay beaker. There was a small crease in his forehead as he concentrated on pouring the appropriate volume of water for the amount of herb present. The steaming tea released the sharp aroma of mint.

He looked up to see me watching him, his hazel eyes calm after the previous day's anger. He rose gracefully and walked over to me, offering the beaker.

'Thank you,' I said, accepting the tea. Despite its aroma, the tea did not taste like peppermint and had an unpleasant, acrid aftertaste. 'Is this peppermint?'

Drey watched me closely as he replied. 'No. It's pennyroyal.'

I choked on the mouthful I had just taken. 'Pennyroyal?'

His face remained expressionless. 'Yes, pennyroyal. The last thing you need is to produce a royal bastard.'

My face burned as I belatedly realised how obvious Kade and I had made our relationship the previous night. I felt ashamed of the discomfort we must have caused Drey with our very public display. But knowing him as I did, this was not a reprimand or condemnation. It was more his pragmatic acceptance of the way things were. I was embarrassed again for having put him in that position. A small part of me wondered whether it was Kade's intention to get back at Drey for not accepting his decision to travel with us; to challenge Drey's authority that bit further. The thought was quickly suppressed.

We travelled through the countryside for two days. As we journeyed further from Liegeport the effects of the war with the Lindvanes became more pronounced. Buildings were poorly maintained and badly repaired, with many abandoned completely. Fields were overgrown with weeds and scrub so that the crops were stunted and withered. As we got nearer the border, fields and woodlands had been torched, the blackened skeletons of trees standing guard over destroyed livelihoods; the faint smell of charcoal in the air despite the crops having been burnt long before our arrival. Very little livestock was seen on the second day, and any we found ran away in fear, but not before we saw their unkempt coats, prominent bones and dull eyes. The few people we met were suffering too; their skin drawn over too-obvious cheekbones, clothes hanging off their thin arms and shoulders, making even the young look frail. Suspicion poured out of their every glance, continuously watching but never making eye contact. Friendly acknowledgement with a wave or a companionable greeting were noticeably absent. The whole kingdom seemed to be holding its breath. Waiting.

The clouds gathered throughout the second day, threatening a late summer storm. The humidity levels rose, draining our energy and making everything seem more difficult. We slumped a little further into the saddles and the horses walked with heavier feet. The first big, fat drops of rain fell as the evening became so dark that it was difficult to see further than the three horse-lengths along the trail.

'We need to stay indoors tonight,' said Kade.

'I know,' Drey replied. 'I was hoping to avoid revealing your presence with us until we had crossed the border.'

He turned to look at Kade. The prince rarely travelled and was commonly known by his reputation rather than his features. Kade was wearing simple clothes that bore no crest to identify his clan. He had grown a stubble of beard during the ride from Liegeport.

'There's a tavern not far from here.' Drey glared pointedly at Kade. 'We will need to remain discrete to avoid the Lindvanes learning of your vulnerability.'

Kade nodded in a submissive manner that I knew to be insincere. 'Yes, sir.'

I was having difficulty controlling Nalya by the time we reached the tavern. The rising tension made her sensitive to any movement or noise. She snorted hopefully as she smelled the clean straw of the tavern stables. I had only just dismounted inside the wooden building when a bright flash of lightning and a timber-rattling crash of thunder caused Nalya to rear. Kade caught her reins as I scuttled out of the reach of her striking feet. We shared a glance, confirming that finding shelter for the night had been a very good idea.

The Goat Inn had a clay statue of a goat, larger than life-size, above the main door. The tavern was spacious and welcoming, with a number of local men and women taking shelter from the storm. The ale was cheap and watered, but it was clear the people came for the company rather than the drink. We sat at a corner table where we could see but not be seen. A young serving girl brought us chicken broth and fresh bread along with three tankards of ale. She smiled shyly at Kade as she placed the food in front of him. Drey rolled his eyes as Kade smiled back, causing her to blush and rush away.

'So much for remaining discrete.'

Kade laughed. 'Relax, Drey. No one is going to look for us here.'

'Hayton has spies everywhere, and I don't trust Villermir's motives. Your disappearance from Liegeport will have been noticed by now. Everyone is going to be looking for you.'

Kade dismissed Drey's concerns with a shrug, returning his attention to the tavern. The mood was sombre. The people talked in hushed voices despite the noise of the storm outside, drinking their ale slowly. There were numerous pauses in the conversations. I watched as Kade absorbed all this information, and I knew what he was planning long before Drey did. My suspicions were confirmed when Kade caught my eye and nodded towards the lute that hung behind the bar. I shook my head, but he just grinned, his eyes sparkling.

As always, attention turned to him as soon as he started tuning the strings. He seemed to swell before my eyes as he drew on the energy of his audience. His voice began low and raspy, drawing them in before closing the trap with his lyrics.

He sang songs of defiance. He told tales of triumph against adversity. He wove spells with stories of heroics during impossible battles. He inspired with tunes about the power of belief and conviction. The atmosphere within the tavern danced to the music of his fingers and voice. The solemn mood was replaced with one of optimism. A taste of victory was just out of the people's reach but was no longer unobtainable. Backs straightened. Heads lifted. Pride returned to their eyes. Kade breathed hope into the blood of those listening, feeding it to every cell in their bodies. I knew the effect would not last beyond that night, but for a few hours these people would feel as if they could take on the Hordes of Mobis. And probably win.

I looked over to Drey, who was watching the prince with obvious pride, and a little sorrow.

'So, is that magick?'

Drey smiled. 'Oh, that's definitely magic.' He turned to me. 'But not the kind you mean. Kade can weave spells that control a room, bringing joy to the joyless, peace to the troubled, calm to the angry. But his magic lies within his own talent. He understands people. He feels their hopes and fears. It will make him a good leader, but also makes him a slave to his passionate heart.'

I grinned. 'He is a good leader.'

Drey sighed. 'Much as I hate to admit it, I think you two are good for each other. You give him focus, and he calms you.'

I frowned in confusion. 'I'm calm.'

He shook his head. 'You're a bundle of eels in the bottom of a bucket. Why do you think horses react so badly to you? There's an air of control about you; a containment. One that could crumble at any moment. You're a huge eruption waiting to happen.'

'Really?' That did not sound like me.

Drey laughed at my expression. 'Oh yes. I sometimes expect to see fire coming out of that mouth.' He laughed again as I pouted, then grew serious. 'I can't help with your dreams.'

I was surprised at the sudden change of topic. 'I never asked you to.'

'I know. But for all the magick I possess, I can't change your dreams. It's destroying Kade, being powerless to help you. It's difficult for all of us. I can't imagine how it feels for you.'

I moved in my chair, more uncomfortable with the conversation than with the hard wooden seat. 'Drey. The dreams are mine. They are mine to deal with.'

'I fear there is more to them than your guilty conscience, Tallen. They seem too frequent, too vivid.'

'Have you seen my dreams? Have you been in my head?' I was getting angry now. My dreams were private, occurring when I was at my most vulnerable.

Drey continued calmly. 'I haven't seen your dreams. I do not know what torments you subject yourself to. But I see their effects in your eyes the next morning. I can see that you have lost a little more of your soul to those dark places.'

I quickly drank the last of my ale. I did not want to be having this conversation. Knowing about Drey's concern and Kade's pity would do nothing to ease my guilt. And the guiltier I felt, the worse the dreams. I turned my attention back to Kade as he found notes of pure pleasure to captivate the tavern's customers, and couldn't help smiling at the sheer joy he got from using his skills to ensure they forgot their troubles for a while.

Chapter Thirteen

It took another two and a half days to reach the southern border of Faulknar. The reason Faulknar did not have to patrol the border with the Travellers' lands became very clear. There was a natural feature running along the entire northern border of the Travellers' territory that made invasion too laborious and, at times, too perilous to contemplate. As far as could be seen a giant scar in the land left chalky cliffs over the plains below, rising to over fifty times the height of a man. Anyone approaching from the Travellers' lands would see a towering white wall, while from Faulknar it looked like the end of the world.

We camped at the top of the cliffs overnight so that we could have the whole day to descend the crumbling paths. We guided the horses down on foot, fearing that a missed step would plunge us to the plains so very far below. The white pebbles rolled under our feet with each step, frequently causing us to stumble. There was no firm rock to hold on to for support. If we strayed too close to the edge, the chalk would crumble away beneath our feet. Nalya snorted nervously but followed the calm lead of the other two horses. I concentrated on the trail and avoided looking down. I soon had a headache from the tension. My legs were shaking uncontrollably by the time we reached the bottom, just as the sun was starting to blend with the horizon.

We made a welcome camp at the foot of the cliffs. The chalk radiated the warmth it had soaked up during the day so there was no need for a fire. Not that anyone had the energy to make one that night. We all lay flat on the ground, unwilling to move even if Mobis had sent his Hordes.

'Was there not a magickal way of getting down here?' I grumbled as a stone dug into my back.

'No,' Drey grumbled back.

'If you think that was bad, wait until the climb back up,' Kade added.

'Oh, thanks for making me feel so much better.'

Kade chuckled in the growing darkness. 'Don't worry, Magpie. You could just fly up.'

I groaned at the pleasurable thought. 'Now that would be amazing. Drey, can you make me fly?'

'No.'

'So what's the point of all this magick, then? You can't make me fly up a cliff. You can't produce a crystal-cool lake that I could just dive into.'

Kade joined in. 'Can't get me a feather-soft bed to lie down on.'

'Can't magick me a large plate of roast boar with all the trimmings.'

'Can't get me a large tankard of cold ale.'

We continued until it grew dark, when Drey shouted at us to be quiet and get some sleep.

The next day involved a trek across the stony plain towards the woods that would offer us some cover. The sharp pebbles littering the ground restricted our travel to a slow crawl as the horses picked their way through. Despite our care, Nalya was footsore and Mael was lame by the time we reached the trees. Kade helped Drey with the horses while I went to gather firewood to make the warm poultice that would be needed for Mael. I had gathered around half of the wood that I needed when I heard a twig snap behind me.

I turned quickly, dropping the wood as I saw five small, dark-haired men with raised swords standing before me. For a heartbeat no one moved. Then movement came quicker than I could track it. I reached for my sword as the smallest man lunged towards me. His blade was at my throat before mine was halfway out of its scabbard. I felt the wet trickle of blood flow down my skin where the sharp point had entered below my chin. Keeping my head and upper body very still, I slowly released my grip on my sword's hilt, allowing it to slip back into the scabbard. My hands shook with a mixture of adrenaline, anger and fear.

The man in the centre of the group stepped forward. He was a head taller than me, with light brown eyes that had a hint of green. He sheathed his sword as he got closer, the decorative hilt catching no reflection of light. He studied me quietly for a number of heartbeats, before turning away.

'Bind her,' he barked as he marched back into the woods.

The first man kept his blade to my throat as another of the swarthy men sheathed his sword while walking towards me. He removed a length of cord that was hanging from his belt. My stomach clenched in response to the hopelessness of my situation. He swiftly bound my wrists and elbows behind my back, looping the cord around my neck. The pressure from my arms pulled at my throat, and I had to concentrate on not choking myself. My fingers felt as if they were being stabbed by small needles as they grew cold from the reduced blood supply. The muscles around my shoulders spasmed as the joints were pulled into unnatural positions. My throat burned as I rasped for air through my narrowed windpipe. My body suffered numerous small torments, and no one was even touching me.

I was made to follow the one who appeared to be in charge. The two men beside me moved to walk either side, while the remaining two walked behind. We headed through the trees, straight towards Drey and Kade. I tried to slow my pace but was encouraged to move faster by the point of a blade in the small of my back. I tried to shout a warning but could not get enough air past the restriction in my throat. Frustration and fear battled within my chest.

We soon made it to the small stream where Drey, Kade and I had set up camp. Nalya snorted at my arrival and Mael tossed his head in agitation. My view of Kade and Drey was blocked by the captor leader's back, but I heard the ring of drawn steel.

'You're a long way from home, Prince.' The title was uttered with too much scorn to be confused with respect.

I felt the air around us grow still and expectant as the hairs on my arms started to rise. The leader grabbed the shoulder of my tunic and pulled me in front of him. I overbalanced and fell to my knees, releasing a grunt of pain as fire ripped through my abused shoulders. A fist grabbing my hair stopped me from falling on my face. Kade stood as still as the cliffs behind him, with his sword aimed at the stranger's heart. Spots at the tops of his cheeks had flushed with blood, demonstrating his fury. Drey had his hands held slightly in front of him, palms facing forward. He appeared to be surrounded by a haze of heat, the air shimmering a hand-width from his body.

A sword was laid at my throat once again, causing my whole body to tremble.

'Her life stands as a forfeit, old man.'

The haze around Drey melted. His body relaxed, but his eyes remained sharp and accusing. 'This is no way to introduce your family, Eldiss.' He spoke in a low, dangerous voice.

'A little security against hostile intent.' The reply held equal danger.

Kade's glare was lethal as he growled, 'Let her go.'

Eldiss was not intimidated. 'I don't think so. Not yet.' He waited to make sure Kade was listening. 'Why are you here, Prince?'

Drey answered. 'We're just passing through. We are no threat to you or your kin.'

Eldiss continued to look at Kade. 'And I'm supposed to just take your word for that?'

'We want nothing from you,' Kade spat.

'Oh, really? So you spent all day climbing down that cliff just so you could climb back up it? Or would you be asking for safe passage through these lands?'

Kade took a step forward, but Drey restrained him with a light touch on his arm. 'Eldiss. We mean you and yours no harm. You have my word as a *zaratos*.'

I had not heard that word before, but at the mention of it Eldiss turned his attention from Kade to Drey. He hesitated for a number of heartbeats, studying Drey. Eventually he gave a small nod. He removed the sword from my throat, slashing the cord between my neck and arms before returning the blade to his scabbard. I needed no other encouragement to run the short distance to Kade and Drey. Drey gathered me to him to stop me falling in a heap at his feet. My legs were shaking so much they were barely able to hold my weight. Kade continued staring murderously at Eldiss as the smaller man walked towards us.

I could not suppress a whine as Drey cut the cords at my wrists and freed my bound arms. He rubbed my limbs as the numbness was replaced with a torrent of pain as blood returned to the starved tissues. Kade briefly turned to me with a look of concern before returning his attention to Eldiss, who now stood a few paces in front of him.

Kade rammed his sword into its scabbard, drew back his arm and released it with all the anger and frustration that had built over the previous minutes. A crystal-clear crack was heard as Eldiss swung round, clutching his nose. Blood seeped through his fingers as he fell to his knees.

Everyone froze.

Then Eldiss started laughing. 'I think you broke my nose, Prince.'

Kade flew at the kneeling man. But Eldiss was quick on his feet and had jumped up by the time Kade reached him. Using his superior strength, the smaller man pushed Kade forward to unbalance him. Kade's agility saved him from falling face first into the dirt. I was certain Eldiss' men would overpower Kade, but they remained standing at the edge of the trees, their arms folded or resting on their sword hilts, as if watching a bout of wrestling. Drey gently restrained me from going to help Kade.

The two men circled each other, evaluating one another's strengths and weaknesses. Kade was taller and more agile but was still furious and therefore lacking in focus. Eldiss was calm and methodical and also the stronger of the two. He would do damage.

Predictably, Kade's patience ran out first. He lunged at Eldiss, aiming for his broken nose. Eldiss easily dodged to the side, smashing his fist into Kade's ribs as they passed. Kade grunted in pain. Drey's grip around me tightened as I struggled to get free.

'Let them be,' he said quietly.

'But Drey…!'

'Kade started this. Let him be the one to finish it.'

Kade quickly turned back to Eldiss, catching him on the jaw before Eldiss could slip away. As the smaller man was off balance, Kade followed up with a double punch to the stomach. Eldiss crumpled to the floor as Kade stood over him.

'Get up!'

Eldiss chuckled before rolling to his feet. 'You hit like a girl, Prince.'

Kade lunged for him again, punching him in the kidneys before Eldiss whipped round and hit Kade in the face. Blood seeped from a small cut above his left eye. He rubbed it away, irritated.

'Why doesn't he draw his sword and be done with this?'

Drey remained calm. 'Eldiss has not drawn his. Kade will not be the first to draw blades.'

'For the love of Mobis. Your stupid rules are going to get him killed.'

'Look for the details.'

I reluctantly took my gaze away from Kade and looked at the men standing by the trees. They were still relaxed, despite the beating their leader was getting. Not one had made a move to help him. I looked back at Eldiss. His arrogant smile was still in place, taunting Kade into making rash moves.

But Kade's anger was dissolving. His attacks were slowing and their force was reduced. The lunges were more calculated, connecting more often but causing less damage. Both men were bloodied, their breathing forced.

Finally, Kade dived in a false attack at Eldiss' face, grabbing the arm that came up to defend his damaged nose. Kade twisted the arm, taking it up Eldiss' back and forcing him to his knees. He grabbed the man's short brown hair and pulled so that Eldiss could see Kade towering over him.

'Enough,' Kade growled.

The smile had gone, and Eldiss looked at the prince with an honest expression for the first time. 'Well played.'

Kade shoved him forward in frustration, then turned his back on the Traveller and walked over to me. He looked deep into my eyes as he cupped the side of my face. The sudden release of tension, and relief that he had not been killed, brought tears to my eyes. They ran down my cheeks as I tried to blink them away. Kade wiped them tenderly with his torn and bloody knuckles.

'We camp here tonight,' Eldiss instructed his men. They quickly disappeared into the woods as he turned to us. 'Your horse is lame and it will be dark soon,' he said by way of an explanation.

Two of Eldiss' men soon returned with firewood and built a fire while I assisted Drey in bandaging Kade's broken ribs and applying ointment to his numerous cuts and bruises. Eldiss laughed again when I refused to provide ointment to his injuries. Drey was bandaging the warm poultice to Mael's hoof when the remaining men returned with the Travellers' horses. These were quickly tethered alongside ours, and one of the men started cooking a meal from the stores in their saddlebags. Dried meat was softened in a broth with grains and beans. Biscuit was added, which also softened as it soaked up the rich juices of the broth. It was a good meal, and the chill of the earlier hostilities thawed in the warmth of the food.

Curiosity got the better of me and I leaned in towards Drey so that I would not be overheard. 'So, is Eldiss the king of the Travellers?'

Eldiss' eyes flickered in the firelight as he smiled at me. He had heard but did not mock me. 'We have no kings as you would understand the term,' he replied. 'There are no claimed territories here, so no one to take stewardship of them. We move throughout the land wherever the food is plentiful, leaving before we harm its potential renewal. The land is free to all.'

Drey continued. 'The Namori travel in family groups. Eldiss happens to be the head of one of the largest.'

'And just happened to be waiting at the border with Faulknar.' The challenge was clearly heard in Kade's voice.

'Your kingdom appears to be at war, Faulknar. And rumour has it, you're losing.' Eldiss was happy to throw the challenge back. 'I guessed you would come calling sooner or later. We won't fight for you.'

'Nobody is asking you to,' Kade snapped back.

'Of course. Because you are doing so well on your own.'

Drey held up a placating hand. 'Peace. We're just passing through.' He diplomatically changed the topic of discussion. 'Shouldn't you be heading to the winter pastures by now?'

Eldiss smiled at Kade before turning to address Drey's question. 'Truth is, if you had waited a couple more days we would have been gone. My brother is watching the Lindvane path. We were to join Yarna and Neela and journey to the warmer territories.'

'Do you meet up with other families?' I asked, curious about the culture of these people that I had dealt with in Faulknar but never taken the time to understand.

'Sometimes our paths cross. We trade with each other, much as we trade with you in the north. For much of the year we are isolated to our own families. But twice, once in the winter and once in summer, as many families as possible come together for a period of feasting and celebration. Horses are traded, alliances made.' He looked at me and winked.

'He means there's a lot of sex,' grumbled Kade.

'Something you could probably do with more of, Prince.'

Kade scowled at the implied insult, but I could not help but giggle as Drey glared at both of us, hoping we wouldn't be encouraged. The talk continued on a superficial basis, with Eldiss and his men telling me about the games and the dancing that were common at the festivals. Eldiss resisted teasing Kade further, and the atmosphere was relaxed and companionable by the time I snuggled into Kade and fell asleep.

The next day Mael was sound enough to walk, although all of us travelled on foot rather than riding in order to rest the horses. The Travellers' horses were tall and sleek, highly strung with a proud head carriage and raised tails. They were mainly grey with black or brown spots and dark grey tails. There was an obvious affection between the horses and the men, with the horses frequently nudging their riders or nibbling at their tunics. They were led on rope halters rather than the metal bits used to control our mounts.

We followed the stream all morning, watching it grow into a wide river. The boulders visible under the surface created eddies and tides that would make crossing it perilous. The forest grew thickly on the far bank, while we followed a clear trail through grasslands and meadows. The air was filled with birds claiming their territories, or shrilling alarm calls when we got too close. Small deer were frequently seen on the far bank, although they were too shy to visit us in the meadows. During the afternoon we left the river, following the trail over more contoured terrain. Summiting the rolling hills allowed a good view of the countryside falling away in front of us. There was no evidence of the cultivation seen in Faulknar, with marked boundaries and linear hedgerows. The meadows blended naturally with the pockets of trees in small woodlands. The hedgerows meandered where they willed, providing food and shelter for uncountable numbers of creatures. The meadow flowers grew tall, vibrant colours attracting butterflies and bees to their pollen. It was easy to forget the war raging destruction and despair across Faulknar, and to enjoy the simple glory of The Lady's nature.

During the early evening we reached the top of the hill that looked down on a meadow cut in two by a small river. Camped by the water were ten wooden carts, each covered with a brightly coloured sheet that formed a half-moon on the back of the wagon. I recognised the shelters from the Travellers that traded in Liegeport but had not seen them mounted onto carts before. Eldiss caught me staring and smiled.

'Makes them easier to transport. We can store everything inside, move at will, and ride in comfort.'

He pointed to the wooden bench in front of the covered trailer. Each had been covered with a cloth matching that of the shelter and looked comfortably padded even from this distance. Three large fires were already burning, the scent of cooking food drifting into the air. A number of women were performing domestic duties, while the few elders tried to control the children that ran around the fires playing with the dogs that joined in noisily with their games. I felt myself smiling at the carefree nature of the scene. A young boy saw us on the crest of the hill and waved enthusiastically, drawing the attention of the others. The camp stirred like a disturbed ants' nest, with frantic tidying away of the washing and mending, while the children were sent into the shelters to fetch pots and bowls.

The evening light was dimming towards dusk when we arrived at the camp. Small lanterns hung from the wagons, adding to the energy of the scene as the flames caused shadows to dance. The aromas of cooking meat had my stomach growling in anticipation.

'It's about time you came home to me, husband.'

A beautiful woman marched towards Eldiss. She had long black hair held back by red ribbons that matched her dress. She was smiling warmly, and her pleasure was matched by Eldiss. Without any concern for Kade, Drey or me, she wrapped her arms around her husband's neck and kissed him passionately. She curled a leg around his as he pulled her to him with both hands on her bottom. The kiss lasted longer than was appropriate.

Eventually, Eldiss broke the kiss. 'May I introduce my lovely lady wife, Yarna.'

She pulled away from him as quickly as she had hugged him, turning to smile at us warmly. 'Welcome. You are just in time for food.'

She did not appear to be at all bothered by the presence of three strangers in her camp. She guided the men to the nearest fire and bade them sit while sending a young girl to fetch them a drink. Other women came to collect our horses, but not before planting equally passionate kisses on the returning men. They smiled suggestively at Kade, while an elder grandmother winked at Drey. Two small boys, who looked like twins, fell into Eldiss' lap as soon as he sat down.

'Papa, did you miss us? Papa, tell us where you've been. Papa, did you bring presents?'

Eldiss was bombarded with questions from his sons. He laughed indulgently as an older girl brought him a beaker of wine. He smiled up at her and she kissed the top of his head affectionately. Kade and Drey were also offered wine, but Yarna waved away the one offered to me.

'We have work to do,' she said, taking my hand.

She took me to a covered wagon with bright images of horses painted on the scrubbed leather. She threw back the flaps covering the end of the shelter and ushered me inside. Two beds were pushed against the walls, allowing a passage in the middle. I sat on one while Yarna went to the far end of the wagon where a large chest was being used as a table. She collected several small metal clips and a handful of blue and white flowers from a dish that was resting on the chest. She studied me for a couple of heartbeats, before nodding and reaching into one of the drawers that were under the beds to remove a bone comb.

'Right,' she said, turning me so I sat sideways on the bed. 'Let's see what we can do here.'

She combed my hair rhythmically, gently removing the tangles that had developed over the last few days. She parted my hair to the right, rather than in the middle where I always parted it. The change allowed my black fringe to fall over my left eye before being tucked behind my ear. Once satisfied all the tangles had been removed, Yarna twisted sections of my hair into the stems of the flowers, holding them in place with the hairpins. She stood back and examined her work.

'Why the frown?' she laughed.

I bit my lip, unwilling to offend her after all the trouble she had gone to. But I did not understand why she had taken the time.

'Why are you doing this?'

She laughed easily again. 'What's the point of anything if we girls can't dress up and look pretty for the boys?'

She winked at me and I blushed at the insinuation. 'After the welcome we got from Eldiss, and the way he keeps stinging Kade, I didn't expect… this.' I waved in the general direction of my hair.

Yarna sighed. She sat on the bed opposite me and took my hands in hers. 'Eldiss does have a gift for annoying some. But he does what he has to do.'

The calm that had been nurtured over the previous day had been superficial, and my anger was easily provoked. 'He didn't have to break his ribs!'

She rubbed my hands with her thumbs while searching for the right words. 'We have watched your war and seen what it has done to your land and your people. We do not want that here.'

'That's not why we're here.'

She looked deep into my eyes to make sure I was listening intently. 'Your war has affected us. Your people no longer trade with us. That's not so much of a hardship. We have this land for all our needs.' She smiled sadly. 'We trade with you because we like to see new places and meet new people.'

'Eldiss has already said that he won't fight.'

'If the war continues, he may have no choice. Once your land has been destroyed, you will look to our green pastures and see no protectors, no overlords to stop you taking what you need. Eldiss needs to decide who to fight, should that day come. To protect all that we are. He will fight for that.'

She held my gaze with an honesty that was humbling. Although Faulknar was a long way away, Yarna feared for her family just as all people did.

'You understand now? Eldiss needs to know what kind of man your prince is. In case he must face him in battle.'

I shivered. I did not want to fight these people. I knew Kade would not. But I also understood the starving farmers in Faulknar, and how tempting the rolling hills of this land would be to them.

'We will do all we can to avoid that.'

Yarna smiled. 'I know.' She gave my hands one last squeeze before jumping up and reaching for another drawer under the bed. 'Enough of this depressing talk. We have men to impress.'

She withdrew two long dresses. The blue one she passed to me while she held a pale yellow one against herself. She grinned in approval and we changed into the dresses. She helped me remove my tunic without disturbing the flowers in my hair and fastened the many buttons that ran the length of the dress' back. It felt strange to be wearing a dress, especially one that hugged my curves and exposed my shoulders. But I had to admit I did feel special as I fastened the buttons on Yarna's dress.

Yarna led the way back to those sitting around the larger central fire. Eldiss jumped up and grabbed her around the waist as soon as he saw her, swinging her round in a circle while she squealed. Kade stood to greet me.

'You look amazing,' he breathed.

I felt him tremble as he took my hand and we sat together by the fire. I was offered food and wine but was distracted by the intensity of the stare that Kade could not help directing at me. He refused to move far from me all evening, ensuring there was always contact in the form of a hand or an arm.

The evening progressed into a loud celebration with music and dancing. Kade was encouraged to sing and entertained all with wild tales of mad deeds. The children juggled with painted rocks, displaying great skill with their complex routines. One of the older boys juggled with flaming torches that sent sparks flying into the night sky. The mood was merry, but I noticed Yarna looking increasingly tense. Eldiss frequently reassured her but she would not settle. She eventually sent her youngest daughter on an errand to one of the trailers. The girl was gone a matter of moments before she ran back to Yarna.

'Neela is really sick, Mama.'

Yarna paled as she turned to Drey. 'My sister-by-marriage. She's carrying Saldor's child. Eldiss' brother. She should have birthed before now.'

Drey nodded quickly. 'Of course.' He called to me as he followed Yarna to the wagon. 'Tallen, collect my herbs. They are with the saddles. Bring them to me in Neela's shelter.'

I ran as fast as I could to get the herbs as the festive mood around the campfire evaporated. Children were sent to bed while the women sat with their husbands, their concern clear on their faces. I took the herbs to Drey.

Neela was lying on the bed to the left side of her wagon. Sweat had stuck her dark hair to her pale face and she fixed her gaze on the shelter roof. She had bitten her lips and they were cracked and bleeding. She gripped the blanket so hard in her fists that the bones were showing through her knuckles. She let out a small whimper as I watched her body convulse as her abdomen contracted.

Drey grabbed the bag from me as Yarna shouted at a young girl I had not seen before. 'Why didn't you come and get me like I told you to?'

With her red, puffy eyes, the girl looked like she had been crying for some time. 'I was too scared to leave her.'

Yarna rubbed her face with her hands. 'Emez,' she said to her daughter, 'take Reema for some food.'

The two girls left and Yarna slumped down on the spare bed. Her hands covered her mouth as her eyes pleaded with Drey to help. Drey ignored Yarna and me, concentrating on what he was doing.

He had removed a stick of charcoal from the herb bag and was drawing on Neela's arms. The symbols he drew looked like the boxes and lines that I saw when I first started to learn to read. He drew five symbols on each arm before replacing the charcoal in the bag. He thrust the bag towards me without taking his eyes off Neela, and I took it before standing as far away from him as was possible in the small shelter. Drey removed the rose quartz from around his neck, holding it between both palms for a number of heartbeats while he closed his eyes. He then traced over the charcoal letters with the point of the crystal. I felt my eyes grow large as the crystal left a glow of silver light around the ciphers, wherever the stone touched skin. Neela's eyes closed as Drey completed the last symbol, and her body relaxed into the bed. Her breathing slowed.

Drey replaced the quartz around his neck. He closed his eyes again before holding his hands out four or five hand-widths apart, a hand-width above Neela's swollen belly. He flexed his fingers, then moved them in a flowing pattern as if feeling a moulded stone. He covered the whole of the area between his hands with his exploring fingers, his eyes remaining closed. He took a deep breath and pressed the air between his two hands.

My jaw fell open as I watched the movements he made with his hands reflected in the ripples of the muscle of Neela's abdomen. As Drey moulded the air, Neela's pregnant belly moved left and right in synchrony with his hands. It was as if Drey were manipulating an invisible baby, causing the child within Neela to follow his directions.

Using the tiniest of movements, the infant that had lain across Neela's abdomen, preventing it from passing into the birth canal, was turned so that its head was pointing down. Drey took painstaking care to fold its limbs into a streamlined shape. He fussed over the details, ensuring the very best chances for the both the mother and the baby's survival. Only when he was satisfied with the smallest of factors did he open his eyes.

His voice was strained. 'Yarna. Bring me fresh river water.'

I found my voice as Yarna left. 'So, this is the point of magick.'

A ghost of a smile rippled over his lips as we both ignored the shouting outside. 'Charcoal and quartz, fire and earth, are used to produce the magick. Water and air will be used to release the spell.'

'I don't know what to say. What you did… It was incredible.'

'The baby's not born yet,' he cautioned.

Yarna returned with the water, which Drey used to wipe the charcoal from Neela's arms. He blew gently to dry the skin, and the silver light faded as he did so. Neela opened her eyes slowly as if waking from a deep sleep. Almost immediately, her body was racked with a contraction. Tears spilled from Yarna's eyes as it became clear that these pains were more natural and productive. Neela reached for her marriage-sister's hand, squeezing as another spasm ripped through her body.

Drey assumed the position between Neela's spread legs, assisting the baby in its escape from the womb, easing the slimy bundle into the world. Everyone's faces erupted into manic grins as the tiny boy cried in protest. The birth had been perfect.

Drey looked exhausted by the time we left the shelter. His face had paled and the lines around his eyes appeared a little deeper. We had barely walked three steps from the cart when we heard the commotion. Kade and Eldiss were standing with their backs to us. Eldiss had his hand on the chest of the man in front of him, restraining him from coming towards us. His face bore a resemblance to Eldiss' but was contorted in anger as he shouted at the shorter man.

'Let me through, Eldiss. I'll rip his head off if he hurts her.'

Eldiss remained calm. 'Let it go, brother. The man is a *zaratos*. He's helping her.'

'It sounds like he's killing her.'

He looked up and saw Drey and me standing outside Neela's shelter. Pushing past his brother, Saldor ran towards Drey, grabbing his tunic before Eldiss could react. Drey remained passive, holding his hands up, placating. Catching up with him, Kade took hold of one of Saldor's arms, while Eldiss took the other.

'Saldor. She's fine,' said Drey in a quiet voice. 'And so is your son.'

Saldor froze for several heartbeats while he considered the information. He frowned at the same time as a smile developed. 'I have a son?'

'See for yourself.'

We all turned to see Yarna emerge from the shelter carrying a tiny bundle wrapped in blankets. She walked to stand beside Saldor, pulling a corner of the wrap down so the small, serene face could be seen. Saldor let go of Drey to hold his son. Tears spilled down his face as he gently rubbed the smooth, chubby cheeks.

Eldiss clasped Drey's wrist with both hands. 'Well played, old man.' Drey nodded in acknowledgement as Eldiss continued, 'Thank you.'

Chapter Fourteen

The advantage of the covered wagons was well demonstrated the following day when we were able to travel while Neela remained in bed with her son. The pace was slow, with the Travellers seeing no reason to hurry. We enjoyed the mild weather while learning about the land and its wildlife, the history and culture of the Travellers. The company was pleasant and the mood was merry after the birth of the child. We stayed with the Travellers for three days before our journeys diverged. I was sad to leave their company and returned Yarna's hug with as much strength and passion.

Kade walked to one side with Eldiss. 'I don't need you to join us. Just don't join the Lindvanes.'

Eldiss laughed. 'Well, that would depend on their offer.'

Kade raised an eyebrow. 'Eldiss?'

The smaller man nodded in defeat, clasping Kade's wrist in the manner of warriors. 'It would be a shame to kill you in battle, friend.'

The prince smiled. 'I think you would find that I would be the one killing you.'

The two men laughed easily, having found a mutual respect during the previous days. Perhaps the beginnings of a friendship. They hugged briefly before returning to the rest of us. Eldiss waved at his brother, who came forward carrying a pair of saddlebags.

'Take this food,' said Saldor. 'A small thank-you for my son.'

Drey nodded his head in acknowledgement. 'Thanks are not necessary.' But he knew that refusing the token would insult the proud man and took the supplies with good grace.

We waited until the covered carts had moved behind the hill, reluctant to continue our journey, knowing the short respite was over and that the dangerous part of our task was yet to come. All three of us were quiet, lost in our own thoughts as we secured the gifted saddlebags to Mael. We slowly rode away, the future's possibilities weighing heavily upon us.

The rain started that afternoon. It began as a persistent mist of drizzle that did not feel like rain, but still made everything wet. By the evening it had increased to harder drops that managed to drip down collars and seep through oil-treated leather. A low mood degenerated into a miserable one by the time we set up camp under treated sheets, eating dried trail rations as the available wood was too wet to make a fire.

The rain continued for the five days it took to get to the Lindvane path cut into the chalky cliffs. The prospect of scaling a soaked cliff in blinding rain was not a pleasant one. As with the descent, we were to leave at first light in order to have the full day to complete the climb. No one slept very well that night and we were ready to face the challenge before the grey light of pre-dawn.

There was no conversation as we concentrated on maintaining our footing on the crumbling rock. The rainy mist made it difficult for me to see Mael's rump ahead of me. When I turned, I could not see Drey behind me. The path was steep as it zigzagged up the cliff. Sweat soon mixed with the rain dripping down my back. Several times I stumbled as the stones moved under my feet, bruising my hands and knees as I hit the ground. Nalya slipped and skidded. Her breath rushed noisily out of her nostrils, but she continued forward bravely.

We were less than a third of the way up the cliff when the path crumbled away from my left foot. My balance shifted as I began to slide over the edge. Instinctively I gripped Nalya's reins tighter as she planted her feet and pulled heroically against my weight. For several heartbeats that struck painfully against my chest, I hung over the side of the cliff. My shoulders screamed in protest while my legs trembled in mid-air. Drey and Kade called out at my cry but were unable to help as the path was too narrow for them to get past the horses. I couldn't answer them as my mind raced with a number of different ways I was about to die. My arms giving way. The reins breaking. Nalya plunging over the cliff after me.

It slowly became clear that Nalya was able to hold my weight, and that neither my arms nor the reins were going to give way. I hesitantly used my feet to explore the cliff face, looking for footholds to provide leverage.

The chalk crumbled as soon as I put any weight on it. With my stomach clenching in fear, I carefully pulled against the reins to lift myself. I prayed to The Lady that everything would hold – Nalya, the reins, my grip. Hand-width by hand-width I dragged myself up the leather straps and crawled over the side of the cliff onto the trail. I lay on the ground, panting as my heartbeat and breath raced out of control. My whole body shuddered, my kneecaps jumping uncomfortably.

Kade demanded information.

'I'm fine,' I was finally able to tell him. 'The path gave way and I fell over the edge.' I heard his involuntary yelp. 'I'm fine. Nalya was amazing. She stopped me falling.'

'Did it never occur to you to ask for help?!'

I was surprised by the tone of Drey's question and confused by his obvious anger. 'I didn't fall over the edge on purpose.'

'I could have helped,' he snapped back, 'if I'd known what was happening.'

My anger at Drey channelled my adrenaline into a more constructive direction. I stood up, shouting at him. 'I was rather busy, and I don't think you pushing past Nalya would have been particularly helpful.'

'There are other things I could have tried,' he retorted. 'Magickal things.'

I turned to look at my horse. She was snorting forcibly, so I could feel her hot breath on my face. The whites of her eyes were visible in the gloom as the tense muscles pulled within her face. Her legs trembled and a faint sheen of sweat turned her shoulders a darker grey.

'Oh, Nalya,' I breathed.

I slowly reached up to gently touch her cheek, before moving slowly down to wipe the blood at the corner of her mouth. She quivered but did not move away. I gradually moved my hand up to tickle her ear, scratching in the soft dip where the ear joined the head. She lowered her head and relaxed her lower lip. Slowly, the trembling stopped.

'Are we ready to move on yet?' asked Drey, irritated.

'Yeah, we're fine,' I grumbled back. 'Thank you so much for asking.'

We had not reached the top of the cliff by the time it got dark, but Drey was reluctant to light torches in case the path was being watched by Hayton's men. Our pace slowed to a torturous crawl, testing every footstep before committing our weight. We strained our ears trying to hear any changes in the sound of our footsteps that might indicate loose soil, or any activity at the top of the cliff that could suggest an ambush. We were exhausted by the time we reached level ground, and thankful for the stable grass beneath our feet. I was ready to collapse as soon as we got to the top, but Drey insisted we continue on to the woods that loomed black a short distance away.

It was another cold camp and we burrowed through a bramble thicket to ensure we were not discovered. We were allocated shifts for keeping guard, and there seemed too many things to do before Drey would allow me to rest. I did not resent the time spent ensuring Nalya was groomed, fed and comfortable.

We stayed close to the woods for the next few days, trusting the trees to disguise our presence. We crossed a countryside quite unlike the one we were familiar with in Faulknar. The flatlands were replaced with rolling hills that got steeper the further we travelled from the chalk cliffs. The small farms supporting individual families were lost beneath large fields that would support more than one community. It would have taken us half a day just to ride between the hedgerows that marked the field boundaries. Several labourers worked in the fields, collecting root vegetables while the rain beat against their bent backs. Overseeing them were two or three men on horseback. They would watch and bark orders, but never help. The horses wore oil-treated sheets over their rumps, clearly marked with the Boar crest.

'Seems Hayton controls his land very closely,' noted Kade.

'The people are prevented from owning land,' Drey explained to me. 'The farms are owned by the lords, who are carefully managed by their king. Hayton removes any lord who does not offer his unquestioning loyalty.'

'Or who helps himself to the produce,' interrupted Kade.

Drey nodded. 'All the produce goes to the capital, Bostown. Hayton's stewards allocate a proportion to the lord who produced the goods, who then has to finance the transport to and from Bostown.'

'Seems a lot of effort.'

'But a profitable one.'

The rain eventually stopped, leaving the ground muddy and the air heavy. The mornings were covered by a thick mist that would not disperse until midday. The nights stayed darker for longer. The woods thinned before disappearing completely, forcing us to ride on small trails and minor roads. We avoided most people, keeping the hoods of our cloaks pulled far over our faces. The Lindvanes did not seem to be a talkative people, and we travelled quite easily without discovery. The trail took us to a river, swollen by the days of heavy rain. The current was fast-moving, foaming past with reeds and branches. The river had breached its bank on the far side, spilling muddy water onto the fields and creating a boggy marshland. The nearside bank still contained the flow, although the mud was being eaten away by the rushing current, making the side unstable.

'There's no way we will be able to cross here,' Drey said quietly.

Kade turned to him as I watched debris being carried away by the water. 'There must be a bridge around here.'

Drey nodded. 'There should be a crossing west of here, but it's a main trade route and will probably be guarded by Hayton's men.' He looked critically at Kade. 'Not really an option any more.'

Kade had the grace to look chastened. My initial treatment by Eldiss had been meted out in order to control Kade, and now safe passage over the river had been denied due to his presence. I tried to smile reassuringly at him, but he avoided my gaze.

Drey continued. 'There may be a smaller bridge eastwards. It takes us further into Lindvane but with the river being so flooded, unfortunately that can't be helped.'

We rode for the rest of the day alongside the river, seeing few people and even less evidence of a bridge. The trail grew smaller and smaller until it was little more than a deer track through gorse and scrub. We made a morose camp that night, deciding to spend half of the next day looking for a bridge, before turning back to the main crossing. We had a day and a half to come up with a plan to get Kade safely past the guards that would be there.

It was mid-morning the next day when we finally found the crossing. Or what was left of it. The wooden struts and planking were intact on both sides of the water, but the force of the swollen river had removed the middle struts. The joining planks had been washed away, leaving a large, gaping hole that prevented us from crossing. We spent several moments staring forlornly at the destroyed bridge.

Kade broke the silence. 'Mael could swim across.'

'Are you insane?' I shouted at him.

'The river is narrower here than at any other point we have seen so far. Mael is the strongest horse.' He shrugged. 'It's here or we return to the bridge.'

Kade and I looked at Drey. He scowled at the river for several heartbeats.

'It's a crazy idea,' Kade said eventually. 'But perhaps we need a bit of craziness to change our luck.'

I couldn't believe it. 'You're both insane.' I turned on Kade. 'You'll be smashed to pieces on the rocks below the surface. You'll break Mael's legs and we'll be stranded in Lindvane. You'll be—'

'You think I don't know that? What other option is there?'

I couldn't think of one. So I sulked.

'We'll tie a rope to Mael's saddle,' Drey instructed. 'If you get across we can use it to help the other horses. If you don't...'

Drey didn't need to finish the sentence. We all knew the consequences of failure. I couldn't bear to watch, but neither could I take my eyes away from Kade as he guided Mael into the water. Almost immediately Mael struggled against the current. The large bay was a strong swimmer, but he was being buffeted by the river debris as well as the pull of the water. For every horse-length he gained across the river, he was carried two horse-lengths down it. He was soon tiring. As was Kade, clinging desperately to the horse's mane.

I felt the quality of the air around us change, seeming to vibrate as I became more aware of its presence. I turned to Drey, who was sitting calmly astride Mupp. His arms relaxed at his sides, palms turned towards the river. He looked at Kade and Mael, but his gaze appeared focused on something much further away. Mael rose a little higher in the water as his forelegs powered against the current. He gained several extra strokes before his strength failed again. The horse disappeared under the water, taking Kade with him. I could not see either of them for a couple of heartbeats that seemed to last forever. Then they resurfaced, coughing water from their lungs.

'Enough of this!' I tightened the rope on Nalya's saddle and encouraged her to walk backwards with gentle pressure on her reins, drawing in the slack. Mael was heavier than my little grey, and there was the added pull of the water. Nalya struggled, but valiantly held her ground. It was enough to stop them drifting further down the river.

Drey also changed focus. No longer looking at Kade, he shifted his gaze to several paces upriver from the struggling horse. The river surged against an invisible barrier. A curve across separated it in two. White water foamed against the invisible boundary, while below it the river became calm and placid. The current was directed away from the pair, allowing Nalya to draw Mael back towards the near bank. Despite his rapidly vanishing strength, the protection from the current allowed the bay to reach the shore safely. It was only when I was noting with relief that Kade had made it back without injury that I noticed the saddlebags had been lost. Kade's sleeping mat and shelter had gone, along with the food given to us by Saldor. Kade had risked his life and Mael's and only succeeded in making the situation worse than it was before.

I slumped a little further into my saddle, before turning to Drey to see what we were to do now. I was shocked to see him looking so pale. His eyes had become darkened wells within a face as white as snow. The muscles drooped, dragging the corners of his mouth down and accentuating the lines in his face. His hands trembled as they lay folded on the saddle.

He felt me watching him and turned with a small smile on his face. 'There's always a price to pay when messing with nature.'

We camped by the river, judging that the need for a fire to warm Kade was more important than the risk of being discovered. I made ginger tea to help restore some of Kade's and Drey's energy. I also added some ginger to Mael's and Nalya's feed. I gave Kade my sleeping mat, curling up next to him to add my warmth to that of the tea.

My dream that night was of a crowded marketplace. It was not a market I recognised, and the people were all strangers. I moved from stall to stall looking at the goods on display – food, clothing, household items. The merchants scowled at me, muttering words I did not understand. Their meaning was clear, however: I was not welcome there. The streets became more crowded, and I was jostled by passers-by as they rushed down the narrow alleyways between the stalls. More than once I was pushed into a stall, knocking things over. The mutterings turned to shouts. More menacing. More threatening. Fists were waved at me as I tried to move out of the way while being blocked by the crowd. People started shoving me out of their way. Their hands hurt me.

Kade stood at the far end of the market. He was clean-shaven and wore a cloak displaying the crest of Faulknar. His face was sad; his eyes like dark puddles. The wind lifted his hair for a moment, blowing his cloak around his legs.

A woman pushed past me and I fell against a stall selling cheap jewellery. I quickly stood up and looked for Kade. He was no longer in view. I started to push through the crowd, trying to get to where I had last seen him. But gripping hands prevented me from moving.

'You stole that pendant,' accused the stallholder.

I shook my head. 'No. No. I didn't take anything.'

'Yes, you did. I saw you take it.' A round woman wearing a plain headscarf joined in.

I tried to pull away but the stallholder's grip did not slacken. 'I didn't take anything.'

A crowd had formed around me. Accusations were coming from all directions, from people who had been nowhere near the stall and could not possibly have seen anything. Their word was believed over mine. I was a stranger. Untrustworthy. People were poking and pinching. I squirmed this way and that but was unable to avoid the bruising contact.

Then I saw Kade watching. He was closer than before but still several stalls away. His sad face seemed to judge me guilty. I struggled harder. I had to convince him that I hadn't taken anything; that they had got it wrong. But there were so many of them. He lowered his eyes and shook his head slowly, then turned and walked away.

I screamed after him, desperately proclaiming my innocence, shouting that it was all a mistake.

He didn't look back.

I awoke in the darkness. Everything was silent. Not even the hoot of an owl. I concentrated on slowing my breathing, quieting the hammering of my heart. I strained to hear Drey's soft breathing, deep and regular. I leaned back, needing Kade's firm presence to ground me.

He was not there.

My heart leapt into the back of my throat as my pulse thundered in my ears. My breathing stuttered as all my muscles tightened simultaneously. I went ice-cold at the same time as sweat beaded on the backs of my hands and down my spine. My mind screamed endless possibilities. I rejected all of them, preferring to believe that he had just gone to relieve himself or check on the horses. I concentrated on my breathing again, counting to five before exhaling and again before inhaling, all the time telling myself that he would be back soon.

He wasn't, and I could no longer wait for him. I got up quietly, so as not to wake Drey. I went straight to the horses to see if Kade was there. He wasn't, and neither was Mael. Panic was starting to tickle the back of my throat. I returned to Drey, touching his shoulder as I whispered his name. He was awake instantly, looking at me with clear eyes.

'Kade's gone.'

He hesitated, trying to judge my concerns. 'He's probably just checking the area. Making sure no one is near.'

'Mael's gone too.'

Drey hesitated again, then nodded. He sat up, his eyes losing their focus. I now knew that meant he was trying to contact Kade through their connection of minds. He quickly shook his head.

'I can't find him. He must be too far away.'

'Drey, I'm worried...'

He stood up smoothly, placing a reassuring hand on my shoulder. 'I'm sure he's just scouting the area. He'll be fine.'

'Would you know? Could you *feel* it if something had happened to him?'

He shrugged. 'I don't know.'

It did little to reassure me. I ducked out from under his hand and started pacing. I couldn't sit around doing nothing.

'Why don't we search the area, see if we can find tracks?' I heard the pleading in my voice.

I knew we were unlikely to find anything in the dark, but it gave me something to do. It stopped me thinking about all the horrible things that could have happened.

Drey started near the horses while I began on the opposite side of the camp. The moon provided some light, but it came and went. Any tracks would have to be large and obvious for me to find them. I checked the bushes and low branches for signs of damage.

A sudden crash echoed through the forest. It sounded like a tree being felled. I ran to where Drey had been searching and found him rubbing his arm.

'He left tripwires.' Drey grinned. 'Clever boy. We would have been warned.'

'We still don't know where he is.'

'But we know he wasn't taken. Wherever he went, he went voluntarily.' He guided me back to the fire. 'We are going to have to be patient and wait for him to return.'

I scowled, hating to be so helpless. I busied myself by building up the fire and making tea. We had almost finished our drinks when I heard movement in the trees. I pulled my sword as I stood, ready for the attack.

Drey held up his hand. 'It's Kade.'

I did not relax or sheath my sword. I was angry, my concern replaced with white-hot rage now I knew he was safe. I heard him tether Mael and the soft swish as the saddle was removed. He stepped into the light of the fire carrying two large sacks.

I ran at him, my sword pointed at his heart.

'Fearsome Father, Tal.' He jumped out of my way, dropping the sacks. 'What are you doing?'

'Of all the stupid, idiotic, irresponsible, ridiculous...' I turned to slap his back with the flat of my sword, missing as he skipped away. 'Did you not think for one minute...?'

He held his hands up, placating. 'I got food.' He pointed to the sacks, which had opened when he dropped them. A cured ham and fresh bread could be seen poking out.

'Oh, that's all right then,' I continued sarcastically. 'You try to get yourself killed, but at least we can eat.'

'I didn't get killed.'

'What if someone had recognised you?'

Kade was getting angry now, the volume of his voice rising. 'What if they had? No one cares about me. I'm the second—'

'...son. I know. But I think delivering your severed head to your father would still send the required message, don't you?'

Kade's anger melted, taking mine with it. We looked at each other for several heartbeats before I lowered my gaze and sheathed my sword. Kade grabbed me in a tight embrace, kissing the top of my head gently. I squeezed his back as hard as I could, biting my lip to stop the tears of relief from spilling down my cheeks. It was a long time before I could speak.

'I can't lose you, Kade,' I said into his shirt. 'I can't lose you too.'

'I know,' he whispered into my hair, gently stroking the back of my head. 'I know.'

We turned to see Drey ripping strips off the ham. Despite my anger at the risk Kade had taken to get it, I had to admit that the fresh food tasted very good.

The next day we travelled back to the main crossing. We could see no option but to face the soldiers that stood guard at the bridge. We would try to cross with the other traders, hoping Hayton's men would not look too closely. If that failed, we would have to fight our way across. After days of rain, we hoped for another miserable day to increase our chances of getting across without challenge. The day stayed stubbornly clear and dry. As did the next day.

We stopped the horses on the rim of the hill and watched the activity on the bridge. There were four soldiers, two at each end, checking those that wanted to cross and inspecting their sacks and carts. No one got through without being seen by the guards. With the number of weapons we were carrying, there was no way we would be able to get across without a fight.

'Let's hope those at the far end are stupid enough to join the first two when the fighting starts,' said Kade.

We rode slowly down the hill, joining the few people making their way to the bridge. My sword and knives were easily accessible but hidden by my light cloak. I could feel the apprehension sitting like a rock in my belly, so I concentrated on remembering my lessons with Langdon. *Watch their eyes. Keep your movements fluid. Don't let them dictate your moves. Be aware of what's going on around you.*

The soldiers were having an animated argument with a stocky farmer pushing a cart filled with geese when we arrived at the checkpoint. The geese were hissing at the guards. The farmer was waving his arms around. The other people in the queue were noisily backing the farmer, and the guards were angrily trying to maintain order.

'My geese need to get to Wolfton today,' the farmer was saying.

'You know as well as I do, livestock are not to be taken out of their village.'

'I can't help that. My geese need to be in Wolfton so His Lordship can feed everyone at the wedding.'

'I have had no instructions that more geese are needed. You may not cross the bridge.'

The guards tried to turn the cart around, succeeding only in getting bitten by the distressed birds. The farmer refused to help, repeating his need to get to Wolfton market. I could see the soldiers at the far end of the bridge watching the commotion nervously, undecided whether to stay at their post or help their colleagues. They glanced towards the geese, then at the empty countryside on their side of the river, and back to the disturbance in front of us. Finally, they looked at each other, coming to an agreement and running to join the others.

'Get ready,' said Drey softly. 'This could be our chance.'

I rested my hand on the handle of one of my throwing knives, guiding Nalya after Drey as he rode towards the bridge.

'Excuse me,' he said politely. 'I don't mean to be a bother, but we are running a little late. Can we pass through while you deal with this problem?'

'Wait your turn,' came the terse reply.

'Yes, yes. I'm sure that's the normal course of events. But I really must insist. We are dreadfully late already.'

Drey rode up to the cart, with Kade and me close behind. The geese erupted into a new fit of hissing, while the farmer started complaining about distressed birds fetching low prices. Drey moved to push through the centre pair of guards. Kade went to the left and I went to the right. But the soldiers were well trained and were not intimidated by our horses.

'You will wait your turn,' said the guard next to me, grabbing Nalya's reins.

Nalya spooked at the rough handling, rearing up until she was restrained by the hold on her reins. I let go of the knife handle in order to maintain my balance. My cloak slipped open, revealing the knives. The guard let go of Nalya, stepping back to draw his sword while shouting a warning to the others. Two soldiers turned towards Kade while the remaining one moved towards Drey. Kade kicked Mael in the soft part of his belly, causing the horse to lash out with his hind legs. The hooves crashed into the cart, sending the crated geese flying across the bridge. The thin wooden crates smashed, releasing the birds and causing mayhem. The geese snapped at the farmer and the soldiers. The horses snorted and skipped to avoid the hissing creatures. The farmer was hysterical, chasing his birds and trying to contain them in the broken crates. The other people waiting to cross the bridge saw their opportunity and surged forward. The soldiers shouted at us to dismount. We all drew our swords.

The villagers saw the weapons and decided that they did not want to get involved with such a serious disturbance. They turned back for their homes, each taking at least one goose so the farmer could join them. Thoughts of going to Wolfton market were swiftly forgotten.

We had the advantage of height from being on horseback, but the soldiers could manoeuvre better. They easily moved out of the way of our sweeping thrusts, whilst managing to block our way across the bridge. Without the distraction of the geese, they demonstrated a skill with their weapons that kept me fully focused. Drey and I only had one attacker each to contend with. Kade had to defend himself against two. But I had no time to see how he was faring. My slashes were blocked again and again, my arms growing heavy with the repeated concussion of metal against metal. I blinked away the sweat that was seeping into my eyes, narrowly avoiding a slice to my leg.

The soldier soon tired of battling me on horseback. I had too much of an advantage. He changed tactics. I watched as he turned to slice at Nalya's neck. A rage I had never felt before swept over me, as if I were being wrapped in a soft cloak. The heat flashed through my muscles to provide them with renewed energy. My vision narrowed on the soldier in front of me. I was outraged that he would hurt my horse, let alone try to kill her.

I felt my lips pull back in a primal snarl as I screamed an ancestral roar. I kicked out at his chest, feeling the ribs give way beneath my boot. In the heartbeat it took for him to rebalance himself, I brought my sword down as hard as I could, knowing it would sink home, slicing from neck to ribcage. Blood and tissue sprayed, covering my face. The metallic scent of blood filled my nostrils. Droplets stuck to my skin, still hot with life.

My sword had been halted by a rib, but the weight of the dead man pulled the blade free. I no longer considered him, instead looking up to see where my next foe was. Drey's attacker was on the floor. I could not tell if he was unconscious or dead. I didn't care either way. Kade had dispatched one soldier. He lay on the ground, bleeding from a stomach wound. His liver had probably been sliced, judging from the amount of blood pooling around him. His unseeing eyes looked at the sun. Kade fought with the last guard. I moved to assist him.

Drey had positioned Mupp to block my path. It took several heartbeats for me to recognise him, and several more to accept he wasn't a threat. The snarl slowly left my face and I lowered my sword, as Kade speared the final assailant in the chest. Drey gestured to me to lead the way and I urged Nalya into a trot across the bridge and into the lush grass beyond it.

The cloak of rage slipped from my body, leaving my legs thumping and trembling. The blood and tissue were setting on my face, pulling at the skin. I started to remember the details of what I had done. The way it felt. The smell of death. The sight of dead eyes.

Saliva flooded my mouth as my stomach spasmed. My head felt roasting hot and sweat beaded between my shoulder blades. Acid flooded my mouth, causing me to gag.

I almost fell off my horse in my rush to get to the ground. As soon as my feet touched the grass, I collapsed to my knees. I vomited. And again. Then again, until nothing more than frothy fluid came up, burning the back of my throat. My whole body was trembling as tears ran down my face.

I became aware of Kade stroking my back. He offered me some water and I swilled out my mouth, not trusting my stomach enough to swallow.

'There's a stream a little further on,' said Drey quietly.

Kade helped me back onto Nalya, staying close as we walked the horses the short distance to the stream. I scrubbed my face and hands until they were raw, the cold water doing little to remove the sticky feeling of blood. Kade thoughtfully brought me clean clothes and I buried the stained ones. I would not be able to wear them again.

Too soon, Drey insisted we moved on. We needed to be as far from the bridge as possible before reinforcements came and looked to avenge their comrades.

Chapter Fifteen

Having crossed the river, we travelled quickly through Lindvane. We started early, finished late and stopped only when the horses needed a rest. We avoided populated areas, staying close to woods and marshland. The incident at the bridge had clearly illustrated the perils we were facing. I could no longer pretend that this was just like taking goods from the Liegeport merchants. I had killed a man. And I suspected that he would not be my last.

The border between Lindvane and Hilman was not as obvious as the chalky cliffs that separated the Travellers' lands. The rolling hills of southern Lindvane had steepened as we rode north, but these were still gentle slopes covered in a rich, fertile soil that was good for agriculture. The border into Hilman was marked by small white stones. A faded tusked boar was painted on the sides facing Lindvane. The Hilman ancestors had chosen a stag to symbolise their clan's characteristics. This was painted on the Hilman sides of the stones. There were no patrols, no guards. Crossing the border was as easy as passing between two of the white stones.

Although the landscape did not change dramatically beyond the border, it was clear that the industry in Hilman was again different to that in Lindvane and Faulknar. The fertile soil extended from the border, but I could see the hills rising into jagged mountains on the horizon. The peaks of these mountains were rocky, with only stunted shrubs able to grow in the thin soil and constant wind. As we travelled through Hilman, the countryside was truly stunning. The mountains were interspersed with beautiful valleys and lakes, but these were not suitable for maintaining crops either. The source of income available from these hills and valleys was livestock. In more populated areas, cattle were kept for meat and milk, while in the more mountainous regions sheep and goats provided these products.

The sheep also provided much of the wool that was exported to kingdoms such as Faulknar for clothing and bedding.

Below the mountains, the Hilman exploited the natural resources of their land. The true wealth of the kingdom came from tunnels where they mined precious stones and crystals as well as the metal needed to make weapons. The minerals found in the mountains of Hilman provided for the basic requirements of the three heraldic kingdoms – Faulknar, Lindvane and Hilman. Trade with this kingdom was important for the domestic needs of Faulknar. It was essential for the continued campaign against Lindvane. We avoided villages and farmsteads. We did not want to risk Faulknar being associated with the theft of the Empathy Crystal.

The domineering presence of the mountains made me feel uncomfortable. Almost as soon as we had crossed the border, and I had seen the rocky peaks in the distance, I had felt intimidated by the power implied by their size. The way they had remained impassive and unchanged with the passing of uncountable generations made me feel very small, like I could be so easily crushed. I felt my posture shrinking in response.

The mountains also provided a clear visual reminder of my dreams. Although I knew that these were not the same mountains I had been trapped under during numerous night terrors, I felt that I would be lost forever under their massive boulders if I stopped concentrating for a heartbeat. I found myself sneaking glances at them, waiting for some evidence that they were sentient and malicious. I knew I was being ridiculous, but I could not stop myself.

Unsurprisingly, my dreams mainly used the mountains to remind me of my shortcomings and failures. The rocky paths we rode on during the day became the starting point of many of my dreams at night. Both Laken and Kade were waiting for me in the caverns deep below the craggy peaks, disappointment and disapproval clearly marked on their faces. I endured night after night of frantically searching for them in the tunnels of my greatest fears. Trapped under the crushing weight of rock. Suffocated by the absolute darkness. Desperately needing their reassuring presence, only to be faced with their rejection over and over again.

I slept less, became more irritable with Kade and Drey, and blamed it all on the mountains.

One dream had been different.

We had been in Hilman for a week, riding through mountain trails that overlooked the western sea. I had suffered with a headache all day; a crushing, energy-sapping throb that felt like my head was being squashed by two rocks. One boulder pressed against my forehead above my left eye, the other pushed up through the back of my skull, both trying to meet in the middle. The day was dull and overcast, with the sun obscured by several layers of cloud. But even that dim light stabbed at my brain, making me screw up my eyes. Making the headache worse. I was glad when we stopped for the night. I was given the morning watch, in the hope that a few hours' sleep would clear the pain.

It seemed as if the dream started as soon as I closed my eyes. It started the same way as the others, with Kade, Drey and me walking up a mountain pass. I could see the sea glittering in the sunlight, as seabirds danced and dived. The dream changed when we reached the end of the trail and found a large wooden door sunk into the rock of the mountain. Drey picked up a branch that was lying to the side of him and tapped on the door three times. It slowly opened to expose a dark tunnel leading into the mountain. I left Kade and Drey on the path and entered. The mild apprehension felt in their company became a more familiar fear as I stepped through the doorway. The door closed silently behind me.

The walls of the tunnel glowed a pale blue, providing enough light to be able to walk without stumbling. I followed the path as it angled down into the mountain. I was taken steadily left by the paths and at each junction, the blue light leading the way. I continued for some time, with the soft tap of my footsteps being the only sound, the pounding of my heart a constant presence.

Then I heard it.

It started as a soft scraping, as if something was being dragged along the ground. The left path led towards the sound. I reluctantly followed the lights; the right path being blocked to me. Then came the scraping sound again, nearer this time and definitely like something metallic or shell-like was being hauled. Then a *whoosh* as a large volume of air was expelled from around a corner bending to the right. The hot air blew in my face, strong enough to move my hair, carrying the scent of warm ash with it.

I took a deep breath, wiping my sweaty palms on my leather trousers. I walked slowly forward to look around the corner, curious to see what was waiting for me there but terrified at the same time. My legs shaking with every step.

I had taken two steps towards the corner when the robed stranger I had not seen in my dreams since leaving Liegeport appeared. She stood in the middle of the path, blocking my way. Her hood was pulled forward, so that even though she was standing in front of me I still could not see her face. All fear concerning the creature in the tunnel disappeared as I became enthralled by her calm, ethereal presence. I took another step towards her. She did not step away this time. She simply held up a hand, palm facing me. She had long, slender fingers and skin as pale as moonlight. I stared at the simple beauty of that hand, totally absorbed by it, until I became slowly, gently aware that I was awake, Kade's arm draped over me as he slept.

The next day we turned away from the sea and I never had that dream again.

It took another three days of climbing up and down mountain trails before we reached the peak we were looking for. Villermir had described the mountain under which the crystal was found and being kept. The two summits clearly separated it from the others in the range, with their rocky points that looked like goat horns. The lower slopes were covered with rough grasses and hardy gorse plants that released their scent when the horses' hooves crushed them. Wildlife was scarce with the cold wind predicting a hard season to come. Small hawks hovered above the shrubs hoping for rodents, but few dives were made. I pulled the collar of my cloak a little tighter, shivering at the breeze that managed to get to the bare flesh of my neck, and followed Drey up the trail.

There was a tiny settlement of wooden shacks and covered shelters halfway up, but no one was visible and we passed through without challenge. Small piles of ash were smouldering from the previous night's fires. There were cleaned cooking pots and water jars arranged nearby, suggesting the settlement had been occupied recently.

'It's a miners' camp,' said Drey, seeing my interest in the basic arrangements. 'There will be a permanent village on the other side of the mountain. This is a rough camp for those working in the mine. They stay up here for several weeks at a time, before returning to the comforts of the village.'

We continued along the well-used track until we could see the entrance to the mine, extending into the darkness of the rock. Drey led us off the trail and through the scrub, pushing through small bushes to hide the horses.

We tethered them to the tough stems of the sturdy gorse before returning to observe the mine entrance. I was starting feel a little sick at the thought of going into the mountain. As I watched the entrance, the darkness seemed to writhe and flow like fog. I closed my eyes and took a deep breath, and was glad when I opened my eyes again that the darkness was just darkness.

Kade touched my hand. 'You all right?'

I nodded. 'I will be.'

Hidden by the scrub, we watched the activities of the mine. Three times during the afternoon, small, stocky ponies emerged pulling carts laden with rocks. A young girl would lead a pony down the trail, past the miners' camp and out of sight around the mountain. A long time later, another girl would bring a different pony, pulling an empty cart, and enter the mine. This continued until dusk, when the men that had been inside the shelters when we passed through the camp came up to the mine. With them were three heavily armed soldiers.

'Seems there is something worth protecting in this mountain,' whispered Kade.

I watched them enter the tunnel, fearing that we would have to fight them too in order to get the crystal. My stomach had been tight all day and my shoulders ached from the tension. Despite my words to Kade, I was beginning to think that I was not going to be able to face going inside the mountain. The thought was suppressed as a number of men and young boys came out of the tunnel. Their faces were so dirty that only their eyes and teeth were visible in the twilight. They were followed by a final girl and pony. The men and boys went to the camp, while the girl carried on down the trail.

Drey turned to Kade and me. 'You should get some sleep. I'll wake you at full dark.'

We burrowed back to the horses, wrapping ourselves in the treated sheets to provide a little extra warmth. I felt Kade's breathing slow almost immediately, but I was unable to rest. I tossed and turned with thoughts of the mountain. The darkness. The crushing rock. It was enough to ensure I would not get any sleep. Despite the chill air, sweat trickled down my back. My nausea became more insistent.

As promised, Drey alerted us when it was fully dark. The moon shone intermittently through the clouds that were blown briskly across the sky. The mine entrance was quiet.

'No one has moved since the shift change. The miners will be deep underground by now.' He looked at us before handing small vials of poison. 'Time to go.'

Drey and Kade stepped forward, but I could not move. The fear of the mountain was too much now that the time had come to enter. My face flushed red-hot and ice-cold in waves. Sweat beaded on my lip as my stomach flipped. I couldn't stop my hands from shaking.

The men had only taken a couple of paces forward before noticing I had not joined them. They turned back.

'I can't do this.' My eyes pleaded with them to understand.

'What do you mean, you can't do this?' demanded Drey. 'You have to.'

Kade was watching me. 'The dreams.'

I nodded. 'I just can't.'

'Oh, Father help me.' Drey threw his hands up. 'You choose now to tell me this?'

'I thought it would be all right. I thought I could handle it.' I bit my lip. 'But now that we're here...'

'We don't have time for this.'

'I know!'

Kade came to stand in front of me, taking my hands in his. 'These dreams. You're on your own, right?'

I nodded, and he squeezed my hands.

'Then this is totally different. We're here with you. I won't leave you, Tal. We can get through this together.'

I looked into his soft, melting eyes, desperately trying to convince myself he was right; that I could do this with his help. I *had* to do this. I nodded, and his beautiful smile banished all my dark thoughts, melting my frozen muscles, untwisting my stomach.

Until I looked back at the mountain. But Kade squeezed my hands again, before turning and leading me towards the mine. I concentrated on my breathing and the feel of Kade's hand in mine. The roughness of his skin. The contours of his knuckles. We walked up to the entrance. Kade winked at me.

And I walked into the darkness.

I squeezed Kade's hand. Hard. My breathing became erratic as my heartbeat raced. But I put one foot in front of the other. I could do this.

'I hope we don't have to fight down here.'

I looked at Kade. 'Why?'

'I can't feel my fingers.'

I yelped an apology, letting go of his hand as if it had suddenly turned into flame. 'Sorry.'

He chuckled quietly, his white teeth showing in the gloom. We had not walked far when I heard Drey groan quietly behind us. I turned to see him a few paces away, and strained to see clearly in the darkness. He was outlined against the tunnel entrance, bending over, his hands pressing against his temples.

'Drey?'

Kade and I walked back to him. I could hear his forced breathing.

'I can't do this. I can't come with you.'

'What?!'

'There are protections here. Wards against those with magick.' His voice cracked with pain. 'The buzzing… it hurts… I have to go back.'

'Drey!' I couldn't believe I was losing him already. 'I'm two heartbeats away from losing my mind down here. I need you.'

'I'm sorry, Tallen. Kade will be with you. You'll be fine.' His voice faltered with the pain caused by the magickal protections. He turned away from us and went back towards the tunnel entrance, his silhouette briefly visible as he left the mine.

'I don't believe it. He acts all disappointed in me, like I'm letting everyone down even though this is my worst fear, one that has terrorised my dreams for years, and then he bolts before the first corner. Typical!'

Kade laughed beside me. 'Tal, you're brilliant.'

'What?' I snapped at him.

'Only you could exchange abject fear for righteous anger in the blink of an eye.'

I had to smile. 'Yeah. Well. I suppose it's not his fault.'

Kade gave me a quick hug. 'Come on. Let's find this damned crystal and get out of here.'

We walked deeper into the mountain. Kade had lit a firebrand, quickly blowing it out so the light would not be seen by the miners or soldiers. The glowing embers were enough to prevent us stumbling. The tunnel twisted round and round, with side tunnels at regular intervals. We could hear the sounds of the miners further up the tunnel. A ringing beat, like a muffled blacksmith's hammer on metal. We followed the sound along the main, wider shaft. Eventually this divided into two. The sound of the working mine could be heard further along the left hand tunnel. The right passage quiet, but I could see a faint glow. We decided to follow this path, hoping to find the soldiers guarding the crystal.

We crept along, concentrating on making no noise that would alert the soldiers to our presence. The embers no longer provided any light, but we could see the end of the tunnel clearly. The three soldiers seen earlier were sitting in front of a large wooden door. Two burning torches were placed in brackets either side. The light illuminated the games of dice that the men were playing. They chatted easily to each other, not expecting any challenge this far from the miners and the entrance. Their relaxed body posture suggested a familiar boredom.

Kade reached in his pocket for the glass vial Drey had given him. We were to anoint the blades of my throwing knives. Contact with the poison through a small cut would leave them unconscious for several hours; long enough for us to find the crystal and escape. A deep cut would be enough to kill. Kade held his hand out for a knife.

I shook my head, holding my hand up to emphasis the point. I had seen a small passageway to the right of the soldiers. I pointed this out to Kade. He nodded. We would explore this first to see if there was another way in. I didn't expect there to be one, but all we had to lose was a little time. Staying in the shadows, we crept into the side tunnel. There was a faint yellow light being emitted from a point several paces away on my left. I indicated this to Kade, but he frowned at me in confusion.

I leaned closer so my mouth brushed his ear. 'The light.'

He twisted his head to whisper in my ear. 'What light?'

It was my turn to frown. 'That yellow light.'

'I don't see any light.'

We walked forward towards a gentle glow. As I got closer I could see that the light covered an area of the wall that was as tall as I was, but only six handspans wide. I reached out to touch it.

My hand passed straight through. I snatched it back, my skin still prickling from the contact with the light. 'Merciful Mother.'

'It's just a wall, Tal.'

'You can't see that?'

He patted the wall several times in random places. 'Wall, wall, wall.'

When he touched the yellow glow, his hand stopped in the same place as it had when touching the surrounding rock. It did not pass through as mine had. It was as if the light was not there for him. He returned his attention to the guards.

I placed my hand on the wall once more. Again, it continued through as if no rock was there at all. I felt a slight stinging sensation on the part of my wrist that was bathed in the golden light. I could not see my hand beyond the light but could feel a cool wind against my skin. I pushed my arm in further, moving it in all directions to see if I could feel solid rock again. I only felt air.

'Kade, check this out.'

I turned sideways to the wall. I could just squeeze through the illuminated gap. I wondered briefly whether this was a good idea, just before I stepped through and into a small cavern, glowing with the yellow light.

'Welcome, Dragonslayer.'

My heart lurched as I reached for a knife, prepared for danger. But there was no one else in the cavern. I could not see where the voice had come from. I scanned every corner, but the chamber was well lit and there was nowhere to hide.

My heart slowed as I convinced myself that I had imagined the voice. Then my attention was caught by the small ledge cut into the mountain wall. The source of the light rested on a polished wooden stand: a crystal the size of my hand. It was the colour of freshly churned butter. The clear surface was smooth but had many sides, each about the size of my thumbnail, all laid side by side. Light streamed from each of these faces. It was the most beautiful thing I had ever seen.

It felt wrong to take the crystal from this setting, but I still reached forward to take it. Just to feel it. To hold it. My fingers felt as if they were being stung by swarms of tiny bees as I moved towards the crystal. The sensation changed as I got within a finger-width of the stone. My fingertips pushed through a glacially cold waterfall before finally touching the gem. It felt surprisingly warm, and soft as a day-old chick. I stroked the tiny facets, smooth beneath my exploring fingers, a soft curve separating each face of the crystal.

I reached forward with both hands and picked up the stone. The golden light dimmed to a small, pulsing glow deep within, illuminating my face as I stared at the Empathy Crystal, searching its core for its story. Its foundation in the rivers of fire. Its slumber in the depths of the mountain. Its discovery by the Hilman miners.

I don't know how long I stood gazing at the crystal before I gradually became aware that someone was standing beside me. I turned to see Kade standing a few paces away, looking at me as if I was an unsolvable puzzle.

'You found it.'

'I saw the light.'

'There was no light, Tal. Just solid rock.' He shook his head slowly, back and forth. 'You were standing beside me. Then you weren't. You vanished into solid rock. How did you do that?'

'There was a gap in the wall. How could you not see it?'

'Tal, there was no gap. Well, not until just now. There was a solid wall, and then I saw you holding the crystal in this chamber.'

We fell silent for several heartbeats.

'How did you do that, Tal?'

I shivered with a sudden chill racing down my spine. 'I don't know.'

I reached into my pocket and removed the piece of midnight-blue silk that Drey had given me earlier. I covered the crystal, extinguishing all light, then waited until my eyes had adjusted before taking Kade's hand. He was shaking as much as I was.

'We had better get this to Drey.'

Chapter Sixteen

We had taken two steps towards the hole in the wall when we heard footsteps coming from the passage outside. We looked at each other in the darkness, realising that the crystal's golden light must have been seen by the guards once the gap in the wall became visible to Kade. There was nowhere to hide in the chamber. A warm glow could be seen as the guards lit their way with burning torches.

'Stand beside the gap,' whispered Kade. 'Hopefully they won't look behind them.'

He almost pushed me towards the newly formed entrance and we flattened ourselves against the rock, one either side of the hole, holding our breath as the soldiers advanced. The light came steadily closer.

'How did this hole get here?' muttered one of the guards. 'I never noticed it before.'

'Never came down this way before,' replied another. 'Would've thought they'd've told us, though.'

'We're guarding a locked door, while all the time a great big hole in the wall would let anyone in.'

A torch was pushed through the gap into the chamber. The firelight sent shadows dancing over the rocky walls. I pushed myself further into the wall, causing its sharp points to dig into my back. Cautiously, two guards crept forward and stepped into the cavern.

'Oh, my thieving masters,' cried the one nearest to Kade. 'It's gone. Seven Hells of Mobis. The stone's gone.'

'What're talking about?' The other soldier came further into the cavern.

'The holy stone we were supposed to be looking after. It's gone.' He pointed to the empty ledge from which I had removed the crystal. 'Oh, we are in serious trouble now.'

He turned to leave.

And saw us.

Kade immediately punched him on the jaw, turning him round so that he could slam his fist down on the junction of the head and neck. The soldier crumpled at Kade's feet without making a sound. The second soldier advanced on me. I ducked under his reaching hand, removing a knife from my belt as I came up behind him. I smashed the hilt of the knife into the same spot as Kade had struck the first guard. But I lacked his strength. The guard fell to his knees, but the blow did not knock him out. He groaned loudly at the pain in his head. Then Kade punched him hard in the temple, and the soldier folded and hit the floor, unconscious.

It was too late. The final soldier was running down the passage to investigate the cry. Kade reached for the vial of poison, but there was not enough time. The guard burst through the gap, almost tripping over the fallen bodies of his colleagues. He quickly assessed the situation and turned towards me and Kade. Kade punched him on the jaw, as he had with the first soldier. But this one was prepared. He braced himself against the impact before returning a stunning blow into Kade's abdomen. Kade folded over, gasping for breath. The soldier grinned as he pulled his arm back for another powerful strike.

Without thinking, I plunged the knife into his unguarded side. The blade slid easily into the soft tissue below his ribcage. Blood seeped through the skin and along the blade, making the handle slippery. The soldier stared at me with unbelieving eyes. He clutched his side in a vain attempt to stop the blood that was oozing between his fingers and soaking into his tunic. I gripped the knife a little tighter before removing it. The blood ran a little quicker. The man's eyes widened as he collapsed to his knees. His face had turned a deathly grey.

Kade took the knife from my hand, wiping my fingers and the blade with his shirt. He placed the knife in his belt, then quietly guided me out of the chamber. I was trembling all over, but I felt numb. I knew what I had done. I had seen the blade penetrating the soldier. But I felt no emotion at all. Nothing.

Kade risked the light from a torch in order to escape quickly from the mine. Drey had the horses ready. We had mounted and ridden past the miners' camp before he spoke.

'Did you get it?'

Kade nodded. 'Yeah. We got it.'

Drey looked at me. I had not spoken and avoided eye contact. 'Trouble?'

'Some.' Kade also turned to look at me. 'She'll be fine.'

I didn't know who he was trying to convince. We all needed the reassurance. It was a sombre party that rode the mountain paths in the hours before dawn.

The sun rose late over the rocky peaks, but it provided enough warmth to melt the chill lodged within me. The beauty of the valleys and the distance we gained from the mine gradually dulled my thoughts of the soldiers. I buried the incident deep in my memories and focused on finding safe footing on the slippery trail. I was exhausted by the time Drey allowed us to camp in a sheltered hollow in the valley below the mine. The mundane chores of fetching water, caring for the horses and preparing a cold meal provided welcome distractions.

Drey was watching me closely as I chewed on a strip of dried meat. I looked up at him.

'What?'

'Can I see it?'

For a moment I was confused as to what he was referring to. Then I remembered the Empathy Crystal. I had tucked it securely into my pocket and forgotten all about it due to the fight in the mine. I reached into my pocket, feeling the soft silk glide over my fingertips. I passed the wrapped bundle to Drey, who almost snatched it from me. I watched him as he stroked the silk reverently, his eyes drinking in every detail of the shape and the folds of cloth over the crystal. His breathing had quickened. His hands were trembling.

He slowly folded back the cloth to reveal one side of the stone. The soft yellow light bathed his face as he smiled in appreciation. His eyes sparkled in the warm glow, his gaze caressing the multifaceted surface of the crystal. He brought a finger around the cloth. As gentle as a snowflake, he touched the surface.

He yelped and almost dropped the crystal, resting it carefully in his lap. The colour had changed from a pale yellow to a dark gold. I smiled.

'I don't think she likes you.'

Drey scowled at me and tried again to touch it. He got within a finger's width of the stone before withdrawing his hand once more.

'It feels wrong,' he said, frowning. 'As I get nearer I get an unpleasant feeling. It feels like a warning.' He smiled a small smile. 'A fair warning. She has quite a bite.' He held up the finger that had touched the crystal. The skin had blistered.

I frowned. This was nothing like my experience of the stone. 'It felt prickly to start with for me. Like the protective wards around the Ki Oval. Then it felt cold, ice-cold.' My fingers stroked the air as I remembered touching the crystal. 'But when I touched it, it felt warm. Soft.'

With clear regret, Drey covered the crystal and passed it to me. 'Seems she likes you, then. Keep her safe.'

I nodded, suddenly protective of this stone that had let me touch her. I placed her securely back in the deep pocket of my tunic.

We travelled quickly, leaving the mountains and valleys of Hilman behind without incident. It was easy to avoid inhabited areas in the sparsely populated kingdom. We were more cautious riding through Lindvane. At first we restricted our movements to between dusk and dawn, sleeping in bushes or caves during the day to avoid detection, but the frosty mornings and early mists added a sense of urgency as the year started to close. We were all restless and eager to get back to Liegeport. We increased the time spent travelling, starting earlier in the evening and finishing later in the morning. But we were acutely aware of the hostility directed at us within this kingdom. Our company became quiet and tense; conversation increasingly short and sharp.

Where luck had seemed to be against us during the initial ride through Lindvane, the return journey made up for its deficiency. We avoided villages and towns with ease. The floodwaters had subsided while we were in Hilman, so that we were able to cross at the ford as originally planned, and avoid the main trade bridge. Within a few days we had crossed Lindvane and were at the top of the chalk cliffs above the Travellers' lands. As before, Kade led the way. It took several heartbeats for me to guide Nalya onto the crumbling path. Her heavy breathing behind me reflected my own tension as we descended the cliff. We slipped and skidded on the loose stones, careful to stay away from the edge. I kept one hand on the crystal to reassure myself that it would not be lost over the cliff edge. It felt warm beneath its silk covering. The initial flood of cold water was no longer present when I felt it. My protectiveness towards it grew as we travelled further from its mountain.

We reached the foot of the cliff without any difficulties. The wide, empty plains of the Travellers' lands stretched before us. The absence of Yarna and Eldiss enhanced the loneliness of the countryside. Without the need to travel at night, we covered the distance quickly, pushing the horses as much as we dared. Food for us and grain for the horses were running low, and the thought of returning to Faulknar kept us riding long after our endurance wavered. The horses grew thin, but continued valiantly.

The sense of relief as we crested the chalk cliff into the kingdom of Faulknar was palpable. Drey led us straight to the nearest tavern, laughing at my expression as we reached the summit of a small hill to see a village nestled into the curve of the river. Our mood lifted instantly, and I could not help the smile that burst across my face. I looked over to Kade to see him grinning back at me.

'I really need a long drink of cold ale,' he purred.

I shook my head. 'Keep your ale. I really need a soak in a hot bath.'

Kade sniffed the air. 'I wondered what that awful smell was.'

'I think you'll find that's you.'

We laughed more at the release of tension built up over the long weeks away from home and the thought of a safe place to sleep, rather than at the poor jibes we were aiming at each other. Drey remained quiet, happy to listen to our friendly bickering. But I had noticed that his posture was more relaxed once we had crossed the border into Faulknar. Despite the overwhelming odds set against us that I had been careful not to think about, he had brought us safely home.

The horses were soon stabled and rolling in the clean straw. Drey, Kade and I walked into the tavern, which was only half full this early in the evening. I breathed deeply, savouring the smells of fine food and stale ale. Drey paid for two rooms for the night, as well as stabling. The tavern owner laughed as I eagerly requested a bath.

'There's a tub already in the room. Aven will be up with the water shortly.'

Drey was left to arrange food while Kade and I rushed up the wooden stairs to the bedchambers. There were eight rooms in total for the guests. We were to have the first two rooms at the top of the stairs. I pushed Kade out of the way, trying to ensure I was the first in the room. He pushed back, and we continued to shove each other as we ran up the steps.

'You didn't want a bath,' I protested. 'You said you wanted ale.'

'But my station requires that I have the first bath with the hottest water.'

'But you're only the second son,' I teased, stepping out of the way as he aimed a playful punch at me. 'The bath is mine.'

We barged through the door, both trying to get through at the same time. The room was sparsely furnished, with a bed, a chest of drawers and a larger chest at the foot of the bed. A mirror and washbasin had been placed on the chest of drawers. The promised bathtub was positioned in front of a roaring fire. The tub was already warm, awaiting the hot water to be brought from the kitchen.

I carelessly threw my saddlebags on the floor and flopped onto the bed, groaning in contentment as the soft bedding supported my aching back. Grinning, Kade tossed his saddlebags down next to mine before jumping onto the bed beside me. I squealed as he pinned me to the mattress, his beard tickling my face. I started to tickle his ribs but got distracted when he kissed me. I released a sigh as his warm, moist lips pressed against mine. I cupped my hands around his back, feeling his muscles tense as he shifted his weight onto his forearms so as not to crush me. His musky scent penetrated through the smells from the trail, relaxing my mind as the touch of his hips and mouth stimulated my body.

We jumped simultaneously as the door banged open. A boy a few years younger than Kade and I came in carrying two large jars of steaming water. A leather strap was attached to the neck of each jar, running along his broad shoulders to support the heavy weight. He walked to the tub and filled it with the hot water without looking at Kade or me. We grinned at each other as the boy left the room without saying a word.

Kade pushed me back onto the bed as I tried to rise so that he could get to the bath first. He dipped his head under the water, pulling back so that his wet hair dripped rivers of water down his back.

'Not fair,' I complained, seeing tendrils of dirt drifting on the surface. 'The water's all dirty now.'

He laughed, scooping up fingertips of water to splash in my face. 'It will be dirtier soon when you get in there.'

I stuck my tongue out at him as he turned to fetch the washbasin from the drawers. He filled the basin with the bathwater and started to shave off the beard that he had grown since we left Faulknar.

I relaxed into the warm water, letting out a sigh of contentment. I heard Kade giggle as I closed my eyes and enjoyed the soft caress of the water against my skin. I sunk down far enough so the water tickled behind my ears, my aching legs, back and shoulders melting into soft wax.

'Don't fall asleep in there,' said Kade.

He had moved to stand beside the bath. The damp had curled his hair at the ends and the skin of his chin was a little paler where the beard had been. He had changed his shirt.

'You might drown. And you should eat something first.'

'So are you concerned about me starving or drowning?'

He smiled down at me, quickly reaching to push me under the water. I surfaced, coughing, and wiped water out of my eyes. But he had already left the room.

I stayed in the bath until the water was cold and my skin was wrinkly. Pimpleflesh covered my arms and legs as I towelled myself dry. Wrapping my body in the towel, I rummaged through my saddlebags looking for clean clothes. I paused when I moved my dirty tunic to one sde and revealed the Empathy Crystal that I had hidden within a deep pocket. I removed the silk covering and sat on the bed, placing the stone carefully on my lap. I admired the way the light reflected off its honeyed surface, slowly stroking each smooth face. Its mysteries remained closed to me.

I looked around the room for a more secure place to hide the crystal. I thought about sliding it between the mattress and the wooden slats below the bed but dismissed that idea. I had found the poison Lord Bridgeford had hidden under the bed in his room by accident. I did not want the crystal to be discovered the same way. The large chest was too obvious, as were the drawers. Maybe behind the drawers would work. They rested against the outside wall.

I got up and dressed quickly in clean tunic and leather trousers, then crossed the room to inspect the floor around the drawers. Any dirt or dust would be disturbed when I moved the furniture and would be an obvious clue for anyone looking for hidden goods. But the tavern was well managed and the floor was clean. I removed the mirror and washbasin, placing them on the floor before struggling to move the drawers without making too much noise. I used my knife to prise open one of the wooden panels covering the wall and grinned when the wood gave way to reveal a cavity between the inner and outer walls. I removed several handfuls of the rubble that had been used to line the walls, leaving a hole big enough for the stone. When the panel was replaced and the drawers returned to their original position, there was no evidence that anything had been touched.

I caught my reflection as I replaced the mirror. My hair had grown and now covered the collar of my tunic. I finger-brushed the damp strands to produce the side parting that Yarna had shown me. I tucked the strands behind my ears but left a little to fall over my left eye and tickle my cheek. I liked the effect.

The tavern had filled while I had been taking my bath. The men looked to be mostly farmers and stockmen, with simple clothing and tanned faces. They talked comfortably amongst themselves, although their conversations were a little subdued and they looked a bit too thin. I found Drey and Kade at a table by a window. Each had a large jug of ale and a plate of stew and fresh bread. Only a moment after I sat down, a serving girl brought my own drink and food. The ale was warm and had been watered down but tasted like nectar after weeks of tepid water that had tasted faintly of the animal used to make the water skins. The stew contained a good amount of meat as well as root vegetables. I was soon feeling pleasantly drowsy with a full belly and a crackling fire. I leaned against Kade, who laid an arm across my shoulders. His chest felt warm under my cheek as I rested my head against him. The gentle pull of my hair as Kade played with the ends relaxed me further. I felt my eyelids getting heavier.

Then I was instantly alert as I felt Kade stiffen. He kept his arm around my shoulders, holding me to him, while he sat a bit straighter and his muscles tensed beneath me.

'What is it?' I asked.

He nodded his head towards the door and I turned to see two soldiers in uniform carrying the Faulknar crest as they approached the bar. The smaller one talked to the tavern owner as the door banged closed. The tavern owner pointed towards us, and both soldiers turned to look in our direction. My stomach clenched as I recognised Rolyan. Judging by the malicious smile he gave me, it was clear he recognised me as well.

'What's he doing here?'

Kade squeezed my shoulder as Drey answered. 'Probably looking for the disappearing prince.'

Rolyan and the other soldier came over to us. The other man was taller than Rolyan, and younger. I had seen him around Liegeport but did not know his name. Two more jugs of ale were brought as they sat down at our table.

'You're a hard man to find, Your Grace.' The smile Rolyan gave Kade held no humour or respect. 'The king has got the whole company out looking for you.'

'And you are the lucky ones that found me.' Kade's voice betrayed an equal lack of respect. 'I'm sure my father will reward you handsomely.'

Rolyan lifted his ale in salute. 'No, sir. The only reward we ask is the honour of *escorting* you back to Liegeport.'

I felt Kade's heart pound within his chest at the implication of that word. Kyllian was making sure his son would be taken back to Liegeport, with restraint if necessary. Kade's arm was a dead weight as I pushed myself upright to face Rolyan. The younger soldier had the grace to look embarrassed.

'Thanks for the offer,' I said, disguising my hostility poorly. 'But I think we know the way back.'

Rolyan turned to me with the expression of a snake sizing up a mouse. 'Oh, but I insist. Terrible ruffians we have on the roads these days.'

I glared back. 'Some of them are even wearing Faulknar colours.'

The colour rose in Rolyan's cheeks as he drew breath to reply. Drey placed a warning hand on my arm as I leaned forward to goad Rolyan into saying something that would lead Kade to punch him. The opportunity was lost as Kade stood up.

'Time for some entertainment, I think.'

He strode over to the end of the bar, where a large cask had been placed on its end. Standing on the rim, he was able to see, and be seen by, all in the tavern. He recited the poem about a rich merchant's daughter who fell in love with a lowly cobbler. The merchant did not feel the cobbler was worthy of his daughter and had him chased out of town. The daughter vowed to die rather than live without her true love. Kade concluded by lamenting that the merchant had lost his daughter and had no shoes to wear. The drinkers laughed in appreciation of the tale, while Rolyan and I continued to glare at each other.

As predicted, Kade was persuaded to tell more stories, which he did with good grace. Drey cajoled and chastised, working at reducing the tension and succeeding in averting open displays of hostility if not the simmering hatred beneath. The young soldier stayed quiet, sipping his ale and watching the other people in the tavern. The evening passed with an expectant feeling, as if a summer storm was about to break out. My movements were a little more controlled than normal, and I watched Rolyan intently.

'It's no good,' Drey stated. 'My old bladder needs some attention.'

He stood up and I moved to let him out, grinning as he passed me. 'You going to be all right in the dark, old man?'

'Such cheek.' He swiped at my head, before looking pointedly at Rolyan and me. 'You two play nicely while I'm gone.'

Drey had barely left the room when Rolyan leaned towards me. 'What stupid game are you playing with the prince?'

'What are you talking about?'

'Well, just because you have ugly orange eyes, I still can't see why he would waste his time with you.'

I leaned towards him. 'You jealous, Rolyan? Will no girl sleep with you and your stupid face?'

'The prince must be a halfwit.'

I snarled as I half rose from my seat. 'You should be hanged for treason. You're an insult to the soldiers fighting on the front line, those wearing the Faulknar colours with pride. When was the last time you saw any action, you coward?'

Rolyan slid across the bench towards me. I saw him reach for his knife, but my hand had not reached the hilt of mine before he pressed his blade against my thigh, the point resting above my femoral artery. He pushed with enough force to cut my trousers and pierce the skin. A drop of blood welled over the sting where the blade dug in. The young soldier had turned white.

'One day you'll be without the protection of your prince.' I could smell the ale on Rolyan's breath as his face stopped a finger's breadth from mine. 'Then we'll see who's the coward as you go snivelling back under the rock they found you under.'

My mouth had gone dry and I was finding it hard to breathe. I was not sure whether this was due to anger or fear. The look in Rolyan's eyes convinced me that he was serious.

'Move your hand or I swear I'll break your wrist.'

Kade was suddenly standing behind Rolyan. His voice was quiet and calm. It would not have been heard by those at the table next to ours, but the danger in it was clearly audible and chased chills down my spine. Rolyan clenched his jaw but removed the blade from my leg.

'I think we would all benefit from an early night,' Kade continued.

Rolyan turned to grin up at him. 'It will be my pleasure to escort you to your room.'

The young soldier sensed the implied insult and the consequences of it, quickly adding, 'I'm sorry, Your Grace. The king gave clear instructions that we were to stay with you once we found you.'

Kade nodded briefly at the young man, holding his hand out for mine. I jumped up, glad for the excuse to escape Rolyan. Kade scowled as I unconsciously rubbed at the cut, which was starting to throb. I stopped and took his hand as we made for the stairs. Rolyan followed close behind us, ducking in front as we approached our room. Kade walked through the door first. Rolyan pushed me out of the way and followed Kade into the room, blocking my entrance.

Kade turned on him. 'What do you think you are doing?'

'The king said not to let you out of our sight.'

'What do you think I'm going to do? Jump out of the window?' Kade pushed him back out of the room.

'Just taking care of your safety, Your Grace.'

'Well, you can take care of it outside.'

I stepped forward but Rolyan extended his arm across the doorway, preventing me from joining Kade.

'Rolyan,' Kade growled. His expression grew murderous as he reached the end of his patience.

'Just saving you from yourself,' replied Rolyan, ignoring the danger in Kade's face. He smiled at me, sickeningly sweet. 'And any possible diseases she may be carrying.'

Kade shoved him across the hallway, allowing me to enter the room. 'Did the king provide specific instructions regarding Tallen?'

'No, but—'

'Then as your superior officer, I have final say.' He turned his back on Rolyan. 'You have overstepped your authority. It will be remembered.'

The door banged loudly from the force of Kade's closing it. I sat down heavily on the bed.

'Not the happy welcome home I was expecting,' I said sadly.

Kade came to sit next to me, gently rubbing my thigh where my trouserss had been cut. 'Does it hurt?'

'No. Rolyan's a bully. He doesn't have the courage to do any real damage.'

I stood up to turn his attention away from my conflict with Rolyan. I did not want his petty jealousies to goad Kade into something stupid. As a distraction, I moved the drawers to check on the crystal.

'What are you doing?' Kade asked from the bed. He had lain on his side to watch me.

'Checking the stone.' I removed the wooden panels and retrieved the Empathy Crystal, placing it on the drawers.

'Why'd you put it there?'

I grinned. 'Takes a thief to fool a thief.'

He laughed easily. 'True. I never would have thought to hide it there.'

I returned to sit next to him on the bed, admiring the fall of his hair around his face. 'Kade?'

'Yeah?'

'That tale you told, about the merchant's daughter...'

'Yeah?'

'Do you think... would you...?'

'Would I die rather than be without you?'

I smiled shyly. 'Yeah. You wouldn't do that, would you?'

He held my gaze, looking deep into my eyes as I looked deep into his, searching for some clue of what I meant to him. Rolyan's comments had struck home. Why was Kade with me?

'In a heartbeat,' he said quietly.

I shivered. 'Don't. You can't. You're a prince. You're an heir to the Faulknar kingdom. You have responsibilities. People depend on you.'

Kade groaned as he threw himself onto his back. 'You sound like my father.'

'Yeah, well, maybe he has a point.'

He reached up and pulled me down next to him, holding me tightly in his arms as he breathed into my hair. 'You're not going anywhere, so where's the harm?'

'I just have a bad feeling.' I was finding it hard to express how scared it made me feel, the thought of my actions affecting his welfare. 'Everything I touch turns sour. People get hurt around me. I couldn't stand to hurt you; if you were hurt because of me.'

He kissed my forehead gently. 'Then let's not hurt each other. Us against the rest of them. Deal?'

I could not be convinced by his easy dismissal of my fears. The old scar of pain was throbbing deep within my chest. I was petrified of what could happen. I could never bear the guilt of Kade being hurt because of me.

I closed my eyes. 'Deal.'

The journey back to Liegeport continued in much the same way. Rolyan insulted me. Kade growled at Rolyan. Drey snapped at all of us. Tempers were increasingly provoked as we got closer to the capital. A few nights were spent at taverns and inns, although most were spent by the roadside. Rolyan and his colleague were always on guard to ensure Kade did not disappear during the night. It left Kade restless and short-tempered. He slept less and became more irritable. His posture stiffened. His muscles were constantly tense. He rarely sat for longer than was necessary. He wore an almost permanent frown. I started looking forward to reaching Liegeport, so that the anticipation of Kyllian's anger would finally be over.

Two nights before we were due to arrive back in the city, we slept in a meadow surrounded by trees. There was a small river running along one side of the clearing, which fed into a lake in the middle of the woods. Kade and Drey had started a fire and were preparing to cook the evening meal. I went to the lake in order to rinse the worst of the dirt from my face and hands, as well as to wash some clothes. The sun was setting behind the trees when I decided to return to the camp.

I turned from the lake to find Rolyan watching me. I mentally checked the position of my belt-knife before walking towards him.

'How long have you been there?'

'Not long.' He was leaning casually against a tree trunk, but straightened as I moved to avoid him. 'You being a good little girl and washing the prince's clothes?'

'No. Kade washes his own.'

Rolyan moved to block my path so I had to walk past him in order to get back to the camp. I sighed.

'Rolyan, I'm tired and hungry. I'm really not in the mood for your games tonight.'

'You think I'm playing?'

He stepped quickly towards me, and I had to move sideways to avoid bumping into him. I caught my foot on the roots of a tree and stumbled towards its trunk. I dropped my clean clothes as I grabbed at the tree to keep myself from falling over. Rolyan pushed me as I was regaining my balance. My shoulder slammed against tree, sending shafts of pain down my arm and making my fingers tingle.

I grew angry. 'Kade will break your neck for this.'

'You breathe one word and I'll slit his throat.'

'You traitorous bastard.'

I turned to punch him in the face, but he was too quick for me. He had anticipated my move and grabbed my wrist, forcing it against the tree above my head. He forced my other hand over the first. I cried out as my bruised shoulder was wrenched; I struggled but he held me firm. He was only a hand-width taller than me, but he held me in place easily. I tried to bring my knee up between his legs, but he kicked my ankles apart so that I struggled to stand.

He leaned in close so that his face was a finger-width from mine. 'I could crush you so easily. You are nothing without your prince to protect you. One day he'll see through your deceit.' His lips were almost touching mine as I backed my head as far into the trunk as I could. 'And I'll be waiting.'

He pressed one wrist against the other, painfully crushing my bones into the wood. He slowly moved his freed hand down my chest, resting in the hollow between my breasts. My heart lurched painfully, stopping for the briefest of moments before beating again, too fast. He dragged his hand down my abdomen and across my thigh, grasping my groin painfully. All thoughts of struggling vanished as I willed myself into a small a space as I could manage. His hips pressed against mine as he whispered into my ear.

'Just imagine all the things I could do to you.'

'Rolyan!'

Rolyan jumped back as the shout came from behind him. I could see the young soldier over his shoulder. His face was white and his hands were clenched into fists.

'What are you doing?'

'This is none of your business, Jared. Run along like a good boy.'

Jared stood his ground. 'No. Its not right. Let her go.'

Rolyan glared at me for several heartbeats before pushing himself away from me. 'One word,' he growled at me before leaving.

I sank to the ground. My whole body was shaking. Rolyan pushed past Jared as the young man walked over to me.

'Are you hurt?'

I shook my head. 'No. No, I'm fine.'

He did not look convinced, but I was unwilling to admit how scared I had been. How easily Rolyan had rendered me helpless. Jared reached out to touch me, then decided against it.

'Come on,' he said gently. 'Let's get back. The food's ready.'

I let him guide me back to the others. I concentrated on getting my heart and breathing under control so I would stop shaking. So that Kade would not know. Kade could never know.

Chapter Seventeen

Drey had arranged it so that we arrived in Liegeport late in the evening. He had hoped that Kyllian would have retired for the night, and that we would have the chance to at least eat and clean up before being called to attend the king. It was a good plan. But it didn't work. The king was still in a meeting when we rode through the city gates. He had told the runner that he would see us immediately. We had barely handed our tired horses over to the yawning grooms when four of the king's bodyguard came to relieve Rolyan and Jared, and escort us to the state meeting room where Kyllian would receive us.

I could feel the heat coming off Kade as we walked up the steps to the royal house and along the left-hand corridor. I was finding it hard to keep up with the pace he set as he marched slightly in front of the guards. No one spoke. The silence was amplified by the lack of servants at this time of night.

Kade did not slow his pace as we approached the closed door to the meeting room. Without breaking step, he slammed into the door so that it banged loudly against the wall as it flew open. The closest guard had to quickly brace his arm to avoid being hit as the door recoiled. Kade ignored the look of surprise on Villermir's face. He was sitting close to the king in quiet discussion as Kade stormed up to his father.

'Why not put me in chains and be done with it?' Kade snapped.

Kyllian's face was still, but his hands gripped the arms of his chair so hard that I thought the heavy wood would break. His eyes flashed in the candlelight as he turned to his son.

'Don't tempt me, boy. But I doubt it would have taught you any manners.'

'Manners!' Kade threw his hands up in the air. 'Maybe I'll show some manners when you stop treating me like a common criminal. Sending guards to hunt me down and drag me back to Liegeport. Murderers have got away with less.'

Kyllian could not contain his rage any longer and stood to face the prince. He was a full head taller than Kade and was heavily muscled, while Kade still had the remains of his adolescent frame and lacked bulk in comparison to his father. Kyllian stood glaring, a hand-width from his son. Neither man was prepared to back down. Kyllian's voice was dangerously low as he made his accusation.

'You defied a direct order from your king. Give me one reason why I should not execute you for treason.'

Kade paled and I saw his breath catch in his throat. Kyllian was deadly serious. I took a breath to defend Kade but was stalled by Drey's cool hand on my arm.

'There is nothing you can do here,' he said quietly so that only I would hear. 'You will only make things worse for Kade. This is between a father and his son.'

With difficulty I took my eyes away from the royal conflict and looked at Drey. He held my gaze sympathetically. His words had been chosen carefully. Kyllian must have been worried for his headstrong son. It had been months since he had disappeared from the capital. Kyllian must have feared the worst. I nodded to Drey, who gave me a small smile and released my arm.

The anger had left Kade as well. He did not lower his eyes, but his voice was soft as he pleaded with his father. 'I cannot be contained.'

'And I cannot be defied. By anyone. Especially by my son.' Kyllian turned his back and returned to his seat. His magisterial authority returned as he instructed the two guards flanking Kade. 'He is to be confined to his chambers. He will meet with no one. He will remain there until I decide what further action will be taken.'

The king turned to face Drey and me, dismissing his son. When Kade failed to move, the guard on each side took his arm, more forcibly than I felt was necessary, and dragged him backwards from the room. It took several heartbeats for Kade to realise that he had been arrested for treason. I watched the realisation creep over his face. He cried out to his father, pleading. But Kyllian ignored him. I took a step to follow but was blocked by the guard standing by my side. I tried to move around him, but he placed a large hand on my chest to prevent me from moving any further. My heart hammered against my ribs in frustration, but I knew there was nothing I could do. Kade had already been removed from the room and the door had closed behind him.

I turned back to find Kyllian watching me. Villermir was still seated at his side, with a satisfied smile on his face. Whatever scheme the priest was planning, things appeared to be going his way. His smile grew when he saw me look at him.

'You found the crystal,' he said for Kyllian's benefit.

All thoughts of Kade vanished instantly as the need to protect the crystal flooded my senses. My hand went reflexively to the pocket where I had put the crystal, while I took a deep breath to clear my head. I didn't want to reveal the stone. But everyone was looking expectantly at me. A block of ice sat in my stomach at the thought of Villermir holding the crystal.

'Tallen.' Kyllian brought my focus back to him. 'Show me the Empathy Crystal.'

Slowly, reluctantly, I removed the silk-covered crystal from the pocket of my tunic. Looking for reassurance from Drey, I removed the silk to reveal the stone. The pale yellow of the crystal picked up the candlelight and danced with the flickering shadows. The room fell silent as everyone held their breath.

'It's beautiful,' said Villermir.

I looked up to see a greedy desire clearly written in his eyes. He stood and walked towards me; reached his hand out for the crystal. I took a step backwards, but he was already too close. He went to take the stone, his fingers brushing the surface, before jumping back with a cry, holding his burnt fingers.

Drey chuckled quietly. 'She does that.'

Villermir glared at him, before returning his attention to me and the crystal. 'Did you find it where I said?'

I nodded. 'Yes.'

'Was it guarded?'

'Yes.'

'So how did you manage to get it?'

I hesitated, looking at Drey for instructions on how much to tell. Kyllian's temper had not dissipated as he turned on us.

'I do not have time to tease out the details,' he snapped. 'Tell me everything that occurred from when you left Liegeport.'

Villermir did not take his eyes off the crystal while Drey told the king everything that had happened on our journey to retrieve the stone. Kyllian scowled when Drey described Kade joining us at the clearing but seemed to accept that he had been a valuable asset when diplomacy was required with the Travellers, and when a soldier was needed to fight the Lindvanes. The story was not totally the same as I remembered it, and Drey carefully avoided telling the part where Kade had gone alone into a Lindvane village to obtain supplies. But the main points were recounted truthfully and Kyllian seemed satisfied.

Throughout the telling Villermir's eyes caressed the crystal, absorbing every detail of the stone as I held it protectively. The only time he looked away was when Drey described the taking of the gem. He told of the hidden entrance that only I could see. He spoke of the icy waterfall when I first touched the stone, and how it had accepted only my touch after that. Drey watched Villermir as he talked. Villermir watched me. Pressure was building between my eyes and I was getting a headache. I just wanted to go to bed.

'How very interesting,' said Villermir. His head was tilted slightly to one side as he tried to read my expression. 'How very interesting indeed.'

'The crystal holds many secrets,' said Drey sharply, making Villermir turn to face him. 'Many that only the Ancients would know.'

'Perhaps it's time those secrets were relearnt.' The tone of Villermir's voice made the statement a challenge. But he had finished studying me for a time. He returned to his seat beside Kyllian. 'What say you, sire? Shall I be permitted to study the crystal's secrets?'

I opened my mouth to protest but realised there was nothing I could say. I didn't think Kyllian would accept my feelings of impending doom as credible evidence. Villermir smiled slightly at me as I searched frantically for a plausible reason why he should not have the crystal. Drey remained quiet.

'If this stone can be used to finish this war with Lindvane, then I shall know of it. You may study the crystal, Villermir.'

The king rose, indicating the meeting was over. Villermir quickly crossed over to me, ensuring he had the crystal before Kyllian left the room. He tucked the silk over the stone without comment and took the stone from me. I watched forlornly as he followed Kyllian, then jumped as Drey placed a gentle hand on my shoulder.

'The crystal should be safe enough,' he said softly. 'I doubt she will be willing to give up her secrets to him.' He squeezed my shoulder and guided me to the door. 'And I don't know about you, but I'm planning on sleeping for a hundred years in my own bed.'

His grin was contagious, and I felt myself mirroring it. The thought of my own bed was very inviting. I would lie down, just for a short while, and then go and check on Kade.

The room was bathed in sunlight when I awoke. I was still clothed as I lie lay on top of the blankets on my bed. The faint scent of lavender suggested that Tarra had been in my room recently. I sat up to see a steaming tub of bathwater waiting for me in front of a fire. I smiled as I saw the pile of neatly folded clean clothes on the chair beside the tub. Tarra had anticipated all my needs perfectly.

After bathing I went in search of food. Unwilling to spend time in the main dining hall, I left the royal house and headed for the docks. I bought a steaming meat pie and was chewing contentedly as I walked along the waterside. I soon saw Tawpin sitting on the sea wall with his legs dangling over the edge.

'Hey,' I said merrily. It was good to see him.

He turned to scowl at me. 'I'm not speaking to you.'

'What have I done?'

'What have you done?' He turned back to look out over the bay while I sat on the wall next to him. 'Nothing, unless you count taking off for weeks without so much as a goodbye. Leaving me to answer all the questions about where you had gone.'

'We went to help Drey's sick aunt.'

'Yeah, well, that wore a little thin once Kade disappeared as well. Everyone suspected you had gone off somewhere together.' Tawpin could not help the excitement creeping into his voice as he recounted the gossip. 'Word around the market was that you two had eloped. Kyllian went insane. Rina, the new chambermaid, said he threw a dagger in temper, and it took two soldiers to prise it out of the fire mantle. The whole household has been walking on ice since Kade left. Without telling anyone. Without telling me.' He turned to me and paused. 'What?'

I was grinning madly. 'I've so missed you.'

He turned back to look over the water. 'I'm still not speaking to you.'

'I'm sorry I couldn't tell you, but I didn't know Kade was going to come with us.'

Tawpin turned back to face me. 'So, you didn't plan it?'

'No. In fact, Kyllian specifically forbade it.'

Tawpin's eyes grew wide as a grin exploded across his face. 'No wonder he was angry, then. And you can guess who was the main target. I'm Kade's page. I'm supposed to know everything. Kyllian had me scrubbing the stables, smoothing the arenas. That took forever! I cleaned tack, scrubbed the cellars. Oh, and I even had to take the manure to the farms. That was disgusting. I'm sure I still smell.' He shuddered at the memory.

I leaned over and kissed him on the cheek, making them flush with colour. 'My hero.'

'Just let me know next time you go running off. I'll plan on leaving the kingdom to avoid Kyllian.'

I smiled apologetically. 'I'll try.'

He scowled. 'You two aren't planning another trip already?'

I shook my head. 'Hardly. I can't even get to see Kade at the moment, let alone go off anywhere with him.'

The sparkle of gossip was back in Tawpin's eyes. 'I went to see him this morning and couldn't get near. He's got two of the royal bodyguards outside the door. Apparently, no one is allowed in. Not even me! I tried to tell them that I'm his page and need to attend my duties. But they just stood there, refusing me access.'

'Kyllian is not overly fond of Kade at the moment.'

'I can tell. Word is that he's even nailed the windows shut.'

'What? What does he think he's going to do? Fly away?'

Tawpin looked at me for a few heartbeats. 'Or climb on the roof to see you?'

'Oh. Yeah. Good point.' That is exactly what he would do. And what I was planning on doing that night. 'Kyllian knows about that?'

'Kyllian knows about everything.'

I frowned at Tawpin. 'Did you tell him?'

'I'm not his only spy. Kade could have told him for all I know. Although it was probably Drey.'

I sighed. 'Getting to see Kade is not going to be easy.'

He smiled at me. 'Well, if there's a way in, the two of us will think of it.'

I smiled back, encouraged by his optimism. We discussed many ideas, each one more extravagant than the last. We thought of climbing down the chimney, but rejected that as the fire was likely to be lit. We thought of tunnelling through the walls but felt it might be too noisy. We thought of poisoning the guards but concluded that getting thrown into gaol ourselves would not help.

We finally decided on a plan and arranged to try that night.

Drey looked at me suspiciously when I declared that I was going to have an early night, but did not pass any comment. We had discussed Kade's internment earlier in the evening and I suspected that Drey had a good idea what I was up to. But he declined to question me, and I was grateful that I did not have to lie to him. I made a noisy show of getting ready for bed, leaving it a long while before quietly climbing out of my window and down onto the second-storey roof. The night was bright, with a cloudless sky allowing sufficient moonlight to see by. The clear night, however, also meant that an icy wind blew around the towers. The cold air pinched my cheeks and I was grateful for the sheepskin gambeson that I huddled into.

I waited under the window of Kade's room. Tawpin was to engage the guards outside his door in a noisy game of dice. He would place a lantern on the sill of the arrow slit that was directly below the door to Kade's chambers. This would indicate to me that it was safe to climb up to the tower, and also prevent the guards from seeing out as I climbed. It was not long before I could see the lantern ascend the stairs as Tawpin brought food and drink for the bodyguards. He waved the lantern several times as he placed it on the sill, making me smile as he ensured I had seen the signal.

I quickly climbed the tower, using the uneven bricks as foot- and handholds. I had climbed up my tower many times but had never climbed Kade's. The bricks were a little smoother and I had to concentrate to ensure I didn't slip and make a noise. I soon balanced on the sill outside Kade's bedchamber, pushing my legs against the far wall as my back leaned against the opposite one. This provided a little stability on the narrow ledge.

I pulled at the shutters, not expecting them to open. As Tawpin had said, they were nailed firmly shut. I rattled the wooden slats, trying to attract Kade's attention. Predictably, there was no sound from inside the room.

'Kade,' I whispered as loudly as I dared.

Still no sound. We had assumed Kade would be in the bedchamber. I did not know how I was going to make him hear me without alerting the guards if he was in the main reception room. I rattled the shutters more violently while I tried to think of what to do.

I tried again. 'Kade!'

'Tallen?'

Relief flooded through my body so that I wobbled on the window ledge. My mind immediately focused as Kade continued to talk through the closed window.

'What are you doing here?'

'Well, I had nothing better to do so I thought I would sit on a tiny ledge, stupidly high off the ground, and freeze to death.'

I heard his quiet chuckle through the wood, and I smiled in the darkness.

'You are completely insane.'

'Yeah, I know. It's the company I keep.' My smile melted. 'How're you doing? You all right?'

'I can't bear being trapped in here, Tal.' The volume of his voice rose and fell, and I suspected he was pacing in frustration. 'I'd rather he flogged me than be trapped in here.'

'Don't say that. Don't ever say that.'

'I can't stand it, Tallen.'

'Hey. It will be all right. Your father is just angry at you, that's all. He'll soon calm down and let you out.'

'My father has been known to hold a grudge for years.'

'Tawpin and I will get you out.'

'I'm not overly reassured by that.'

I laughed. 'Come on, Kade. There are worse places to be trapped. He could have thrown you in the dungeons. I'd be very happy to be forced to stay in your room.'

It was Kade's turn to laugh. 'You are impossible.'

His voice settled close to me as he sat on the inside window ledge. I rested my head against the shutters. A burning ache throbbed in my chest at the thought of him being so close, but I could not see or touch him. I wondered if Kyllian had known it would be as much a punishment for me as it was for Kade.

'I tried to speak to Drey. You know, by thinking to him, like we did in meetings. But I can't do it.'

I sighed. 'I tried to get him to speak to you too. Pass on a message that I haven't forgotten you; that I wish we were together. But he refused. Said that Kyllian has passed his judgement and it's not for him to go against his king.'

'That sounds about right. Drey is first and always the king's man. Knowing him, he is also trying to teach me a lesson. I'm sure he hasn't forgiven me for leaving Liegeport when I should have stayed safely here.'

'Not a nice way to even the scores.'

Kade remained silent for a while, before continuing on a different subject. 'Has Drey had a look at the crystal yet? Can he tell if he can gain any magickal advantage from it?'

'He hasn't had the chance. Villermir wormed his way into getting the first look.'

'What?!' Kade's voice rose in height, suggesting that he was now standing. 'How could you let him have it?'

'I didn't have much choice. He charmed Kyllian into allowing him to study it. I didn't think your father was in the mood for demands from me.'

'I suppose you're right.'

'Villermir just wants to make sure Drey doesn't have it.' I shivered on the ledge. 'I've got a bad feeling about Villermir having the crystal. Even if he can't get it to work, I'm afraid it'll give him too much power.'

'How?'

'I don't know. I just really hate the idea of him having it.'

'I know what you mean. He already has too much influence, if you ask me. Especially over Kerk. He fills my brother's head with ideas of divine right and how the people should worship him as a God-appointed ruler. With Villermir, naturally, telling Kerk what to do to fulfil God's wishes. It worries me that Kerk believes so much of what Villermir tells him.'

'How can it be so easy for him to manipulate people the way he does? Half worship the ground he hovers above; the other half have an uncontrollable fear of him.'

Kade laughed quietly. 'I can guess which half you fall into.'

I smiled in the darkness. 'The man gives me pimpleflesh whenever I see him.'

Kade's voice rose and fell again and I guessed he had returned to his pacing. 'Tal, I'm afraid of what he could do with that crystal. He doesn't need it to work for him. He can use it to demand all manner of things. He could claim the crystal talks to him or gives him special powers. No one would be able to deny it. The people would follow him. Faulknar would be left with a puppet on the throne.'

'Not if he didn't have the stone.'

Kade was quiet for several heartbeats. 'What?'

'I stole it once. I can steal it again.'

'No. That's not going to happen.'

'Why not? It can't be as bad as travelling through Lindvane to steal a sacred relic from the Hilman.'

'This is different.'

'How? This time I won't have two kingdoms after me.' I swallowed against the lump in my throat. 'Just Villermir.'

'Exactly. He's not going to let you just take it. He'll have protections.'

'I know,' I said quietly.

Neither of us spoke for a long time. The muscles in my lower back started to spasm under the strain of maintaining my awkward position on the ledge. I cried out as they cramped when I tried to move to a more comfortable position. The release of pressure from my compressed bottom muscles allowed the return of blood, bringing uncountable needle-stabs with it.

'You all right?' The concern was clearly audible in Kade's voice.

'Yeah. This isn't the most comfortable of places to sit.'

'And you must be freezing.' His voice was very close to my ear. 'Go to bed, Magpie. Just promise me that you won't go after the crystal.'

I was prepared to make no such promise. 'Goodnight, Kade. I'll come back tomorrow night. Hang in there, all right?'

'Tallen! You didn't promise.'

It was several days before I had the chance to go after the crystal. Drey kept my days busy with checking his stores of dried herbs to ensure no damp had crept in while we were away, allowing mould to develop. He sent me on errands to fetch jars and glass flasks, then made me fill them with the potions and ointments that would be needed over the winter to treat aches and pains brought on by the cold. Late evenings were spent on the window ledge, talking with Kade. He was desperate for news of the city and of the war with Lindvane. Every night he would try to make me promise that I would not go after the crystal. Every night I managed to avoid lying to him.

It was a week after returning to Liegeport that I decided to check on the crystal. I had not seen Villermir since he took the stone, but this was not unusual, particularly if he had a new project to occupy his time. Drey had sent me to the stables with some powder for a horse with a cough. The rain was cold, almost sleet, and I shivered as I hurried across the courtyard. I walked down the barn containing the horses in order to get to the tack room where the head groom could be found. The horses, predictably, snorted and rolled their eyes at me but I ignored them. Bow, the head groom, laughed at me as I joined him by an empty stable.

'Bit of a foul day to go for a ride,' I said, indicating the empty stall.

Bow nodded. 'I wouldn't fancy being out in this.' He frowned as he thought. 'Tempest has been gone, must be… three or four days now.'

'That's Villermir's horse?'

Bow nodded.

'When's he due back?'

The stocky man shrugged, running a hand through his dark ginger hair. 'Didn't say. Must be going for a while. His saddlebags were bulging.'

'Seems a strange time to be going on a journey.'

'Maybe. But it's not for you or me to question what Villermir gets up to.'

He pulled a face that made me laugh as I handed him the powder for the horse. It would seem that Villermir was not as absorbed by the crystal as I had thought. Unless he had taken the stone with him. I shivered at the thought. Why would he take the crystal anywhere? Where would he go? My planned visit to the temple took on a new urgency. I made my excuses to Bow and quickly crossed the city to the Temple of Baila, where Villermir had his quarters.

The colours of the temple were muted by the grey clouds and falling rain. The familiar feeling of nervousness grew as I approached the imposing building. My stomach clenched and my breathing became shallow and rapid. I swallowed repeatedly against the acid threatening to burn my throat and took a deep breath as I pushed against the brass door handles and entered the temple. The calm inside was particularly noticeable after the tension I had felt outside. There were a number of people on their knees at their devotions, heads bowed, eyes closed, arms crossed over their chests, with hands resting on the opposite shoulders. The only person to notice my arrival was Coen, Villermir's scribe. His small, dark eyes glared out of his angular face as he looked up from the small desk that he was sitting behind. The desk was ornately carved in expensive dark wood. Two pots of ink were placed to Coen's right, along with a number of quills. Three large leather-bound ledgers were stacked to his left. The candlelight reflected off his shiny forehead. He returned to the ledger that was open in front of him.

I quietly walked around the back of the temple and along the left-hand side of the benches, sitting at the end of the middle row. Devotees rose occasionally, finishing their worship and paying their donation to Coen before leaving. Worshippers were required to provide coin in exchange for communion with their God. As devotions were encouraged at least three times a day, Coen was handling a large sum of money every day. I looked around at the riches this money had bought. Gold was everywhere – candleholders, statues, sculptures depicting the power and might of their God. I was again impressed at the detail on the stone sentinels, expecting them to come to life to annihilate me as a non-believer.

I studied the doors that led out of the main atrium. I knew that several of these doors led to storerooms and private rooms where meetings could be held, or counselling could be given in private. I also knew one of them led to the private courtyards of the Baila priests, where Villermir kept his quarters. There were no identifying features on the doors, with one elaborately carved door looking like all the others. There were four doors along each side of the temple with a further two either side of the altar. The courtyards were located behind the temple, with access only available by going through the main building, so I assumed the door I needed was one of the ones near the altar. I had no idea which one.

It seemed wrong to send thanks to The Lady in the hallowed place of worship to the One God, but she had definitely sent me her luck. While I was considering ways of getting through one of the doors unnoticed, two of the lower priests came through the door nearest to the left side of the altar. Their plain black robes were banded with one light grey stripe to signify achievement in the first level of religious studies required of the Baila priests. There would be four more levels for them, taking a further eight years, before they were awarded a temple of their own. They talked in hushed tones in the doorway for several moments, allowing me to see beyond them into a darkened lobby and daylight beyond it. That was the entrance to the priests' private apartments. Villermir's rooms would be in the centre of this courtyard.

The junior priests finished their conversation and separated. One went through a door in the left wall of the temple, while the other left through the main doors, nodding to Coen as he passed him. I waited until Coen had returned to his ledger and the worshippers were all bowed in prayer. Making no sound, I rose from the bench and slipped into the shadows of the nearest alcove. My soft leather boots allowed me to move silently from shadow to shadow as I crept closer to the altar. I waited for several anxious heartbeats to ensure no one was watching, then carefully opened the door and slipped through.

My eyes quickly adjusted to the dim light of the lobby, identifying small wooden benches along each wall before the room opened out into a stone archway. I peered around the smooth, pale stone wall into the empty courtyard. There were two long, single-storey buildings, one to my left and one opposite me. A closely cut grass square separated these buildings from the temple and the row of five two-storey houses on my right. Dominating the courtyard was a large two-storey stone house, with a coloured tile roof and a large coloured-glass window above the main door. I was convinced that Villermir would live in this ostentatious building.

The courtyard remained empty as I walked along the pathway in front of the houses. My heart hammered painfully in my chest as I expected someone to shout at me, questioning what I was doing there. But all remained quiet and serene. I listened at the door of the big house, but it was impossible to hear anything through the thick wood. Seeing no other option, I took a deep breath and opened the door.

The hallway was empty. Light from the coloured-glass window sent flickers of orange and gold onto the wide staircase that covered most of the far wall. A thick tapestry rug, depicting a crowd in devotion to the One God, was on the floor in front of the staircase. The boards around it were polished to reflect the light like glass. There was a lack of further ornamentation, with the room implying simple practicality. To the left was a carved wooden archway leading to a large dining room with a long table and numerous chairs. It seemed Villermir would host social gatherings. To my right was a closed door. Even standing several paces away from it, I could feel the hairs on my arms lift and the beginnings of the crawling feeling over my skin.

This feeling increased as I moved towards the door. Apprehension tugged at my stomach and closed my throat. I knew that sensation meant this room was protected. There would be consequences if I entered. Taking another steadying breath, I reached for the brass handle.

The spark of lightning that exploded under my fingers took me by surprise. I cursed and jumped back, before fear of discovery made me bite my lip. Chastising myself, I reached for the handle again. Ignoring the sharp stab of the protections, I turned the handle and entered the room. I closed the door quietly, rubbing my tingling fingers. The room was furnished like a library. There were two small wooden tables in the centre, and a larger one in front of the window. Shelves of books, ledgers and scrolls lined two of the walls, with a large wooden cabinet either side of the door I had just walked through. A pair of silver candleholders rested on the large desk. I recognised the staring eye of the Box of Binhos beside one of these holders. A rose quartz pendant nestled at the base of the other.

A persistent buzzing sat between my eyes as pressure built at my temples. I unconsciously rubbed at my forehead while I looked around the room, trying to determine where the Empathy Crystal would be kept. I felt no connection to the stone.

The cabinets were the obvious choice to hide precious artefacts, so I started there. The buzzing increased as I approached the one to the right of the door. I rubbed at my eyes and frowned in pain. The upper half of the cabinet was enclosed by glass, revealing shelves containing small statues, crystals, goblets and containers. Each was elaborately decorated and looked to be very old. The crystals were often in their uncut state, chunks of rock ripped from the earth. One of the polished stones was the size and shape of an egg. It was unbelievably black with ripples over the surface, like pools of ink reflecting the small amount of light not absorbed by the liquid. The black egg drew my attention, drawing me into the depths of its dark centre. A feeling of dread and despair flowed through my veins as my muscles grew heavy and it became difficult to breathe.

Reflex prevented me from toppling, correcting my balance and stopping me falling into the cabinet. It broke my gaze on the egg and I became aware of the room again. I took a deep, unsteady breath to clear my head. The pain at my temples became an anchor preventing me from dissolving into the black crystal.

I reached nervously for the small golden tassels that acted as handles on the cupboard doors below the glass-covered shelves. Every sense I possessed screamed at me not to touch the cabinet; to walk away from the mysteries held within it. I dismissed these concerns as the voice of a protective shield, similar to my crawling skin and the lightning bolts.

I touched a tassel.

Sound seemed to vanish for a heartbeat. The air grew heavy around me, like a thick blanket thrown over my head, stifling me.

Then the world exploded.

The loudest bang I had ever heard smashed through my head. I felt myself being thrown backwards. But I was enveloped by the cold, black depths of the egg crystal before I hit the floor.

Chapter Eighteen

I felt the soft sheets supporting my back and the pillow behind my head. My breathing was slightly restricted due to the sheets being tucked tightly around me. My sense of smell returned first: medicinal herbs and a faint scent of ash tickled my nose. I smiled as I felt a cool hand on my wrist, guessing that Drey was sitting beside me. My hearing returned soon after that, with the familiar sounds of the city's infirmary. Glass jars rattled, herbs were pounded, quiet moans were being comforted by the healers and priestesses. I mentally checked myself for injuries, finding only a stabbing headache and tightened skin on my face and right hand. I sighed, knowing I had to face Drey. I opened my eyes.

And saw nothing.

Panic punched my stomach into the back of my throat, causing me to gag on the acid that burnt the soft tissue. Drey's firm hand pressed against my chest as I sprang forward to sit up.

'I can't see. Drey, I can't see.'

The pressure of his hand increased until I was lying back down on the bed. 'Remember this feeling,' he said quietly. 'Perhaps it will stop you from meddling in affairs that do not concern you.'

My panic had not subsided. 'But, Drey—'

'The blindness is temporary,' he continued. 'You should have some vision restored by midday. Although I would venture that your sight will be blurry for some days yet. Villermir's defences pack a hefty punch for those who are unprepared.'

The chastisement was obvious. I had been hasty and careless. Drey was right; I had no idea what type of protections Villermir had left to protect his treasures. I could have been killed. I frowned as Drey quietly let me explore all the many ways in which Villermir's defences could have maimed or killed me, not to mention anyone who was nearby.

'But Villermir has gone.'

I could sense Drey shaking his head by the small sounds of a rustling collar and the change in his breathing. 'The wards do not need his presence.'

'No… I know that.' The stabbing headache was not helping as I rubbed my forehead in frustration. 'I mean, Villermir has left Liegeport. Bow said he was probably going to be gone for some time. I know he's taken the crystal. I couldn't feel it…'

'Hush.' Drey's hand was on my wrist again, squeezing a little harder than was comfortable. 'This is not the place to talk of such matters.'

'But, Drey, if he's left with it—'

'Hush,' he repeated, hissing through his teeth. 'Rest assured that Kyllian and I share your concerns.'

The headache was getting worse. 'Kyllian?'

'The whole city is aware of the mess you made of Villermir's house. The king demanded an explanation.' He ignored my groan but lowered his voice. 'I was aware that Villermir had left the city. I suspect he is about to cause mischief, but I'm not yet sure how. We can be certain that he will hear of your intrusion and will be particularly cautious now.'

I curled my hand around his fingers. 'I'm sorry. Seems as if, in trying to help, I've really messed things up.'

'Yes, you have.' He chuckled. 'But then I have learnt to expect that from you.' He squeezed my hand and I felt him rise. 'We will talk about this later. For now, you need rest. Sleep, Tallen.'

I relaxed back into the pillow as I heard his footsteps click away from me on the stone floor. The panic I'd felt earlier had subsided into a ball of worry sitting like a rock in my belly. I knew Villermir would use the crystal to cause trouble, and it seemed Drey felt the same way. Strangely, his confirmation only added to my dread. I rubbed between my eyes with the heels of my palms in an effort to lessen the pain in my head. It wasn't long before a healer came with some tea to ease the pain and send me into a deep, restful sleep.

Drey had been right about my loss of sight. My vision returned when I awoke later that day, although everything was blurred for another three days. Drey insisted I stayed in the infirmary, I think more to ensure I was under constant supervision than from any concern for my health. The idle time left me with nothing to do but fret, so by the second day I was pestering the healers until they put me to work mixing herbs and preparing poultices. I had to admit that the simple tasks left me tired and caused a recurrence of the stabbing headache. I slept deeply each night, untroubled by my usual night terrors.

It was late afternoon on the fourth day when Drey found me infusing healing herbs into the material used for dressings and bandages. He frowned at the slight tremor that remained in my hands.

'I'm fine, Drey. Just bored with being in here.'

'Hmph. Be careful what you wish for.' The frown melted as he continued. 'Kyllian wants to see you. There have been… developments. I think you should attend the Council of War meeting.'

I dropped the dressings. 'You've found Villermir?'

Drey tilted his head as he glared at me in exasperation. 'Again, this is not the place. Hold your questions until we have returned to the royal apartments.'

I bit my lip. 'Sorry.'

He flapped his hands at me. 'Never mind. Kyllian is waiting.'

After several days of the subdued lighting in the infirmary, the clear, crisp afternoon was too bright for my damaged eyes. I was forced to shield them with my hand as Drey carefully guided me through the streets to the main house. I was glad when we walked through the main doors and the bright sunlight was obscured. Drey led me up the stairs and along the hallway to the king's private chambers. I had never been in there before and felt that it could not be a good thing that we were meeting there.

Drey paused before entering. 'Ready?'

I took a steadying breath. 'Ready.'

Drey gave two quick knocks on the door before entering. Kyllian was standing at a small window with his back to us, giving me time to look around the room. Although the furnishings were expensive and of obvious high quality, the decoration was sparse and functional. There was only one wall tapestry to soften the stark walls. The royal standard of Faulknar stood proudly as the central focus of the room, over the fire that warmed the cold stone chamber. A door leading to further rooms stood closed at the far side of the fire. A sturdy oak table stood near the far wall, under another window, and was covered in ledgers and maps. A matching oak chair sat behind it, the red leather sagging from repeated use. Five comfortable red leather chairs were arranged around the table. Langdon and Kerk were already seated. Kerk gave me an encouraging smile as I walked in, and I returned a grateful one. Langdon and Drey exchanged anxious glances as Drey and I sat in two of the remaining chairs. Kyllian's private equerry hovered protectively near his liege.

'I hope you are feeling better, Tallen.' The king did not turn from the window.

'Much better, thank you, my liege.' I played nervously with a blister on my right hand.

'That's good news. It seems I have need of your services yet again. Drey, please bring Langdon and Tallen up to date.'

Drey bowed his head reflexively, although Kyllian could not see him. 'Yes, sire. There have been reports of Villermir in Lindvane—'

I stood up in protest. 'That conniving son of a diseased water rat. How dare he…?'

I stopped in mid-sentence as I caught the glare Drey directed at me. I mumbled my apologies while Kerk smirked at me. I scowled in a mixture of anger, disbelief and frustration. I knew Villermir would use the crystal to cause trouble. I did not think he would use it to commit treason.

Drey waited for me to sit down before continuing. 'Villermir has been sighted in Burford Hythe. Hayton's uncle has an estate there and I believe Villermir is experimenting with the Empathy Crystal. We have to assume that he will try to use it against Faulknar.'

I bit my lip hard, to avoid cursing in front of the king.

'There have already been reports of unusual events in the area. Rivers have burst their banks without the aid of rain. Small hills appear overnight. People claim the ground has been shaking beneath their feet.'

'How well protected is this estate?' asked Kyllian. His fists clenched tightly behind his back were the only sign of his anger.

Langdon replied. 'Reports state that a company of Hayton's household guards are training there. Twenty men, but highly trained. They will be difficult to overcome.'

Kyllian nodded, turning to face us. He looked at me. 'And so, it seems I have a need for stealth rather than strength.'

Drey remained quiet, presumably more aware of the dangers than I was.

'Of course, my liege,' I said at once.

Kyllian smiled a small, sad smile. 'Of course.'

There was a short silence before Kerk spoke for the first time. 'Who else are you going to send?' The question was more loaded than the words would suggest. It seemed to be a continuation of a conversation that had been held before I arrived. He did not break his gaze as his father sent him a challenging stare.

'It's not an option.'

'It's the only option,' persisted Kerk. 'Who else can you trust with this?'

'I have a hundred guards...'

'But who can you truly trust?'

Kyllian shook his head and started to pace. 'I will not allow it.'

Kerk remained still. 'We have no choice,' he said quietly.

Kyllian turned to look at his son. The anger had left the king, to be replaced with sorrow and a touch of pride. Kerk appeared to have aged with his final statement, the skin seeming heavier around his eyes and mouth. Kyllian and Kerk remained looking at each other for several heartbeats. A whole conversation was being exchanged between their eyes.

Finally, Kyllian dropped his gaze, submitting with a barely perceptible nod of the head. I released the breath that I hadn't realised I was holding. He turned to his equerry, who nodded before leaving the room. The conversation turned to the practical considerations of crossing into Lindvane and surviving long enough to reach Burford Hythe. Drey would again accompany me. He would be needed to deal with Villermir while I took the crystal. There was no longer any pretence. Villermir would use magick to protect the crystal and Drey would be needed to defeat these protections. Whatever gifts I had in holding the crystal would be ridiculously inadequate compared to Villermir's powers. He no longer had any reason to hesitate in destroying both me and Drey. He would also be expecting us to come after the stone. As would the highly trained soldiers guarding the estate.

The chances of success were looking very small.

The discussion finally stalled. We had run out of plans to be described, organised and arranged. We all lapsed into our private thoughts, desperately trying to think of all the ways the task could go wrong so we could plan effective ways of dealing with them.

I looked at Drey. 'How in the Seven Hells are we going to do this?'

He smiled sadly. 'We have to try.'

'Great. That doesn't increase my confidence.' The smile grew wider and I felt myself responding. 'Well, you know the full terrors of what Villermir can do, so I suppose that makes you more insane than me.'

We were interrupted by a knock at the door and the equerry returning. He was followed by Kade.

I jumped up before realising what I was doing, and turned red with embarrassment when I saw Kyllian watching me with a disapproving frown. Kade was unshaven. He had dark circles under his eyes and his cheeks were more pronounced. He appeared to have lost weight as his clothes hung loosely on his thin frame. The fight had gone from his attitude as he looked at his father. I was shocked to see his hands were trembling.

'Tallen is needed to retrieve the Empathy Crystal once more,' Kyllian began. I saw the muscles ripple as Kade clenched his jaw. 'Villermir has taken it to Lindvane.'

'What?!' The word was spat as flames of fury flickered in Kade's eyes.

Kyllian ignored his son and continued. 'Tallen is required to obtain the crystal. Drey is needed to neutralise Villermir. Which leaves the company of guards Hayton has placed at the Burford Hythe estate.'

The silence was palpable as Kade considered what was being said. Kyllian hesitated a heartbeat more.

'You are to protect the lives of my thief and senior adviser.'

The colour melted from Kade's face and the trembling became more pronounced. 'Yes, my liege.'

'And you are to protect the life of my youngest son. Do you understand?'

Two spots of colour exploded on Kade's cheeks. I felt tears prick my eyes.

'Yes, sir,' he said quietly.

Kyllian continued. 'It's against my better judgement. But your brother presented a compelling argument.'

Kerk grinned at Kade. I bit my knuckle in an attempt to resist the urge to throw my arms around all three of the royal men. Kyllian waved his hand in dismissal.

'Get out of my chambers. You are to leave tomorrow morning. Kade, I expect you to spend that time with Langdon.'

Langdon nodded in acknowledgement.

'Drey, I have matters yet to discuss with you.'

Langdon, Kerk, Kade and I quickly left the room. As soon as the door closed I threw my arms around Kade's neck, kissing him noisily. Langdon and Kerk groaned dramatically as we headed for the training grounds.

We left before dawn the next morning. The mist hung heavy in the air as the frost glistened in the torchlight. The horses' breath puffed like dragon-smoke as they pawed at the ground and shook their bridles impatiently. I huddled into my warm woollen cloak while Nalya rubbed her eye against my chest.

I had made a point of meeting Tawpin to explain that we were leaving and that Kyllian had agreed to allow Kade to accompany me. I smiled as he walked across the courtyard, bundled in a warm cloak and scowling at the cold, damp weather.

'You up at this time of day?' I teased. 'I am honoured.'

Tawpin grunted. 'You'll be the death of me.' He coughed dramatically. 'I think my lungs are filling with water.'

I laughed. 'You didn't have to come.'

He shrugged. 'Wanted to say goodbye. You know. In case it's the last time.'

'Oh, thanks for the confidence,' I joked, but Tawpin wasn't smiling. 'Hey. I'll be back. You'll not get rid of me that easily.'

He waited several heartbeats before holding me tightly in a firm embrace. He maintained the hug for slightly longer than was comfortable. I gently pushed him away.

'Come on now. People will start talking.'

He took a shaky breath and his eyes glistened suspiciously. As if he was fighting back tears.

'You just take care of yourself.' He kissed me lightly on the cheek before walking briskly away. 'And you take care of her, Your Grace,' he snapped at Kade as he strode by.

Kade stopped fastening his saddlebags to the rear buckles of Mael's saddle. He turned to me, eyebrows raised questioningly. I shrugged in reply, as confused by Tawpin's behaviour as Kade was. Kade returned his attention to his horse.

'He always is emotional when he gets up this early.'

I mounted Nalya and walked her over to Kade and Mael. I watched him lengthen the stirrups and check the girth before scratching the gelding behind the ear. He smiled up at me as Drey led Mupp through the archway, accompanied by Kerk.

'Bit busier than the last time I left,' Kade said, indicating his brother.

'Seems there will be no end to the well-wishers this morning.' I grinned back. 'We must really be doomed!'

Drey focused on attending his horse as Kerk moved round Mael to speak to his brother.

'Miserable morning for a ride,' he began.

'I'll take this over being trapped in my rooms. Thanks for speaking to Father for me.'

Kerk shrugged. 'He was easily persuaded. He's just trying to calm you down.' A small grin flittered over the prince's lips. 'I told him Mobis would dress as a maiden and dance the summer waltzes before that happens.'

Kade playfully punched his brother on the shoulder. 'I'm not sure if that's a compliment or an insult.'

The brothers smiled at each other, the affection between them clearly visible in their eyes. Kerk clasped Kade's forearm in the manner of warriors. The smiles slowly faded from their faces as they looked at each other. A memory flashed to the surface of my mind, causing a trickle of cold water to slip down my spine. I shivered and Nalya sidestepped in irritation. I had seen that look before. Kerk was looking at Kade the way Sharpie had looked at Laken, all those years ago. I did not like the way it made me feel. As if something important was ending. I took a deep breath and concentrated on the swirls of mist obscuring the walls of the courtyard.

'Take care of yourself, brother.'

Kade broke the handshake and slapped Kerk on the arm. 'You take care too. Try to leave the place standing until I return.'

The mood was lifted with Kade's gentle tease. We were ready to leave. Kade and Drey mounted and Kerk was soon lost in the grey cloud as we left the courtyard.

The mist remained for three days, making the journey miserable and the nights spent under oilcloth worse. Muscles cramped from hours spent huddling to prevent moisture dripping down our necks and onto our already soaked tunics. Leather leggings became saturated and refused to dry, chafing the soft skin at our knees. The dried meat supplies grew wet and spoiled, leaving the trail rations bland and unappetising.

But our misery compared poorly to that of the farmers and villagers we passed as we travelled towards the border. It had been less than a season since we had travelled south to take the crystal from the Hilman. That season had treated those in the west harshly. Or maybe it was the burden of supplying the army as it marched towards the front line. The bare fields and skeletal trees reflected the sunken faces and dark eyes of those we saw. Hard work and lack of food accused us from the stares of those working in the fields or herding malnourished animals to market. Drey distributed herbs and salves to those most in need, but we were travelling with minimal supplies and had no food to spare for the hungry.

Two days before reaching the border we spent the night at a small tavern on the outskirts of a market town. The Woodcutter's taproom was full of villagers using the tavern's fire to keep warm. Talk flowed freely, even though the ale was lacking and closely rationed.

'Only one jar each, I afraid,' apologised the innkeeper. 'Grain harvest failed and the troops took most of the rest.'

The ale was weak and the broth was watery, but it felt good to be out of the damp, knowing the horses were resting in comfortable beds of straw. I snuggled into Kade and watched the customers as I let the many conversations drift around me. Men and women complained of domestic hardships. The poor harvest. The hungry children. The ailing elders. There seemed to be a tradition of helping each other and services were offered to mend a fence or the loan outgrown clothes. An elderly woman freely shared the location of a recently discovered patch of edible mushrooms in the woods on the far side of the town. A younger man offered some of his firewood, cut from the forest that day.

It was late, and I was half asleep when I felt Kade stiffen. I became instantly alert to the heated conversation taking place at a nearby table. Talk had left domestic affairs and had turned to the war. Specifically, the lack of progress that appeared to have been gained considering the loss of life and hardship suffered. The abilities of the military and their leaders were being questioned.

'Seems we've been fighting for years,' complained a stocky man with a thick black beard and matching eyebrows, 'just to lose more ground to the Lindvanes.'

The lady to his right nodded in agreement. The firelight accentuated her cheeks. 'We're losing more boys every season. Veren, from two farms over, has lost all three of her sons. And Macey has lost two of her boys, with another coming home in a terrible state. Lost an eye and will never walk again.'

'These generals need to get their act together.' Another man at the table joined in. 'They sit in their furnished shelters eating our food while our men are sent to fight a losing war. It's disgraceful. They have no idea what they are doing. We'll all be ruled by Hayton before Kyllian does anything.'

I felt Kade's chest rumble in anger but heard no sound. His breathing was shallow and heavily controlled. None of his fury was evident as he spoke calmly to the group.

'What would you have him do?'

The villagers turned to glare at Kade for interrupting their conversation. But finding no aggression in his manner, they considered his question. The man with the bushy beard blustered as he tried to decide on an effective strategy.

'Well,' he stammered. 'Anything would be better than this, sitting around waiting to be raided. We should attack them for a change. Give them a bloody nose.'

His friends nodded encouragement until Kade answered quietly, 'And risk more lads from the farms?'

'So. Bring the trained soldiers from the south rather than use our boys.'

'And leave the southern villages unprotected?'

'Well...' The man was flushed and sweating as none of his friends came to his aid. 'I don't know. That's what these lords are supposed to do: take charge and do something.'

Kade gave a small smile of triumph as those seated at the table began to look embarrassed by their previous criticism of the war and of Kyllian. Nobody wanted the deaths and injuries that were occurring. The resultant hardships affected the poor first, but everyone was being hurt by the prolonged engagement with Lindvane. Wishing was not going to make the problem go away.

The final man at the table spoke. He had remained quiet and unnoticed until then. He was taller and more muscled than the others. His clothing was simple but well maintained. He held himself still, making his few words more meaningful than the blustering of the farmers.

'Seems whichever way the king turns will mean losses. This stalemate means the pain is bearable but drawn out. A throbbing ache in the guts.' He looked at Kade. 'Perhaps the time has come to rip the dressing off. Short, sharp pain heals quicker.'

Kade was paying close attention. 'What kind of pain is needed?'

'Extreme,' replied the stranger. 'The time for volunteering is gone. Every man in Faulknar needs to fight for his kingdom.'

'Conscription?'

The tavern had gone quiet and Kade's soft word was heard by the whole room. The stranger nodded.

'Train all that are able to fight for their freedom. Then take this force into the heart of Hayton. Break Lindvane's back before he breaks ours.'

'That would be painful for many.'

'But decisive. Cut off the diseased limb to allow the body to heal.'

Kade dipped his head in acknowledgment of the strong view, as the stranger finished his drink. He rose to leave, bowing to Kade before disappearing into the crowd. Kade looked at Drey, who raised his eyebrows.

I slept badly that night. The dream seemed particularly vivid as I travelled through the maze of tunnels under the mountain. I was hot and sweating as I turned left again and again. My breathing was erratic. I was fighting for every breath by the time I entered the large cavern. Laken was already waiting for me. He was unharmed and wearing a clean white shirt over his dark leather trousers. The look of anger on his face chilled my blood. My heart lurched to a stop momentarily, before beating painfully against my chest, running faster to make up for the missed beats.

'Laken, I—'

'Don't speak to me,' he growled. 'You have no right to speak to me.'

I trembled as he walked towards me. I could see a strip of leather wrapped around his knuckles and gathered in the palm of his hand. My stomach spasmed in fear as I realised what was coming. I tried to back away, but my exit was now blocked by solid rock.

'You have forgotten me. Carrying on with that royal idiot. He makes a fool of you. That makes a fool of me.'

'No, Laken—'

'*I said, don't speak!*' he roared at me, releasing the bundled leather to strike at my face.

I brought my arms up to protect my head, taking the blow on my forearms. I huddled into a protective ball. Again and again he snapped the leather, leaving angry welts on my arms and shoulders.

Laken was panting by the time he stopped. 'You need to be removed. You think you can save the world but you only make it worse. Everyone would be better off with you out of the way.'

He grabbed my arm and dragged me towards a hollow carved into the cavern wall. The space was only large enough for me to stand with my back to the rock, toes level with the walls either side. Laken kept a restraining hand on my chest as he used his free hand to pull the side wall in front of me. I couldn't believe what I was seeing. Solid rock was sliding like a door across the cavity, enclosing me in an upright coffin.

'No, Laken!' I screamed at him. 'Please, *no!*'

I beat against the rock as it closed in front of me. The darkness was absolute. My back pressed against the rock. My arms were pinned in front of my chest. I tried to beat against the stone once more, but I was unable to move my arms. I pressed as hard as I could, making my throat sore with the screams I knew Laken could no longer hear. The walls seemed to press in on me as I struggled for air, my lungs refusing to inflate.

I awoke gasping, my heart hammering against my ribs and echoing in my ears. Kade was holding me so tightly, pinning my arms between our chests. My shoulders were aching from the forced posture. I stopped struggling and listened to his erratic breathing; a slight hitch on inspiration. His grip relaxed when he realised I was awake, but he did not let go. Both of us were trembling in the aftermath of my dream.

We stayed like that for a long time, until dawn oozed into the room around the window shutters and I saw the patchwork of bruises I had left on his chest.

Chapter Nineteen

It took another two days to reach the camps on the border. Kade had dispatches to deliver to Keenan at the main camp at Hunter's Down. We were to rendezvous with Keenan's scouts to determine the best route to the Burford Hythe estate.

The camp spread over three fields along a wasteland land straddling the border between Faulknar and Lindvane. This area of wasteland spread from horizon to horizon, the flat land churned into mud from the numerous horseback sorties that had taken place. No tree, bush or shrub remained in the desolate strip that would have taken a man half a day to walk across. Smoke from the enemy camp rose in the afternoon sunlight. No barracks could be seen, but I knew the Lindvane soldiers had dug deep trenches into the peaty soil to provide shelter from any stray arrows. The colours of the Lindvane dukes flapped in the gentle breeze, although the crests were too far away to be identified. This did not detract from the fact that many companies were opposing Keenan.

We rode into the Faulknar camp with the early winter sun in our eyes. The shelters were arranged in small groups of canvas triangles around a central fire. Entrance to the group was guarded by the standards of our own dukes. Keenan's banner with its regal white lion stood proudly defiant in the centre field, protected by those of the most influential families of the west of the kingdom. The falcon of Brunfield. The bear of Gascombe. The stallion of Humphston. The soldiers of these three dukes filled the massive field at the heart of the camp.

Flanking the centre field were two smaller camps, each containing several hundred soldiers. The standards for the less influential dukes and lords identified smaller groups of shelters. Amongst the huddle of oil-stained wool, men and horses hurried around, giving the camp the appearance of an ants' nest. The smell of ash and charred remains from the funeral pyres at the far end of the furthest field could not quite mask the undercurrent of waste from the men and horses. Barked orders and colourful curses could be heard as we approached. Soldiers of all ages, from beardless youths to grey-haired seniors, worked quickly and efficiently at maintaining the camp. Caring for the horses. Repairing weapons. Performing repetitive drills to condition mind and body. Our presence was monitored by everyone.

We were met by a soldier, his blond hair greying at the temples. The lines carved around his eyes and mouth told of hardship in an otherwise young face. His left eye was pulled by a scar running from eyebrow to jaw. He walked with a pronounced limp, swinging the right half of his body rather than bending at the hip. The man was less than ten paces away when I finally recognised him as Gheth. I hadn't seen the young soldier for years, but I was surprised at the changes the war had forced on him. I no longer saw the carefree youth that I had known in Laken's company. He smiled warmly as we dismounted.

'What in Mobis' Seven Hells are you doing here?' He gave a brief salute with a fist over his heart, before clasping Kade's forearm.

'I have dispatches for Keenan.'

'The lord general will be very pleased to see a friendly face. Come. I'll take you straight to him.'

Gheth called to two grooms as he turned, instructing them to take good care of the horses. He led us through the maze to the largest shelter in the centre of the field. Thick wooden poles provided structure as heavy, oiled leather hung from the timber. The stitched hide was roped to wooden pegs driven deep into the ground, leaving only one entrance at the side. This was guarded by two large soldiers, heavily armed and scarred from combat. They saluted Kade and Gheth before moving aside to let us through.

Keenan's accommodation was spacious, a quality accentuated by the lack of furniture in the main room. Smaller rooms had been created with the use of curtains to provide more private chambers, but the main area allowed him to hold War Councils with his dukes. Brunfield and Gascombe stood either side of a large table in the centre of the room, which was covered with a map and small wooden counters. Gascombe was a small, balding man with broad shoulders used to wielding a sword. His nose had been broken several times, although mainly due to tavern brawls. I knew Kade thought highly of his strategic knowledge and fighting skills. Brunfield reflected his falcon standard. He was also small, but lean in comparison to Gascombe's bulk. Many a tale had been told of his skill on a horse, and his ability to ride into the heart of battle, strike a deadly blow and retreat with the minimum of losses. He had a fresh wound at his hairline and his left arm was strapped across his chest.

Keenan looked up, scowling at the interruption. The scowl was quickly replaced by a wide grin when he saw his nephew.

'By the twelve lower Gods in the Halls of Eternity, it's good to see you, boy.' He marched round the table to clasp Kade's arm affectionately. 'Drey, welcome. Your counsel is sorely needed, my friend. And the beautiful Tallen. I hope you and Kade are not giving my brother too many sleepless nights.' He laughed at the face I pulled. 'No matter. Kyllian was never that fond of sleeping.'

'I have dispatches from Father,' said Kade, handing Keenan a leather-bound bundle. 'There are letters from the quartermaster and chief steward as well.'

Keenan groaned. 'Telling me of all the things I can't have, no doubt.'

He passed the bundle to his equerry before returning to the map on the table. Drey and Kade moved to join him as the dukes shifted to give them room. There were no chairs, so I sat with my back to a timber pole to listen to the discussion. I watched the equerry read the missives, frowning at the letters before placing them on a writing desk at the far end of the room. The correspondence bearing the Faulknar seal remained unopened.

Brunfield continued the conversation we had interrupted, using the counters to demonstrate companies of men. 'Tyree has moved his company to the river at Gransden. Seems Welling is gathering his resources for a final rout before winter. Earl Reed should have it covered but it could get messy down there.'

Keenan indicated a group of counters halfway along the border. 'Can we move Earl Cam's men from Yellin to even up the odds?'

Gascombe shook his head. 'Cam's running light as it is. That last attack has left a hole that Eldion is exploiting for all he's worth. The villages down there are suffering heavy losses.'

Keenan drummed his fingers against the table in frustration. No one spoke for several moments, during which the sounds of the camp could be heard through the shelter walls. A leather-clad scout came through the entrance, bowing to Kade and Keenan before saluting the dukes.

'News from Petton, my lords.' He passed the dispatches to Brunfield, who was standing closest. 'The town was attacked two nights ago. Over half the buildings have been burned and numerous civilians were killed along with a third of Cranston's army. I sadly report that the earl did not make it.'

Keenan's face sagged with the weight of the news as he rubbed his tired eyes. 'Lady Taplin and the heir?'

'Safely wintering with her sister at Edenburrow.'

'The Gods be thanked for that.'

The scout was dismissed as Keenan's equerry lit candles to chase away the shadows from the room. Brunfield absently massaged his bandaged arm as everyone considered the latest setback. Gascombe rubbed at his temples before clearing his throat.

'My lord. May I suggest we retire to instruct the men on the morning's sortie? Some rest may be the best strategy for tonight.'

'Of course. Brunfield, Gascombe, get some food and brief your men. I'll see you at dawn tomorrow.'

The dukes bowed to their general before leaving the room. Brunfield patted Kade on the back, sharing a smile as he left.

'Come.' Keenan swept his arm towards one of the smaller rooms. 'Let us retire to a more comfortable setting. Carver, please bring us some food and wine.'

The equerry bowed his head and followed the dukes. Keenan led us into the room in the centre of the three smaller rooms. He held the curtain to one side to reveal several chairs arranged around a thick woollen rug. A small table was placed between each pair of chairs, and many of these were covered with letters or maps. There was no fire, but each chair had a thick fur blanket that could be used to keep away the chill as the night deepened. Carver had already lit the candles, giving a cosy feel to the temporary shelter. Keenan flopped heavily into a chair, and Drey, Kade and I gratefully followed his lead.

'So. What news of Liegeport?'

Kade relaxed into his chair as he told of the court gossip. 'Dockers are fighting. Merchants are complaining.'

'No change there, then.'

'Lady Amma came to complain to Father that she has been widowed for two years and he still hasn't arranged a suitable marriage for her.'

Keenan barked a quick laugh. 'Oh, I would have loved to have seen that. Poor Kyllian. Amma has been after him since we were children.'

'Breya is chasing Kerk around to get him to try on wedding outfits. She wants him in ruffles. Do you believe that?'

'I believe that girl is capable of getting anything she wants.'

'Tarra keeps her in order,' said Drey quietly.

I watched the sad smile ripple over Keenan's lips as he nodded to Drey. Information was passed with a look between the two men, but was quickly dismissed as Kade turned the conversation back to the war.

'And how goes it here?'

Keenan sighed. 'Slowly. We kill a few of Hayton's generals. He takes a few of ours. We start a sortie. The next day he starts one. It feels like a game of rabbit and fox. We chase him to ground, only for him to pop up somewhere else.'

'You think he's stalling?' asked Drey. 'That he has something else planned and is buying time?'

'I don't know,' said Keenan, shaking his head. 'Maybe it's because we're heading into winter. But...'

'You fear something else?' Drey leaned forward, encouraging the lord general to continue.

'He has greater numbers than we do. The border is being maintained by the dukes here in the west, but...' He rubbed his tired eyes. 'The western dukes have committed their full companies, around five hundred men apiece. The central estates have sent maybe half that. By the time we get to the east coast, they're sending fewer than fifty men.'

Drey shook his head sadly. 'Lindvane seems a long way away to them. Maybe they are more concerned with the Gallowglass raids.'

'You don't need soldiers for the sea raids. You need scouts, runners, deterrents. Men are dying here. I need numbers!' Keenan slapped the palm of his hand on his thigh in frustration.

'We could make them come.' Kade looked at his uncle, assessing his mood. 'Conscription.'

Keenan looked up to meet Kade's eyes. He nodded in acceptance. 'Conscription. I've thought the same. Kyllian will hate it. But I can't see us standing against Hayton any other way.'

Before he could say more a deep rumble vibrated through the ground, up my legs and into my chest. Although Keenan did not seem concerned, I saw Drey and Kade exchange worried glances. The rumble grew louder, causing the empty chairs to wobble and the shelter leather to snap against the wooden frame. The candles threw wild shadows around the room as they rocked in their holders. I could feel the ground shaking beneath my feet. A sudden crack, the sound of lightning tearing across a summer sky, rang in my ears, leaving a buzzing for several heartbeats after the original concussion. The vibrations stopped and the ground was immobile again.

'What, in all that is Holy, was that?'

I looked at Drey, who had turned pale. His hands were shaking, although he quickly covered them with his fur blanket when he saw me looking.

'Earth tremors,' said Keenan calmly. 'They've been happening once or twice a week since the last full moon.'

'That could be the reason for your stalling,' said Drey, continuing when he saw Keenan's confused expression. 'The king has provided all the details in his letters to you. But the short version is that Villermir has taken the Empathy Crystal to Lindvane.'

The muscles along Keenan's jaw rippled as he ground his teeth and his eyes flashed in anger. 'I never trusted that pious son of a…'

'Quite,' continued Drey. 'But I don't think any of us realised the level of his treachery.'

'And I assume that's why you're here?'

Drey nodded in agreement. 'Apparently Villermir has the crystal at Burford Hythe.'

'That's several days from here.' The lord general chewed the skin around his fingernail as he thought. 'It's also heavily guarded. Do you need men?'

'No. We've got Kade.'

Keenan looked up to see Drey smiling at him.

'I know you need everyone here. We're aiming for stealth. With a bit of luck, they'll never know we were there.'

Keenan did not look convinced. 'So, it seems Faulknar is indebted to you once again, Tallen.'

I shifted uncomfortably in my chair. 'Faulknar owes me nothing, my lord.'

'On the contrary. You have already risked your life for my brother. Several times, I believe. Yours is not the glory of battle, yet it may be the more important.'

I could feel my cheeks burning as the blood rushed to colour my face. 'Really, it is of no consequence. Anyone would do it.'

Keenan smiled kindly, noting my embarrassment. 'Still. Your loyalty is noted and appreciated. Never forget that.'

'Yes, my lord.'

I was rescued by Carver bringing food and wine. The discussion turned to more pragmatic issues regarding our journey into Lindvane.

The next morning brought rain. The horses pawed at the mud as they stood at the edge of the wasteland. The far camp was obscured by low cloud, making the day feel heavy and oppressive. The men lined up facing Lindvane. The cavalry would ride out first to engage the enemy, followed by the pikemen and finally the foot soldiers. The ranks extended as far as I could see on either side of me. Each unit – cavalry, pike and foot – was several lines deep. The banners hung limp with the weight of the rain, but their colours still motivated the troops. I saw fear in many faces, but also determination and pride.

Gascombe gave the order to advance. Half a field away, Humphston repeated the order. The lines moved forward together, the horses raising their forelegs high as their riders fought to keep them in pace with the pikemen behind. The army moved in eerie silence, with the jingle of bits the only sound. Keenan and Brunfield remained with Drey, Kade and me at the edge of the wasteland. While Keenan and Brunfield directed the battle from afar, we were to wait until the opposing forces engaged before slipping past into Lindvane. Hopefully Hayton's men would be too preoccupied with the sortie to notice three riders on the fringes.

Keenan's army had made it over halfway across the wasteland before the alarm was raised. The noise of the camp stirring to life reached us on the sidelines. Shouted orders drifted on the slight breeze. Horses whinnied as they were hastily tacked up. Hooves pounded as they galloped towards the battle.

The noise of contact was immense, even as far away as we were. The thud of sword against shield. The scream of blade against blade. The shrieks of wounded horses and men. I swallowed against the acid burning at the back of my throat. Mael skipped in irritation as Kade balled his hands into fists on the reins.

'You have a greater duty than this, boy,' said Keenan sympathetically. 'Your day in battle will come. But dying here today is not your destiny. Faulknar needs you to bring back the stone.'

It was several heartbeats before Kade acknowledged his uncle's words with a small nod of his head. He continued to stare out over the wasteland as the colours of the standards became lost in the chaos of battle. The pikemen had joined the fight and were removing the enemy cavalry. Riderless horses added to the confusion. Who was fighting for which side became lost as the foot soldiers sliced and carved their way through the mass. The rain turned red above the clash of metal and the crack of bone.

'We go now,' snapped Kade through gritted teeth.

Mael leapt forward at the touch of Kade's heels. Mupp and Nalya soon followed and my attention was taken from the battle as we tried to catch up with Kade. He had unsheathed his sword and leaned forward in the saddle, ready for anyone who dared to stop him. I copied his position, moving myself between Drey and the fighting armies. I was sure he could take care of himself, but he carried no sword.

We were not lucky enough to go unnoticed. A small group of five cavalry split from the main battle to chase after us. I felt the hair at the back of my neck stand up as the air around Drey became different, more expectant, like the clean air before a thunderstorm. I had no chance to see what was causing the change. Two soldiers were charging at Kade while the other three were on course to intercept Drey and me. Ignoring the cramps in my stomach, I readied myself for the contact. I swung my sword, connecting with the blade of the warrior aiming for my head. The shock wave that vibrated up my arm focused my attention as I followed the swing through to slice his horse on the flank. It skittered sideways, unbalancing the rider and giving me the heartbeat I needed to slice across his abdomen. Nalya skipped sideways to avoid the soldier's backswing. But the stroke lacked any force. His strength had leaked out of his wound, along with his blood and guts.

Refusing to dwell on something that no longer posed a threat, I turned Nalya around to face Drey. One attacker was already on the floor. Nalya bore down on the final Lindvane. I used her momentum to power my thrust. The air seemed to shimmer around the soldier, causing him to freeze as his sword raised to strike Drey. Nalya swerved to avoid crashing into them, and my killing blow sliced into the soldier's shoulder, taking his arm off at the joint. The man didn't make a sound as he toppled from his stationary horse.

I wheeled Nalya around, lifting my right leg over the saddle in order to dismount and finish the soldier. Then I was halted by a sudden thrust of air to my chest. I looked up to see Drey glaring at me.

'Leave him. We don't have time.'

He kicked Mupp into a gallop after Kade. Nalya followed the other horse without any instruction from me. I scrambled to return to my seat in the saddle. Kade had killed both his attackers and was waiting for us to join him. We rode away from the battle and the destruction disappeared into the rain.

We rode steadily north-west, heading for the heart of Lindvane. We travelled by night, trusting the horses to find sound footing. It was slow, but safe. Where there was sufficient tree cover we would occasionally travel by day. I watched the labourers toil in the large fields, turning the soil and planting the seed for next year's crop. There was a lack of young, healthy men. The work was mainly carried out by women and children. A few elder men were seen along with the occasional Traveller, their darker skins and long black hair identifying them as strangers in this land. The few Travellers labouring in the fields worked away from the Lindvane farmers, keeping themselves to themselves. The friendly banter rarely included the southern helpers. I suspected that the Travellers had been hired to replace the men sent to the front line, and that their presence was resented; a constant reminder that Lindvane's men were dying while the Travellers took their earnings.

The rain stopped after two days, leaving the nights bright and clear, but cold. I was grateful for my many layers of warm clothing as well as the heat generated by Nalya. A strong wind blew over the countryside, bringing the almost constant smell of onions from the fields. Drey called it a lazy wind as it seemed to want to blow straight through you rather than go around. The Lady provided a waxing moon to bathe us in plenty of light and our distances increased each night. The scenery gradually changed as we made our way across Hayton's kingdom. The flat, open fields at first began to undulate, looking like the rolling waves of the sea in the darkness. The waves grew larger until defined hills rolled along the horizon. The lights of settlements generally marked the summit of these hills, so we made our way between them, staying in the shadows and barely making a noise.

It was four days into our journey when I commented on how fortunate we had been in avoiding patrols or late-drinking villagers. Kade's teeth flashed white in the moonlight as he smiled at me.

'It's not luck,' he said quietly. 'Concentrate. You should be able to feel it.'

He nodded towards Drey. Drey had spent most of the nights relaxed, drooping slightly in the saddle. His eyes were open but the lids were sagging. He seemed to be almost on the point of dozing off. With the arrogance of youth, I had put it down to his age. After Kade's words I reconsidered my assessment. Drey's manner was more that of a man in a trance. His posture was still but not relaxed. His muscles were taut, and when the moonlight shone on him I could see the lines of concentration around his eyes.

I closed my eyes and opened my senses to detect what Drey was concentrating on. I identified the normal occurrences of the night. The sound of leaves being rustled by the wind. The soft pad of the horses' feet on the moist grass, releasing the scents of broken plants and disturbed mud. Frowning, I concentrated to determine the fainter sounds. The squeak of an alarmed mouse in the undergrowth. The whisper of displaced air as an owl swooped. The bark of a fox hunting in the far hills.

Dismissing these sounds, I explored further, allowing my mind to drift where it willed, riding the currents of the wind. The tantalising hint of a different tone; one that ran counter to the normal rhythms of the countryside. Tentatively, I reached towards it.

And almost lost it in my surprise.

A faint hum, as insubstantial as the ghost-lights that played over the marshes; as gentle as a butterfly's stroke. The sound radiated from Drey, expanding further than my peripheral vision. Tiny ripples, as fragile as spiderwebs, flickered across my closed eyelids. I breathed the faint scent of magick.

I opened my eyes to find Kade watching me carefully. 'I felt it.'

'Drey's scouting the territory for us; a more refined version of what you've just done naturally. Drey can send out his consciousness to detect the auras of every living thing. He can identify sheep, dogs, farmers and soldiers long before they are able to see us. He's been keeping us safe.'

'I never knew.' I was shocked by the casual use of magick, practised so close without me realising it. 'I'm glad he's here.'

'Me too.' Kade grinned.

The protection granted by Drey lasted until we were almost upon the estate at Burford Hythe. The large house could be seen at the top of a tall hill. Smoke rose from its many chimneys to mix with the clouds. The green fields of the private estate bordered on orchards and pastures for cattle and sheep. A river flowed lazily around the foot of the hill to the right of the house, before opening into a large lake. To the left of the house was a thick forest that would provide cover for us as we approached.

The presence of armed soldiers had increased as we neared the estate. Drey instructed us to hide in thickets at least once every night. Single runners passed us frequently, carrying messages to and from the house. As we neared the property these were joined by small groups of between three and five soldiers. The crests on their tunics and saddle numnahs identified them as Hayton's bodyguards. The boar emblem was highlighted with red tusks and eyes to mark them as members of his elite force. Each man had been hand-picked for his unquestionable loyalty and exceptional combat skills.

We were still a day's ride from Burford when Drey alerted us to a large number of guards heading towards us. The grey light preceding the dawn had removed our protective cover of darkness, so Kade suggested we camp for the day and hope the soldiers pass us by. We led the horses off the forest trail and deeper into the trees, finding a clearing that allowed a good view of the trail but was bordered by tall grasses to provide cover. Kade took the horses further into the forest before tethering them to the trees. We were careful not to leave a track in the grass that could reveal our presence. We burrowed into waist-high bracken behind a small rise, content that we were sufficiently hidden from view.

I awoke to the sound of horses rattling their bits as their hooves thumped on the trail. My heart raced as I glanced at Drey and Kade beside me, watching the riders approach. Careful not to make any noise, I rolled onto my front. The sight of ten Boar bodyguards riding into the clearing made my stomach lurch and I started trembling. The soldiers looked unassuming in their woollen cloaks, but each had a sheathed sword and at least one dagger in his belt. Most were tall and broad at the shoulders with closely shaven haircuts to accentuate their stern faces and watchful eyes.

The guard leading the group raised his arm. 'We'll rest here,' he said, leading his horse into the clearing. 'Dekker can take a look at Elion's horse; see why she's gone lame.'

I watched, barely daring to breathe as the men gathered at the far end of the clearing. Two of them examined a lean chestnut mare while the others stretched tight muscles and shared water from a leather skin. The smaller of the two men examining the mare gently ran his hands down her left foreleg while the other tickled her nose. She tossed her head in irritation as her fetlock was flexed.

'Well? What's the damage?' called the man who appeared to be in charge.

The smaller man shook his head. 'Nothing serious. The joint's a little swollen. Probably knocked it on something.'

'When can we ride?'

'After noon should be fine.' He turned to the horse's rider. 'Take her to the river. Stand that leg in the cold water for a while. That should take down the swelling and make her feel better.'

The smaller man stretched his back and accepted water from his senior as the young guard took his horse across the clearing. I chanced a quick look at Kade, worried about our horses. Would they call to these others? I could see concern in his face as well. Fortunately, halfway across the soldier turned his horse away from us, leading it through a thicket in the opposite direction to where Kade had taken our horses. Kade relaxed his taut shoulder muscles and very slowly released the breath that he had been holding.

I returned my attention to the soldiers gathered by the trail. While the leader and Dekker talked together, four soldiers were grooming their horses and taking care of their hooves. The remaining three took the rest as an opportunity to release some energy. A thickset man with an easy smile casually threw some mud at the taller soldier opposite him. The tall man dramatically protested this unfair treatment, before returning a clod of turf. The third guard, who looked much younger than the rest, laughed at his comrades. This unfortunately drew their attention and two mud-balls came his way. Before long there was an all-out battle of flying mud and grass, the accuracy of their aims matched by the athleticism of the soldiers as they twisted to avoid the debris.

Their shouts and laughter were halted by a sharp reprimand from the man in charge. Leaving Dekker, who was failing to hide a smile, he walked over to the soldiers.

'What is this? Entertainment for young children? You are the king's bodyguards. Act accordingly, or by the power of the One God I'll knock your heads together.'

The guards had the grace to look embarrassed. Brushing lumps of mud from their uniforms, they avoided looking at each other or their commander. He maintained their discomfort for several heartbeats.

'If you have so much energy to burn off, at least do something useful. The woods will be full of berries and mushrooms. Add variety to the trail rations. Just make sure you bring back the edible varieties and not the toxic ones.'

He flipped his hand in dismissal and the soldiers grinned at their mild punishment. I felt Drey stir as the men walked away from their horses and the other guards. Kade leaned towards me and whispered in my ear.

'Drey thinks this is too risky. We need to move.'

I nodded in acknowledgement, thinking that moving from our hiding place was too risky. But I also realised that with soldiers roaming the forest, even if we managed to stay hidden, it would not be long before our horses were discovered. We moved so slowly, backing out of the bracken without causing the ferns to sway. Once under the protection of the trees we could move more freely, swiftly but silently making our way to the horses.

I gave silent thanks to Sucellos, the God of good fortune, that our horses had been trained from foals not to whicker in greeting as we returned. They remained as silent as we were, as we tightened their girths and released their reins.

'We've got two headed this way,' breathed Drey, unnecessarily adding to our sense of urgency.

We could no longer maintain our stealth as we mounted and the horses walked over dried grass and dead twigs. The noise was amplified by our oversensitive nerves, but nevertheless the sound brought shouts from the nearby soldiers. We turned the horses towards the heart of the forest, but I had not moved three paces before the thickset guard ran into view. His easy smile was no longer visible as he drew his sword smoothly.

'Drey, get her out of here.'

Kade turned Mael's head towards the soldier, unsheathing his own sword as he kicked the gelding into a gallop. Drey reached over and grabbed Nalya's reins before I could react and join the attack.

'No argument, Tal. We have to go now!'

I clenched my jaw against all the protests I wanted to make. Leaving Kade to face the threat alone hurt as a physical pain squeezing my heart. Still I nodded to Drey before kicking Nalya into a canter away from Kade.

The second soldier soon appeared before us, throwing his dagger at Drey. The blade fell short as Drey instructed me to keep riding. My heart squeezed a little tighter as I turned Nalya away. I heard a sharp crack, like the spitting of a fire, and convinced myself that Drey was going to be fine.

Nalya bravely negotiated the fallen branches and tree roots as we rode deeper into the forest. I had no time to miss my friends as I concentrated on avoiding low branches that wanted to whip at my face.

I had travelled no more than fifteen horse-lengths from Drey when the final soldier appeared in front of me. My relief at facing the youngest guard was short-lived when he was joined by another on horseback. I urged Nalya on, aiming at the young soldier, hoping to get to him before the rider could. I drew my sword and focused on the man on the ground while remaining aware of the horse heading straight for me.

I sliced downwards as Nalya ran past the soldier. The momentum forced my sword along his with a scream of protest. The blade slid towards the hilt before swinging away, catching him on the cheek and causing blood to flow from the wound. The young soldier followed through with his swing, slicing Nalya on her rump. She swung round to remove her hindquarters from the threat, leaving me blind to the rider who was now behind me.

I positioned Nalya so I could strike again at the man on the ground. In the heartbeat before jumping into a canter, the mounted soldier flashed past on my unprotected side. Rather than aim for me, the guard swung his blade at Nalya, turning her grey neck crimson.

Her scream of pain joined my roar of anger. Her knees folded as I felt the bite of a blade deep in my thigh and the warm spread of blood. I swept my sword in retaliation but Nalya had stumbled away from the soldier. My blade carved harmlessly through the air. My mare fell heavily, trapping my leg under her as my head smacked against the ground. My vision dimmed for a heartbeat as a fireball of pain exploded in my skull.

The young soldier stood over me, smiling slightly as I raised my sword in a weak defence. He raised his sword for the killing blow. I felt strangely calm as he brought the weapon down.

Then Kade's head appeared over the young man's shoulder. His face was contorted into a rictus mask of rage. His lips pulled back to reveal his teeth in an animal's snarl. His eyes were as dark as ink. He raised his sword over his head with both hands on the hilt.

And then there was nothing.

Chapter Twenty

Pain exploded in my leg. Flames radiated from deep in my thigh, extending as far as my spine. I tried to twist away but was prevented from moving by pressure across my chest. My eyes refused to open as sparks of golden light swirled against the blackness. I tried to tell them that I was awake, to plead with them not to remove my leg. But the words came out as a faint groan, daggers stabbing into my brain.

'Be easy, Tal,' whispered Kade. 'Drey's just cleaning your leg.'

Somewhere, buried deep, I received the warmth of knowing Kade and Drey were well. The sensation remained buried under numerous aches, stabs, crushes and flames of pain tearing into my body. I was vaguely aware of gentle pressure along the insides of my arms; patterns being traced onto my skin. I sunk further into the blanketing darkness.

I awoke next to the smell of warm honey. My eyelids felt coated in clay, but I managed to open them. The room was dark. Shadows played in the rafters, cast by the fire I could hear popping quietly. I tried to speak but my mouth and throat were so dry the sound came out as a rasping croak. Kade gently eased me up to sit with my back supported by his chest. The change of position, although smoothly performed, made the room tilt suddenly before swimming back into focus. I closed my eyes and took a shaky breath.

'Here,' said Kade, passing me a beaker of cool water. I saw that his knuckles were bruised and swollen. 'Small sips now.'

The water settled my stomach as well as lubricating my throat. I saw Drey stirring a small pot over the fire, releasing more of the warm honey scent. I could not make out the details of the room outside the circle of light cast by the fire, but we appeared to be in a wooden building similar to the woodcutter's cottage outside Liegeport.

'Where are we?'

'We found this shack about half a day's ride from the clearing.' Kade took the beaker from my trembling hands as I relaxed into his warmth. 'From the amount of wildlife living in here, it seems to have been deserted for quite a while.'

'Probably used as lodgings in the summer but rarely visited in the winter.' Drey turned from the fire to assess me critically, eventually smiling reassuringly. 'That's what we're hoping, anyway.'

'How long have I been asleep?'

Drey flicked his gaze up to Kade before replying. 'Over a day.'

'A day?!'

I tried to rise, shocked at how much time had been lost, only to have the room tilt sharply again. Dark rings closed in from the edges of my vision. I forced myself to breathe deeply until they faded back out of sight. Kade placed a hand on my forehead, gently pressing me back against his chest.

'All's well.'

'But the soldiers – they'll be looking for us.'

Another look passed between Drey and Kade. 'No one is searching for us at the moment. We're safe enough for now.' Drey took a deep breath, changing the subject as he rose. 'Anyway, you need to concentrate on getting better.'

He removed the pot from the fire and placed it on the floor by the bed. He placed a strip of linen into the pot, using a stick to ensure it was fully submerged in the liquid. Sitting beside me on the bed, he lifted the blanket to expose my injured leg. Despite the large bandage, I could see there was extensive damage. The skin above and below the dressing was swollen. Blotchy purple bruises covered most of it, with dark blue veins radiating from them. Drey removed the bandage, taking care to move the leg as little as possible. Even so, each jolt sent daggers of pain up and down my leg. I gripped fistfuls of the blanket and tried to keep still so Drey could work.

Fascination replaced revulsion when he removed the final layer to reveal a puffy, bleeding wound. The skin had been sliced into a half-moon flap of tissue. The swelling had pushed this flap upwards so that the edges were separated by two finger-widths. Blood pooled in the cavity left inside the muscle before trickling down my leg. The flesh pushing out of the wound was pink and bubbly. I could see no sign of infection. Drey looked up to see me watching him and smiled.

'It looks worse than it is,' he reassured me. 'I've included a few spells in your dressings to speed the healing along. You lost a lot of blood and the wound went deep. Without intervention, it would be weeks before you could use that leg again.'

He did not have to say that we could not spend weeks in enemy territory. Kade kissed the top of my head while I considered Drey's words.

'Drey made sure you slept well,' Kade said into my hair. 'Your body needs all the energy it can get to heal your wound. You're going to be very boring company for a few days.'

Drey tested the temperature of the new dressing before placing it over the wound. The honey gave the linen a warm, golden hue as well as providing all the components my body would need to heal. The warmth spread instantly through the abused tissues. The constant ache was dulled for a few heartbeats. Drey then covered the honey poultice with a clean square of linen and placed a silver coin in the middle.

He winked at my frown of confusion. 'Magick.'

He placed his hand over the coin, leaving a hand-width's space so I could still see the coin.

'*Ruith*,' he whispered to the coin.

All pain was forgotten for an instant as I watched, disbelieving. The coin melted without any heat, absorbing into the linen so that the white sheet sparkled with silver flecks in the firelight.

'He's just showing off,' said Kade, his voice rumbling pleasantly against my ear.

Drey grinned, then wrapped my leg in strips of clean linen. He whispered words, too quiet for me to hear, into each layer of the bandage. Small clouds of pure white smoke dissolved into the material. My breathing grew deeper with each fold of cloth and I fought to keep my eyes open. Kade pushed me away from his chest but maintained my sitting position with his arms as Drey scooped out the last of the honey solution from the pot with his fingers. He stood up so he could access the back of my head. I could feel the hair clump around an area the size of a small coin. The place where I hit my head on the ground when Nalya collapsed. I started to ask about her, even though I felt I already knew the answer. My memories were all wrapped in a thick fog. Perhaps she hadn't been hurt as badly as I thought.

Drey's probing fingers ignited sparks of pain over my scalp.

'Ow!' I reached up to protect the sore area, but he slapped my hand away.

'You need to be more careful, Tallen.' He smeared the sticky liquid over the wound. 'You keep hitting your head like this, you may just knock some sense into it.'

'I doubt that,' replied Kade.

I tried to protest but Drey's spells were pulling at my eyelids again. My limbs felt heavy and sank into the bed as Kade laid me flat. My head felt like a massive boulder. I gave in to the pressure and closed my eyes, clutching Kade's hand as sleep dragged me back into the darkness.

'Sleep well, my injured Magpie.'

It was still dark when I awoke. The fire had gone out and I saw no light from any windows. My thoughts seemed clearer than before and the pain was restricted to my leg, but I still felt as weak as a butterfly in a gale.

'Kade?'

'He's not here.' Drey's voice sounded strained, coming from the other side of the room.

'What do you mean, he's not here?'

'He left this afternoon.'

Maybe my thoughts were not as clear as I had thought. Drey wasn't making any sense. Why would Kade leave? Where would he go? I was starting to get a headache.

'Drey, I don't understand. Why has he left?' I tried to sit up but lacked the strength to even lift my head from the pillow. 'What do you mean, this afternoon? How long have I been asleep?'

'You've been asleep another full day. I told you, your body needs to repair.'

'But where's Kade gone? Why hasn't he come back by now? It's dark.'

'Tallen!' Drey snapped at me, halting my endless ramble of questions. 'He went to the estate. He was concerned about the wasted days. He went to scout Burford Hythe.'

'He went where?!'

Anger provided the strength I needed to sit up. Ignoring the pain in my leg and the encroaching black rings, I turned to Drey, who was still hidden in the shadows.

'How could you let him go there? On his own!'

'I didn't have much choice!' He took a deep breath to suppress the anger in his voice. His tone was one of concern when he continued. 'There was no other choice. We can't stay here much longer. Kade bought us some time, but that time's running out. They'll start looking for us soon.'

He walked over to sit beside me on the bed. His face was mottled by deep shadows, but his posture was a little deflated. Defeated.

'You are confusing me. How did he buy us time?' I asked quietly. 'Drey? Why aren't the soldiers from the clearing looking for us?'

'He killed them. Kade killed them all.'

'All of them?'

Drey sighed in the darkness, taking my hands. He slowly rubbed his thumbs over the skin as he thought about how much to tell me.

'Kade is an excellent swordsman. But that day…' He shook his head. 'He was something different. I've never seen him like that. It was like he was possessed.' He squeezed my hands. 'He thought you were dead.'

'But all of them?'

'They will be missed soon. Then the whole countryside will be crawling with soldiers. We have to be gone by then.'

'Then help me up.'

I struggled to swing my legs over the side of the bed, but Drey placed a restraining hand on my chest.

'The best thing you can do is sleep.'

'I can't sleep knowing Kade is roaming around Lindvane on his own.'

Drey smiled at me. 'You'll sleep. *Suain.*'

I drew a breath to protest but sleep took me back into the dark oblivion.

The sun left a rectangular patch of light on the floor the next time I stirred. I could hear the birds singing while Drey chatted away to the horses. The cold wind brought in air to cool my hot head. I threw back the wool blanket and fur cloak covering me to allow more cool air to touch my heated limbs. There was a throbbing ache within my thigh and my scalp was tender when I touched it. But elsewhere the pain had gone. My thoughts were clear and my breath came easily. I had a moment of dizziness as I sat up and swung my legs over the side of the bed. The floor felt pleasantly cold beneath my bare feet. I needed the support of a nearby chair to rise to a standing position, hesitantly placing weight on my damaged leg. Flames stabbed through the muscle, but it held my weight.

I wrapped the woollen blanket around myself to protect my modesty, even though Drey had cared for me for at least three days. I walked to the door, welcoming the contrasting sensations of the warm sun and the cold wind on my face. Drey was checking the feet of a bay mare with a white smudge on her nose. She had been ridden by one of the Lindvane soldiers. Standing patiently beside her was Mupp. I saw no sign of Mael or Nalya. Drey looked up to see me watching him.

'Nalya?' My voice cracked on the word as tears pooled in my eyes, suddenly emotional at the violent loss of my little grey.

He shook his head, lowered the bay's foot and walked over to me, gently guiding me to sit on a large log that appeared to have been used as a seat before, with a smoothed indentation.

'You'll need a horse.' He nodded towards the bay. 'She's a calm, steady mare.'

The horse was flaring her nostrils at my scent. Her eyes were wide enough to show the white sclera. I had my doubts that she would let me ride her.

'How are you feeling?'

'Amazing, considering.'

'Your body has done a lot of healing. Don't take it for granted for a few days.'

I smiled at him. 'I won't.' I hesitated for a few heartbeats to ensure the sincerity of my words. 'Thank you, Drey.'

He waved his hand in dismissal. I looked over to the trees bordering the small clearing in front of the cottage. The leaves had fallen, leaving empty branches. The bracken had turned brown in preparation for winter.

'Drey?'

'Yes?'

'Do you think we would know if anything had happened to Kade?'

Drey sighed and sat on the ground next to me. 'I don't know,' he replied simply.

'I was thinking… with your link to his mind…'

He shook his head sadly. 'I'm afraid it only works over a short distance. I've tried but get no answer. He's just too far away.'

'But you hear stories of loved ones, far away, that know when a person dies.'

Drey took my hand. 'I have no proof for or against those stories. But I believe we would have felt something if harm had come to Kade.'

But I did feel something. A cavernous space engulfing the whole of me, pressing against my chest, making it difficult to breathe; pressing against my stomach, making me feel sick. Cold fingers of dread caressed the back of my neck. When I looked at Drey I could see the same emptiness in his eyes.

We left at dusk that evening. After several attempts at approaching the bay, and her biting, kicking and rearing, it was decided that I would ride Mupp and Drey would take the acquired horse. Mupp snorted and constantly maintained one ear turned in my direction. We eventually left when the last songbird had gone to roost.

The night was clear, and we cantered for most of it. The forest ended soon after leaving the cottage and we chose speed over stealth. The roads to Burford Hythe were well travelled during the day but deserted at night. We passed several small settlements containing five or six roundhouses. Lights shone from their single windows, keeping the perils of the night at bay. The sky was beginning to lighten when we entered the woods to the left of the estate. There had been no sign of Kade.

We slept fitfully during the day, hidden within bramble bushes. The horses were tethered to small shrubs, their reins attached to their headcollars by sections of thin cord. If the horses got scared, the cords would snap, allowing them to run free without the fear of trapping their legs in the reins. This would also work if we failed to return from the house.

Leaving the horses behind, we travelled the remaining distance to the estate on foot, arriving at the forest edge during the late evening. With the protection of the tree cover we could study the building and the people moving around it. The house had a main section that was three storeys high. The stonework had been carved from the main entrance to the multiple chimneys blowing smoke into the twilight. Decorative patterns had been chiselled into the cornerstones, while images of small animals were carved into a number of bricks across the wall. The archway over the door proudly displayed two boxing bears, the standard of Duke Tywell, uncle to Hayton and unwavering in his support of his nephew.

The rest of the house was less intimidating, looking like it had been added hurriedly as the need arose. A wooden structure extended away to the right, nearest the woods. It rested uncomfortably against the main building. A plain door was set in the centre of the single-storey structure. A row of windows overlooked the garden. The left side of the house had two additional wooden structures, each with its own door and standing two storeys high. Their chimneys released smoke, suggesting occupancy.

There were four guards on duty. Two stood by the main door while two walked the perimeter of the gardens. The route taken by these guards was regular and predictable. The men at the main door were relaxed, leaning against the stone arch as they chatted companionably. It appeared that the estate was well protected within the heart of Lindvane and by the status of its duke. The guards did not seem to be expecting any trouble.

We waited until it was fully dark before leaving the cover of the woods. The clouds had gathered during the evening, making the night a uniform grey that would conceal our presence from the soldiers at the main door. The patrolling guards passed out of sight behind the single-storey building and we made our move. Crouching as we ran to lower our profile, we made for the door of this building. We hesitated while Drey checked for people inside. I wiped my sweaty palms on my dark leggings while I waited anxiously for him to do his magick. Eventually he nodded and eased the door open, moving it finger-width by finger-width to avoid making any noise. When the door was only a quarter of the way open we were able to slip inside.

We stood by the closed door, trying to listen past the sound of our pounding hearts for any signs of activity. My eyes grew accustomed to the dimmer light. It revealed a long, narrow room running the width of the building. A large table dominated the centre of the room, which may have once been used for the servants' meals. It was currently covered in pots, boxes, sacks and clothing. The room was being used as a storeroom. The thick layer of dust that covered everything suggested it had not been visited for a long time. More goods were stacked along the walls, but the floors were clear, allowing us to cross the room without stumbling.

There were two doors leading from this room. A sturdy oak door with iron hinges and lock was positioned to the left of the wall that probably joined the main house. The other door was more basic: thin wood with a simple latch. Since entering the building, I had felt the soft touch of something brushing my mind. It fled whenever I tried to grasp it but returned as soon as my attention turned elsewhere. It was like the feeling of someone being in the room when you can't see anybody there. The feeling increased in intensity as I approached this plain door. I looked at Drey and saw a frown of confusion.

'My skin is positively crawling with tiny creatures at the amount of magick in this room,' he whispered. 'I've never encountered such blatant use before.'

He placed his hand close to the door while taking care not to touch the wood. A faint green light glowed from his palm as he moved it over the door. The colour darkened when he hovered over the latch.

'This door is warded,' he said as his frown deepened. 'Nobody is walking through here without getting a mighty headache.'

He brought his other hand up to cover the back of the one hovering over the latch. He closed his eyes for several heartbeats before taking a deep breath.

'*Fuasgail*,' he breathed.

He opened his eyes as the green light faded and then dissolved into a thin mist. Drey turned to me and winked as he opened the door. The air smelt stale as I entered the narrow passageway that led away from the door. Further rooms could be seen as darker areas along the corridor. Drey led towards some stone steps leading downwards. As we stepped onto the first of them, small crystals resting in cavities on both sides glowed a pale orange. The lights illuminated the steps leading to the right and seemed to extend below the main house. My head was starting to ache with the tension behind my eyes. I suspected it had more to do with the magick that was so obvious here, than with me straining my eyes due to the low lighting.

I counted fifty steps down into an atrium. This space seemed to be more frequently used. The air was fresher and there was a woollen rug in the centre of the floor. More orange lights cast dim illumination over the room, allowing us to see several passages radiating from the atrium.

'It's hard to tell if anyone is around,' said Drey, making me jump. 'There is so much noise from the protections and the lights. It's hard to filter the important markers from the trivial. I can't feel any presence nearby.'

'Which way do we go?'

Drey spun round, looking at all the options. 'I don't know. The whole place feels like a trap. I feel like I've fallen into a pit full of insects, all crawling over my skin.' He smiled reassuringly at my horrified expression. 'It makes it hard to concentrate.'

He hesitated a few more heartbeats before walking confidently towards a tunnel. 'This way.' He paused at the entrance to bow enthusiastically. 'Ladies first.'

'Thanks very much,' I said sarcastically, fully realising that I would spring any trap first.

I had not walked more than ten paces when there seemed to be a momentary lack of sound, as if the air had been sucked out of the tunnel. Then a sharp crack sounded behind me. I spun around with my heart pounding almost through my chest wall and was paralysed by what I saw; by the fear of something so powerful.

The entrance to the tunnel had been sealed by a large boulder of what looked like ice. I could feel the heat radiating from it curl my eyebrows and make my eyes water. I could get no closer than five paces from the rock. Trapped inside, Drey was frozen in a posture of torment. His face was contorted into a scream of agony, his eyes tightly closed. Small blue veins radiated from his neck, wrists, waist and ankles. They looked like miniature lightning bolts frozen into the ice. His hands had convulsed into claws halfway to shielding his head. The tendons in his neck stood out like small cords of rope.

I sank to my knees. Drey had been right. It was a trap. If Drey had been beaten by the magickal protections of this house, there was no hope for me. I felt crushed by the weight of failure.

Chapter Twenty One

I remained sitting in the tunnel for a long time, staring at Drey trapped within the icy rock. I stayed there until it became obvious that the world would not end; until I could no longer convince myself that Drey would break free, that I would think of a way to help him. Until I could no longer ignore the insistent pull at my mind; the desire to go on, to find the crystal. I resisted as hard as I could, not wanting to accept that I had lost both Kade and Drey. That I was totally alone. I had been totally alone twice before. Neither occasion had been good.

Finally, I could ignore the call of the crystal no more.

'I will come back for you,' I said to Drey, hoping he could hear me.

My eyes stung with sudden tears as I turned away and continued down the corridor. I no longer walked quietly. I no longer checked for soldiers. I no longer cared if I was caught. I felt as if I had lost everything. I stiffly placed one foot in front of the other, trusting my direction to the tugging in my head.

Such was my state of mind that I almost walked past the room. A golden light flickered over my eyes, breaking through my morbid thoughts. The pressure in my head had gradually increased while I had been walking, to the point where I could almost feel a physical pressure pushing me into this room. The hairs on my arms stood up as I got pimple-skin in anticipation of the trap I knew would be waiting. Part of my brain was screaming for me to leave the tunnel, leave the underground maze, leave Burford Hythe and go far away. But this was smothered by the greater part of my brain that didn't care if it was a trap; if Villermir had left defences that would rip me apart. Just didn't care.

I walked up to the doorway so I could see further inside. I wondered briefly if I would be able to detect any wards guarding the room. But all thoughts were forgotten as I saw the crystal. The Empathy Crystal rested in a wooden cradle on top of a plain table. The stone was against the wall opposite me, but I could clearly see the many small faces of the honeyed crystal.

From habit, more than desire, I checked the room for hidden assailants. There was a door next to the crystal. It was closed. I had no way of knowing whether it was locked, but I assumed it would not be. As I stepped into the room I saw several darkened alcoves that could have hidden someone. But no one rushed forward as I came into view. I had felt no tingle of magick on my skin as I walked through the doorway and this continued as I crossed the room. I stopped within an arm's reach of the stone, taking a moment to bask in its golden light; to admire the flawlessness of each facet. To wonder at the power contained within.

I slowly reached forward, my fingers questing toward the rock, itching from the need to touch it once again. My hand closed around the crystal.

And passed straight through it.

I snatched my hand back, unsure of what had just happened. The stone looked solid enough, but my hand had passed through it like it was made of smoke. My heart hammered in my chest as I rapidly drew in lungfuls of air. My brain whirling with questions of how that could be.

My breath stopped suddenly as I heard a quiet chuckle coming from a shadow to my right. I drew my sword as Villermir emerged from the alcove and stood laughing at me. With a snarl, I lunged towards him. The door next to the crystal burst open and two bodyguards crashed through, their swords raised. The first through the door slammed his blade onto mine. The scream of metal caused vibrations to travel up my arms as I fought to maintain my hold on the weapon. The second aimed the hilt of his sword at my head, intent on taking me down rather than killing me. I staggered frantically out of the way, feeling the rush of air as the steel brushed past my face and scraped down my arm. Twisting to keep the two soldiers in front of me, I saw two more blocking the door I had used to enter the room. Neither moved to confront me but it was clear they would prevent any attempt to escape.

I swung my blade at the first guard, who was preparing another blow at my sword. The blades connected with a shower of sparks. I maintained my hold but the force spun me around, away from the second soldier. I was too slow to turn to face the new threat. Pain exploded between my shoulder blades, sending flames racing down my arms, burning away all feeling. My sword clattered to the ground as my numb fingers lost their grip. I fell forward onto my knees but was caught short before hitting the ground by the second guard grabbing the back of my tunic. I cried out as my arms were wrenched behind me, the soldier lifting me up to stand as the energy drained from my legs. The first smiled at me as he removed my belt containing my dagger and empty scabbard. I tried to struggle but was effectively restrained and only succeeded in sending waves of needle-stabs down my arms and into my fingers. The soldier bent to pick up my fallen sword, bowing his head slightly to Villermir before stepping back into the doorway.

Villermir walked slowly towards me with a satisfied smile on his face. He stopped a few paces from me and shook his head.

'Tallen. Did you really think I would just leave it lying around for you to take?'

Despite my previous lack of success, I still struggled to break free. 'You traitorous bastard!'

I spat at his face, then cried out as my arms were forced closer together behind my back. Red-hot pain ripped through my shoulders. Villermir looked unimpressed by my feeble efforts.

'Really?.' His tone was openly mocking. 'Is that any way to speak to a God-appointed priest?'

'False priest. You'll burn in Mobis' Seven Hells for what you've done.'

Faster than I could blink, Villermir lashed out and backhanded me across the face. The stone in his ring caught me on the lip, tearing the skin and filling my mouth with blood. The look of anger on Villermir's face made me shrink back into the guard who was holding me from behind.

'Do not pollute my air with talk of your heresy.'

He took a deep breath and the mocking smile returned. He reached forward to wipe the blood that had trickled down my chin, rubbing the sticky fluid between fingers and thumb.

'Perhaps we can convince you to place your trust in the One God while you stay with us.'

'I have no intention of staying here, you traitor.'

Villermir leaned closer to me, whispering conspiratorially. 'I don't think you have a choice.'

I turned my head to bite his face, but he pulled back, laughing.

'Oh, Tallen. This is going to be so much fun. For me anyway.'

'What are you talking about?' The sting from my cut lip and the pain of my crushed arms were joined by a headache building between my eyes. 'What have you done to the crystal?'

'What, this?' Villermir swept his arm back to indicate the softly glowing Empathy Crystal. 'This isn't real. The real crystal is well away from your thieving hands.'

I frowned in confusion. He was making no sense. Villermir moved towards the crystal and the guard swung me around so I could still see him. Making sure I was watching, Villermir punched at the crystal. I flinched. But his hand passed through the rock as easily as mine had.

'This is just an illusion, my dear child.'

He clicked his fingers and the crystal vanished, leaving the table and wooden cradle empty. He chuckled as I stared in disbelief at the empty space where the crystal had stood a heartbeat before. With a dramatic flourish, Villermir spread his hands so that the palms were facing upwards. As I watched, the stone blinked into being again, resting comfortably on his hands. He clapped his palms together, the crystal disappearing before his hands met. He pointed to the guard holding my sword. The rock was floating above the soldier's head. I was beginning to feel sick.

'Didn't I say this would be fun?' The crystal vanished again as Villermir turned to face me. 'Oh, come on now, Tallen. Do keep up. The crystal is an image created in your mind. It's not real. No one else can see it. Your vivid imagination is producing pictures at my request.'

'What are you talking about? I don't understand.'

He tapped my forehead. 'I place the suggestion in here. And your clever little mind convinces you that you are seeing the real thing.'

A wave of burning hot anger flooded through my body, instantly chased by ice-cold fear. 'What do you mean? I would never let you into my mind.'

'Oh dear. Yes, I suppose Drey would teach you about being allowed into the mind. He's all for maintaining the balance of nature and ensuring free will. How naive. The One God gave us nature to use as we please. And look where free will has got us. Blindly fumbling around in the dark. We don't have the ability to deal with free will. The One God needs to guide and protect us.'

I watched as Villermir glowed with religious fervour, gaining strength from the power of his convictions. The glow faded as his thoughts turned back to me. A vicious smile distorted his lips. He drew back his hand, and I flinched to avoid the blow.

The hand never connected.

'Fear,' he purred. 'While your mind's awareness is busy protecting you from abuse, I gain entry through hidden pathways.' He lowered his hand. 'Your time in North End provided fertile ground for me to exploit. It was so easy to condition fear into you. A few well-timed smacks and you practically trembled every time I walked into the room.'

The freezing fear chased away all heat from my anger. I shook uncontrollably as I thought of how easily I had been played since that first lesson in the library.

'You set me up.'

The smile broadened. 'Patience is a virtue, my dear. From the moment I saw you I had to possess you. That meddling Druid frustrated many of my attempts. But then, he's no longer an issue, is he? Once you touched the Ki Oval, I knew I could get you to retrieve the Empathy Crystal. My friends here in Lindvane ensured your safe passage into Hilman to obtain the stone for me, and again made sure you were delivered safely to me here. The Hilman, naturally, have been informed of your theft and are joining Hayton to destroy Faulknar.'

He paused to allow me to absorb the level of his treachery. How easily he had manipulated me.

'But the real joy? The true goal? It was always to venture into that complicated mind of yours. What secrets are you keeping? What are you capable of?'

'I will be pleased to disappoint you. You've known me most of my life. You'll find nothing special in me.'

'I disagree. I believe I will find your mind fascinating.'

The quiet, purring quality of his voice had removed my sense of threat of immediate danger. I had relaxed into the soldier's grasp. It left me totally unprepared for the sudden assault on my senses.

It felt as if I had been punched in the head. My vision lurched sideways, the room spinning out of view as streaks of light played across my retina. My body felt tossed aside by a storm-wind, no longer feeling individual limbs but a sensation of being contained in a paper-thin shell, blown one way, only to violently change direction a heartbeat later. Images were moving so fast before me that they blurred into flashes and swirls of colour. I felt acid burn the back of my throat as the effect of the vertigo made me gag.

Bright red fire exploded across my senses. Burning. Blinding. A crushing force compressed my brain. Shards of glass embedded into my eyes. Volcanic lava sucked into my lungs with each breath, searing the sensitive tissues on inspiration and again on expiration.

Then, as quickly as it had come, the assault ceased.

I felt as weak as dandelion seeds on a summer breeze. The support of the bodyguard was the only thing keeping me upright. I was panting as if I had just run as fast as I could up ten flights of steps. Black dots swam across my vision. I tasted blood where it had drained from my nose. Every muscle jumped sporadically as my skin prickled with beading sweat.

It took a long time before I managed to control my breathing and heart rate enough to reduce the black spots and see Villermir watching me intently.

'What did I say?' he purred. 'Fascinating. Such an extreme reaction to a gentle exploration.' He smiled, causing my body to increase its trembling. 'Let's see what happens with a more forceful poke.'

The floor fell away under my feet. I was falling so fast, the wind pushing against my skin and making it difficult for me to breathe. My eyes watered as the rush of air dried them. Flashes of green, gold, blue and red sped past. There was no way of knowing what generated these colours. I started twisting this way and that, falling head over feet to the left, then to the right. Then backwards, feet over head, round and round until I had no idea which way was top or bottom, left or right, up or down. I was completely disorientated.

I slammed to a halt.

Acid burned the back of my throat again as I hung suspended in the total darkness. I felt my paper-thin self being pulled in all directions, muscles screaming as they were stretched beyond their natural limits. Joints cracked in protest. My skin peeled away. My lungs froze in full expansion.

In a blink of an eye I was back in front of Villermir. My mouth flooded with saliva as I retched and vomited bloodstained fluid onto the floor, adding to the puddle that was already there. Inside and out, I felt as if I had been trampled by a herd of stampeding cattle.

Villermir gently lifted my limp head. I had no strength to resist. I had to concentrate to keep my eyes open as his face floated in and out of focus.

'Quite a performance, my dear.'

The mocking quality of his voice had vanished. I was unsure whether it had been replaced with concern or pride. It would seem my reaction had not been what he had expected.

'Such a powerful response from someone who has not been trained. I've never heard of such defences being mounted by any of the order's initiates.' He chuckled to himself. 'Not even me.'

He released my head, letting it sag forward. I could see his hands shaking. The skin was as pale as parchment as he wiped his palms on his tunic. I lifted my head to focus on his face. A small trail of blood leaked from his right nostril. Another had clotted on his right earlobe.

Villermir saw me notice the blood and quickly wiped it away.

'Take her to the lower cell.' He waved his hand in dismissal. 'And get her cleaned up.'

I was only vaguely aware of the route taken to the cell. As I no longer had the strength to walk, the other guard helped to drag me through the doorway next to the table. The corridor looked like all the others I had travelled in this house: smooth stone walls lit by pale, glowing crystals. Several sets of shallow steps led to open areas containing a number of solid oak doors. I was quickly lost within the maze. It was clear that I would be unable to find my way back to the room we had just come from, much less escape from the house.

The final set of steps fell away into the darkness. There were no crystals to illuminate this part of the tunnel. One of the guards set fire to a brand that was resting in an iron bracket at the top of the steps. The jumping shadows added to my feelings of dread at being trapped below ground.

At regular intervals the steps widened to accommodate a door on each side of the passageway. We passed at least five pairs of doors before reaching the bottom. There was only one door at the foot of the steps. It stood open and I could see inside as we approached. The cell was a thin rectangle, three paces across and six paces long. A small wooden bucket had been placed in the furthest corner, and I could still smell the faint scent of urine. A sleeping space had been carved into the wall. A thin straw mattress and a threadbare blanket provided a little comfort from the cold, damp stone. There was nothing else in the room.

The guards shoved me into the cell. I could not help the cry I gave as my knees cracked against the rock floor when I fell. The door banged closed, the sound echoing loudly for a heartbeat before being sealed away by the heavy wood.

I was in total darkness.

I could not see my hand as I waved it in front of my eyes. My breathing stuttered as panic forced my diaphragm into spasms. The room was not cold but my whole body shivered uncontrollably. I was unable to move to the sleeping bench, so I curled up into a tight ball, holding myself together as I fell into my private hell of despair.

I awoke an unknowable period of time later. The left side of my body had grown numb against the stone floor. Sensation screamed back into the tissues as I rolled over and allowed the blood to flow again. I couldn't help whimpering at this new wave of torment, adding to the abused shoulders, bruised knees and cramped muscles. My mouth was completely dry, and my lips were cracked and swollen. I swallowed to produce some saliva, but only succeeded in opening up the cut made by Villermir's ring. I felt warm blood trickle down my chin, but lacked the motivation to wipe it away.

No light entered the cell. The air smelt stale. The only sound was the quiet rasp of my breath. I could not see the walls or the ceiling, but I felt them pressing down on me. My breathing became more laboured as panic threatened to overwhelm me. I knew the cell was getting smaller and smaller, the ceiling lowering until it was just above my face. I had to raise my arm to prove I was not being crushed. My mind refused to believe the sensory information sent by my grasping fingers. I could not feel the rock above me. But I might within the next heartbeat.

I kept my arms extended, swapping the left for the right and the right for the left, as my hand grew cold from the blood draining back towards my heart. I counted my breaths to stop them speeding out of control. *Inhale, count to three. Exhale, count to three.* Over and over again, focusing my mind away from the terror that threatened to tear it apart. To suppress the scream waiting within my lungs that would shatter my senses.

Insanity offered a welcome retreat from the horrors in my head. It was so hard not to give in to the temptation. Exhaustion eventually took command and I drifted into the equally black oblivion.

The peace did not last long. Within moments I was thrown into my dream world. Colours were muted as if I had already forgotten what they looked like. The maze of tunnels reflected the passageways under the Burford estate. I wandered aimlessly, doubling back on myself, walking in circles, getting more and more confused. Panic bubbled at the back of my throat, the sensation so familiar it was almost welcome. I quickened my pace, eventually running down the corridor. And the next. And the next.

I was hopelessly lost. I would never escape.

I cried out for help. Pleaded with Kade to come for me. Begged for Laken to save me.

Nobody came.

Time gradually drained away my fear. My mind finally accepted the facts. I was not being crushed. No one was here to hurt me. Villermir had not entered my head. My head felt light and slightly separated from my body as I sat up, resting my back against the stone below the sleeping bench. I still could not face being within the enclosed space of the carved-out bed, so I pulled the mattress onto the floor and wrapped myself in the thin blanket. It provided small comfort but gave me a little control over my situation. That made a big difference to my mood.

The imagined terrors gave way to more practical concerns. I had no idea how long I had been at Burford Hythe and when I had last been able to quench my unrelenting thirst. My throat felt scoured by sand. Each swallow rasped at the delicate tissue, but I could not help myself repeatedly swallowing to ease the discomfort. It consumed my full attention. I tortured myself with thoughts of cool, refreshing drinks. Foaming ale at the Blue Boar. Crystal-clear spring water flowing smoothly over my swollen tongue, trickling down my parched throat. My stomach clenched tightly in anticipation of the liquid that never came.

My fluid fantasies were interrupted by the opening of the door. The light from the burning torch seared my eyes after so long in the dark. I closed them, but still needed to cover my closed eyelids with an arm to avoid the dim light sending needle-stabs into my brain. I relied on my hearing to inform me of the single soldier that entered the cell. He lifted me up by the arm. The grip was firm but not overly forceful. My eyes gradually adjusted to the light as I was half marched, half dragged up the stone steps to the crystal-illuminated corridors. I tried to concentrate on the pathways taken but was soon confused by one tunnel looking the same as all the others. My head ached and my vision blurred as I was taken back to the heart of the network below Burford Hythe house.

I was panting for breath and my legs were trembling by the time we stopped in front of a pair of simply carved doors. The soldier knocked twice, waiting for a mumbled response before entering.

We walked into a room that was a similar size to the one that had housed the illusionary crystal. But this room could not have been more different. Villermir was dressed in a thick woollen robe, the colour of crushed blackberries. Elaborate embroidery confirmed the quality of the garment. He sat behind a sturdy oak desk that was covered in loosely rolled scrolls and leather books folded open. More books and scrolls had been discarded on the floor around his well-padded chair. Two glowing crystals illuminated Villermir's workspace, while another two provided light for the rest of the room. I recognised a map of the three heraldic kingdoms that had been tacked to one of the walls, but did not recognise the area depicted in the older map on the opposite wall. There were two simple cabinets resting against the wall behind the desk. One had inkpots and quills scattered over its shelves, while the other displayed a small shrine to the One God; a gilded carving of golden rays of light shining from a yawning mouth, showering the kneeling worshippers with glory. I felt myself staring at the glass goblets and decanter of water that was on the shelf below.

'Leave us.' Villermir dismissed the bodyguard and indicated that I should sit in one of the seats in front of him. He studied my appearance, wrinkling his nose slightly. 'I see no one bothered to clean you up. No matter.'

He rose from his chair as I sank into the one indicated for me that was positioned in front of his desk. He turned his back on me and opened the door of the right cabinet. I had to bite my lip to stop myself crying out as I heard him pour liquid into a goblet. He turned back to me and placed the cup on the table between us. I could smell the water. I held my body tense to prevent myself from grabbing the goblet, to resist begging for the drink.

He shook his head slowly. 'Such determination. I have to admit, you have an impressive willpower.' He indicated the cup. 'Take it.'

In my rush to grab the goblet before he changed his mind, I almost knocked it over and spilt the contents. With both hands I grasped the cup and gulped a large mouthful of the cool liquid. My stomach rebelled at the sudden appearance of water, causing me to retch. But I was not going to relinquish the precious fluid. The second mouthful was taken more slowly. I closed my eyes to savour the soothing presence as it drained down my parched throat. I barely resisted the temptation to purr at the pleasant sensation.

Villermir was watching me with his head tilted slightly to one side as I opened my eyes. 'Better?'

I hurriedly replaced the empty cup on the desk, only just realising how much power I had given him by accepting the drink. How much he controlled my future. How I was totally reliant on him. A small spark of anger still burned deep inside as I glared at him.

He failed to acknowledge my feeble defiance. 'I've been studying references to the Empathy Crystal. The Ancients used the stone to create valleys and build mountains. It was used to drain floodplains and irrigate infertile soil. The Empathy Crystal has the power to shape continents.'

He paused for me to consider his words as he walked around the table to sit on the edge in front of me. He leaned forward, causing me to shrink back into the seat.

'Now why would you have the power to control such a crystal?'

'I can't control it,' I protested.

He leaned back and folded his arms across his chest. 'Perhaps not at the moment. But it allows your touch. Why would that be?'

I remained silent. I had no idea why the crystal tolerated my touch when it repelled all others. I was more discomforted, however, by the thought of how tempting it would be to tell Villermir if I did know the reason. Of how much I was already willing to let him dominate me.

'The Ancients were destroyed millennia ago. No trace of them exists after the Rebellion.' He sighed and tilted his head to one side again. 'But the Ancients had human helpers. Men and women who could channel the great power. The Druids. The priestesses. The Aquiline. The Dragonslayers. The Fire-walkers. The Empaths. Is that you, Tallen? Are you a distant relative of these humans? Are you an empath?'

'No.' I almost laughed at the absurdity of the concept. But a small part of me wondered whether there could be any grain of truth beneath all the insanity. 'No.'

'Let's find out, shall we?'

Between the space of one heartbeat and another, Villermir and the room blinked out of existence. Lindvane was replaced by Methhold. It was a warm summer's day, with a deep blue sky without the distraction of clouds. Small, swift birds darted across the meadow after insects. The people were sitting in a large circle in the centre of the village. The men sharpened tools or carved, while the women pounded herbs or scraped leather for clothes. Children were running around amidst the barking dogs, squealing carelessly in play. I recognised these people. Parnell, the village elder, smoked his clay pipe as he watched his people work, a small smile of pride stroking his lips. Veeley, his wife, sat beside him. She always had an extra sweet treat for me. There was Sharnie, who lived in the roundhouse next to us. She would spend more time than she could spare teaching me about the plants and animals that lived in the woods nearby. She was holding Ciarnan, my sister, rocking her gently in her lap. Ciarnan was a small child, not yet three years old, her blue eyes eagerly taking in all the sights to be seen. She was playing with a small wooden toy dog made by Sharnie's husband. My mother sat next to her, stroking her soft black hair before turning to smile at me. I was frozen by the sight of her gentle blue eyes. Her long black hair framed a tanned face, and her tiny hands beckoned me to join them.

Tears streamed down my face as the room at Burford returned. The loss of my family and friends felt like a physical wound within my chest. I had somehow backed myself into a corner, sitting on the floor with my back against the wall and my knees pulled tightly to my chest. Villermir watched me closely from the other side of the room, still perched on the edge of the desk.

'Please... Don't,' I sobbed. 'Please stop.'

I was returned to Methhold. I was watching my mother standing over Sharnie as the younger woman lay on the bed in her roundhouse. Sharnie had her eyes tightly closed. Her blonde hair stuck to her sweating forehead. Her face was pale with two red blotches over her cheekbones. She moaned quietly as my mother pressed gently on her abdomen. Mother smiled reassuringly at me before closing her eyes. She raised her hands so that they hovered just above Sharnie's body, trembling slightly as she slowly moved them up the abdomen towards the chest. I had seen her perform this act several times but had never seen the pale colours of Sharnie's aura respond to the touch. A ghost image of the woman shimmered with faded rose and brown. In contrast, my mother glowed with swirls of apple green and turquoise. Mother's hands continued up until they reached the small hollow at the base of Sharnie's throat. The young woman suddenly bent over the side of the bed, vomiting into a bucket that had been placed there. The fluid was black and smelt sour. The red spots faded from her cheeks and her face became a more normal colour. The glowing auras faded from my vision as Mother folded her hands in front of her, smiling warmly at Sharnie.

'So.' Villermir's voice brought me back to Burford. 'Your mother was a healer. Have you inherited some latent talent from her?'

I had curled myself into a ball, lying on my side facing Villermir. 'I don't know. I don't know anything.'

'Oh, Tallen. You know so much. It's all hidden in that pretty little head of yours somewhere.'

'I'm not hiding anything.' I could hear the desperation in my voice. I was ready to tell him everything if he would stop the pain generated by my memories. 'Please stop. I can't stand it.'

My body shook with the threat of the sobs that tore through my chest. The tears flowed freely, dripping onto the floor as I hugged my stomach as hard as I could. The image of my mother's smile lingered when I closed my eyes. Villermir called for the guard.

'Enough for now. It seems I have further research to do.'

My body had lost all its rigidity and the soldier had to raise me from my position on the floor. He easily picked me up and carried me back to the cell.

Chapter Twenty Two

Time that seemed to last forever while I was in the cell seemed like no time at all when I was taken back to Villermir. He was waiting for me in the same room as before, the desk still covered with books and scrolls. He watched me closely as I walked in, as I carefully avoided looking at his eyes. I knew what was coming and was already finding it hard to breathe normally. I sat in the chair I had used the previous time and studied the cracked skin around my thumb. Villermir made me wait a long time.

'The fact that your mother was a healer, while very interesting, does not help me.'

I still refused to look at him.

'You see, I can find no reference to healers being gifted by the Ancients. Your mother may have been capable of minor magicks but not on the scale needed to access the Empathy Crystal. It would appear your talent does not come from her...'

Without warning I was taken back to the Methhold of my childhood. It was Samhain. The large fire was burning brilliantly against the dark autumnal night. The steady beat of the drums marked the time for the dancers twirling around the fire, their arms raised in praise for the harvest. The smell of roast boar teased my empty stomach, but I knew it would not be long now before we could taste the succulent meat. I held my mother's hand tightly as the village elders walked menacingly among us, their faces hidden by stylised masks of bird, mouse and fox. The shadows from the fire added to the dark wells of their eyes, convincingly suggesting that the Halls of Eternity and the Hells of Mobis were only a small step away.

The drumbeat grew faster. The dancers spun dizzyingly quickly. The bright colours of their skirts and tunics flashed in the light of the flames. Sparks leapt into the sky as the logs popped and snapped. The elders started chanting, their mouths covered by the masks so that their voices seemed to come from all round the gathering. Low, rhythmic notes of words I did not understand. A language that had not been commonly spoken for countless generations. I shivered as pimpleflesh rose on my arms and the hair at the base of my neck stood up. Mother laughed kindly at my fears, wrapping her arms around me as she pressed me against her; a warm presence to keep the perils of the Sacred Night at bay.

'Halt!'

We all turned towards the voice as the drums fell silent and the dancers stopped. I bit my lip, trying to see the familiar, friendly grandfather in the apparition in front of me. The ritual robes made him look larger than I remembered. The thick pelt of a silver wolf hung from his shoulders. The lupine face, still wrapped around its skull, sat on top of his head so that two pairs of eyes watched us. His hazel staff was held in his right hand, the base resting on the ground, the cage of twisted roots level with the hollow eyes of the wolf. The rose quartz crystal, the size of a man's palm, reflected the firelight from its timber cage. My grandfather held the rapt attention of everyone present, waiting, while we all held our breath.

'It is the night of Samhain. The walls of the living are thinning and soon those that have been taken from us will be among us once again. Our ancestors will return to offer guidance and wisdom. Daemons will tempt those of weak character.'

I shivered and pressed closer to my mother.

'Stay true to the teachings of Our Father Sun and Our Mother Moon. And rejoice in the gifts offered this night.'

He raised the staff high above his head. The crystal caught the light from the fire and turned blood red. All across the sky the stars fell to earth, bringing the spirits of the ancestors back to the land of the living. I watched the white spots streak across the clear sky, a glittering trail of light following them. The sight seemed to warm me more than the fire.

I watched as my grandfather placed the staff back on the ground. He smiled as wisps of smoke appeared between the villagers. I held my breath as the smoke thickened to become faint outlines of people. No one seemed to see them. I looked at my grandfather, who winked at me, sharing the secret that only we two could see. Figures, some wearing strange clothes, joined in the dancing. They did not eat or drink, but otherwise seemed to enjoy the festivities as much as the living. The ancestors walked the earth again on the Sacred Night, at the call of my grandfather…

Villermir banged his hand on the table. 'Enough of this.'

The sudden change in focus left me feeling sick for a couple of heartbeats. I took a deep, steadying breath, looking up to see Villermir's scowl of frustration.

'It would seem that talent runs in your family. Your grandfather showed advanced gifts as a shaman. But this still does not explain your affinity with the Empathy Crystal. Your power is latent, not learnt as was your mother's and her father's. There's more to you than these rustic magicks.'

Villermir stared at me for several moments. I carefully avoided looking at him but could still feel the heat of his glare. My skin itched with the intensity of his gaze. I could feel myself shrinking into the chair, trying to make myself as small as possible.

'Perhaps we should try a different approach for now.' He sighed as he leaned back in his chair. 'Let's see what is behind those barriers of yours. Fear allows me into the rest of your mind; let's see how far it will get me past those wards.'

I looked up as movement flickered in my peripheral vision, then almost fell over the chair in my haste to scramble away. Laken walked from the shadows of the doorway, the familiar look of disappointment on his face.

'Please…' I did not know if I was pleading with Laken or Villermir.

'You worthless piece of rubbish.' Laken advanced on me.

My back banged against the wall as I stared in horror at my night terror made real. I pressed as hard as I could, sliding along it until I reached the corner and there was nowhere else to go.

'You abandon your friends and wallow in self-pity. You're a disgrace.'

I whimpered at the accusation, my knees giving way so that I crumpled onto the floor. Laken stopped a couple of paces away from me, a look of disgust clear on his face.

'Your dreams were so easy to control,' murmured Villermir.

I took my eyes away from Laken to look at Villermir in confusion. 'What?'

'Your own feelings of inadequacy were easily manipulated.' He sighed, frustrated at my lack of understanding. 'He's not real. Just another suggestion in your head to stop you being so damned self-contained.'

Villermir waved his hand dismissively and the look of disdain left Laken's face. It was replaced by a stupid grin. He tilted his head comically to one side before starting to dance a lively jig. I grabbed the hair at my temples in horror.

'Stop it,' I shouted. 'Stop it!'

Laken stopped. His face went blank as he stared at me, hands hanging limply by his sides. I could not believe that man in front of me was not Laken. The lines around his blue eyes; the set of his mouth – it was all so perfectly how I remembered him. My eyes stung as tears started to flow. How much of what I remembered was true? How much had been corrupted by Villermir? How easily he had found my soft, vulnerable centre.

'Time to open your barriers.'

'I don't know how,' I begged, anticipating the vertigo and disorientation I had felt the last time Villermir attacked my protections.

'We'll see.'

Laken's face crumpled into a grimace of pain. He cried out as he fell to his knees. Fire erupted in my chest as I watched him convulse in agony from an unseen attack. The veins stood up as his hands clenched into defenceless claws.

I drew a breath to plead with Villermir to stop, but the words never left my mouth. The floor tilted away and I slipped into a kaleidoscope of swirling blues and oranges, pinks and yellows. My stomach rebelled at the clash of colours. I tasted acid at the back of my throat. A paralysing pressure built up in my head, compressing my forehead between the eyes in an effort to meet with the back of my skull that was pushing forward into the centre of my brain. I closed my eyes to block out the colours, but the light flashed against my eyelids, increasing my nausea. I spun round and round.

I was curled up on my side, holding my head as if it was about to burst. I slowly opened my eyes. The dim lighting in the room was enough to cause stabs of pain. Laken was gone. Villermir was standing, leaning heavily on the table. He wiped the sweat from his forehead as he stared at me. I curled tighter.

'I don't know how to give you what you want.' I was ready to give him everything. I had nothing left with which to fight him. I just wanted the pain to go away. I just wanted him out of my head.

Villermir said nothing as he left the room. The lights extinguished as he slammed the door, leaving me in welcome darkness.

Sometime later I was taken back to the cell. I followed obediently, my mind closed to all but the essentials. One foot shuffled in front of the other, walking only fast enough to keep up with the guard. Seeing only enough to avoid stumbling. Breathing only when necessary. Heart beating only as required.

I calmly accepted the darkness of my cell. Counting the five paces to the nest I had made with the mattress and blanket, I curled myself into a tight ball and tried to think of nothing. Not to think of how alone I was, not to think of how much power Villermir had over me, not to think of how he controlled my thoughts. Not to think of Laken.

I tossed and turned. Sleep would not rescue me from the thoughts terrorising my mind. I dozed fitfully, my racing heart waking me almost instantly.

When I finally succumbed to exhaustion, I dreamt. The maze of tunnels under the mountain was unusually quiet. One passageway would be roughly chiselled from rock, while the next would be the smooth stone of Burford Hythe. I was taken steadily left, deeper and deeper, finally reaching the atrium.

Laken was waiting for me.

He stood, silently, in the middle of the cavern. I stopped several paces from him and waited, trembling, for the accusations. But he just stood there. His face was so sad. It was accusation enough, and I couldn't stand it.

'You're not real!' I shouted at him. 'Villermir placed you in my head.'

Laken flinched as a cut slashed across his cheek. I watched blood form a drop that ran down his face. My shattered heart broke again at the sight.

'You're not real,' I repeated, quieter. 'You don't exist.'

Another cut appeared, mirroring the first but on the opposite cheek. Laken continued to look at me, his arms hanging limp by his sides.

'Tallen.' He took a step towards me. 'Please—'

'Stop it!' I walked backwards until my back pressed against solid rock. 'You can't feel it. It's not real.'

I was desperately trying to convince myself. But the pain I felt was real as another wound appeared: an angry slash across his bicep. Blood soaked into the cut edges of his shirt. A single tear rolled from his eye.

I pulled at my hair in frustration as I slid down the wall to sit on my heels. 'You're not real,' I whispered.

Another wound, across his chest this time. The only reaction from Laken was a sharp intake of breath. More sorrow was in his eyes as he silently pleaded with me to make it stop. I couldn't bear to see him like that. The only way to stop my heart from lacerating my chest was to accept the Laken in front of me was not real. But with each thought came a new wound. Laken's skin was flayed and bleeding. My tears were flowing freely now. A vicious repetition, turning round and round: the more Laken was hurt, the more I had to convince myself that he was an illusion created by Villermir. Each time I had that thought another wound would slice into Laken, broken and bleeding in front of me. I could not bear it if it was real. I caused more damage believing it was false.

Villermir's laughter bounced off the rock walls, echoing down the corridors.

I was physically and emotionally drained when I was next taken to Villermir. My vision spun whenever I stood up. My bones ached. My muscles cramped. I had scratched my skin until it was raw and bleeding. My lips were swollen and cracked. The headache would not go away. I was ready for Villermir to kill me. I had nothing left to give.

As we got nearer to Villermir's room, the headache grew more insistent; a gentle but persistent tug at my mind. The hair stood up on my arms and I felt the crawling sensation I associated with magick. My energy and focus returned with a sudden anticipation, a need to protect, although I didn't know what.

That became clear as soon as the soldier opened the door. The Empathy Crystal rested in a wooden cradle on the desk in front of Villermir. I held my breath for a heartbeat, knowing instinctively that this was the real crystal and not the illusion I had seen before. I briefly wondered how I could have been mistaken, but my attention soon returned to the crystal and how close it was to Villermir. I could almost feel my back arching like a threatened cat's. I fought the urge to hiss at him.

Villermir was watching me closely, clearly fascinated by my reaction to the crystal. He licked his lips and rubbed his fingers in anticipation.

'Touch it,' he purred.

I hesitated, fearing a trap. For several moments we faced each other.

With obvious effort, Villermir placed his hands on the table, palms resting flat against the wood. He sat back in the chair to create some space between him and the crystal. I knew that it would make no difference if it was a trap. But I was also tempted to touch the crystal once more, to check that all was well. I reached forward, hesitating a heartbeat more, before resting my fingertips on the warm stone.

I heard my breath release as a contented sigh as warmth spread from my fingertips, up my arms and into the very core of me. It seemed as if a river, turned golden by the sunset, flowed up my veins. I felt a smile spread across my lips as my eyes half closed with the acceptance of the crystal.

Villermir grabbed my arm.

The sensation changed instantly. The golden river became polluted by his touch. Like ink dropped into water, dark coils swirled within my blood vessels, contaminating the areas they touched. I snarled in anger and tried to remove my hand from the crystal, but Villermir's grip was too strong and maintained the contact. I cried out in frustration as Villermir travelled on the currents created by the Empathy Crystal; currents that took him to forbidden areas, revealing secrets he should not know.

'I knew it!' he cried, ecstatic. 'You have the power of the Ancients. A true descendant. Glory to the One God. This is unheard of.' His breath caught. 'A protector.'

I roared in protest that he should know of matters that had been kept secret even from me. I would not dwell on his discovery but renewed my efforts to expel him from my mind. I tore my hand from the crystal, imagining a force radiating from me, pushing Villermir away from the crystal and out of my head.

Villermir slammed into his chair so hard that both were sent crashing to the floor. Without the restraint of his grip, I fell backwards, landing on my back with a thud. The energy from the crystal fled my body and I was left shaking at its loss. The barriers to my ancient potential were slammed firmly closed to all.

'No,' roared Villermir as he stormed around the table. 'I need more. Tell me more!'

I was terrified by his look of insane anger as he came towards me. I backed away quickly, as far as I could, my bruised back banging into the wall as Villermir barrelled after me.

Villermir flicked his hand dismissively and fire exploded from my arms.

I screamed as the heat scorched my skin, curling my eyebrows, stinging my eyes. I screamed again as I felt Villermir's attack on my mind like a hammer blow. He waved his hand again. The flames vanished. I had a heartbeat to realise that my skin was undamaged, before a horde of creatures from Mobis' torments descended upon me. Winged monsters, the size of small dogs, stabbed with taloned hands. Sharp teeth in grotesque faces slashed into my tissues, blood draining freely from their mouths. High-pitched squealing that hurt my ears. Pinching and biting as they flapped around my head. Red-hot rods of pain stabbed into my brain as Villermir tried to force his way through the barriers.

'Villermir, please,' I begged. 'I don't know how to give you what you want.'

Villermir withdrew the pressure from my mind and dispersed the creatures. I lay on the floor, curled protectively and panting hard. It took several heartbeats to realise the creatures had left no marks. More of Villermir's mind games. I looked up at him. His hair had stuck to his forehead where sweat glistened in the crystal glow. He was also panting as he glared at me, his jaw clenched tightly; I didn't know whether from anger or frustration.

'I have given you everything I can.' Tears flowed down my cheeks as I admitted defeat. 'I don't know how to lower the barriers. I never even knew they were there. You have to believe me. I would give you everything if I could. I have told you all that I know.'

Villermir watched me closely, narrowing his eyes as he considered my words. He relaxed his jaw and wiped the sweat from his forehead.

'Yes, I do believe you have given me everything you can.' He returned to sit on the desk, facing me. 'The wards are more powerful than anything you could have created. A legacy from your Ancient past? Perhaps. Although I feel they may have been applied more recently. They are too complete. Too precise.' He stood up, adding dismissively, 'Definitely not Drey's work.'

Villermir opened the door to speak to the guard waiting outside. 'Bring him,' he instructed before closing the door again.

He returned to his position resting on the edge of the table. I carefully avoided eye contact as Villermir watched me. My breathing had almost returned to normal, but I could not stop shaking, my whole body trembling in anticipation of what might come next. He just watched as I lay on the floor, defeated.

'I don't know what else to do. I don't know how to lower them.'

'Yet, I suspect you still resist me. You're stronger than I think even you realise.' He tapped the table with his fingernails while he thought. 'A protector. Very interesting. What powers would a protector have, I wonder? How to harness that power…'

I pressed my fists into my head in frustration. 'I have no power. I have no idea what you are talking about. I'm not resisting you.' Even then I resented saying the words out loud. 'I can't. I can't fight you any more. I can't take any more of this.'

Villermir's expression turned from curious to cold. 'Well, we are about to find out.'

I screwed my eyes shut. I just wanted all this to go away. I couldn't play games with Villermir any more. I was physically and emotionally crushed. He had broken the very core of me. I had no strength or desire to fight him. I just wanted all the pain to end. I ignored the sound of the door opening, the shuffle of feet. It no longer concerned me. I felt as if nothing concerned me now.

I was wrong.

A small, quiet gasp broke through my misery and grabbed my full attention. My eyes snapped open and my focus was once again sharp. It would seem that Villermir was right. I had access to resources that I did not know I possessed. I had stood and moved two paces towards Kade before the blade at his throat brought me to an abrupt stop. It was clear the threat was to control me. Kade was beyond resistance.

Kade was being supported by one guard, while the other held his sword at his neck. His hair was matted and he had several days' worth of beard. One eye was swollen shut with puffy, black eyelids. The other looked at me, immeasurably sad and defeated. His cheeks were bruised and battered. His lips had split in several places. A drop of blood slipped down the sword's blade where it had pierced the skin. His knuckles were inflamed and misshapen. A large gash showed starkly crimson against the pale skin of his forearm. His breathing was irregular, one side of his chest moving more freely than the other. I suspected broken ribs. His abdomen was held tense and I expected damage there as well. Kade's body was battered and broken. But the worst thing was the look in that one open eye. The sag of the shoulders. Kade's spirit had been crushed. He had been totally destroyed.

I felt an animal snarl vibrate within my throat. The soldier looked coldly at me as he pressed his blade further into Kade's throat. More blood seeped from the cut as Kade failed to silence a whimper. I imagined numerous savage ways of removing the soldier's head from his shoulders. Of removing limbs, one joint at a time. Of causing unspeakable pain for the wrong committed against Kade. I took small comfort from the nervous swallow in response to my glare, as the guard released the pressure from Kade's neck.

'Very impressive, my dear,' mocked Villermir. 'It seems the strength of protection extends beyond Ancient relics. Most impressive.'

I turned to glare at him. I could feel my teeth baring in a primitive challenge but lacked the emotion to care about being more civilised. I would have happily ripped his throat out with my teeth at that moment. The mocking smile faded from his face.

'I'm glad you have recovered your strength,' he continued. 'Perhaps we can explore where that came from. The trigger appears obvious.'

'You didn't have to hurt him,' I snarled. 'You shouldn't have destroyed him.'

Villermir sighed. 'It was not my intention. But your prince provoked my bodyguards.' He shook his head. 'Not a good idea.'

I took a step towards Villermir but was again halted by Kade's cry of pain as he was forced to his knees. He shielded his ribs with his arms as his head was pulled back. I shook in frustration, not knowing whether to focus on Villermir or Kade.

'My guards have very volatile tempers. Kade resisted their attempts to restrain him, and things got a bit… carried away.'

My attention returned to Villermir, still relaxed against the table.

'Has he never told you about his irrational fear of being contained?'

I saw a brief flicker of rebellion as Kade attempted to stand. The defiance was short-lived and his posture soon reflected his submission once more. My fingers itched for the hilt of a weapon.

The mockery had returned as Villermir continued his tale. 'It's a very sad story. Worthy of a tragedy sung by the best bards. Although I suspect Kade would be too modest to sing his own story.'

'What are you talking about?' I snapped impatiently.

'It all happened a long time ago. Kade was just a young boy. Must have been about five years old, would you say, Kade?'

Kade remained silent. He no longer looked at me.

'Some pirates from Gallowgla decided to kidnap the queen and ransom her back to Kyllian. The king and Kerk had gone hunting, while Kade and his pregnant mother walked a favoured coastal path. The pirates had not anticipated Frenjia's spirit. She put up quite a fight before they could smuggle her aboard their sloop. Kade was taken too and had to watch his mother being… mistreated at the hands of these men. He was helpless to aid her.'

Kade had closed his eyes. He seemed to be barely breathing.

'Of course, the brigands were caught and subjected to the full wrath of Kyllian's justice. But not before Frenjia had lost the child. She never recovered from the infection and blood loss. She died several days later. So very tragic.'

What happened next occurred so fast that it was all over in the space of two heartbeats. But when I remember it, time seems to slow almost to a standstill, every detail magnified, every movement etched indelibly into my memory.

Kade exploded from his kneeling position, shoving one guard backwards while taking the sword from the other. The soldier who had pierced his neck died instantly as the blade was forced through his abdomen and up into his chest, piercing the heart. Kade removed the sword smoothly, turning in a fluid motion to slice at the other man's jugular before he could regain his balance. I had taken a step towards Villermir as he stood up from the table, his hands raised as Kade dispatched the second guard. The area around Villermier shimmered as he forced the barrier towards Kade. The air screamed in protest before slamming into Kade's chest as he turned to face the priest.

His body rocked as the shimmering force punched into him. He half twisted towards me before crumpling to his knees. His arms fell limp by his sides, the sword ringing as it hit the ground. He was starting to sway as the life drained from his body. Sweat stuck his brown hair to his face. His bruises became more prominent as the surrounding skin drained of blood, turning a deathly grey. His chestnut eyes lost their focus. He fell forward.

Kade was dead.

Chapter Twenty Three

A white-hot fury smothered me. I barely heard my scream echoing off the walls. I ignored the tremors that rocked the ground beneath my feet. My only concern was the silver, sparkling light that was forced out of Kade's body by the impact of Villermir's assault. The glow wrapped around Kade like an aura, becoming fainter as it drifted away. The light compressed to a single cord as he fell forward, the cord severing as he exhaled his final breath.

Working on instinct, without understanding, I reached for this dimming cord of light. I was too far away but it didn't stop me stretching my arms forward, straining muscle and tendon in an attempt to close the gap. I did not understand the absurdity of it all as my arms stretched beyond their natural limits, fading as the distance grew until they were a pale grey imitation of the silver haze floating away from Kade. My grey smoke intertwined with his silver mist, taking my vision on a vertiginous ride into another realm. My peripheral vision faded so that the only points of focus were my faded arms, blindly reaching for the trail of smoke and mist disappearing towards the horizon. Further and further I stretched; on and on drifted the shimmering haze, steadily increasingly the speed at which we were travelling. Images flashed by too quickly for me to identify. Still I followed the light. The rush of air over my arms felt icy cold, as if I was standing in a blizzard. Strange that I should feel sensation in arms that were mere ghost images of the body I'd left behind at Burford Hythe.

Suddenly the scenery changed. A momentary tug at my senses felt as if I had passed through an invisible wall. But then the feeling was gone instantly.

The landscape was vast, so that although I could still feel the speed at which we were travelling and the near-images flashed by in streaks of colour, the distance remained in focus and I could see the detail of this new reality. My grey smoke chased after Kade's silver mist without any voluntary input on my part. It allowed me to study my new surroundings.

The heat was oppressive. An unseen sun blazed over a desert landscape of bleached rock. There were no plants or creatures visible in the vista. Beige rock had been blasted by the furnace heat of the constant wind, blowing particles of sand against any exposed surface. Mountains were being reduced to boulders by eons of constant attack. My ghost arms felt scoured of flesh, each nerve ending screaming in protest as the sand scraped the skin. On and on we sped through this never-changing landscape, the stripped rocks undulating gently like sand dunes. The sky was bleached a pale amber by the unremitting glare of the sun, painting the whole landscape the colour of toast.

Far in the distance a spot of black hovered over the horizon. Kade's silver spirit was aiming straight for it. The spot gradually grew larger as we neared, punctured occasionally by flashes of lightning, a torrential storm raging in the black disc. The white flashes became hypnotic as we raced towards them, the darkness growing and growing until it was the size of a small town. Still we streaked towards it, never changing course, never changing speed. I never closed the distance between myself and Kade's cord of light.

We slammed through the bubble. Again the momentary pause, as if suddenly walking through mud, before the scenery changed again. We still travelled fast, but slower than before. The landscape was littered with craters and large rocks. Kade's light weaved around the obstacles at lightning speed, with me following a heartbeat later.

The oppressive heat remained, but this was generated by a nightmare vision of fire and molten rock. The sky boiled with swirls of red and orange. I seemed to look into a liquid fire. Explosions of steam sent fireballs of burning rock into the air, crashing down moments later, sending showers of debris into the pools of lava, hissing and spitting like a pit of angry snakes. The scoured skin on my ghost arms now peeled away as it was scorched by the inferno.

Rivers of fire flowed through the valleys cut into the black rock, bubbling and popping as they released clouds of sulphurous gases. The acrid smell added to the suffocating heat as we raced towards a new black spot. Flashes of yellow lightning slashed across its ebony depths. As our speed had slowed a little, I had the time to notice the blue haze that followed each explosion; ripples through the inky darkness. Kade's light aimed towards the growing black horizon, never deviating from its target, a comet racing across the night sky.

We passed through this portal as we had the others, the increased resistance slowing our speed yet again, taking us to a new reality within Mobis' Seven Hells. The air was more temperate with no wind or fire to sear the ghostly nerve endings in my arms. But the relief was momentary as the winged creatures that Villermir had sent to attack me swooped over the blazing trail of light that was Kade. The creatures bared their teeth and slashed with their talons, but never made contact. They soon tired of antagonising the silver mist and returned to flying over the rocky hillside. Small avalanches of pebbles and scree rolled down the hills from the downdraught of their wings as they dived and banked on the thermals.

Hiding in caves and crevasses within the hills were dark grey shadows; shades of humans avoiding the slash of talons. They moved independently and individually and seemed aware of their surroundings and the horrors sent to torment them, although no identifiable features could be seen. The scream released by one of the shadows when it was caught and ripped apart by a winged daemon was sickeningly human. Chunks of shadow fell to the valley floor. I watched in horror as the pieces coalesced to re-form the shadow. The process could be repeated for eternity. The drama replayed as I looked all around me, as far as I could see in every direction.

I focused on Kade's light as we travelled towards a third black spot. The lightning flashed green with an afterglow of deep purple. For the first time I heard the crack of thunder that accompanied each display. I felt the vibration ripple across my skin before the deafening crack. It sounded as if mountains were being ripped apart. I became anxious as we approached the next tear between the realms, afraid to be so close to the energy being released within. We passed through with the now familiar momentary pause.

Our speed had slowed to that of a galloping horse. Still I could not decrease the distance between me and the silver light. My speed matched Kade's precisely. The new world was dark, covered by a black sky with no stars visible. A pale silvery sheen bathed the rocky precipices but left no shadows for shelter. The dark grey shades drifted from rock to rock without any apparent purpose. The reason was soon revealed as enormous fanged daemons materialised behind a shade, tearing it into chunks, screams mixing with the snarls and grunts of the monsters as they fought for scraps. Cloven hooves stamped on the ground as scaled hands grasped their prey. Long snouts slashed into the shade while blazing orange eyes sent waves of hatred into their victim. In the space of two heartbeats it was over. The daemons vanished as the shade reformed. The scene was quiet. The shades moved to different rocks; the daemons appeared and destroyed another victim. It happened again and again. Despite the shades' lack of human features, the violence still affected me deeply. I felt the acid burn my throat, far away in Burford.

Kade stopped abruptly. His silver aura enlarged until it was roughly the same size and shape as the man he had been. His featureless shadow-face looked around as if getting its bearings in a strange city. I could not see a dark spot on the horizon that might offer another reality. When I turned to look behind I could see the fading shadow of grey linking me to my body. It disappeared into the distance, and I could not see the portal back to the other hells. This world was effectively isolated from the others. A slowly disappearing smoke cord was the only indicator of where we had come from.

Kade's shadow wandered slowly away from me. I felt his essence slip through my fingers as a gentle tug pulled me backwards along my smoke trail.

There was no way I was leaving him here.

Resisting the sudden desire to return to Burford and my corporeal body, I stretched towards Kade. I was no longer following him as my contact with his light was broken. I was being drawn slowly backwards. I concentrated on reaching for his shade, clutching with my questing fingers but passing through his insubstantial form. Again I tried. Again my hands grasped mist. Roaring in frustration, I stretched every muscle, every joint, every sinew.

My fingers clutched material.

The mist felt like thin fabric between my fingertips. I balled the material into my fists. Kade's shadow halted, hesitating before trying to move on. I tightened my grip, pulling back towards me with all the strength I possessed, the abused tissues in my arms howling in protest. Kade was dragged into my embrace. I held his spirit so tightly.

I concentrated on the pull of my body; remembered the feel of cold, hard stone beneath my knees, the flicker of crystal light on my closed eyelids. We were pulled backwards, away from the daemons that appeared in greater numbers as we attempted to escape their realm, snapping fangs brushing against skin, clawed fingers reaching for Kade's shade. We were dragged faster and faster, flashing through the portal into the next reality, winged creatures swooping around us. But we were moving too fast. Back across the rocky outcrops, through the portal, across the molten rock and rivers of fiery lava. Another portal. The parched desert flashed by so quickly, into darkness.

We floated in a void, having lost all sense of direction. My only reference was the silver shadow held tightly in my embrace. My arms felt like they were covered in burning pitch. My muscles screamed from overuse. My head swam in disorientation.

I would not let go.

I opened my eyes as Kade took a deep, rasping breath. We had returned to Villermir's study at Burford Hythe. The room was clouded in a fog of dust as chunks of stone fell from the ceiling. Rubble was scattered all around.

'Are you back?'

'Yes,' I replied hoarsely, not fully understanding that the voice was Drey's. I swallowed against the rods of pain spearing the back of my throat. 'Yeah, we're back.'

Sound was momentarily sucked from the room before a deafening crash. The dust smothering the room, caused me to cough as I inhaled the gritty air. There was rubble strewn all around. The two guards lying behind Kade were covered in small pieces of debris. Behind them the wall was pitted, the holes resembling those that are created when fingers are pushed into bread dough. Slivers of stone had been removed from between the holes to produce a network of jagged edges and cracks.

Another crash rained pebbles on my head from the ceiling. I lifted my arms to protect myself and cried out in pain. I looked at my arms in horror. The skin remained only in patches, some of it blackened and charred. Other areas were red and bleeding. Craters littered my limbs, revealing torn tissue and leaking yellowish fluid. My fingernails were split and my fingers curled loosely over my palms. The damage extended to between two and four finger-widths above my elbows. The abused tissue throbbed with every heartbeat, sending flames of pain deep into my armpits. The slightest move sent those flames exploding through my body.

The stone cracked above my head, the sound sending spears of pain from my ears to the centre of my head. Kade grabbed my tunic and dragged me to the far wall where a large slab of stone rested. It had fallen to lodge against the wall, leaving a triangle of gap underneath. He threw me under the shelter as another part of the ceiling crashed down on the floor where I had been moments before. I pressed my back against the narrow side of the stone while Kade sheltered opposite me. I reached forward to touch him, to hold him, needing the reassurance of his solid presence. He raised his hand between us, the palm arresting any forward movement with a clear gesture. He reduced the command to just his index finger when I stayed still. But it was the look in his eyes that paralysed me more effectively than the raised hand. His face displayed confusion and pain, but his eyes revealed something else. Fear. A fear of me.

A scream of metal drew my attention away from Kade, as the door was ripped from its hinges. From under the stone slab I could see Drey and Villermir standing opposite each other. Each had adopted a stance with one foot slightly in front of the other to ensure balance. Their hands were raised in front of them, again with one slightly in front of the other. I watched as Villermir drew back his arms towards his chest, curling his fingers into loose fists. He pushed them forward sharply, spreading his fingers as if pushing against a large boulder. The momentary absence of sound preceded the shimmering of air between the two priests. A ripple passed from Villermir towards Drey. A blue shield of air became visible in front of Drey, deflecting the force of Villermir's thrust harmlessly away from the Druid. The unspent power slammed into the wall to Drey's left, showering him with dust and debris. A large crater had been punched into the stone.

Drey repeated the action just demonstrated by Villermir, pushing out from his chest to send ripples of shimmering air towards his adversary. Villermir's protective shield glowed dark red as it deflected Drey's power towards Kade and me. Stone exploded from the wall above us, but we were protected by the slab. Villermir attacked Drey once more, with the force deflected against the door. The door exploded, sending splinters of wood into the room and the passageway outside. Rubble fell on top of the shattered door from the hole created in the wall next to it. Drey immediately counter-attacked.

Although Villermir's chair had been smashed and his papers blown all around the room, the table and the Empathy Crystal had escaped damage. The crystal's amber glow had reduced to a flicker as if to avoid drawing attention to itself. I could not bear the thought of it being damaged by the surrounding chaos. Clenching my teeth against the pain in my arms, I crawled out from under the shelter. I managed to stay behind Villermir's line of sight as he concentrated on Drey. Very slowly, I moved closer to the crystal.

I was within five paces of touching it when my body suddenly refused to move. My limbs felt cast in iron, my head encased in steel. I could not move despite the panic storming around my mind. Villermir turned to me as he aimed a blast of air into Drey.

'Will you never learn?' he mocked.

He turned his attention back to Drey, changing tactics as he used each hand to release a volley of small blasts rather than one big assault. The effect knocked Drey off balance as the air slammed into his shield of protection. Drey staggered a few steps backwards, away from the destroyed door and the way out.

Seeing Drey disadvantaged, Kade rushed out from under the rock shelter. He had raised the stolen sword above his head in a position that he could slice Villermir from his shoulder to the opposite hip. Without turning towards the new threat Villermir released a pulse of energy towards Kade. The prince was sent flying backwards. He slammed into the wall and fell in a heap on the floor. He stayed very still but I could see his chest moving, shallow and rapid. I howled in frustration, unable to help Kade or grasp the crystal.

Suddenly, a soldier armed with a sword and a large knife filled the doorway. I could see two others behind him. One held a war-axe above his head.

'Don't let them leave,' instructed Villermir as he wrapped the crystal in its silk before picking it up.

He directed his power at the stone above Drey's head. Rubble rained down, knocking Drey to the ground and covering him with debris. Villermir left with the crystal. The soldiers stayed in the corridor, guarding the exit, as he passed. They would not come in, but we would not leave. Still I could not move.

Drey emerged from under the rubble like a mole, coughing the dust from his lungs. He appeared unharmed as he went over to Kade, still crumpled on the floor where he had fallen. He placed a hand on Kade's shoulder.

'Your Grace. We have to go.'

A wave of ice-blue light flowed over the prince. He took a deeper breath before stretching out. Drey helped Kade to stand, clasping his forearm before returning the sword. A brief conversation passed between the two men's eyes. Kade nodded slightly. He took another deep breath before turning to confront the bodyguards.

Drey walked over to me, looking deep into my eyes as my brain screamed in frustration and fear. Villermir was no longer there but I still couldn't move. My joints would not work no matter how hard I tried. I feared I would be left behind as Drey and Kade went after Villermir. I begged Drey not to leave me; I pleaded with him to help me, but he couldn't hear me.

'Tallen. Look at me.' He spoke as if we were the only people in the world. As if there was no danger. 'Concentrate on my voice. Just listen to my voice. Think about your breathing. Breathe in. And breathe out. Nice deep breaths. Breathe in. And out. There's nothing but you and me. Just relax, Tal.'

The soothing tone of his voice and the velvety softness of his hazel eyes calmed the chaos in my head. My breathing came more freely. I felt the pain in my arms, the fire of my blood pumping round my body, my muscles cramping from sustained tension.

I stumbled forward and Drey caught me before I fell. Warmth radiated from his touch, reducing the throbbing in my arms to a dull ache. He winked at me.

'Let's get out of here.'

Drey moved aside, allowing me to see the doorway. Kade had managed to kill one of the soldiers, but the other two were forcing him back into the room. The larger one raised his war-axe to cleave Kade in half. Kade turned to face this threat, leaving his left side vulnerable to the guard attacking with a broadsword. As Kade slashed the arms holding the axe, the swordsman drew back for the kill. Drey released a blast of air that knocked the sword from the soldier's hands as he was thrown against the far wall. He did not rise. Kade dodged out of the way of the descending axe, twisting around before thrusting his sword into the belly of his combatant. He viciously sliced upwards to increase the blood loss. The guard stood for a heartbeat before swaying and falling to his knees. With a feral snarl, Kade beheaded him.

Drey gently pushed me towards the exit. Once in the corridor we could hear the sound of feet running, echoing off the stone walls. Drey paused for a heartbeat before confidently leading us away from the destroyed room.

'This way. Quickly.'

He did not look back to see if Kade and I had followed him. There was no other option. We ran down the maze of tunnels, dust and debris falling on our heads. Drey never hesitated to take a passageway when we came across a junction. The sound of feet remained behind us. The chase continued down tunnel after tunnel and my head swam as I struggled to keep up. We raced up the stone steps and burst into the storeroom beside the main house. I braced myself for the attack that I was sure was coming, but no one waited for us.

The pale grey daylight coming through the windows provided enough light to navigate the room without stumbling. We paused to catch our breath, listening for any sound that might predict an assault. I heard nothing. Kade looked out of a window and assessed the grounds before turning to Drey.

'I can't see anyone. The place looks deserted.' He shrugged. 'Not that that counts for much.'

Drey shook his head. 'I can feel nothing. We can only hope that Villermir is too preoccupied with saving himself to worry about us.'

He didn't sound hopeful and I was not convinced. My breath was coming too fast and my heart raced out of control. I could not slow either as my mind suggested endless possibilities of how Villermir could be waiting to destroy us. The decision was made by a crash and a mumbled curse from the bottom of the stone stairway. Kade, Drey and I exchanged hurried glances, accepting that known dangers from below outweighed the potential danger outside. With a brief nod from Drey, Kade opened the door and we ran into the gardens of the estate. My back itched with the thought that Villermir could be watching. The day was overcast, but bright enough to offer a clear view of the gardens. We had no defence as we ran towards the relative safety of the woods. I prayed to the The Father and The Mother, and all the Lower Gods in the Halls of Eternity, promising everything in my power if they would just keep us safe.

It would appear they were listening. We crashed through the dry bracken and into the darkness of the woods. Drey led us to where we had left the horses, but neither of us was surprised to see that they had gone. Kade had set Mael free before entering Burford. He would not have him in the hands of Villermir. I sank to my knees. All energy left my body at the thought of walking to Faulknar. Days of vulnerability in enemy territory. The threat of death or capture all around. I could not be taken by Villermir again. I felt myself sway as waves of heat and cold flowed over my head.

I fell forward, welcoming the black oblivion.

It was dark when I awoke. A small fire, barely more than embers, emitted a little light. More importantly, it radiated some heat. The night had turned bitterly cold with the setting of the sun. I had been covered in ferns and grasses to contain some of my body heat, but we had no supplies. The clothes I had worn during my detention provided some warmth but we had no blankets. At least I was used to being hungry.

Kade lay still on the far side of the fire. I couldn't tell if he was asleep or unconscious. His chest rose and fell rhythmically, although there was still a slight rasp when he inhaled. He had been covered with a blanket of bracken.

'He's asleep,' Drey said quietly from the shadows. 'He'll be fine.'

I nodded in acknowledgement. I slowly raised myself up to sit cross-legged, being careful not to brush against my arms. My vision tilted for a heartbeat while the blood fought to reach my brain. But it soon settled. I felt more clear-headed than I had for a while. I avoided thinking about why that might be. I inspected my arms. Drey had torn strips of material from his tunic and covered my scorched skin. The fingertips felt tingly, like exposed skin on a frosty morning. The skin felt tight and I was unable to straighten my fingers without gasping in pain.

'You've made quite a mess of your arms,' continued Drey. 'I've weaved some spells into the dressings and given some healing, but I fear they will take a long time to heal.'

I took a breath to reply but the air caught in my sore throat and caused a coughing fit. Tears were streaming down my face by the time I was able to stop. I felt as if I had swallowed burning lava. I could see spots of blood on the bandages.

'Drey...' I hesitated, not knowing how to ask what I wanted to know. 'Are you well? In the tunnel, when you were in that rock of ice, you looked...'

Drey was silent for several heartbeats. I started to feel guilty that I had broached the subject. I frowned in confusion when I heard him quietly chuckle.

'My dear child. You have literally been to Mobis' Hells and back again. And your first question is to ask if I'm well?' He sighed. 'Villermir was very clever. He used my own attempts at escape to inflict his torments; lightning pulses to stun and bleed away my energy. It was like walking in quicksand. The more I fought, the harder I was bound. He took me so very far away...' He drifted into silence.

'But you escaped.'

'Yes, I did. And for that I believe I have you to thank. Far across time and space, I felt the pull of something twisting out of shape. A tilting of the natural order of things. You should not have been able to do what you did. The world hasn't seen magick like that for a very long time.' He chuckled again. 'I think Villermir was quite surprised at the size of the fangs within the snake he was tweaking.'

'I won't regret what I did,' I said sharply.

'And neither should you. You achieved something quite special. But it does raise uncomfortable questions. I fear the hands of the Gods in this conundrum. You seem to have a destiny; one I have no idea about. But it would appear fate has found you and will use you for some greater purpose. I fear those destined for the Gods' work travel a lonely path.'

'Villermir called me a protector. I feel the need to protect the crystal, and Kade. He said I may have inherited some power from the Ancients.'

Drey remained quiet. His shadow shifted uncomfortably.

'You knew!' I accused.

'I suspected.'

'And you didn't think to tell me?'

'There was nothing to tell.' His voice remained calm and quiet in the darkness. 'They are called the Ancients for a reason. They left this world a very long time ago and took their magick with them. There are some of us that still practise the old arts, but our abilities are a mere breath compared to the storm that could be unleashed by the Ancients. Continents were sculpted. Oceans formed. It was a time when Gods walked the earth.' He paused. 'Those times have been lost for countless generations. They will soon be nothing more than myth. We have no place in that story.' He paused again, a heartbeat longer than before. 'And then there's you.'

I shuddered as his words blew an icy wind through my bones. I refused to believe that I was anything different, anything special. But as I looked at Kade, I couldn't deny what I had done. My damaged arms gave evidence as to where I had been. Kade's quiet breathing told of what I had achieved.

'When you are ready to talk,' Drey's voice broke through my thoughts, 'know I will always be here for you.'

I dismissed his concerns with a shrug. 'I'm fine.'

'You've been to a place no one should come back from. Seen things you should never have seen. And Villermir doesn't play nicely. I suspect he has been playing his nasty little games with you for some time.' He hesitated. 'Talking about it may make you feel less alone.'

I doubted that, but I didn't dissuade Drey. He had good intentions. I just couldn't believe talking about it would remove the horror of what I had seen, reduce the fear of what could be done, restore my confidence that my thoughts were truly mine. Talking would involve remembering, and I would not do that. The memories were locked away, safely hidden from sight. I intended to keep them there.

It took a further two days to reach the woodcutter's hut that we had used before. It had started to snow, intermittently at first but steadily by the time we reached the hut. Although the day was cold, Kade had a sheen of sweat covering his face. He was deathly pale with grey tinges around his eyes and mouth. His breathing was shallow and forced. I was exhausted and stumbled more steps than I placed firmly. My arms throbbed painfully despite Drey's attentions. My world had reduced to the struggle of placing one foot in front of the other. When we reached the hut I noticed Drey's hands were trembling uncontrollably. He struggled to lift the latch. Although he had no obvious injuries, I suspected that his time at Burford had demanded a heavy price.

I could not believe how simple things could mean so much. Being inside the cottage, out of the snow and wind, seemed the richest luxury imaginable. The blankets retrieved and draped over my shoulders felt like the softest silk. The dried fruit tasted like the sweetest pastry. I was grateful to crumple onto the floor and not have to move.

There was only one bed in the cabin. After much persuasion, Drey finally accepted it. He was taking sole care of Kade and me. There would be no way we could make it without him. He fussed over us a little longer before succumbing to his exhaustion. He was asleep within a heartbeat of lying on the bed.

I felt Kade watching me. He had not spoken to me since leaving Burford. But then he had barely spoken at all. I had frequently felt his eyes on me, but he always looked away when I tried to make eye contact. He had remained several paces away from me since leaving the estate. I did not blame him, but I could not forget the look of fear in his eyes.

'What?' I demanded, looking up.

He held my gaze. The fear was still evident in his eyes. He searched for something familiar in a face changed beyond recognition.

'I'd never seen eyes the colour of yours before,' he said eventually, causing chills to race down my spine. 'The daemons had orange eyes. A shade brighter than yours.'

I had started trembling.

'What does that mean, Tallen?' His voice turned hard and cold. "What are you?'

Chapter Twenty Four

It continued to snow for two more days. The journey became one of survival. We no longer cared about being spotted by enemy patrols. The cold held a more immediate danger. We travelled by day and slept in barns at night. We stole what we needed – food, clothing, blankets. We trekked in silence across a subdued, white landscape. The squeaking of our feet as they compacted the snow was the only sound as the wildlife stayed in their warm dens and nests. I quickly lost feeling in my toes and fingers, the symphony of aches, stabs, cramps and throbs providing constant company. We rarely spoke. The weight of our sombre mood and unfavourable odds pressed heavily on our shoulders. We all walked with slightly stooped backs.

On the third day the snow turned to sleet and the ground to squelching mush where we walked. My head stayed bowed in an attempt to remain dry, but the icy meltwater invaded every gap in my clothing. Despite the heat generated by the exertion of walking, my teeth still clicked together uncontrollably. The sweat on my back seemed to freeze when it mixed with the persistent sleet. Kade's lips and the tip of his nose had turned blue and I suspected mine showed similar signs. Somewhere my brain was screaming that we were getting dangerously cold, but its protests were smothered by the concentration needed to place one numb and frozen foot in front of the other without falling.

We stopped early. Drey led us to a small cave before dark. The space was shallow but well covered by trees. We could have a fire. It provided more smoke than heat. Nobody complained. It was more warmth than we had had in days. We all huddled as close to the embers as we could without burning ourselves. My teeth finally stopped rattling, but the pain of my thawing extremities caused my eyes to water. Drey melted snow to make willow-bark tea to help ease our aches, before melting more snow for a watery vegetable broth. I sighed as the warmth spread through my tired muscles. I watched Kade's eyes closing as he sat opposite me, the fire chasing shadows across his face. His cheekbones were too prominent. His eyes were shadowed sockets. His head trembled slightly.

Drey reached over and took the cup from Kade's swollen hands. 'Get some sleep. We're safe enough here.'

Kade barely had time to nod in agreement before folding into the mattress of dry fern. I wrapped the blanket a little tighter around my shoulders, not wanting to sleep yet so I could savour the feeling of warmth deep inside me. My treacherous eyes had other ideas, the lids becoming harder and harder to lift. It wasn't long before I had to admit defeat and join Kade in welcome slumber.

I awoke with a start. My racing heart told me there was something wrong, but my brain was unable to determine what. I looked over to Drey for reassurance. His face wore an expression of concern, but he calmly held out a hand to keep me still. He returned his attention to Kade, and I followed his gaze. Kade was sitting up but his eyes were closed. He was trembling and his forehead glistened with sweat. His hands were repeatedly clenching into fists. He twitched violently, causing the sharp rustle of fern that would have woken me. I watched, horrified and fascinated at the same time. It seemed he was sleepwalking without moving, his eyelids flickering as if dreaming.

My heart jumped again as Kade snapped open his eyes. The irises had rolled upwards so that only a sliver of brown could be seen. The white sclera glowed eerily in the firelight. He glared straight ahead, where I happened to be sitting. I was transfixed by the sightless stare.

'There's fire. People screaming.' Kade's voice was steady, maintaining both tone and pace. The hairs at the back of my neck and along my arms stood up. 'Ships are burning in the harbour. They're trying to put out the flames. The storehouse is smoking. Flames can be seen in the windows. Some are running towards the city. Fire in the houses and shops. The heat is forcing people into the street. It's so noisy. Timbers breaking. Dogs barking. Men shouting. Women crying. The door to the royal house is broken. It's dark inside. No lights are burning. Two soldiers are lying dead. Their throats have been cut. The house is quiet. There's blood on the stairs. A tapestry is torn. More soldiers are dead in the main hall, and a man in black. Kerk's door is open. Another man in black lies in the reception area. Jeck is lying face down in the doorway to Kerk's room. There's a crash. A chair being knocked over. A man in black is fighting with Kerk. He has a small dagger. Kerk is holding it away from his neck. The man in black is stronger. Kerk's grip slips. The blade slashes his throat.'

Kade gasped as his eyes rolled back down. He was shaking, his eyes searching for an identifiable feature. He took several deep breaths before recognition returned.

'What was that?' he panted. 'Did I dream that?'

'Didn't look like a dream to me,' I said quietly.

Kade turned blazing eyes on me. 'And what would you know about it?' he snapped.

My reply was equally sharp. 'I have had a dream or several.'

'So you know everything now. No one can have bad dreams apart from you. Scared someone will take the attention away from you for a moment?'

Drey held his hands up to placate Kade as I drew breath for another retort. 'I don't think it was a dream either. You described everything you saw.'

Kade placed his shaking hands over his mouth. 'Fearsome Father. Kerk...'

Drey kept very still. 'It may be a connection with your brother; an empathic link with someone close at a time of great emotion.'

'Over this distance? You and I need to be in the same city to connect. Kerk is a kingdom away.'

Drey shrugged. 'It's not unheard of. But yes, it is unusual.' He looked at Kade carefully. 'Unlikely.'

Kade tensed his voice, turning hard with suspicion. 'Then what?'

'It may be a vision of things yet to come.'

Kade growled deep in his throat. He turned his glare on me, his eyes flashing dangerously with rage. For the first time, I was truly scared of Kade. He stood up and Drey had to place a hand on his chest to stop him crashing through the fire to get at me. I felt myself shrinking, making myself smaller as I remained frozen in place by the hate in his stare.

'What have you done?' he demanded. 'What have you done to me?'

It took another eight days to reach the border. The cloud had rained itself dry, leaving clear skies and cold days. The overnight frosts remained until mid-morning and froze again soon after dark. Our pace grew slower as our energy faded. I knew Drey was frustrated by our slow speed but was showing as much deprivation as Kade and I. Our clothes hung loosely on frames that were too thin. Lifeless eyes were set well back in darkened sockets. Kade had developed a cough that would leave him pale and struggling for breath. Drey trembled continuously, increasing his frustration as he dropped things repeatedly.

I escaped the constant torments by letting my mind wander in daydreams. The images I conjured were so vivid I could forget the cold and the hunger, my aching back and throbbing feet. I soared over mountains and through valleys. I swooped so low over lakes that I could almost touch the rippling surface. I rose on thermals and played in the clouds. The snow on the mountain peaks was afforded beauty due to the distance. I was able to glide between the snow-dusted crevasses before returning to the warmer valleys below, making the deer in the meadows run away from my shadow.

I spent so much time in this imaginary world that I barely registered being picked up and carried. My mind recalled a memory from long ago; a previous time when I had been so tired.

'Laken?'

The arms held me tighter to the warm chest, releasing the scent of oiled leather, woodsmoke and spices. It was an unfamiliar smell, but it was reassuring all the same. I relaxed my head into the warmth of the strong embrace and fell asleep.

All was quiet when I awoke. I kept my eyes closed, not wanting to reveal myself until I had assessed my surroundings. The bed was soft and the sheets were tucked tightly around me. My arms lay on top of the sheets, their dressings comfortably applied. The light on my closed eyelids suggested daylight but I could hear no sounds of activity. I breathed in the scent of woodsmoke and spices, frowning as I tried to place where I had smelt that before. I snapped my eyes open.

'Morning.' Keenan smiled at my sudden recognition.

'Your Grace.' I tried to sit up but was held in place by the sheets tightly tucked around my chest and under the mattress.

'Rest easy, Tallen.'

'Kade and Drey? Are they here? Are they well?'

'They're fine. Drey, the tough old goat, is up and about already. Short of a few good meals, but he's fine. Kade will need a little more time.' He paused, studying me carefully. 'You three appear to have had quite an adventure.'

'We failed. I failed.'

Keenan held up a hand to stop me. 'The three of you are back in one piece. I consider that a victory. The matter of the crystal has suffered a setback, no more.' He smiled reassuringly. 'For both parties, it would appear. We have had no earth tremors for quite a while. Seems Villermir is licking his wounds as well.'

We lapsed into a comfortable silence as I looked around the military infirmary. There were two rows of five beds in the shelter. Only one other bed was occupied. The soldier was asleep or unconscious. His head was heavily wrapped in bandages.

'How long have I been asleep?'

'You were found by the scouts a short distance north of here. I don't know how Drey got you past the Lindvanes but you were far enough north to miss the main camp. You were brought to the camp yesterday, around noon. You've been asleep since then.'

I frowned, trying to remember returning to Hunter's Down. 'You carried me?'

Keenan chuckled softly. 'Kade and Drey had enough strength left to protest against being carried.' He smiled at me. 'You didn't.'

'I thought you were Laken,' I said, more to myself than to the lord general.

'I know,' he said quietly.

I took a deep breath to banish the sad memories. 'Thank you.'

Keenan waved his hand in dismissal before turning to a young soldier who had brought a steaming cup. Keenan took the cup and dismissed the soldier. He turned to see me wrinkle my nose at the acrid smell.

'It's good for you.'

'Smells like it,' I replied, unconvinced. 'What is it?'

'Something for the pain and to help you sleep.'

'I don't need to sleep,' I protested, gasping at the pain when I tried to sit up.

Keenan thrust the cup at me. 'Yes, you do.'

The look in his eyes made it very clear that he would not be dissuaded. He helped me into a more upright position to enable me to drink the liquid. I shuddered at its bitter taste.

'Sleep well, Tallen.' Keenan took the empty cup and settled me back in the bed.

'Do I have a choice?'

He laughed. 'No.'

I didn't feel sleepy when Keenan left. I inspected the stitching on the sheets. I tried to move my fingers, but the bandages held them still. I closed my eyes and returned to the mountains of my daydreams, drifting over rocky peaks, floating over green meadows. The image soon faded as sleep claimed me again.

The next few days followed a predictable pattern. I was woken to be fed, then dozed in a healing sleep. I felt a little stronger each time I awoke. I started to get restless, kicking the restricting blankets off. My arms itched under the dressings and I was frustrated at not being able to move my fingers. The soldier with the head bandages was no longer in the infirmary and I had the place to myself. I had managed to wrap myself in a blanket and walk around the shelter on three different occasions. The room was fifteen paces wide and thirty paces long. It took me until the third occasion to walk the length and back without having to rest on one of the beds.

Drey caught me on the fourth occasion.

'You are obviously feeling better. Ready to leave the infirmary, perhaps?'

'I would have left earlier if I had any clothes,' I snapped, embarrassed at being caught out.

'Which was precisely the reason we took them.'

Drey helped me back into bed, arranging the pillows so I could sit up. He looked much better than I remembered. His pallor was more natural and his hands no longer shook. His eyes were bright and critical again, assessing my health and the potential damage done by exercising too early. He eventually gave a small nod, accepting that I had come to no harm.

'How's Kade?'

Drey sighed. 'He's healing. Villermir's guards gave him quite a beating. It will be a while before his ribs have repaired. But the cough has gone. He's getting there.'

'And his… dreams?'

'He's not had another. Keenan has received no news from Liegeport. Perhaps it was just a bad dream after all.'

'But you don't think so.'

He paused. 'No. No, I don't.'

'And it's all my fault.' I pressed my head back into the pillow as tears pricked my eyes. I blinked them away.

'It's not your fault, Tallen. A lot of things happened to Kade at Burford. He's been changed by his time there. He needs to come to terms with it all. Just give him time, Tallen. He'll come through this all right.'

But what about us? Would we be all right? Would it ever be comfortable between Kade and me again? Would he ever trust me again? I knew it was a selfish thought, and that I should be grateful that he was alive and healing. And I was grateful. But the gratitude did not fill the gaping void left by Kade's rejection.

I changed the subject. 'So can I leave this bed?'

Drey frowned. 'Let's see how your arms are doing.'

I tried to convince him that they were healing well as he removed the dressings. I had to bite my lip to resist the urge to scratch as the bandages were unrolled. Drey gently removed the final layer to reveal a patchwork of glistening pink skin. Normal skin traced between the shiny patches like veins in a leaf. The healing tissue felt tender when Drey touched it, but otherwise it only itched. I couldn't resist rubbing the skin quickly on the sheets.

'If you scratch those arms, I will tie them to the bed,' Drey snapped. I stopped instantly.

Drey frowned at my hands. The skin had healed, curling the fingers towards the palms. I yelped in pain as he carefully tried to straighten them. The fingers would not move.

'Looks like we need to work on these,' he said as he tried to extend the fingers again. 'But yes, you can leave the infirmary. Keenan has provided a sleeping shelter for you, next to mine.'

He applied light dressings to my arms and hands, leaving the fingers exposed to encourage movement. He left to arrange clothing for me, with strict instructions not to scratch.

Three times a day for the next few days, Drey came to rub oil into my hands and stretch the skin covering my fingers. It often left me sweating, but I could see the small improvements made. It grew more comfortable holding eating utensils and I was soon able to dress myself. Boredom saw me helping out around the camp, fetching and carrying what was needed. The gentle exercise did much to maintain the flexibility of the joints worked on by Drey.

The camp had quietened for the winter. Many of the minor lords had returned to their estates, leaving a small portion of their men behind to guard the border. Lord Gascombe had also returned home with an honour guard, although most of his men had stayed at Hunter's Down. The camp had reduced to one field. Sorties were rare with no one wanting to risk horses' legs on uneven, frozen ground. Many duties centred on maintaining the camp. The drills aimed at maintaining fitness and reaction speed.

Kade avoided me and I did not seek him out.

I also spent time with the horses, knowing that I would probably need one to ride back to Liegeport. I was happily surprised to find Mael and Mupp tethered with the others behind a mound of earth that had been constructed to provide the horses with some shelter.

'Well-trained horses, those,' said Todd, the captain overseeing the care of the horses. 'Caused quite a stir when they turned up one morning. Amazing how they find their way back to the last safe place, where they got their last good meal.'

I happily braved the kicks and bites to give each horse a tight hug around the neck, breathing in the beautiful scent of their coats in the crisp morning air.

'The lord general was quite concerned when he saw them,' Todd continued. 'We all feared the worst, I'm afraid. We were all mighty glad to see the prince back safe, as well as you and the king's adviser.'

I let him ramble on, his constant chatter providing some comfort as I groomed the horses and cared for their feet. Despite the time I spent there, none of the horses accepted my presence. Only three tolerated me enough not to kick at my approach, and only one of those would let me ride her. I missed Nalya terribly.

Drey was late for the midday session on my fingers. He was frequently absent-minded and absorbed in whatever he was doing, enough to miss appointments. But until now he had been reliable when it came to healing my wounds. I paced my sleeping shelter while I silently debated whether I should take the opportunity to avoid the discomfort. My fingers were gaining more and more movement. I was sure three times a day was a little excessive. But this had to be judged against the trouble I would get into if I missed a session. I cringed at the length of the lecture I knew I would be given. I decided to go and look for him.

I found Drey in the first place I looked: his sleeping shelter. The accommodation had room for a bed and a chest to store bed linen and spare clothes. Drey's also contained a small writing desk and four chairs. It took a few paces for my eyes to adjust to the more subdued lighting inside the shelter. Drey was sitting with his back to me. Kade sat opposite. He was clean-shaven and his hair had been cut short. He was pale and visibly shaking. He looked up at me with such intense hatred that I took two paces backwards.

'What's wrong?'

Drey turned so he could see me. He looked very tired. 'Kade has had another vision.'

Kade turned his attention back to Drey, scowling as a growl rumbled deep in his chest. I gained courage from the removal of his glare, and silently moved to sit next to Drey.

Drey sighed in frustration. 'Well, you can't claim this was a dream. You were awake. You were in the middle of a sentence.'

Kade lowered his eyes to his hands that were folded in his lap. He started picking at the dry skin around his thumbnail.

'What happened?'

Drey continued as Kade stayed silent. 'We were discussing how soon we could return to Liegeport. Understandably, Kade is eager to return home.' He watched Kade closely. 'He just stopped in the middle of a sentence. His eyes rolled back and...'

'What did you see?'

Kade's jaw tensed, sending ripples though the muscles. Drey sighed again, before continuing to compensate for the prince's silence.

'Same as before. Liegeport under attack. The city burning. Strangers in black clothing directing the chaos. And Kerk...'

'We have to go back to Liegeport.' I looked from Drey to Kade and back again. 'If this is a prophecy we may be able to warn them. To stop it.'

'Oh, well done. No one had ever thought of that,' snapped Kade, glaring at me once again.

'Well, what amazing plan did you come up with, oh royal one?' I snapped back, equally venomous.

'I don't know. Maybe hanging you for treason would break the curse.'

'So you're worried about yourself, then, and not your brother.'

Kade lifted his lip in a snarl, rising to confront me. Anger was an old friend to me and I was willing to meet the challenge.

'Enough!' Drey stood to prevent any further hostilities. 'It seems you two are feeling much better. Perhaps the long ride to Liegeport will cool your tempers.'

Keenan refused to allow us to leave, suggesting that we stay in the camp for a couple of days. The sky had covered with heavy, snow-laden clouds and the wind had increased its force. There was likely to be significant snow and drifting over the next few days. I could see his wisdom. We would not be able to travel in a snowstorm, and it would be better to remain in the camp rather than be exposed on the road. Still, I was restless to return to Liegeport.

The rider arrived two days later. The camp runner found me checking supplies for spoilage. I raced to Keenan's accommodation, finding that Drey, Duke Brunfield and Duke Humphston had joined the lord general. The rider was seated and holding a steaming cup. He looked ready to collapse, with mud smeared all over him. He unconsciously scratched at the drying mud on his cheek above his soiled beard. A plate of food was untouched beside him.

Kade burst into the room, making the oiled leather sheet that served as a door crack behind him. He had been practising with the sword which he held, forgotten, in his hand. His fleece-lined leather gambeson revealed arms covered in fading bruises. Sweat stuck his hair to his temples.

'What news?' he demanded.

The rider stood, glancing between Kade and Keenan, wondering which one to address. He settled on Kade.

'Your Grace, the news from Liegeport is bad. I have ridden continuously since yesterday morning, changing horses as they tired to ensure news reached the lord general as soon as possible.'

'Tell me.'

'Liegeport has been attacked. A small band of men infiltrated the city. They set fire to strategic points including the docks and warehouses to create panic. In the chaos they invaded the royal house. The king's equerry was killed trying to protect his liege. The king was safely removed from the city.' He paused. 'I regret to inform you that your brother did not find safety. He was killed in his rooms.'

Kade breathed in deeply. 'How did he die?'

A look of horrified shock rippled over the rider's face before he resumed the mask of his profession. 'His throat was cut, my lord.'

Kade went from pale to grey. He swallowed hard before turning on his heel and leaving the shelter. I had taken two paces to go after him before I remembered that he no longer welcomed my company.

We left before the sun had moved further across the sky. The journey back to Liegeport happened so fast and at the same time took forever. We pushed the horses as hard as we dared, but we could not replace them with fresh mounts, so had to rest them often. The roads were soft and mushy during the day but froze solid at night. We were careful not to bruise the horses' soles by stepping on uneven mud that had failed to thaw with the rising of the sun. Extra care and attention was given to Mael and Mupp by everyone, not just Kade and Drey.

The company racing to the capital numbered six. Drey, Kade and I were accompanied by Keenan and his two personal bodyguards. Brunfield was to send a company to follow us at a slower pace but be available if military force was required. Keenan was as tight-lipped as Kade, and dangerously efficient at organising camps or hostelries. The set of his mouth was a little too tight, his forehead carried the permanent hint of a frown, and his blue eyes had lost their zest for life. The loss I saw in Kade's eyes was reflected in Keenan's. But while Kade snapped and sulked in equal measure, Keenan focused on his work. He ensured that he always had a task to complete and we felt obliged to follow his lead. Under his gentle leadership, we worked well as a team.

It took four days to reach Liegeport. The city came into view as it had so many years ago when I first came to the capital. We crested the small hill and I smelt the tang of salt from the sea. The sandstone royal house looked unaffected, its towers pointing defiantly into the sky. The windows appeared dark with the sun having moved around to the south but the colours of the Faulknar banner welcomed us home.

The rest of the city had not been so lucky. Fire had spread to many of the houses, leaving large areas of blackened timber. The poorer quarters where the houses were jumbled together were the worst affected. Some areas had been completely destroyed. Shelters of light-coloured material had been erected all over the city, small islands dotted within the sea of destroyed neighbourhoods. The main gates were closed. It seemed a little late for that.

The port had been more extensively damaged. Two large ships had burnt almost to the waterline, blackened stumps rising from the sea. The storerooms had been completely destroyed. All that was left was the charred outline of where the buildings had stood, the ground littered with the burnt remains of the food and furnishings stored within them. It was a major setback for the city at the start of winter. But the damage was minor compared to the blow dealt by the destruction of the quays and jetties. There would be no more supplies from the cities along the coast. Liegeport was facing a hungry season.

The seabirds circled without any concern, their calls mocking the despair of the people below. As we rode closer to the city we could smell the ash in the air, tickling the back of my throat, even though it had been over a week since the attack. The click of the horses' hooves sounded unnaturally loud as we entered the subdued city. Despite being just after noon, the streets were quiet. Doors were closed and windows shuttered. It felt very strange to see the usually proud and confident capital act as if it was hiding from some childhood monster. Dangers lurked in the shadows. Strangers were judged a threat based purely on their unfamiliarity. The few people that were around looked at us with poorly disguised anger, showing little respect for the prince and the lord general. It was clear that the townspeople laid some of the blame for the attack at the feet of the royal family. I suspected that the frustration I had seen in the faces of the people throughout the kingdom had finally made it to Liegeport. The enemy had delivered a blow to the heart of Faulknar. Those of the royal city no longer felt safe. War had touched their families and their homes. They expected their royal family to protect them. I wondered if they knew how the royal family had also been affected; how they had lost one of their own.

The inner circle of the city seemed to have suffered less damage. The stone buildings had been more resistant to the fire than the wooden buildings had. Many of them were occupied by the military, who had a more pragmatic approach to the dangers of war. The stables were functioning efficiently as usual, although the greeting afforded to Keenan and Kade was more restrained than would normally be given to the well-liked and respected royals. Forearms were clasped, backs slapped, but the weight of responsibility was clearly seen in the soldiers' faces. The horses were quietly taken from us and we were escorted to the royal house.

Chapter Twenty Five

We were taken immediately to see Kyllian. We had no time to refresh ourselves or change our mud-stained clothes. The steward accepted our charge from the soldiers at the door of the royal house. He descended the stone steps to greet us, dismissing the guards as he bustled us into the house. He rubbed his hands nervously, I suspected to resist the urge to shove us in an attempt to get us to move faster. His agitated energy was reflected in the other staff in the house. Heads were nodded respectfully to Kade, Keenan and Drey, but eyes remained downcast. They went about their business hurriedly. There was no celebration, or even relief, at the prince's return.

We were taken to the state meeting room along the eastern corridor. The steward knocked rapidly on the solid wooden door, then closed his eyes momentarily and took a deep breath before opening it. He blocked the doorway while he bowed to Kyllian, making us wait in the corridor.

'Your Majesty,' he began. 'The party of four is here and has been brought directly to you as requested.'

Averting his gaze from Kyllian, he stepped aside and ushered us in. I was the last to enter the room and the steward quickly ducked behind me, closing the door as he left. It was a grey, overcast day and little light came through the windows behind Kyllian. The subdued lighting seemed to add to the atmosphere in the room. The tension was oppressive, increasing my heart rate in anticipation. I could see the men standing beside me, all of us maintaining a controlled posture, muscles tense, breathing quick and shallow, our heads bowed, unable to rise until Kyllian permitted it.

The king kept us waiting.

I had time to study the thick, woven rug that covered the polished wooden floor. The tables had been moved to the sides of the room. The chairs were stacked neatly beside them. That left a large rectangle of space for the king to assess us. I resisted the urge to shuffle under his gaze.

'So,' he said finally, allowing us to lift our heads. 'Did you get the crystal?'

I opened my mouth to reply, lifting my eyes to look at the king in his formal robes of black trimmed with white fur. The words melted in my throat and I was left gaping like a stranded fish. Sitting next to Kyllian was Breya. Dressed in the mourning colours of black with red trimmings, her carriage was anything but sorrowful. Her posture was regal, her stare direct, her right hand placed lightly on Kyllian's arm. I could not understand why she would be there.

Kade answered for me. Picking up on his father's tone, he replied with equal formality. 'I'm afraid we did not, sire.'

'You failed.'

There was a world of accusation in those two words. I glanced at Kade, who had paled at the king's statement. His jaw muscles were rippling. His shoulders tensed to prevent clenching his fists. He would not give so obvious a submission to his father.

'Yes, sire.'

Kyllian exhaled noisily through his nose, clearly expressing his displeasure. 'So it was all for nothing.'

For the first time, I noticed the blankness in the king's eyes. His face seemed elongated, his jaw lengthened, his cheeks prominent. Stubble covered his chin. His eyelids were lowered slightly, adding to the shadows playing over his eyes. His hands gripped the arms of the chair tightly, the bones showing white through the skin of his knuckles.

'My liege,' began Kade, 'I believe we did everything possible to retrieve the crystal.'

'But it wasn't good enough, was it?' Kyllian leaned forward. 'As usual, you just weren't good enough. Did you even try? Or did you just go to the nearest tavern to sing to all the pretty ladies?'

Kade spluttered. 'Father, I hardly think—'

'Precisely. You hardly ever think. That's the privilege of being the second son, I suppose. Leave the thinking to the firstborn while the second son just has to follow orders.'

Keenan stepped forward. 'Kyllian, that's not fair. The boy was following your instructions.'

Kyllian turned to glare at his brother. 'And what would you know? You ran away from your responsibilities at the first opportunity. You've been playing at being a soldier ever since.'

The two brothers stared defiantly at each other. Kyllian's rage was clear to see. A darkened patch of pink on each cheek was the only evidence of Keenan's anger. He held the glare of his sworn liege, both men stubbornly refusing to yield.

Kyllian broke first, briefly lowering his eyes before returning to accuse his son. 'The role of the second son is to protect Faulknar. The capital was attacked and where were you?' He looked at Kade and Keenan. 'Both of you?'

'I didn't know...' Kade began before realising that he had known. He had been warned. My stomach spasmed at the expression of raw grief on his face. 'I couldn't get here in time.'

'No. You were busy failing at the task you were given.'

'Your Majesty.' Drey's voice was very quiet but still carried in the highly charged room. 'Villermir knew we were coming. It was a trap. Kade barely made it out alive.'

Kyllian continued to stare at the prince. 'And yet here you stand. Which is more than can be said for your brother.'

I gasped at the viciousness of his words. Kade shuddered next to me. His jaw clenched tightly but he could not stop the tears from breaking the dam of his lower eyelids.

'Father, please...' His voice broke.

Drey stepped forward. His tone was carefully measured as he said, 'Kyllian, perhaps now is not the time for this conversation.'

'Ah, my master Druid. And where were your Gods?'

Drey remained calm. 'The ways of men are but one concern of the Gods.'

Kyllian would not be deterred. 'Perhaps they were concerned with the misuse of the Empathy Crystal? Did you determine Villermir's plans for it?'

Drey's shoulders dropped a little further as he conceded. 'No, sire. I did not.'

'No.' Kyllian leaned back in his chair as if accepting defeat. 'Is it any wonder my kingdom is on its knees when my chief adviser and my own family cannot deliver on their promises? Perhaps it is time I listened to the people. The old Gods are impotent; their influence long gone.' He paused, looking at each of us as we absorbed his words. 'Faulknar is hereby under the protection of Baila. Other religions will no longer be encouraged.'

Kade's sorrow was swept away by anger, the colour returning to his face in the form of bright red blotches spread over his neck. He moved towards his father but was restrained by Keenan's hand on his arm.

'How can you say that?' He threw his free arm up with incredulity. 'How can you support Baila when the high priest is a traitor?! Are you insane?'

Kyllian stood so suddenly that his chair was knocked backwards, crashing loudly as it smacked the floor. 'How dare you question my decision?! A religion cannot be condemned on the actions of one man. Kerk believed in the teachings and I will make sure his religion thrives.'

'Then there appears to be nothing left for me here,' said Kade quietly. He turned to leave, turning his back on his father.

Kyllian roared in anger. 'You have not been dismissed!'

As he had before, Kade obeyed his father when I knew he wanted with all his heart to run away. Keenan watched his nephew carefully as Kade slowly turned to face his king. Without submission, Kade inclined his head.

'Yes, my liege.'

Breya stood to set Kyllian's chair back on its feet. Touching him gently on the shoulder, she indicated that he should resume his seat. Kyllian smiled warmly at her and sat.

'My liege,' she began, 'I'm not sure that now is the correct time to voice such concerns, but I would not have any confusion between us at this time.'

Kyllian inclined his head indulgently at her. 'What is on your mind, my dear child?'

Breya smiled self-consciously. I narrowed my eyes in suspicion. Breya was never shy. She was playing the king.

'I'm afraid I don't understand matters of state...'

Now I knew she was up to something. Breya understood politics very well and was always ready to twist convention to meet her needs.

'...but I believe the agreement with my father stated a union between Greenwood and the heir to Faulknar.'

Kyllian frowned. 'That is correct.'

'Well...' She lowered her eyes. 'Since Kerk has...' She lifted a shaking hand to her mouth, closing her eyes as if too overcome to continue that train of thought.

I found myself staring. I knew she was not distraught at her betrothed's death, but I could not believe she would use it to further her own ambitions.

Kyllian patted her arm tenderly. 'Go on, my dear. What is your concern?'

Breya composed herself before continuing. 'I was just wondering if, with Kade the new heir to the throne, would the contract now be between Kade and myself?'

I staggered a step backwards as her meaning became apparent. The blood drained from my head, making me feel dizzy. But I did not imagine the brief flicker of triumph in Breya's eyes as she looked directly at me. The contact was fleeting, and she soon returned to the 'naive girl' act for the benefit of Kyllian.

'I admit, I had not given it much thought. But yes, I believe you are correct. The agreement with your father was for you to marry my heir. That would now be Kade.' Kyllian lowered his head to look into Breya's eyes. 'Would that be agreeable to you?'

Breya nodded. 'I will do what is required of me. For the good of the kingdom.'

Kyllian smiled encouragingly at her. 'That's a very brave thing for you to do.'

Kade was very still, his voice barely more than a whisper. 'Do I get a say?'

The wrath returned to Kyllian's face immediately as he glared at his son. 'You will do as you are told. You failed in your duties as a brother and Kerk paid the ultimate price for your inadequacy. May the One God strike me down if I do not make sure you fulfil your duties as my heir.'

Kade's nod of agreement was barely perceptible but clearly displayed his submission and defeat.

I returned to my room in Drey's tower after finally being dismissed by Kyllian. I lay on my bed and cried until I thought there could not be any water left in my body. Long after dark I heard Drey quietly enter the room, but I pretended I was asleep. He waited in the doorway for a long time before leaving without saying a word. I slept very little that night.

The next morning I awoke to Tarra bringing the hot water for my bath. She fussed for several moments before sitting on the bed beside me.

'I was going to bring your bath last night. Thought you would be needing it after your journey. But Drey said not to disturb you.'

I smiled at the concern she showed me. 'Thank you. It was good to sleep in my bed again.'

She played with her fingers for a few heartbeats. 'If you ever need to talk about anything, I hope you would consider me a sympathetic ear.'

I raised an eyebrow at her. 'Did Drey put you up to that as well?'

She smiled and relaxed. 'Yes. But the sentiment remains.' She paused and the smile melted. 'I heard what Mistress Breya said yesterday. That she is to be betrothed to Master Kade.'

I stayed silent, my mood descending rapidly.

'Drey also hinted that you'd had a tough time before returning home. I know you like to keep these things to yourself, Tallen. But if you change your mind, I'm always willing to listen.'

I was a little embarrassed but appreciated her intent. 'Thank you, Tarra.'

She patted my leg through the blankets before leaving me to soak in the bath. Having cleaned away the grime from days on the road, I made my exit from the house.

The day was damp and misty as I walked through the deserted city. It suited my mood perfectly. I pulled my woollen cloak tighter around my shoulders, tucking my hands under my armpits to keep them warm. Few merchants were walking the street, carrying half-empty baskets of bread or vegetables. We all kept our heads down, failing to give even a nod of acknowledgement.

I left the city by the smaller of the gates that led to the coastal path, high above the bay. The gate was closed, unusual for this time of the morning, and the guard was required to unlock it for me. He grumbled about being forced to come out in the cold but held it wide open for me. The flint in the city walls glistened as the moisture caught the weak sunlight. The guard locked the gate immediately after I had passed through.

The tension I'd felt within Liegeport melted as I crunched over the gravel path leading to the clifftop. The mist had beaded the leaves with silver. The spiderwebs carried a fortune in jewels made from dew. A sparrow drank from water collected at the base of a bramble-bush leaf. I took a deep breath in, savouring the smell of wet earth and the sharp tang of the sea. I slowly breathed out, wishing I could expel all my troubles with the puff of steam my breath released.

At the top of the cliff was a large, flat meadow. For countless generations it had been used for the funeral pyres of the people of Liegeport and the surrounding villages. There had been no distinction between royalty and servant, lord and farmer. All were cremated under the guidance of the Druid of Liegeport. Drey had conducted the rituals for as long as I had been in the capital. The ceremonies were held when the wind blew west to east, taking the smoke, and the freed spirit, out to sea and into the Halls of Eternity. My heart sank lower in my chest as I saw the sacred place had been claimed by Baila. There were three stone cairns, the slate rocks piled high to form giant pyramids. One towered above the other two, standing an arm's length taller than me. The others came up to my waist and were set together, further from the cliff edge. It was as if they had been positioned so as not to spoil the view for the largest cairn.

I had collected some winter roses, and placed some at the base of the nearest cairn. The white petals with a blush of pink at the tips contrasted with the dark earth and the blue of the boulders, the light colour making a defiant statement on such a dreary day. All three cairns had an iron pole protruding from the centre, declaring who was buried beneath. The first displayed the lion of Faulknar above a hovering falcon. I didn't recognise the heraldic design. With a start, I realised it must belong to Kyllian's equerry. I never knew his name. Never bothered to find out who he was.

'I'm so sorry,' I said, touching the stones reverently.

I moved on to the next cairn and placed some more of the winter roses there. The iron pole again bore the lion of Faulknar, but also the oak tree of Gazelea, Jeck's family. With the larger cairn belonging to Kerk, I realised that only the fallen nobility had been buried on the clifftop. None of the townspeople had been afforded memorials on the sacred site. It would appear that the One God made a distinction between those with titles and those that served. Perhaps the distinction lay solely in the interpretation by his priests.

'Sleep well, Jeck.' I touched his cairn in farewell. 'I'll join you for a tankard when we meet in the Halls of the Lower Gods.'

I wondered if Jeck's spirit would find its way to the Halls of Eternity Smoke had always been used to guide the spirits to their ancestors. Without a sanctified fire, would they be permitted to enter?

'Oh, Jeck.'

The thought of him contained within the cold earth forever was more than I could bear, so I moved on to Kerk's cairn and placed the remaining flowers there. The prince's naming pole displayed the Faulknar lion inlaid with silver to reflect the light. The effect made the lion ripple as shadows passed over it. Below the lion was a small golden crown in place of the one he would no longer wear. The third image was the crossed swords of Kerk's personal heraldic design. Priceless onyx, diamond and turquoise were set in the hilts of the swords; the crystals of passage to the higher planes.

I smiled. 'Appeasing both faiths then, Kyllian?'

Despite the king's protestations regarding the demise of the old Gods, he still offered them the crystals to ensure safe passage for his son's spirit. I placed my hand against the damp stones, closing my eyes. After the previous night, I had no more tears left inside me, just a deep sadness that caused a physical pain each time I breathed. I felt overwhelmingly tired. Tired of all the sorrow. Tired of all the pain. Tired of not being able to help those I cared about. Tired of not being good enough. Tired of being sorry.

The pale haze of the sun had moved into the trees and had emerged from the other side when a runner found me. The young girl shifted impatiently from foot to foot as she relayed her message.

'Lady Greenwood requests your presence.'

I frowned in confusion. 'Breya?'

'She says to meet her in the formal gardens.'

'Me? Breya wants to talk to me?'

The girl huffed impatiently. 'Yes. You. It took me ages to find you. She will have been waiting in the cold all this time. She's going to be so angry.'

'Don't worry.' I rose slowly and painfully. My muscles had cramped from being immobile for so long in the cold and damp. 'I'm sure her temper will be taken out on me. The blame will be mine alone.'

'I hope so.' She huffed again before running back down the trail.

I followed more slowly, not looking forward to the meeting with Breya. It could not be a good thing that she wanted to see me. I tried to think of what I had done wrong.

I had the beginnings of a headache by the time I returned to the royal house. The formal gardens were at the back, enclosed by a wall to provide privacy. The lawns were carefully manicured into symmetrical shapes with pale gravel paths separating them, allowing the ladies to walk the gardens during any season without damaging their expensive gowns. Breya was seated in the wooden arbour in a sheltered corner of the gardens. In the summer, richly coloured roses released their scent, but during this season their cages of thorns were poorly covered by the dark, curled leaves.

Breya was talking quietly with Rolyan. She was enclosed within a warm, fur-lined cloak. The black cloth covered her completely so that only her head and small, black shoes were visible. Her blonde hair curled softly around her neck.

'What do you want, Breya?' I demanded.

'Some manners from you would be good,' growled Rolyan, taking a step towards me. 'You will address her as Lady Greenwood.'

I glared at him as a small smile rippled over Breya's mouth. She released a hand from the sleeve of her cloak to rest gently on Rolyan's arm.

'Don't waste your breath, Rolyan. She has never displayed appropriate manners. I doubt she will start now.'

'You brought me here to complain about my manners?'

The smile widened. 'No. I've summoned you to talk about your future.'

I frowned. 'What do you mean?'

'What will you do now?'

Rolyan looked at me with predatory eyes, causing cold water to run down my spine. 'Now you are without the protection of the prince.'

I started to shake, finally realising how much Kade's influence had protected me in Liegeport. Remembering that that protection had been revoked. And it had been noticed already.

'I mean,' continued Breya, 'your only use to Faulknar was as a thief, and you've failed at that. I will be queen, and I will not tolerate charity to those that offer no value. Everyone supported by Faulknar has to contribute to the kingdom. You give us nothing.'

'It would be advisable for you to leave sooner rather than later,' Rolyan added. 'You wouldn't want to make a scene.'

I had turned ice-cold. 'Do I have a choice?'

Rolyan smiled. 'No.'

Breya watched as I considered her command. Where would I go? What would I do? Who would help Drey? My stomach clenched violently. Who would look after Kade? I looked at Breya.

'And Kade?'

Her smile was full of triumph. 'Do you understand yet? There is nothing you have that I cannot take.'

I saw no reason for delay. I left that evening. I had not unpacked yet and only added some more clothes to my bag. There was nothing else I needed to take. After Breya's comments about charity I did not take any food or money. After the journey to Lindvane, I knew the countryside would provide for me.

Tawpin stopped me on the stone steps as I left the house.

'Tallen. Wait.' He ran over from the stables to join me. He looked at the bag hanging from my shoulder before raising accusing eyes to my face. 'You're leaving!'

Despite my concerns that I had cried all the moisture from my body, tears stung my eyes once again. 'I'm sorry, Tawpin.'

The accusation in his eyes turned to concern. 'What happen, Tal? Kade is… wrong. He won't talk to me. He won't talk to anyone. What happened with you two?'

I took a shuddering breath. 'Too much. None of it good.'

We spent uncomfortable moments looking at each other, trying to find the right words to express how we felt, failing to find words big enough to deal with all the heartache and broken promises. Tawpin stepped forward and embraced me in a desperate hug. I returned it with as much force, trying to hold on to all that I had once had; to delay leaving all the broken pieces behind. I gripped so tightly while my tears soaked into his cloak.

'Don't go, Tallen,' Tawpin whispered into my neck, breaking the spell.

I sighed and pulled away from him. 'I have to go, Tawpin. Breya has made that very clear.'

He scowled. 'That interfering sow…'

I shook my head sadly. 'She's just protecting her own. And she's right. I can't stay. I can't watch Breya and Kade…' I paused, biting my lip against the tears still threatening to spill. 'Take care of him for me.'

'Tallen…'

'And take care of yourself.' I playfully hit him in the chest. 'Try to stay out of trouble, yeah?'

We looked at each other for a few heartbeats longer. Tawpin took my hand and kissed the knuckles.

'Don't leave thinking you have no friends at Liegeport.'

He leaned forward to kiss me on the cheek. I felt his warm, wet tears on my cold skin. The contact was brief before he ran up the steps into the house. I was suddenly so very alone.

Epilogue

The screeching bellow ripped through the air seconds before the warehouse exploded into a lethal rain of timber shards. Arrows of wood embedded in flesh as flames leapt up into the mockingly cloudless sky. The cries of disembowelled men silenced by the cacophony of sound released by the collapsing building. The sunlight reflected off iridescent scales as the dragons swooped and soared over the port. Wooden toy houses to the giant beasts. The downdraft from the membranous wings was enough to fell a muscled stevedore as they skimmed the merchant houses and meeting halls. Causing shadowed darkness as their massive bodies covered the sun.

Hands flinched to cover ears as another scream radiated from the dragon's mouth. Human flesh offered little protection as small trails of blood leaked through cramped fingers. The dragon slowly turned. The light of the flames dancing over its emerald scales. Its underbelly was two shades lighter than its legs, and black talons at the four corners of its body flexed in anticipation. As the dragon curved, its tail snaked leisurely into a row of rooftops and ramparts. The structures toppled as easily as a child's building blocks.

But the people did not cower in fear. While their hearts pleaded to run, their brains understood there was nowhere to go. If they were to die, they would die with swords, spears and bows in their hands. At high points of the port, platforms had been erected to support giant bow-like ratchets. Within these nestled harpoons the length of a horse. Two men were required to crank the handle that tightened the bow; two more to place the harpoon in its cradle. All four held their ground as the monster came closer. Gold and black scales rippled as its wing muscles contracted and relaxed, the intelligent ebony eyes focusing on the target. The men waited until the last possible moment, until the dragon opened its mouth and they could see the heat haze that preceded the flames; could smell the ozone above the acid on its breath.

They released.

The harpoon flew straight and true. The dragon's roar of victory sealed its fate as the iron-tipped shaft sunk deep into the back of its throat. Such was the power of the shot that the harpoon dug deep into the soft tissue at the top of the mouth, and penetrated the thin bones of the encasing skull. The force of the impact knocked the dragon off its trajectory and away from the tower. It cleared the city walls before impacting the peat earth with a tremendous thud. The ground shook as the behemoth rolled over and over, sending up clouds of turf as it dug into the fields, finally coming to rest at the base of the huge crater it had created. Soil rained over the fallen beast to cover it like a shroud.

On the other side of the port, a monstrous scream ripped across the sky, echoing off the buildings and driving nails of pain into the brains of all who heard it. Air was sucked into a *whooph* as time hung suspended for a heartbeat, then crashed back as a fireball ignited the dockside and flat cargo ships within the harbour. Debris flew in all directions, sending flaming spikes into the bodies of those fallen nearby. A young woman ran from a burning building, her clothes and hair on fire, hands flapping uselessly, before collapsing in the agony of her pitted and melting skin.

While most of the town was dealing with the dragons, others saw opportunities. Looting and mugging could be concealed by the surrounding death and destruction. Hand-to-hand battles dodged flying masonry. The ring of steel added a higher pitch to the symphony of burning buildings. People were dying from cracked skulls and visceral stabbings as well as from flame and claw.

Hour after hour the people fought. The sun rose to noon before sinking towards dusk. Five dragons became four. Became three. Then just two remained. Desperation caused the people to engage the trebuchets, knowing that if they missed their mark, flaming oil-soaked missiles would barrel into the city. Two weapons were loaded on the dockside where the curve of the harbour cupped the edge of the town. Two hammocks filled with ballast awaited ignition, waiting for the right moment. Waiting for the dragon the blue of a summer sky, with scales highlighted in silver, to fly into range. Approaching, then retreating, it tormented the city, the crack of wings snapping taut as the creature soared upwards, spewing streams of fire. The crackle of burning flesh and the stench of charred bodies caused the men to retch. The unconcerned dragon glided effortlessly between the trebuchets and the harbour. The men ignited oil coating the rocks and released the swings. The dragon missed its wingbeat as it was buffeted by flaming boulders, the impact causing it to rotate and twist towards the harbour. Unable to maintain its height, the beast crashed into the water, sending a tidal wave over the docks. Its cerulean wings submerged, the weight of the dragon quickly dragged it to the deep waters beyond the safety of the harbour.

The final dragon watched its fall, the deep reds and purples of its scales fading to paler shades as it realised the loss of all the others. The decision made within the space of two wingbeats to keep it stationary, before it turned to leave. Powerful thrusts soon took it to the edge of the port, but a harpoon was released before it cleared the city walls. As the beast flew overhead, the shaft embedded into the soft junction of the belly and hind leg. The monster screeched in pain as it tumbled off balance and crashed into the ground. Landing awkwardly, the crack of broken bones split the air immediately before another cry of pain from the dragon. The left hindleg hung at an unnatural angle as creature used its other three legs to launch into the sky and fly away from the destroyed town.

The dragon released a final scream of frustration as it glided over a rise to the west of the port, where a small group of people stood watching the burning city. Dressed in robes of white, black, red or blue, they slowly turned their backs on the ruins of the royal port and walked away.